LADY CAROLINE—who lured Nicholas Minnett into her bed through the most corrupt wager a man ever made and a woman ever demanded that he pay in full.

SERAPHINE—who made a devil's bargain with Nicholas for all the love her husband never gave her and taught him a lesson about his own burning need that he could never again escape.

ANNE—the beautiful woman who had belonged to Nicholas's best friend and whom he desperately tried to protect against both her desires and his own.

AURORA—who was a dream of beauty and purity to Nicholas Minnett, until she woke him to the shocking truth in the locked bedroom of the most notorious libertine in Paris.

Nicholas Minnet was a man for all women, but in the orgy of a world gone mad, there was only one woman who could save—or destroy—him....

THE
CAPTAIN'S
WOMAN

Big Bestsellers from SIGNET

THE
CAPTAIN'S
WOMAN

by
Mark Logan

ORIGINAL TITLE
Tricolour

A SIGNET BOOK
NEW AMERICAN LIBRARY
TIMES MIRROR

Copyright © 1976 by Christopher Nicole

All rights reserved. For information address St. Martin's Press, Inc.,
175 Fifth Avenue, New York, New York 10010.

Library of Congress Catalog Card Number: 75-40796

SIGNET TRADEMARK REG. U.S. PAT. OFF. AND FOREIGN COUNTRIES
REGISTERED TRADEMARK—MARCA REGISTRADA
HECHO EN CHICAGO, U.S.A.

SIGNET, SIGNET CLASSICS, MENTOR, PLUME AND MERIDIAN BOOKS
are published by The New American Library, Inc.,
1301 Avenue of the Americas, New York, New York 10019

First Signet Printing, June, 1977

1 2 3 4 5 6 7 8 9

PRINTED IN THE UNITED STATES OF AMERICA

Author's Note

Nicholas Minnett and the House of Minnett are fiction; the events of this novel and most of the main characters are fact. There was even a member of the French Legislative Assembly named Condorcet, although he was a philosopher rather than a lawyer, a Girondist rather than a Jacobin, and he did not marry a girl called Seraphine. Other fictional characters are marked with an asterisk in the accompanying cast.

The characterizations of those men and women to be found in history, no less than the descriptions of the events in Paris between 1789 and 1792, are as accurate as space and an exhaustive study of the period will allow.

The sea scenes belong to the fictional part of the book, but are also based on fact; the author has spent years sailing the Channel and the Brittany coast. Only the Seine *mascaret* is based on report rather than observation, for the reason that it no longer exists in the form described. The Napoleonic Government, only a few years after the period of this book, undertook to tame this rogue river by means of walls and dredging, and although even today ships of all sizes are recommended to meet the tidal wave under way rather than at anchor, the *mascaret* no longer represents the threat it did.

Cast in Order of Appearance

*Harry Yealm *English smuggler*
*Nicholas Minnett *English gentleman of French descent, heir to the banking House of Minnett*
*Tom Price *English seaman, boatswain to Harry Yealm, and to Nick Minnett*
*Dick Allardyce *English seaman*
*Peter Lownd *English seaman*
*Seraphine Condorcet *Wife of Louis Condorcet*
*Louis Condorcet *French republican lawyer and soldier*
*Dr. Planchet *French surgeon, father of Seraphine*
*Pierre de Benoît *French provincial nobleman*
*Etienne de Benoît *His son*
*Aurora de Benoît *His daughter*
George Augustus Frederick *Prince of Wales*
William Pitt *Prime Minister of England*
*Lucy Minnett *Sister of Nick Minnett*
*Lady Caroline Moncey *Friend of Lucy Minnett*
*Percy Minnett *Father of Nick and Lucy, owner of the banking House of Minnett*
*Joachim Castets *French agent*
*Anne Yealm *Wife of Harry Yealm*
*Sergeant Popel *French republican soldier*
*Priscilla Minnett *Wife of Percy Minnett, mother of Nick and Lucy*
*Lord George Moncey *Brother of Caroline*
*George Gorman *English tailor*
Marie Antoinette *Queen of France*
Marie Thérèse de Bourbon, Princess de Lamballe *French aristocrat*

vi

Honoré Riquetti, Count Mirabeau *French republican politician*

Charles James Fox *English politician*

Frederick Augustus, Duke of York and Albany *English prince and soldier*

Richard Howe *English admiral*

*Mr. and Mrs. Landon *English innkeepers*

*Eric *Nick Minnett's valet*

*Stevens *Caroline Moncey's maid*

*Mr. and Mrs. Morley *Minnett housekeepers*

Henry Addington *English politician*

*Jacques L'Onglon *French republican lawyer*

Jean Marie Roland de la Platière *French republican politician*

Jeanne Manon Roland *His wife*

Charles François Dumouriez *French republican politician and soldier*

Marie-Joseph de Motier, Marquis de Lafayette *French republican soldier*

*Alan Crosby *English doctor*

*Jonathan Turnbull *Chief clerk to the House of Minnett*

George Grenville *English politician*

Louis XVI *King of France*

Louis Xavier Stanislaus, Duke of Provence *Brother of Louis XVI*

Hans Axel Ferson *Swedish soldier*

Jeanne Louise Campan *French lady of the bedchamber*

*Philippe de Montmorin *French émigré soldier*

Jean-Louis Charette (pseudonym of François Charette de la Contrie) *French aristocratic soldier*

Camille Desmoulins *French republican politician*

Maximilian Robespierre *French republican politician*

George Leveson-Gower, Duke of Sutherland *English ambassador in Paris*

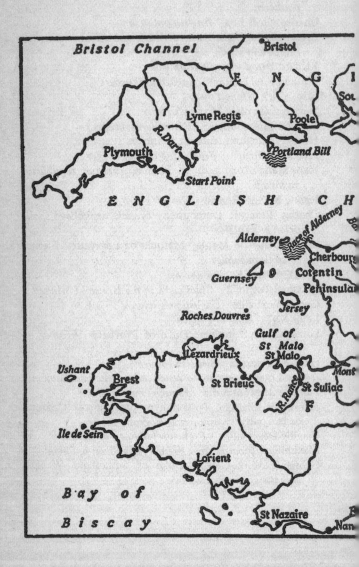

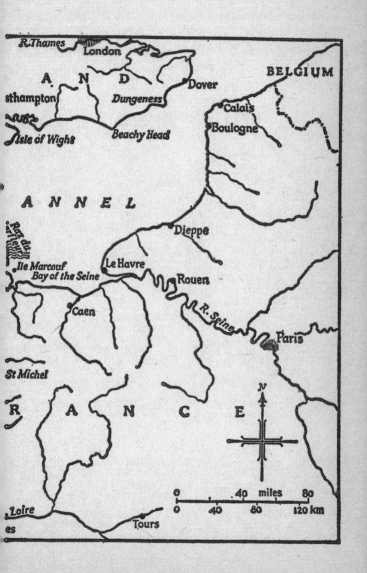

One

Heavy black clouds swept north out of the Bay of Biscay, clustered in the approaches to the English Channel, drifted east. Over the thrusting fist of the Cotentin Peninsula they coagulated into huge oily masses behind which the setting sun disappeared to plunge the March afternoon into an early twilight.

As yet there was little wind, but the sea was restless, anticipating the coming storm. The swell surged past Cherbourg and into the Bay of the Seine, heaving majestically toward the long Normandy beaches. The Isles Marcouf, just south of the fishing village of St. Vaast, were already submerged in flying spray; behind the barren little islets the sea remained calm, but the *Golden Rose* rolled to her anchor, anxious to be away before the wind could trap her.

She was eighty feet overall and two-masted, rigged fore and aft for speed, while from her bluff bows and along the whole length of her varnished topsides she suggested strength. Given sufficient room, she would meet the coming gale on even terms. She had been built in Devon six years earlier, had been launched into the River Dart in the very month of September 1783 which had given the American colonists their independence. Her timbers were oak.

She represented Harry Yealm's boyhood dream, which he had worked for all of his adult life. Now she was his, and he had no fears for the night; but he had been a seaman since the age of twelve, could read the signs in the sky and knew that it was going to be a long way home to

Lyme Regis. He pulled his woollen cap lower over his ears and peered into the gloom at the just visible shore. "Where are they, then?" he grumbled.

"There." The young man beside him pointed at the boat which could just be seen, running down to them under a single lugsail.

"You've eyes in that head, Nick," Harry shouted, his discontent disappearing. "I'll be right glad to get out of this bay, I'll tell you that. I reckon the wind is going northeast before midnight."

"I'll show the light." Nicholas Minnett brought the flickering lantern above the bulwark, three times in rapid succession. He felt the excitement rippling through his system, and knew Harry felt it also. The two men were as different as it was possible to imagine. Where Harry Yealm was short and heavy, Nick Minnett was tall and slender; at twenty-three he was fourteen years the younger. Where Harry's features were blunt, Nick's were fine; an oval face made an ideal setting for the high forehead, the somewhat long, straight nose, the pointed chin. Only the mouth, a shade too wide, disturbed the symmetry, but it matched the eager gray eyes. Each man wore the woollen cap and heavy smock of a fisherman, yet it was easy to tell that Nick's were used for sport, where Harry's clothes were a part of his work. And where the seaman spoke with a West Country burr, Nick maintained the accentless tones of an Oxford education. But they shared a love for the sea, and if Harry, no doubt, occasionally wondered what it must be like to live in a large house in London and be heir to the greatest financial empire in the world, he was also sure that here on the deck of the *Golden Rose* Nick was at his happiest.

The lugger was close, and the sail was being handed. "Are you there with a fender, Tom Price?" Harry called.

"Aye aye," said the boatswain; he and the two deck hands prepared to bring the boat alongside.

"A dirty night, captain." The Frenchman on the tiller spoke English. "You'll remain at anchor?"

"And be taken by your coastguard come sunrise?" Harry said.

The lugger bobbed on the swell, separated from the ketch by the stuffed canvas fenders. Tom Price had already unlashed the boom and tackle; the net was being slowly lowered, while the Frenchmen prepared to load it with their casks.

"What news, monsieur?" Nick asked.

The skipper shrugged. "The Assembly, monsieur. There is nothing but the Assembly."

"And have you no faith in it?"

"Monsieur, you have a parliament which meets regularly, and still mistakes are made. Our States General has not met at all for four hundred years, and they are going to cure all of France's problems with a snap of their fingers? It is not logical."

"Quite a philosopher," Harry muttered, watching the net swinging as Tom Price and Dick Allardyce heaved on the capstan. "Easy now. That claret won't taste much if it ends up in the bilges. You've the money, Nick?"

Nick passed the leather satchel down to the French skipper, who jingled it against his ear, then grinned and stowed it under the transom. "Bon voyage, messieurs. Next month, perhaps?"

"Next month," Harry Yealm agreed.

"I'll be back at college," Nick said.

"Aye, well, there's always the summer. You'll raise that anchor, Tom Price. Stand by your halliard, Peter Lownd." He lifted his head to a gust of wind off the shore. "Let's be away."

The lugger had cast off. Now the *Golden Rose* herself came to life as the anchor clanked into its hawsepipe; Nick and Peter Lownd hauled on the main halliard to hoist the sail while the ship still lay to the wind. Minutes later the foresail was also set, and then the mizzen; the *Golden Rose* gathered way, heeling to starboard as the breeze swept across her larboard bow.

"You'll take the helm, Nick," Harry said. "I'd best be below to make sure those casks are properly stowed."

Nick braced his feet, wrapped his fingers around the heavy spokes, looked up at the taut sails above his head. Harry watched him for a moment, then nodded in satisfaction. Not that he had any doubts. Percy Minnett maintained a holiday home not far from Lyme Regis, and Harry had taken Nick to sea since the young man had been old enough to stand, had taught him everything he knew, not only in the handling of a ship but in navigating the treacherous waters of the Normandy and Brittany coasts. "With the wind where it is," he said, "we'll give the Raz du Barfleur a wide berth. Lay off until the headland comes abeam, and then bring her as close as you can."

He swung himself forward, down the hatch to the hold, and Nick was alone. Now the darkness was coming fast, and with it the wind. The ship was surrounded by surging whitecaps, and every few seconds she dipped her bow and a rattle of spray came aft. He licked the salt from his lips, and looked west. Only on the top of the swell could he see the winking lights of the shore, but they were already four miles off, he calculated. "If you'll harden those sheets, Dick," he shouted at Allardyce, "we'll come up a point."

"Right you are, Mr. Minnett."

Nick put the helm to larboard, and the wind seemed to grow stronger as the ketch turned closer to it, thrumming the rigging. Up and down, up and down went his hands, allowing the ship to move with the waves, sliding into the troughs, tossing her bows as she mounted to the next rolling whitecap, always correcting the helm to maintain his course. Soon it rained as well, teeming out of the low black clouds, blotting out the land, leaving him and his ship alone in a world of water.

It became necessary to maintain concentration. He usually did this in a variety of ways, from construing a Greek sentence to mentally listing his father's principal debtors. This night he found himself thinking about women. He seldom wasted the time; women either were elderly, friends of Mother; young, friends of his sister Lucy;

available, as the ladies he and his fellow students occasionally sought out after an evening at a tavern; or Aurora. Not one had ever suggested a pleasure comparable with helming *Golden Rose*.

But suddenly the sex were threatening to become important. Tom Grenville and Frederick Russell had both married the year they had left Oxford. He was not due to go down till next year, but he was the last male Minnett; and it seemed the whole world was getting married. Even Harry Yealm, a widower for ten years, had last autumn taken a new wife, a girl half his age. Anne Yealm was a delight; she was the daughter of a lighthouse keeper and knew the sea. Harry had chosen well. Nicholas Minnett must also choose well, someone able to sustain the social burden of ruling the House of Minnett. For the life of him he could think of no one able to do that and at the same time compensate him for giving up sailing.

Except possibly Aurora de Benoît. The knowledge that he had actually spent the last two days off the French coast, if more than a hundred miles from the Château Benoît, made him quite nostalgic. Aurora was a childhood sweetheart, and the sister of a friend; she enjoyed the outdoor life as well as anyone. Of course old Pierre de Benoît was head of one of the oldest families in Brittany, while a hundred years ago the Minnetts had been goldsmiths in La Rochelle. But the Count himself had never seemed to care about the difference in background any more than the difference in religious outlook, and certainly the relative positions of the families had changed; where the Huguenot goldsmiths had emigrated and become England's leading bankers, the Benoîts had suffered the general decline which had afflicted the French economy for so long. Pierre de Benoît was one of Father's principal customers.

He discovered Harry beside him. "It's veering," the captain bawled. "We'll come about."

The orders were given, Nick put up the helm, and *Golden Rose* turned into the wind, stopped, and then gathered way again as the foresail was sheeted home on the larboard winches. Now the wind came in from the starboard side, as the ship steered northwest. "She's fine." Harry spat tobacco over the side. "Those froggies were punctual after all. And the wine looks good. Assembly. Bah. Ever been to Paris, Nick?"

"With my father, two years ago; when Necker would raise money."

"Which you didn't lend, I hope. Did you take the Seine?"

Nick shook his head. "The packet to Calais."

" 'Tis simpler, to be sure. The Seine, now, there is a river. I took the *Rose* up to Rouen, once, and got stuck in by the *mascaret*."

"I've heard of it. But I'm not sure what it is." Nick leaned on the helm to bring the ketch back on course, ducking his head as a larger than usual wave broke on the bows and came surging aft over the deck.

"The biggest wave you'll ever meet, on a river. What happens is, the river is flowing out toward the sea, so that when the first of the tide starts up it meets the water coming down. The tide is the more powerful so it keeps on rising, as far as Rouen and beyond, and where it meets the flow of the river it pushes up a wall of water. Of course it depends on the weather. But you get the river running hard, like after heavy rain, and the tide on a big spring, when they meet, why, 'tis said no ship can live in it." He peered into the blackness. "Mind you . . ."

"What?" Nick asked. Now his arms were growing heavy, as his cheeks were chilled beyond feeling.

"I've a notion it could be done. Say with a strong easterly wind. You'd not make it at under ten knots."

"There'd be something," Nick said. "To take the *Rose* through the Seine bore, eh, Harry?"

"Aye. But not something you or I will ever be likely to attempt, God willing. Now you go below and get warm."

Nick was glad to release the wheel; his fingers remained bent with cramp as he slid back the hatch and ducked into the light of the cabin, where the lantern swung to and fro from its hook.

"A wild night," Tom Price said. "Here you are, Mr. Minnett, sir, wrap yourself around that."

It was a chunk of cold ham, together with a thick slice of French bread and a steaming mug of hot rum. Nick drank, and chewed, and felt the warmth spreading through his body. He lay down with a sigh, closed his eyes, and was brought up again with a start as the cabin filled with a tremendous booming thunder.

"Heckie," Price shouted. "We've lost a mast."

Nick rolled out of the bunk, joined the rush for the companionway, looking aloft as he reached the deck. The masts still stood, and the sails were filling.

"There's the bastard," Harry said, wrestling with the helm.

Nick peered into the darkness, saw the ship, not more than two hundred yards away, surging out of the north.

"Never saw her until she opened fire," Harry said.

"But why?" Nick shouted.

"A revenue cutter," Harry bawled. "She wants us to heave to. We'd best look smart, or it'll be Poole Prison."

"You mean you'll run for it?" Nick demanded.

"Your father would not thank me for surrendering you to the revenue. Stand by those sheets, Dick Allardyce."

"Aye aye, captain," came the shout.

Nick slackened the larboard jib sheets, while Allardyce paid out the mainsheet and Lownd released the runner which kept the shroud taut when the ship was working to windward. Harry put the helm down, and the *Golden Rose* swung away from the wind, gathering speed all the time. But now the revenue cutter could see what they were about. The *Golden Rose* gave a long shudder which took Nick by surprise and threw him into the scuppers. Only then did the noise reach him, and in that instant the ketch swung back into the wind, sails banging against the shrouds, while a wave broke on the bow.

Nick gained his knees, holding on to the bulwark, looking aft, realizing that the cutter had fired into them; the after gunwale was shattered, although the ball had struck only a glancing blow before plummeting into the sea. But the wheel was spinning unattended, and Harry Yealm was on the deck.

"Aft," Nick shouted. "Aft, Tom Price."

He staggered for the wheel, and another wave hit the ship, throwing her on her side, bringing the boom slatting across. "The helm," Harry shouted, "or she'll lose a mast for sure."

Nick looked down at the blood running down Harry's back, where a splinter of wood from the torn gunwale had been driven into him like a knife. But the ship had to come first. He grasped the spokes, put the helm down with all his force. "The larboard sheets," he shouted. The *Golden Rose* would not answer until she had gained way.

Lownd slid across the deck and sheeted in the sail once again. The next wave broke on the starboard gunwale, flooding the deck, surging green water over Harry Yealm and around Nick's ankles, but also pushing the bow round. The mainsail ceased its dreadful flapping and Nick felt a responsive hardening on the wheel. They had been lucky; the masts still stood, and not a sail had split. Harry's gear was all in good order.

Harry. His friend was against the foot of the mizzen mast, Tom Price kneeling beside him. "How is he?"

"Grievous hurt, Mr. Minnett," the boatswain replied. "We'd best heave up and give the cutter best."

Nick had almost forgotten the cutter. The coastguard had supposed the ketch was surrendering when she had swung into the wind. Now she fired her bow chaser again. But this shot was wild.

"Aye," he said, feeling anger and despair filling his belly, wishing he had a cannon himself to return fire, to hang for a pirate instead of going to prison, no doubt. "Slack those sheets."

"No," Harry yelled, his face contorted with pain. "You'll not surrender, Nick."

"You're bleeding, captain," Price said.

"Then bind me up, you old fool," Harry said. "Christ, man, 'tis only a puncture."

"Then there's the weather," Price said. "No disrespect, Mr. Minnett, but this is getting up to a gale."

Nick chewed his lip, fingers locked on the spokes; the *Golden Rose* dipped her bow and sent a volley of spray flying aft as she made off west, the wind gusting thirty knots on her starboard quarter, the night a raging inferno of wet sound.

"What do you want me to do, Harry?"

"Listen, boy. This ship is all Anne has, should anything happen to me. I spent every penny I could raise, building the *Rose*. There are no debts left, but no money either."

"Why should anything happen to you, old friend?"

"No reason at all," Harry said, "but you'll not surrender my ship. Now get me below, Tom Price, and bind up this cut. Then you'll take Mr. Minnett's orders. He's your skipper, now."

The boatswain looked from Nick to Allardyce and Lownd, and shrugged. "You'd best give me a hand, Dick. Peter, see to the sheets."

They carried Harry Yealm below, and Nick gave a hasty glance over his shoulder. The cutter's lanterns could be seen, bobbing on the waves, about three cable-lengths astern.

"Douse our lights," he told Lownd.

"That's breaking the law, Mr. Minnett."

"Then they can add that to their warrant. Douse them."

Lownd obeyed. But no sooner had he extinguished the stern lantern than the cutter fired again. The ball splashed into the sea alongside, sending a cascade of water over the deck, bringing Price and Allardyce from the cabin.

"Free those sheets," Nick bellowed, and put down the helm to allow the ship to run dead before the wind. Here the motion was easier and there was less spray, but she required a deal of holding to prevent her yawing too much; to broach to in these seas would mean at the very least the loss of a mast.

"'Tis the Race of Alderney ahead," Price grumbled. "There's no place to be in this wind."

"We need thirty miles for the Race," Nick said, half to

himself. "We'll have lost the cutter before then and can come back to course. Did you get the splinter out?"

"Then would the bleeding really start. 'Tis good English oak. It'll not fester, providing we find a surgeon tomorrow."

Nick listened to the roar behind him as a larger than average wave began to break. He tightened his grip on the helm, stamped his feet to make sure of his balance, felt the ship lift as she was picked up by the crest.

"You'll not hold her," Price screamed, seizing a shroud.

The *Golden Rose* hurtled forward, sheets thrumming, canvas tight, white water boiling on either side, then the wave was away and she was thrusting her bowsprit into solid green, tossing it aft as her bows came up.

"May God have mercy on our souls," Price muttered.

"Do you see the cutter?" Nick's arms and legs were tight with weariness, and a metal band seemed to be constricting his thighs.

Price peered astern. "She's there. I can see her canvas."

"Then she can see ours," Nick muttered. But what to do? The wind was rising all the time. The normal course of action for a boat like the *Rose*, caught out in a Channel gale, would be to heave to in deep water, and wait for the wind to drop. But here he was closing the land at something over ten knots, he estimated. The coast of the Cotentin Peninsula, and the British islands, Guernsey, Jersey and Alderney which lay within the Gulf of St. Malo, was nothing more than an endless succession of granite reefs and isolated rocks amongst which the tide surged at speeds which sometimes approached ten knots itself.

"She'll not carry this canvas much longer," Price shouted. "I'd best take a roll in the main."

Nick chewed his lip. But they were not pulling away from the cutter even with all sail set. "We'll stand on a while," he decided.

"Man, you're crazy," Price cried. "You'll have the masts out, and where will we be then?"

"Precisely where we'll be if those revenue men come on board, Tom."

The night wore on, the wind steadily increased. The *Golden Rose* surfed down the side of so many waves Nick lost count; he reacted to each gust with instinctive ability now, keeping her always dead before the wind, every few minutes casting a glance aloft to make sure nothing had parted. But she was a well found ship.

Yet always the lights of the cutter showed astern. They were professional seamen, and their ship was equally well found. They would not give up the chase. And ahead was the narrow, boiling passage called the Race of Alderney.

"Lights," Allardyce shouted. "Well up."

"Not enough for Cherbourg," Price objected.

"The French show a light on Cap de la Hague," Nick said, desperately trying to remember everything Harry had told him. "Then it is seven miles of open water to Alderney."

"Open water?" Price bawled. "Look there, Mr. Minnett."

For now the cloud bank began to break to allow the moon to scatter across the sea, they could see the seething mass of white water which lay directly ahead, stretching from the blinking light to the distant black hillock which was Alderney.

"Bring her up, Mr. Minnett," Allardyce begged. "That tide runs at eight knots."

"Aye," Nick said. "And will he follow?"

The three seamen stared at him, and then over their shoulders at the cutter.

"You're mad, sir, with respect," Lownd said.

"To come about now would be to turn under his gun," Nick said.

"But to go through the Race . . ." Price said.

"She'll do it," Nick said. Perhaps to encourage himself; the moment for changing his mind was already past. Driven onward by the gale, *Golden Rose* was now picked up by the tide as well. She ran at the passage like a galloping horse, and he realized that he would not hold her.

"The helm," he snapped. "Lend a hand, Tom. Allardyce, Lownd, grab hold, and be ready to let the sheets fly."

For this was a maelstrom, not a sea. There was no pattern to the waves, as in the ordinary ocean. The ship would surf down the back of a huge stern sea, as they had been doing all night, and find no second wave beyond. And then, after bounding through this moment of suddenly calm water, they would see the entire ocean appear to drop away in front of them, and *Golden Rose* would fall like a stone, fifteen feet or more, into the deepest trough Nick had ever seen. He looked aloft to make sure his spars were still there, and saw the next wave towering, up and up, foaming in the crest, determined to drive this upstart wooden intruder still further towards the bottom. Then the entire ship disappeared to bulwark level, and sea foamed about their necks, and he prayed that none of the hatch covers would carry away.

But *Golden Rose* shook herself like a dog, and pushed her bows up, ready to take the next crisis. Nick looked over his shoulder. Still the cutter was there, always there.

The night seemed endless. The Race of Alderney was only eight miles long, and with the tide traveling at maximum speed they must have been through in half an hour. Then the seas remained big, but they resumed some order. He could at last release the helm and accept a glass of rum from Allardyce.

"Look there," shouted Lownd, "she's lost a mast."

They clung to the rigging and stared into the wind. The cutter was rolling about two miles astern, her foremast down in a cluster of sail and cordage.

"She'll not catch us now," Allardyce said.

"They may need help," Nick muttered.

"Not them, Mr. Minnett," Price said. "There's twenty men on board her. They'll have a jury rigged in an hour; and they're in no danger, drifting south of Alderney."

"And what will they do then, do you think?"

"There'll be no beating back against a north-easter with a jury rig. My guess is they'll run down to St. Peter Port in Guernsey. We can slip them now, Mr. Minnett."

"Back to England? That's another twenty-four hours' work, and the skipper is still losing blood."

"Well, sir, we sure can't make for the islands. That cutter will have the word out against us before she's properly moored."

Nick turned his head to look at the distant cliffs of the French coast, ten miles to larboard. No harbors there, for a ship the size of *Rose*. But only forty miles farther south . . . he burst into laughter.

" 'Tis no laughing matter, Mr. Minnett," Price objected.

"Fool I am for not thinking of it before," Nick cried. "We'll make for St. Malo, and up the Rance. The Sieur de Benoît will find a doctor for us."

The wind began to drop as they passed between Guernsey and Jersey; here they were sheltered by the French mainland. Yet the seas stayed high, and Nick used the telescope to inspect the coast as they approached the walled city of St. Malo.

"I hopes you remember the marks," Tom Price muttered; the coast off the mouth of the River Rance was encumbered for some five miles out with an archipelago of rocks and islets.

Nick checked his compass. "Southeast by east," he said. " 'Tis what the skipper always steered. And there is the Jardin Tower, hard by Isle Cezembre. Now we have but to find the Balue church behind it, and we are in the channel. There." He pointed again, and altered course to larboard to bring the two marks into a transit. "Harden up that sheet, Dick," he called. "We're here."

And God, how glad would he be to anchor; not only on account of Harry Yealm. He was utterly exhausted. Except for a brief rest this morning once they were in the lee of the land, he had been at the helm since Harry's wound. That must have been toward midnight; it was now past noon again. His arms felt like lumps of lead, his shoulders ached, his belly muscles were so tight he had been unable to digest his breakfast.

And yet, he was happy. If only Harry was not below,

bleeding and in pain, he thought he would be ecstatic. It was more than merely the exhilaration of having ridden a gale in triumph. It was the thought of St. Suliac, and old Benoît, and Etienne of course, and Louis Condorcet, and Aurora.

The two families traced their friendship back thirty years, to the day of Minden, when Pierre de Benoît, then a cornet in the French army, had fallen prisoner to Uncle William, the only Minnett to take up soldiering as a career. Pierre de Benoît had spent his captivity on parole at the Minnett house in London, and become a firm friend of Father's. Now that he was the ruler of his domain, the friendship had wider ties. He borrowed from the House of Minnett, of course—so did most of the French nobility— but also Nick and Etienne were much the same age, and Aurora was only a year younger. They had alternated holidays in each other's home as children, although they had seen less of each other in recent years.

He brought up the helm and sent Allardyce forward to adjust the sheets. With the wind still astern, *Golden Rose* slipped easily past the gaunt rocks and even gaunter light tower of the Jardin, and turned towards the walls of St. Malo, gleaming in the midday sun.

Aurora. He had not seen her for over a year. He thought of a mass of pale golden hair, fine and floating in the slightest suggestion of a breeze, of a laughing face, perhaps too soft in its outline for beauty, but intensely attractive, of boundless energy and radiant health, of . . . he realized that he knew little else about her. She had always been a playmate, an eager follower of the ideas and antics of her brother and his friend.

A flap from the sail recalled him to his task. The city was to larboard now, and the broad River Rance was opening in front of him. The river flowed fast, and indeed possessed a bore of its own on certain tides; but today it was calm enough, and the rising tide was taking the ship upstream at a good speed.

"How soon before the tide turns, do you reckon?" he asked Price.

The boatswain studied the rocks, estimating their height above water. "Maybe an hour."

"Damnation. We'll not make the château. We'll drop anchor off St. Suliac. Louis Condorcet will help us. Prepare to hand sail."

The still stormy sea disappeared behind them. Now they slipped along between wooded banks; the water was brown. And there were the chimneypots of the village looming around the next bend. The Château Benoît was another two miles farther on.

"Break out the boat," Nick called. "We've no time to lose."

"Aye aye," Price said, and went forward to remove the lashings from the dinghy. There'd be no more argument, Nick reflected with some satisfaction. He had brought them safe to anchor.

St. Suliac was abeam. He spun the wheel to larboard, and the ketch came gracefully round. "Down mainsail," he bawled. "Let go."

The chain rattled through the hawsepipe, and the heavy anchor splashed into the still water. The canvas clouded on to the boom, and Allardyce and Lownd scrambled up with the sail ties.

"And the jib." Nick released the helm. For a moment he swayed with weariness.

"Will you be all right, Mr. Minnett?" Price was anxious.

"Oh, aye." Nick opened the hatch, peered into the damp interior of the cabin. Harry Yealm lay on his side, facing the bulkhead; he breathed evenly, but made no sound. The back of the wounded man's jacket was stained with blood, and not all of it was dry. "I'd best make haste. You're in command, Tom."

He closed the hatch, scrambled over the side, and stroked the dinghy towards the shore. *Golden Rose* nodded quietly to her anchor, her crew busily stowing the canvas.

The dinghy came in to the jetty, and willing hands waited for him to hand up the painter; *Golden Rose* was no stranger to this river.

"It blew, last night," said one fisherman in French.

"So it did," Nick agreed. "Monsieur Condorcet is in town?"

"Oh yes, monsieur. I think he is at the meeting."

"Could you find him for me? Tell him Nicholas Minnett seeks him urgently. I will try his home."

He hurried up the village street. Louis was another old friend, even if he was no more than a country lawyer, son of a St. Malo advocate. No doubt the Benoîts disapproved, although the Breton nobility were on better terms with their tenants than those in the rest of France. But then, the Benoîts certainly disapproved of his friendship with a common fisherman-cum-smuggler; they could not understand how an English gentleman could find it so easy to place himself under the command of an inferior, why talent should count more than birth. And the idea that Nick should feel exhilarated because he had brought Harry Yealm's ship through a gale would be as incomprehensible to them as his pride, the last time he had visited here, at matching a crack shot like Louis Condorcet. "After all," Etienne de Benoît had pointed out, "you could never challenge the fellow. Had you sufficient cause, you'd have to use a horsewhip."

"It could be a military matter," Nick had argued, for the sake of it.

"Again, nonsense. In the army, he would be a private soldier and you an officer."

"Could he not be promoted?"

"Good Lord, no. A man is what he is born to be, what his father and grandfather were before him. I shall be Sieur de Benoît because my family have always been Sieurs de Benoît. Louis is a lawyer because his family have always been lawyers. In France we do not believe in change."

"In England," Nick told him, "it is not enough to be born better. We must constantly remind our inferiors that we *are* better. And if we do not, then do they remind us."

"Ah bah, England," Etienne had remarked, without

rancor. "England is England, and France is France. Thank God."

He reached the little cottage just off the village street, banged on the door. "Louis. Louis. Open up."

The door opened, and he gaped. The girl, for she was hardly a woman, had loose black hair and a gamine-like face, dominated by a pair of utterly delightful black eyes. "Monsieur?"

"I seek Monsieur Condorcet. Urgently."

The girl smiled; her eyes sparkled. "My husband is not at home, monsieur. But he will shortly be back."

"Your husband? But . . ." She was, after all, a woman, even if her high-necked blue gown did little for her figure.

She gave a fascinating little laugh. "Oh yes, monsieur. Louis is my husband. And you are the English milord, Nicholas Minnett. Louis has told me of you. Come in, sir. Come in. My name is Seraphine."

"I need a surgeon," Nick explained, ducking his head to enter the low-ceilinged hallway. "The captain of my ship is badly hurt."

"But of course," she said. "Maurice. Maurice." She went down the corridor to the kitchen, and the boy came in from the back. "He does the garden," she explained. "Maurice, you will hurry for Dr. Planchet, eh? Tell him I sent you, and that he is to go to the ship in the river, immediately. Off you go, now."

Nick removed his woollen cap and scratched his head. "This doctor, will he come so quickly at that summons?"

"Of course, monsieur," Seraphine assured him. "This doctor, he is my father, eh?"

"Oh. Good heavens." His gaze wandered round the room, large, and containing an enormous iron cooking range, in which the coals glowed. The walls were bare stone, but it was warm, and everything was polished and clean. The young woman filled a mug with cider from the cask in the corner, stooping, her gown pulled up to reveal her ankles, her hair flowing out from beneath the white cap. He thought that never had he seen such an attractive picture.

"I did not know Louis was married," he said lamely.

Seraphine straightened, held out the mug. "Your cheeks are blue, monsieur; drink this. We have been married six months."

He sipped. "All the world has been married six months."

"Monsieur?"

"My captain, the man who is hurt, was married about that time."

"Oh, la la," she said. "The poor woman."

"Girl," Nick said. "She cannot be older than you." And what a contrast, he thought. Anne Yealm, so tall and strong, with a mane of fiery copper hair and yet an amazingly quiet disposition; Seraphine Condorcet, small and dark and a bundle of energy. For she was already busy again, stirring a pot which simmered on the stove.

"Then even more, poor girl," she said. "And she is separated from her husband. Alas, Monsieur Minnett, that fate will soon also be mine."

"Louis is not here?"

"Oh yes, monsieur, he is here. Presently. But soon . . . why there he is," she cried. "Louis. Monsieur Minnett."

"Nick." Louis Condorcet burst into the room, sweeping his wife from the floor as he hugged her. He was a big man, as tall as Nick and somewhat broader, as he was several years older, with long melancholy features and thoughtful green eyes. He wore the black coat of the advocate, and a severe tricorne; his cravat was spotless white and the wig he now handed to his wife was neatly curled. "I met Papa Planchet. He spoke of a sick man."

"Harry Yealm, with a wooden dagger in his back."

"My God. We must get down there. Seraphine. Give me back my hat, girl. A wooden dagger? But how?"

"A brush with a revenue cutter. Our hold is full of claret."

"Ah." Condorcet smiled, and his entire face changed; the rather grim expression he habitually wore faded into little dimples racing away from his eyes and mouth. "There will be guests for dinner, Seraphine. You'll add a rabbit to the pot." He winked at Nick. "I've three hanging in the shed. A single bullet each, eh?"

He hurried for the door. Nick hesitated. "We shall not be imposing?"

She held out her hand, and gave a half curtsey as he took it. "You are Louis' friend, monsieur. And mine also, I trust." Her fingers tightened for a moment.

He felt his cheeks burn, and cursed himself for a fool. So she was a natural flirt. She was also Louis' wife. He released her hand, crammed his cap on his head, and ran outside. "He will be well, Nick," Louis said over his shoulder. "Harry? Why, he's as strong as an ox."

"He's lost a deal of blood." Nick joined his friend on the quay. The dinghy was already alongside *Golden Rose,* and the doctor was climbing on board. "Ahoy," he bellowed. "Bring her back, Tom."

Price waved, and Allardyce got into the boat; the doctor went below.

"Harry will be well," Condorcet said again. "And it is good to see you, Nick. Why, it has been a year."

"Aye. Harry got himself a new wife."

"But that is splendid. He mourned too long. And I have also found a wife. Do you not think she is charming?"

"She is lovely," Nick said.

"Do you know," Louis said, "the Count himself came to the ceremony? And Etienne, of course. Oh, they are good people, Nick."

"And Aurora?" But he was still thinking of Seraphine.

"Ah no. She was in Paris. You know she has been presented at Court?"

"I knew she was due to be," said Nick.

"But more. She caught the eye of Her Majesty herself, and is now a lady in attendance. Oh, very great she is become. But no matter. I am off to Paris myself, within the month."

"Your wife mentioned something about your leaving. Paris? You are appearing in a case?"

Louis laughed, and clapped his friend on the shoulder. "Oh, indeed. I am appearing in the biggest case in history. I am representative for St. Suliac."

"You'll have to explain."

"Why, you'll have heard, even in England, I hope, that the States General have been summoned."

"Even in England," Nick admitted.

"Well then, they must be composed of representatives, no? And St. Suliac must have its representative. And I am he. We go to make a new country, Nick. A new world."

Nick could not help smiling at his friend's enthusiasm. "Then you forsake the law for politics?"

"Only for a season. And in any event, this is a task for lawyers. For too long we have been governed by amateurs. Now they must turn to professionals, to balance the budget, to right the wrongs, to give the people a new direction, eh? But once that task is completed, then I will return."

It occurred to Nick that Louis was rehearsing a speech. But the dinghy was back alongside the dock.

"How is Harry?" he asked as he got in.

"He is awake, Mr. Minnett," Allardyce said, "groaning something terrible."

"A brush with a coastguard, you say," Louis remarked, sitting in the bow. "And you escaped?"

"Ah, monsieur, Mr. Minnett handled her like a toy. Took her through the Race with all canvas, and it blowing forty knots."

Louis smiled at Nick's blush. "Perhaps we shall yet see you abandoning the counting house for His Majesty's navy, to become a scourge to us poor fellows when next there is a war."

"There speaks a typical froggie," Nick said, "already looking to the next conflict. But truly, had I a brother, I'd be tempted. The sea does something to a man. I cannot put it into words. It makes you twice the man you are on land."

"Or half," Louis pointed out. "Oh, the sea is a great

separator, I'll grant you that; but only a minority get on with it, and I am of the majority. Even this dinghy sets my belly rolling." They were under the stern of the ketch, and he gratefully seized the backstay to pull himself up. "What cheer, Monsieur Price?"

"Welcome aboard, Mr. Condorcet," the boatswain said. "The captain's in his bunk. The doctor sent us off, but said you was to go down whenever you returned, Mr. Minnett."

"You'd best come along, Louis." Nick opened the hatch, descended the ladder. The doctor, a little man with the black eyes of his daughter, although his hair was speckled with gray, held his finger to his lips. "Does he sleep?"

"He fainted when I withdrew the weapon." Planchet pointed to the table, where a bloodstained wedge of oak rested.

"By heaven, Papa," Louis exclaimed.

The doctor continued to wrap bandages round and round Harry's body. "He screamed when I touched it, and then fainted. I can scarce stop the bleeding. It is a terrible wound."

"Are you saying he will die?" Nick demanded.

"One is hopeful. If he rests, and I am here. And I will stay. You'd best send your people ashore for a spell, Mr. Minnett."

"Of course. But I must stay also."

"What nonsense. What are you going to do, save worry yourself into bed beside him? Go ashore with Louis."

"Papa served in the navy as a lad," Louis explained.

"No doubt," Nick said. "I still feel . . ."

"And I have said what I wish done," Planchet said. "Louis tells me you are a friend of the Count."

"Indeed I am. But . . ."

"It would be discourteous, would it not, to drop your anchor off St. Suliac and not pay a call upon so distinguished a friend? Besides"—at last he seemed satisfied with the bandage, and tied it in a neat little knot— "Mademoiselle Aurora is there."

Nick glanced at Louis in some embarrassment.

"We speak of you constantly, dear friend," Condorcet said. "I was going to tell you, but at some more appropriate moment."

"There is none better than now." Planchet stood back from the bunk, and pulled his lip; the white bandage had already turned pink. "Leave your friend to me. If he can be saved, I will do so."

"He is a good doctor," Louis said. "Had I not anticipated free medical treatment for the rest of my days, I had never troubled his daughter."

"Ah, begone with you," Planchet growled.

Nick climbed the ladder, told the crew what had been agreed.

"You'll dine with us, all of you," Louis said. "We'll seek you in the tavern, at dusk. Mr. Minnett and I are going to pay a social call."

Allardyce rowed them ashore.

"And what do the Benoîts think of you undertaking a political career?" Nick asked.

"It would be best the subject was not raised, Nick," said Louis. "The Count is a splendid fellow, but he feels the conduct of French affairs is best left in aristocratic hands. And as for Etienne, why, I'll wager that, were I not accompanying you, he'd turn me from the door."

"Oh, come now," Nick protested. "He is your friend."

"There are no friends in France today, Nick," Louis said, his face suddenly serious. "There is only politics."

Louis Condorcet borrowed his father-in-law's horse for Nick to ride the two miles to the château, accompanying his friend on an elderly mare. They followed the towpath, with the rushing brown water on their right, while on their left the woods waited, damp and empty at this time of the year, except for the rabbits. It was a place of noisy silence, as the whisper of the water dominated all other sounds, even muted the horses' hooves. Compared with the hustle and bustle and stench of London, and indeed Paris, Nick thought it a paradise.

But perhaps this was at least partly because of the

presence of the Château Benoît. They came upon it suddenly, its old gray walls thrusting through the trees, and thence to their right into the river itself, where there was a landing stage; it was possible to come alongside when the tide was full. The gate stood open; it was difficult to suppose the gates of the Château Benoît ever being shut. They walked their horses under the archway, and were met by the ostlers.

"Ah, Monsieur Condorcet," cried the blacksmith. "What is the news of the meeting, monsieur?"

"Why, I am elected." Condorcet swung himself to the ground, slapped the man on the shoulder. "I am your representative."

"Well, glory be to God," said the man, and crossed himself.

Louis laughed. "Now is that an insult or a compliment, would you say, Nick?"

"Monsieur Minnett?" The blacksmith peered at the young man. "It cannot be."

"I'm sorry to say it is, Jean. Is the Count at home?"

"The Count is here," boomed that deep voice he loved so well, and Nick faced the house, and the porch, and the short, stout man who stood there, while now the Alsatian dog left his side and came forward, slowly, sniffing to make sure this was indeed a friend.

"Uncle Pierre." Nick reached for the brown, weather-beaten hands, smiling at the equally brown face which seemed to dissolve into a thousand wrinkles as the Count smiled. "How good to see you."

"You should have sent word you were coming, Nick. You are to stay?" The Count looked past Nick as if seeking a clothesbag.

Nick shook his head. "I am here by accident."

Louis had joined them. "A fight with a revenue cutter, my lord."

"A fight? My God. But you are all right?"

"I am. Poor Harry Yealm is sore wounded."

"We'll have Planchet to him," the Count announced.

"Condorcet, discover that rascally father-in-law of yours . . ."

"Patience, my lord. Papa is already by Harry's bunk, doing what he can. But the wound is bad. Nick must be distracted."

"Distracted? Ha. You'll come in, Nick. I have a surprise for you. Oh, you too, Condorcet. We'll take a glass of wine."

A footman, in the green and gold livery of the Benoîts, held the door for them, and another was waiting inside the gloomy hall, where the stands of armor and the age-darkened portraits of past Benoîts alike helped to suggest an early dusk. A third carried a tray on which was a decanter and several crystal goblets.

But Nick was looking toward the staircase at the far end of the hall, and the young man on his way down.

"Etienne." He hurried forward, arms outstretched.

"Nick? Can it be possible?" Etienne Benoît was no taller than his father, although he remained considerably thinner, and his face had not yet become wrinkled; it was not a handsome face, as the features seemed somewhat close together, but it was strong. Unlike his father, his clothes indicated his rank; his vest was dark blue velvet, and his coat sky blue; his watch chain was gold, and his cravat spotless white. "You are to stay?"

"A call, dear friend."

"He is in *Golden Rose*," the Count explained. "Harry Yealm is hurt."

"Wounded in a fight with the English coastguard," Condorcet said.

"A fight?" Etienne wondered. "But why?"

"We would not stop when hailed," Nick said. "Our holds are filled with best claret. It would have meant confiscation of the ship—and no doubt prison."

"Prison?" Etienne demanded. "For the heir to the House of Minnett?"

"Well, perhaps not. But certainly for Harry and his people."

"And so you elected to run for it and damned near got

killed," the Count remarked. "What your father will say . . ."

"I would be much obliged, Uncle Pierre, if my father never learns of it. He supposes we are fishing the banks south of Lyme Bay."

"Fishing," the Count said. "What an occupation for a gentleman." He led them into the winter parlor, where a log fire blazed in the grate, sending slivers of light darting across the room to punctuate the chintz antimacassars on the upholstered chairs. "Look there." He pointed through the window. "My potatoes are already showing. This is going to be a good year. Five cows are in calf, and it is not yet April. There is progress. Eh, Condorcet?"

"Oh yes, my lord, it will be a good year," the lawyer agreed, and raised his glass. "I give you France."

"I'll drink to that," Nick agreed. "And I will say again, how good it is to be here. And now, Uncle Pierre, I have heard . . ."

"France," Etienne de Benoît said, and drained his glass. "Let us hope she survives. You've news of the meeting, Louis?"

"Oh indeed, Etienne. I have been chosen."

There was a moment of shocked silence, and the footman hurried forward with the decanter.

"You?" Etienne demanded. "I did not know you intended to stand."

"Why, are you not satisfied with a country practice?" the Count asked.

"Indeed I would be, my lord, were circumstances different. But as Etienne has just said, these are sad times for our country. It is my duty to assist in any way I can."

"And joining the rabble in Paris is a help?" Etienne asked.

The smile left Condorcet's face. "I am now one of the rabble, monsieur," he said. "And it seems that it is up to us, as it has been left to other brains, other ambitions, for too long."

"You think so?" Etienne insisted. "Let me tell you, Condorcet, you know not what you do. You think a nation is like a large lump of putty, and when you grow tired of its shape you seize it and pull it about, in a moment. That way lies disaster, my friend. That way you do not know what you have, until you have it."

"One must try, monsieur," Condorcet said.

"Gentlemen," said Aurora de Benoît from the doorway. "You are not arguing again? Can there be nothing but politics?"

Nick started forward, and checked. Her face had not changed, and the eyes, deep blue and sparkling, were as he remembered. But the voice, soft and clear, now possessed a quality of confidence which might even amount to arrogance. The long golden hair which used to float around the shoulders was gathered on the top of her head; it was secured there with a silver band, and the short and slender body was lost beneath the enormous panniers which extended her crimson gown.

Her manner had changed to suit her voice. "Nick Minnett," she said, and swept toward him, her right hand extended.

Nick lifted it to his lips. "May I dare call you Aurora?"

"It is my name." But already she was turning to Condorcet, and Nick was amazed to see a sparkle of color in her cheeks. "Monsieur, you are a stranger in this house, it seems."

Most remarkable of all, Condorcet was also blushing. "My time is scarce my own, mademoiselle."

"Politics," boomed the Count. "As you say, my dear, there is nothing but politics."

"As of this moment the subject is closed," said the girl. "You will stay to supper. Nick? Louis?"

"Oh, but . . ." Nick began, and was checked by a quick shake of the head from Condorcet.

"We shall be flattered, mademoiselle."

"Nick, walk with me, and leave these gentlemen to continue their quarrel. You'll tell me about Lucy? And Madame Minnett? They are well?"

She moved for the glass doors leading to the terrace, and the footman hastily opened them for her.

"As well as ever. Lucy will be twenty-one in October, you know. There will be a ball, to which you will be invited."

She tapped her cheek with her fan, and the doors closed behind them; she drew her stole closer around her shoulders. They faced the river, and the dying afternoon.

"I doubt that will be possible, Nick. You will have heard I am now waiting on Her Majesty?"

He stood behind her, at the balustrade. "Louis was telling me. But surely . . ."

"She is very demanding. And it is my duty. Now what of you? Annette was telling me there has been a fight at sea. She listens to everything, you know. Pirates?"

He laughed. "Coastguards. We are smuggling wine."

She turned to face him. "I wish I could understand you. You could buy all the wine in France from your allowance."

"That is scarce the point. There is the adventure . . ." He paused to frown at her.

"I do not understand men. Some are too timid, some are too bold . . . That Condorcet."

"Louis?"

She turned back to look at the water. "He came to see me, a year ago. An official call, with a card, and everything. A lawyer, my God. He told me it had been suggested that he should marry, for the sake of his family; but he wished me to know that he would not, did I so command him."

"Good heavens," Nick said. "Louis?" But it made sense. If he had fallen in love with their childhood sweetheart, then why not Louis? "What did you say?"

"I laughed. I command only my equals, Louis, I told him. I think marriage to Seraphine Planchet is entirely what you deserve. Do you know, this is the first occasion he has entered our house since that time?"

"You were perhaps a little brusque."

"I was extraordinarily angry, if you must know."

Nick told her about Harry Yealm's marriage.

"Oh, really, Nick, have you no *friends?*"

"They are friends. You are thinking of the sons of my father's friends. I am afraid we have little in common."

"You do make me so angry," she said, smiling. "You have some sort of a curse running through your veins, I declare. Look at you, Nicholas. When dear Uncle Percy dies, the bank will be yours. What, will you visit Paris to see Monsieur Necker in the *Golden Rose*, with Harry Yealm at your side?"

"It would be the most pleasant way of doing so, certainly." He reached for her hands, and after a moment's hesitation she allowed him to take them. "But Father feels as you do. He thinks I have been allowed to 'run wild' long enough. He suggests I follow the prevailing fashion."

Now she did frown, and pulled herself free. "I beg of you, say no more."

"But . . ."

"You have indeed spent too long in the company of sea captains and advocates. Were you not my oldest and dearest friend I should really never speak to you again. If you have anything to say on such a subject, it must be to Papa. You do know that, Nick?"

"Of course I know that. But I would not ask for your hand without first discovering whether you wished me to do so."

"I do not see that my feelings enter into it at all."

"You mean you would marry whoever your father decided, be he old or young, handsome or ugly, healthy or diseased?"

Now her anger was genuine. "I have sufficient confidence in Papa to know that my future is in good hands, monsieur. In any event, it is in better hands than even his."

"Then I may speak with him?"

"You may do what you like, sir. The answer will be the same. The disposal of my hand is the prerogative of Her Majesty. I think your best course would be to have yourself presented at Versailles."

Nick gazed at her open-mouthed, but was distracted by the noise within the house. And a moment later the glass doors were themselves thrown open. Condorcet appeared.

"I beg your pardon, Aurora. Nick. Tom Price is here. Harry is dead."

Two

The music swelled out of the orchestral gallery; it escaped even the closed windows to ripple across the Lane and echo amongst the silent trees of Hyde Park. Within the house the noise was deafening, as the couples made their stately parade, separating and returning, arms raised high to form an arch beneath which others rushed, feet scuffing the polished mahogany, while sweat stood out on foreheads and elaborate wigs scattered powder on to the floor.

Nor was the kaleidoscope of color any more restful than the noise, for apart from the brilliant gowns of the ladies, the men offered sufficient contrasts, the black coats of the civilians being set off by the scarlet jackets of the military, while the pale blue livery of the Minnett footmen, circulating between the guests in a most perilous fashion with their trays of champagne held high, seemed positively sombre.

"Gad, sir." The Prince took a glass. "A Minnett ball is an occasion. Damn me, I'm glad I came after all." He beamed at the dancers, and toasted a returned smile from one of the ladies. He was a handsome man with his mop of curly fair hair dominating his splendid features; there was only a trace of liquor redness in his cheeks, and at twenty-seven his figure bore comparison with any man's in the room.

"And did you not intend to, Your Grace?" Mr. Pitt was only three years the elder, and yet looked an old man already, his long face sombre with responsibility, his long body seeming to stoop.

"Ah bah," George said, "he'll not increase my advance. Now there is gratitude, eh? We gave his family refuge in their time of need, and here I am touched for a mere fifty thousand . . ."

Pitt allowed himself a smile in which there was more than a hint of malice. "But then, Your Grace, we are celebrating Miss Lucy's twenty-first birthday. The wealthiest heiress in England."

"Gad, sir," the Prince said, and walked away. The fellow was infernally rude. To pretend that Maria could be forgotten, treated as if she did not exist because the old madman would not give his permission . . . He pulled at his lip as Lucy Minnett reached the end of the line, and bowed to him before she turned. She was a pretty wench. But a banker's daughter . . . Papa would never give his consent there either, though the Government might favor such a match. He cast Pitt a surreptitious glance; just how much, for example, was the Prime Minister's debt?

His attention was taken by the girl behind Lucy, taller than the guest of honor, with a mass of curly yellow hair piled up on her head, sparkling with emeralds; the younger generation was beginning to abandon wigs, he reflected, just as they had already abandoned hoops in favor of no more than a bustle. And a good thing too; a man could at last be sure where their legs were. But he was more interested in the plunging décolletage which promised a glimpse of nipple as she bowed, and which did allow an inspection of a magnificent expanse of heaving blue-veined whiteness, at once compressed and projected by the tight bodice of the pale green satin gown.

"Gad," he muttered. "Nick. Come here, boy. Who is that glorious creature?"

Nicholas inspected the dancers. "Lady Caroline Moncey."

"Charles Moncey's child? Good God. Why have I not met her before?"

"She seldom comes to town, Your Grace."

"Aye. Old Charles quarreled with Papa. Gad, sir, but

that such a creature should be buried in the depths . . . Where is it?"

"The seat is in Wiltshire, Your Grace."

"Wiltshire? My God. The end of the world. But as she is here . . . Nick, you'll present her."

"Willingly, Your Grace. You'll remember she has a brother, who has a confoundedly hot temper."

"Gad, sir," the Prince remarked. "As your Lucy has a brother who is a wet blanket. Begone, sir. I'll present myself."

But when he looked for her at the end of the dance, he could not find her. "I saw him ogling me," she gasped, closing the door of the study to a crack.

Lucy giggled; she had all the Minnett looks and charm, spoiled only by a refusal to take any aspect of life seriously. "I can think of at least twenty women in this house who would give their virginity to be ogled by Prinny."

"And it would involve just that," Caroline agreed. "Mine is for sale, dear Lucy, at a higher price than that lout can pay. Now, should sweet Nicky choose to tilt his lance . . ."

Lucy gave a peal of laughter. "Nicky? You'd be bored stiff. Which is more than he would ever become."

Caroline Moncey closed her fan with a snap. "I'd wager I'd have him stiff as a board in seconds. He is such a handsome boy. And I recall him as a gay one, when last we met."

"Ah," Lucy said, "but now he feels the weight of the world on his shoulders. His best friend died, but six months ago."

Caroline frowned at her. "Nicky's best friend? I can think of no gentleman of my acquaintance dropping off."

Lucy screamed with delight. "Nicky doesn't have friends like you or me, Carrie. This fellow was a fisherman. Can you believe it? If you'd find yourself in bed with my brother, you must be ready for the smell of fish."

"Oysters, you mean?"

"I mean hanging over the side of some little boat in the

Channel, working like any port sweeping. Oh, he is a total worry to Mama. And this fellow, Harry, or something, was his friend. But they got involved in a storm last Easter, and the man was injured in some way, and died, and Nick had to bring the boat back to Lyme Regis, and break the news to the widow . . ."

"Elbow-deep in fish grease." Caroline laughed in turn.

"No doubt. It made him awful serious, on a sudden. But there is more. You'll have heard of the Benoîts?"

Caroline shook her head. "Should I have?"

"They are customers. There is a son, Etienne, quite a nice boy. And then there is a daughter." Another peal of laughter.

"Then Nicky *is* capable of becoming stiff."

"Perhaps. But Aurora has become a great lady and will scarce look at him. She'd not attend the ball, because she is busy at Versailles."

"Bah," Caroline said. "She is not here because they have no money. None of the French nobility have any money, especially since this last trouble, as you should know better than I."

"Me? I take no part in the business. Accounting? That is clerk's work. Oooh, the Prince." Hastily she closed the door and turned the key. A moment later the handle turned.

"What will he do?" Caroline whispered.

Lucy shrugged, her mouth wide. "He will be furious. But he owes Papa more than almost anyone. So . . ."

"What a pleasant position to be in," Caroline mused, "especially when you consider that he will undoubtedly one day be king." She seized her friend's hand and dragged her on to a settee. "Lucy, we must do something about Nick. He is too nice a boy just to moulder away. As you say, accounting is for clerks; but I will wager that if he is not distracted he will become the clerkiest clerk in all the world. He is too serious."

"Why . . . I suppose you are right. You? And Nick?" Lucy frowned. "You are the elder."

"By a year. I doubt he knows it. Or will, save you tell him."

"Oh you may count on me. But . . . you are setting yourself a steep slope to climb."

"But you will help me," Caroline declared. "So let us at least discover if he likes me at all."

"I really think you should dance, at least once, Nick," Percy Minnett suggested, with that mildness which invariably deceived his customers. "I agree that it is a senseless pastime, but of social value. I'd not have you arrogant, Nick, ever."

"It is not arrogance, Father, truly. It is . . ."

"Grief? Six months is an ample period of mourning. And we delayed this party for the end of it."

Nick sighed. "Not only grief, Father. The whole world seems a sadder place this year than last. When I think of that business in France, ending seigneurial rights . . ."

"I'll not call the Benoîts, boy, if that troubles you. But believe me, if you spend your time worrying about our clients, you will be gray by thirty. A man must amuse himself, occasionally. Why do you not go back to sea for a day or two?"

"I am due at Oxford on Monday."

"Leave it a week, if you wish. Is Harry's boat still in Lyme?"

"I doubt it. Mistress Yealm will have sold it by now. It is all she has to sell."

"She's young," Percy Minnett said, "and a good-looking girl, as I recall. She'll wed again soon enough. But whoever now owns the ship will know you have conned her, and well. You'll find a berth."

Nick smiled. "And you don't condemn me for going to sea?"

"I told you, a man must amuse himself. If fishing amuses you, well and good. There are worse hobbies."

"Do you know, I might . . ." Nick found his arms seized. "Lucy? Carrie? Have you no partners?"

"We are escaping the Prince," Lucy hissed. "You'll help us?"

"Of course he will," Percy Minnett said, "but I'd best not be privy to your scheme." He went toward the orchestra.

"You are too late," Nick said. For Prince George was on the far side of the room, frowning at them.

"Then come on," Caroline shouted, and dragged him through the glass doors on to the terrace and down the steps to the lawn, while Lucy pulled his other arm. "We have arranged a party." Several of the guest carriages were already moving down the drive, each filled with shouting, laughing young people. "You go with Tom Pelham, Lucy," Caroline decided. "Nick can drive me."

"Drive you where?"

"To a place where we can really enjoy ourselves." She was already at the step to the Minnett's perch phaeton; a groom held the horse. Now she looked over her shoulder. "You'll not refuse to take me, Nick?"

Her pelisse swung open as she turned, and she was breathing heavily from her run across the lawn. Her coiffure was just starting to collapse; he observed that she had taken the precaution of removing her jewelry. But she was an utterly beautiful woman. So Mama said that the Monceys had bad blood; that could be merely because the Earl had quarreled with the King, umpteen years ago. Mama had never tried to stop the friendship between Caroline and Lucy.

And besides, something of her contagious gaiety was beginning to penetrate his reserve. As Father had truly said, he had mourned too long. The fact was, he felt as much guilt as grief. Had he surrendered, Harry's life might have been saved. A term in gaol was preferable to an eternity in a grave. And then Anne, her face, so fine and strong, seeming to dissolve as he had blurted out what had happened; the silence in all Lyme as the news had spread. Nick Minnett sailed for sport, and smuggled for sport; but it had been Harry Yealm's life, and it had cost him his life at the end.

He sat beside Caroline, and the groom closed the door. He picked up the whip and jerked the rein, and the horse turned for the drive.

"You have no coat," Caroline said, seeming to discover this for the first time. She unfastened her pelisse and spread it around his shoulders as well as her own, huddling against him.

"Really, Carrie, I cannot possibly . . ."

"What? Permit the heir of the House of Minnett to catch cold? Should I ever be forgiven?"

He cracked the whip above the horse's back to increase his speed. The other carriages were already lost to sight.

"Take the Dover Road," she instructed. Her chin rested on his arm; a gust of wind blew her hair across his mouth. Her perfume smelt delicious. "Do you know vingt-et-un? 'Tis all the rage."

"I have played it," Nick said.

Her arm went round his waist. "Lucy tells me you are for your last year at Oxford." Her fingers slid over the front of his vest, gently plucked at his cravat. "And then what will you do?"

"Join Father in the business, of course."

"And become the most important man in the kingdom." His cravat had been untied, and her fingers touched his throat. Then she released him, and fell back in her seat, arms spread wide. "Oh, to have so much money. The lack of it is a curse; but you'd have no notion of that."

"Nor can you, surely." He glanced to his left.

"Lack of money is merely a reflection on the amount of money one requires to spend," she argued, and sat up again to hold his arm and bring her face and her scent and the occasional wisp of her now totally collapsed hair into his face. "We are arrived."

The road had topped a heath, and beneath them was a posting inn, its yard a cluster of other carriages and hard pressed ostlers, its windows allowing a gust of noise to escape. "Will you stop?"

"Here? We are within sight of the building."

"They are not looking out," she explained. "And I would ask a favor."

He dragged on the reins, and turned toward her. She placed a hand on each of his cheeks and drew his head down. "From the moment I saw you, this evening," she whispered, her breath shrouding his nose, his eyes, his ears, his mouth, "I promised myself a kiss."

He had driven ten miles, the wind rushing about his ears, his head filled with wine, his mind with the army of beautiful women who had danced before him; and his memory could still be inflamed at his amused rejection by Aurora de Benoît. He had indeed been tempted to ask Father for a mission to Paris, armed with a letter which would have secured his place at Versailles. But Harry's death, and affairs in France, and particularly Paris since the storming of the Bastille, had left him confused . . . He touched her lips with his, and found his mouth forced open, and her tongue licking his teeth, exploring with a delighted wonder, as her hands left his face once again to search his body. He closed his own hands over hers, trying to withdraw his mouth without success, while his instincts cried out to let her have at him, and indeed, to have back at her, without restraint.

She laughed, a gentle gurgle of amusement deep in her throat, and slid away from him. "I swear you are not such a dry old stick after all, Nick Minnett." Gently she eased her coat from round his shoulders.

He could still taste her. "Do you, then, seek only to tease, Caroline?"

She half pursed her lips, and then laughed again. "As you say, our arrival may have been overseen. And now we know that perhaps we can entertain each other, why, we must attempt to recreate the opportunity. Now let us make haste."

He drove the phaeton into the yard, his mind in turmoil. He assisted her down, and she smiled at him, and at the ostlers, before sweeping into the inn.

"Carrie," screamed Lucy Minnett, running forward to embrace her friend. "We had given you up for lost."

"Perhaps we missed our way," Caroline smiled.

"Hooray," one of the men shouted, and they clustered round Nick to slap him on the back. "There's a fate any man could envy."

"We did not miss our way," Nick shouted, his cheeks glowing. "The horse was tired." This produced a fresh outburst of laughter.

Caroline clapped her hands. "The cards," she shouted. "Let us have at them. And why is there no ale?"

"It is here, Carrie," shouted another young man. "Mine host was reluctant, but he accepted the House of Minnett as our surety."

The innkeeper, accompanied by two young women, plump, red-faced and perspiring, hurried forward with foaming mugs.

"Good English beer." Caroline buried her face in a tankard.

Nick drank more cautiously. "Beer," he muttered at his sister. "On top of all that wine?"

She pinched his arm. "We are here to enjoy ourselves. I do believe you have never learned the meaning of the word." She pushed her way into the crowd which was gathering round one of the long tables as the cards were produced. "Make way. Nick would play."

"How can we toss against Nick?" someone laughed. "His credit is inexhaustible, and ours was long spent."

Another gale of laughter, and he discovered that the mug in his hand had been replaced by a full one.

"But you might win," Lucy explained. "And then you could at least be sure your debts would be paid."

"I'll not play," Nick insisted, and was distressed to discover that his tongue seemed to be growing in size.

"Of course you will," Lucy whispered. "They really want to take your money, and you'll not allow that, will you? Come on, the deal. The deal."

He leaned back, to sigh, and found his head resting against another soft body. His second card was the King of Hearts. Idly he turned over the hole card, and had it wrenched from his hand by the girl standing behind him. "An ace," she shrieked. "An ace."

Nick sat up, stared at the winning combination, and then at Caroline Moncey, seated opposite, smiling at him, tongue appearing for a second between her teeth before disappearing again. "I suspect you have a talent, for gaming, Nick. But have no fear. I shall oppose you with the utmost resolve."

Nick dealt, and called, and bid, and sold cards, and twisted them, Lucy ever at his elbow. It seemed impossible for him to lose the deal, and whenever he looked to his right there was another foaming tankard of beer. He felt the room start to float around him, while money accumulated in front of him, and a succession of faces drifted across his gaze.

But always one face remained, smiling, occasionally crying out in delight, more often muttering in despair. In time it became the only face left, but by then his brain was awash in a tumultuous brown sea, and he could scarce understand what she was saying.

"You have the luck of the devil," she cried.

Nick leaned back, found the soft body still behind him. "Am I then the winner?"

There was a fresh shout of laughter from all around him. "Why, Nick," someone said, "you have robbed us of our last pennies."

"I cannot believe it," Caroline declared, staring at him. "Pure luck. And luck will always turn. A last hand, Nick?"

Nick shrugged, moving his shoulders up and down the softness which sustained him. "As you will. Then I am for bed. Landlord, you'll find me a room; I'll not make it back to town tonight."

"But what will you bet, Carrie, sweet?" Lucy inquired. "You've no money left."

She pulled at her ears. "Why, my rings are gone as well. You have left me destitute, sweet Nick. But I'll not admit defeat. Will you wager all you possess, against all I possess, Nick?"

She floated in front of him, rising and falling; now his hearing seemed affected as well, for surely she had left her earrings at the house. "I know not what you mean. We'll have a hand." He dealt her a card, took one himself.

"Come one," she said. "Come on." He turned her second card face upward; a three. "Aha," she said. "Why, you must have a hundred pound there, Nicky. I shall be rich."

Nick turned his own card; a nine, took a peep at his hole card; a knave.

"Well, well, well," Lucy said. "What will you, madam?"

Caroline's tongue came out, pink and wet. "I cannot buy, so I must twist," she said, and turned over her hole card, a four. "Now then, Nick, deal easily, as you live and die."

He turned her third card face up; a seven.

"Fourteen," Lucy chanted. "You'll not make it, Carrie."

"You may come again, sweet Nick."

He dealt a two.

"Aha," Lucy said. "Now you have it. What are the odds on a five or less?"

Caroline stared at Nick. "What have you tucked away there?"

"Shall I tell you?"

"I will accept the hand of fate," Caroline said, sepulchrally. "I stick on sixteen. Now then, Nick do your worst."

Nick turned over the knave, and was greeted by a tremendous roar from the onlookers. "Nineteen. A win. Carrie, you have lost this night."

"Everything I possess," she said sadly, placing her elbows on the table. "Why, I am a perfect slave, as of this moment."

"A slave," they chanted. "A slave. Command her, Nick."

Nick burst into laughter, wondering why as he did so. "I cannot command myself. Landlord, that bed you promised me."

"It will be my pleasure, Mr. Minnett. If you can make the stairs, sir . . ."

Nick pushed himself up, half fell, seized the landlord's arm.

"But what of your winnings?" Lucy cried. "And what of us?"

"Get away with you, to bed. I shall come up tomorrow. As for my winnings, oh, take them back. I was but lucky." He staggered for the stairs, the landlord's arm around his waist. "Confound it, man, but your floor rocks like a ship."

"It is not far, Mr. Minnett. The first landing."

A door yawned, and a candle flared. He fell forward, and the bed seemed to rise to meet him. "You will have to assist me, fellow."

But there were other voices, and other hands, and a sliding away of consciousness, although he doubted that he actually slept, but rather tossed on the sea of brown beer, rising and falling, making him imagine that he was on the deck of *Golden Rose,* in a rising gale off the French coast. Harry Yealm smiled at him. Then the storm subsided and he was back at the Château Benoît, walking toward Aurora, only this time her arms were spread wide, waiting for him, and strangely she wore no clothes, although her nakedness could not be identified. It was there, soft and cool, shrouding him in gentle scent and throbbing flesh, bruising his lips and lying heavily on his belly, then slowly subsiding beside him to leave him at peace. He must be awake since chinks of light penetrated the curtains.

He sat up, seemed to leave his head behind. He held his hands to his eyes, forced himself to breathe evenly, waited for the bed to cease swaying. He moved his hands, looked down at himself, naked, legs lost beneath the rumpled sheet, and at the arm which lay across his thighs, slenderly rounded.

Slowly he turned his head. Caroline's hair clouded over her face, fluttering as she breathed. Below was an expanse of slowly heaving breast, and then a pouted belly looming above a matted wonderworld which in turn dominated the long slender legs; she lay entirely on top of the coverlet.

"Oh Christ," he muttered, and moved her arm. He staggered across the room, emptied the ewer into the basin, scooped cold water on to his face, felt his morning beard scraping his hands. For a moment the room resumed its swaying, and he had to hold the washstand to stop himself from falling.

He heard movement behind him. "Nick," she cried. "Oh, you *lover*."

"Sssh, for God's sake," he begged. "You'll wake the house."

"Do you not suppose they know we are here?"

He regained the bed, and sat down, watched her drag hair from her face. It was impossible not to look at her. She was utterly entrancing, utterly feminine, utterly abandoned.

"How came you here?" he asked.

"You won me at cards, Nick. Surely you remember?"

He frowned, and she laughed. "I do believe you do *not* remember."

"I . . ." He licked his lips, and had them lost in her mouth, as his body rested on hers, as her hardening nipples drove into his chest, as she seemed to entrap him.

Violently he pushed himself away from her, sat up again, legs dangling. "I remember. Christ, I was drunk."

Her fingers stroked his back, lightly, her nails tracing patterns on his flesh. "We were all drunk."

"And I . . . I won at cards." He turned. "And you?"

She gave a peal of delighted laughter. "I am yours now, Nick, for ever and ever."

"You must be out of your mind. We hardly know each other."

"What nonsense. I have known you for years."

"Well, we have been acquainted, of course. And there is the scandal. Did I . . .?"

"You do not even remember that? That's no compliment to a poor girl. Oh, Nick, you have the sweetest, the most determined weapon in all the world. Not," she hastily added, "that I have experience of such things." Her arms went round his waist, and her teeth bit gently into his side.

"Have at me again, I beg of you. I am quite desperate with love for you."

He seized her wrists and forced her hands apart, left the bed and began to gather his clothes.

"What are you doing?" she demanded.

"Getting dressed. And I should like you to do the same."

"I am comfortable here."

He pulled on his breeches and felt a little safer. He could even face the bed again. "I was drunk, and I was lucky. I apologize."

"You *apologize*?"

"But then," he said thoughtfully, "you also were drunk, as you say, or you would not have indulged in that ridiculous wager, much less honored it."

She stared at him, her brows drawing together, her face slowly hardening.

"You must see that to suppose anything can grow from this is quite impossible," he said.

"I think your words are singularly ill chosen," she remarked. "I have more than a fear that I have already been impregnated. Certainly your thrusts were like to have ruptured my womb."

"Oh Christ," he said. "But I cannot remember."

"Which is why I suggest you try again. You'll not pretend to be unable, with a towering bulge such as you display there."

"Carrie," he said, sitting on the edge of the bed and taking her hands. "I know I would have remembered."

"My God." She withdrew her hands, and pulled the sheet over her body. "They always said a banker could never be a gentleman. No doubt a midwife will be necessary soon enough; she'll answer your doubts."

He sighed, and accepted defeat. "What would you have me do?"

"The burden is mine," she said, still speaking coldly. "I shall be a good wife, I promise you. I got drunk, and deserve my fate. What Papa will say . . . I shall be whipped. And ostracized. A Moncey, wed to a banker."

"Married? Wife?" he shouted, and his head began to throb.

"I am afraid it must come to that. We are both entirely compromised."

"Compromised." Slowly, a host of memories came to him, of Caroline Moncey's name linked with a variety of men. "I think you make too much of the matter." He left the bed and finished dressing.

"Too much of finding myself in bed with a strange man?"

"You have just pointed out that I am not a strange man."

"Yet is my maidenhead lost."

"Oh, indeed? And can you swear it got mislaid last night?"

"You . . . you . . ." She left the bed herself in a flurry of scattering sheets and pillows, and ran at him, making a truly unforgettable picture of flying hair, flashing eyes, swelling breasts, long legs and heaving belly.

He caught her wrists. "I but sought to explain that the situation is not half so cut and dried as you seem to fear." She spat at him. "And to convince you that marriage between us is impossible, I will wager we are not the only couple last night to wake up between the sheets. Nothing will be said of it."

"You think so? And what, may I ask, have you got against marrying a Moncey, Nicholas Minnett?"

"Nothing, Carrie. Truly. Save that I do not love you."

"Love? What in the name of God has that got to do with it? I'd be a poor woman could I stoop to love one such as you. But marry you I will."

"And I have said you will not, and there is an end to the matter. I will arrange it; the landlord can be bought." Gently he sat her on the bed. "As for those louts from last night, why, we shall simply agree that we slept at the inn, but in different rooms. Believe me, Carrie, for you and I to wed would be the height of folly for us both. Now get dressed."

He released her arms, and she smiled; the beauty seemed to disappear in the contempt of her mouth and eyes. "An

end to the matter. That is what you think, Nick Minnett.
And suppose I confess to the truth?"

"I have said I shall deny all knowledge. Nor shall I be
lying."

"Oh, you have explained a great deal. Now you will
listen to me. I did not go to the trouble of having you
play the sharper merely to be thrown aside like a sack."
She bit her lip at his frown, then tossed her head. "So
there it is."

"You planned it?"

"With the help of your own sister. You have been a
bachelor too long, Nick. Oh, it was great sport, watching
you win without knowing how it came about. It was even
greater sport, last night, having you all to myself."

"You . . . you harlot," he shouted.

"On the contrary. You should be pleased to possess a
woman who knows her own mind. And Nick . . ." she
reached for his hand again. "I will be the very best of
wives to you. I swear it."

He pulled his hand free, backed slowly across the room.

"Nick," she said, kneeling on the bed, cupping her
breasts. "Stop being a fool and come back to bed."

"With you? I'd as soon sleep with a tigress." He
wrenched the key from the inside of the door, stepped
into the corridor, slammed the door behind him, turned
the key, and dropped it into his pocket. He discovered
he was at once sweating and panting for breath.

Presumably Lucy, silly girl, had but supposed she was
assisting in a practical joke. No doubt that went for all of
them there last night; but it was a joke which could
rebound on him. The House of Minnett was a pyramid
of trust, built by his great-grandfather, expanded by his
grandfather, and brought to its present state of prosperous
omnipotence in the money markets of Europe by his
father. A Minnett who drank and gambled, and even
smuggled, for sport, might be regarded with amused toler-
ance; for the Minnett heir in any way to tarnish the reputation of the House for absolute honesty and discretion

would be to bring down the wrath of an entire graveyard of ancestors. He stamped down the stairs, found the landlord waiting, looking anxious, and holding a large sheet of paper.

"Good morning to you, Mr. Minnett. I hope you slept well?"

"When I slept." Nick cursed himself for a fool; there was quite the wrong thing to have said. "What have you there? The accounting? God's teeth." He snatched the paper. "Seven pounds?"

"Well, sir, there is last night as well."

"You mean not one of those rascals contributed a penny? Well, I've but five on me. You'll have to accept a note. Fetch me some ink and paper." He turned for the taproom. "And meanwhile, you can prepare my phaeton. I wish to leave on the instant."

"The . . . phaeton, Mr. Minnett? But that is gone."

"Gone?" Nick ran to the door, wrenched it open. The yard was empty save for a single tired looking mount tethered to the steps and greedily investigating a nosebag. "By heaven, but they are wretches. I must get to London, landlord. Will you rent me this nag?"

"Oh, not that, sir. That belongs to a traveler, from Dover and in haste. He has merely stopped for breakfast." The landlord pulled his nose. "But I have an animal, Mr. Minnett . . ."

"Then I shall make your note for ten pounds," Nick said. "Fear not, he shall be returned. You mentioned breakfast."

"Yes, sir. He is old, you understand, and not very speedy."

"He'll do." Nick pulled open the door to the taproom.

"Yes, sir. But he'll not carry both you and the young lady."

"I'll send for her when I return the horse. Now make haste, man. Eggs." He sat at the table, discovered himself opposite the traveller. "Good day to you, sir." He frowned at the clothes, then at the man himself, small and dark, wearing a moustache. "You're French."

"Does that offend you, sir?" The man had little accent.

"Quite the contrary." One of the landlord's daughters brought in pen and ink and paper, and he carefully wrote out a promissory note. "You can give me news. Especially of Brittany."

"Ah, Brittany." The stranger shrugged. "Why, sir, no doubt things are as bad there as everywhere else."

"Bad, sir? Here is your note, landlord."

The landlord placed a plate of steaming poached eggs on the table.

"How bad, monsieur?"

"You could describe the whole thing as a massacre."

Nick raised his head, slowly, his fork still on its way to his mouth. "Who has been massacred?"

"Why, most of the provincial nobility, for a start. Well, perhaps not entirely massacred, you'll understand; but some have died, to be sure, and all have been burned out of house and home."

"Killed?" Nick cried. "Burned out? Is there war?"

"Oh, indeed. Civil war; or there will be. You have not heard? You should know a decree was passed ending all seigneurial rights. That were bad, to be sure, in that it impoverished the entire landowning class. But worse, as the tenants had in many cases deep grudges against their erstwhile masters, they have risen all over the country, and as I said, are indulging in a perfect orgy of burning and looting."

Nick put down his fork. The food had become quite tasteless. "There was small reason for hate in Brittany."

"Perhaps. The cause is licence more than hate."

"But . . . what are the nobles doing about it?"

The stranger finished his breakfast, sighed and leaned back with a contented expression. "What would you have them do? As I said, where they would resist, then are they slaughtered like pests."

"You approve of these happenings?"

"On my word, sir, no. I am but telling you what has happened."

"And can they not at least remove themselves from danger?"

The stranger began work with a silver toothpick. "Where would you have them go? In Paris they are prisoners of the mob."

"Well, then, if they are in any event being made destitute, why do they not leave the country?"

"A great number are doing that. Or at least, endeavoring to do so. I suppose for those living close to the borders of Austria or Savoy, it is no difficult matter. But it is not legal."

"Damn your legality," Nick shouted. "What of those who live on the coast? Can they not take ship?"

"Supposing they can find a vessel. But all ships are under the jurisdiction of the government."

"My God." Nick looked up as the landlord entered.

"Your horse is ready, Mr. Minnett. But there is a terrible banging on the door upstairs. It would seem to be locked."

Nick threw the key on the table. "Let her out once I am gone. Give her what she wants and take it out of that note. You'll excuse me, sir; I am most grateful for your information." He went outside, hesitated on the step. The landlord's horse was indeed a sorry creature. And where should it carry him? The Château Benoît, in flames? Pierre and Etienne, murdered? Aurora . . . He ran down the steps and vaulted into the saddle.

The landlord was behind him. "Mr. Minnett. Mr. Minnett. The London road is that way."

Nick kicked the old horse in the ribs. "There are more pressing necessities than London, sir. I am for Lyme Regis."

It was marvelous to be in the fresh air, hatless and coatless, urging his mount toward the west. Remarkably, before this morning he had felt no urge to return to Lyme; the town was too closely associated with Harry and *Golden Rose*. But now he had a reason, and as Father had said, Nick Minnett should have no difficulty in persuading the *Rose*'s new owner to put to sea.

And then, what? He could not believe that anything had really happened in St. Suliac. Pierre de Benoît had always been the most popular of seigneurs, and even were he not, Louis Condorcet would have made sure nothing happened to the family or the château.

But Louis was probably still in Paris, unaware that anything might be wrong. Well, then, old Dr. Planchet . . . but there were too many possibilities to be considered. He was only sure that he must find out what had happened, and help the Benoîts if he could.

He stopped for the night in Poole, rode his exhausted horse down the hill behind Lyme Regis just after noon on the second afternoon. How good it looked; there was hardly any breeze, and the sea was no more than a gentle surge, with a trace of mist obscuring the horizon. The little town nestled behind its breakwater; the tide was low and most of the boats were dry.

And there was *Golden Rose,* sitting up on her legs. He frowned. The ketch sadly needed paint, and her furled sails drooped, as if they had not been set for some time. But he lost sight of the harbor as he rode down the main street, in turn attracting attention, for he still wore his evening clothes, his hair was scattered and his cravat untied, and there was mud splattered on his pantaloons. And, he remembered, a two-day growth of beard on his chin. Several people recognized him and called a greeting, but he merely waved and urged his horse on to the cottage by the mole. He threw the reins over the post— the poor animal was too tired to wander, in any event— and rapped on the door. And listened to the bolts being drawn.

He frowned again. Harry Yealm had always been a careful man. His house had never lacked paint any more than his ship, and his garden had always been neatly tended. Well, to be sure, there were still roses beside the door, but the walls were peeling and dark with damp, and there were shingles missing from the roof.

The door swung in. "Anne? My God, girl, but what is the matter with you?"

Her auburn hair was loose on her shoulders; he would have recognized her anywhere. And yet, not so easily when close. Her face was flawless, long and strong, as if chiseled from marble; but the cheeks were sunk and there was no color. Her green eyes were the most lively he had ever seen; today they were dull and disinterested, scarce seeming to know who it was. And that tall, powerful body, for she was not much shorter than Nick himself, seemed no more than a bag of bones, on which there hung a sadly threadbare black gown. "Anne?" he asked again. "Can it be you?"

"Mr. Minnett?" For just a moment her eyes sparkled. "What brings you to Lyme?"

He looked past her into the gloom. The October afternoon was damp rather than cold, yet there was no fire. Indeed, there was nothing in the room at all, save a box. "What has happened here?"

"Why, nothing, sir. I'd ask you in, but I'm that busy . . ."

He gripped her shoulders, very gently moved her to one side, and stepped inside. It was indeed bare, if clean. The door to the kitchen stood open; there too the fire was out, although there was a pot on the range. Here there was at least a table, and a single chair. He scratched his head, listened to the front door close. "I . . . I'm cleaning, you see, Mr. Minnett."

"You're a poor liar, and that's a fact," he remarked. "May I?" The bedroom door was shut.

"You've no right, sir," she protested.

He opened it anyway. The bed remained, but nothing else. "You've been robbed?"

"Oh, good lord, sir, not in Lyme. It's just that, well, with Harry gone, I found I had no need for furniture."

"Who bought the *Rose?*"

"Well, Mr. Minnett, times are hard, and the fishing has gone off this summer, and . . ."

"She's still yours?" he cried, his heart leaping.

"Well yes, sir, Mr. Minnett."

"And you've been selling everything else you possess to keep from starving?"

"Good lord no, sir. I do my needlework . . ."

"I'm sure you do very well. But I need the *Rose,* Anne. Will you sell?"

"To you, Mr. Minnett? What would you do with her?"

"Sail her, for a start. And today. The gear is all right?"

"Oh yes, sir. But . . ." she clasped her hands together. "I have no idea, for selling it to you."

"Harry must have put a price on it."

"He spoke of four hundred pounds. But not to you, Mr. Minnett. He'd sooner give it to you. I'm sure that's what he would want."

"I'll pay a thousand, Anne, if I can take possession now."

Slowly her mouth opened. "A . . . a thousand pounds?"

"I'll have to owe you the money for a week or two, until I can arrange the matter with my father; but if you'll agree, you have my word." He held out his hand. For a moment she hesitated, then gave him hers. It was firm and dry, and strong. But there were tears in her eyes.

"You've no right to be so generous, Mr. Minnett."

"To you, Anne? 'Tis not generosity; 'tis a duty, and one I've neglected too long. Now listen, I'm starving, and I'll need food if I'm to cross the Channel."

Slowly she withdrew her hand. "You're welcome to the pot."

"Oh, nonsense," he shouted, and felt in his pocket. "Here's two guineas. Go and buy some food, and some firewood. I like to be warm. Hurry now. I must catch the next tide."

Once again she hesitated, then she picked up her shopping basket, tied her bonnet beneath her chin. "And you, sir?"

"I'm to the quay to raise a crew." He threw an arm round her shoulder, squeezed her against him. "I'll keep the ship here in Lyme, Anne. 'Tis her home port. You'll be my agent. Now wipe up those tears and let's get to it."

Another hug, and he hurried down the street. What a strange world it was, to be sure, and what a thoughtless one. He had deliberately avoided thinking of Anne, or the *Rose,* all summer, because of the grief, and the guilt, their memory would awaken. But the guilt had been for Harry's death, not for Anne starving. And now . . . he felt a sudden tremendous surge of excitement. The ship was his; he had no doubt Father could be persuaded—hadn't he already hinted at the idea himself? "Tom," he shouted. "Tom Price."

The boatswain sat on the quay, smoking a pipe, together with three no less weatherbeaten friends. "Well, Mr. Minnett," he said, getting up. "It's good to see you, sir." He inspected Nick's soiled clothes. "There's no trouble?"

"Not here, old friend. What is the news from St. Malo?"

Price shook his head. " 'Tis all murder and mayhem over there."

"You've been in?"

"Not I, sir. My new skipper don't go for the frogs. Jemmie Wainwright tried to put into Granville last week, and was fired on."

"Shot away his backstay," said one of his companions. "Mad, those frogs."

"Always have been," said the third man. "We've no business with them, save at the end of a gun."

"You've seen the *Rose,* Mr. Minnett?" Price pointed. "Sad."

"She's still sound?"

"Oh, aye. It'd take more than six months on the beach to rot that hull; but she shouldn't be left so."

"She's going to sea again," Nick said. "And this evening. I'm bound for St. Suliac, Tom. What are Allardyce and Lownd doing nowadays?"

"Well, sir, they're out with their new skipper. But . . ."

"Then see if you can round me up a couple of good hands, Tom. And you'll come along as boatswain."

"Me, sir? We're not welcome over there any more, Mr. Minnett."

"There's no one in St. Suliac will fire on *Golden Rose*."

Price was shaking his head. "They've changed, Mr. Minnett. And there's my old wife . . ."

"At least find me a couple of hands."

"There won't be anyone willing to enter the Rance, Mr. Minnett," said one of the other men, "not after Jemmie Wainwright had his backstay shot away."

Nick stared at them, his brain clouding in impotent anger. Then he turned, ran back up the street, and met Anne at the door of her house, her shopping basket full. "What's happened to everyone in this place?" he cried. "Tom Price won't sail with me."

She unlocked the door. "I've some cured pork here, Mr. Minnett, and a loaf of bread, and some cheese; it's not your kind of fare, I know, but 'tis the best I could do at short notice."

"And it sounds delicious." He followed her into the kitchen. "You as well."

"But it is your food, sir, bought with your money."

"And I'm inviting you to lunch. I don't suppose you thought of a jug of beer?"

"I can go again."

"Water will do. Sit you down, and eat, Anne Yealm." Nick worked the pump and filled the wooden mugs, watched the woman slowly seat herself, gaze at the food, and then start up again.

"There's only one chair."

"And you'll use it," he said. "What, me sit down after two days in the saddle? Now tell me where I can find two seamen."

She chewed, slowly. He wondered when last she had tasted even bread and cheese. " 'Tis Harry's death, as much as anything. No matter what we put about, everyone knows it was a brush with the revenue. They always said he chanced too much. Now they've got the notion that the *Rose* is an unlucky ship."

He broke off some bread, added a piece of cheese, and tried to imagine what Caroline Moncey would make of a meal like this, in these surroundings. "Is that the true reason you haven't been able to sell?"

She flushed; the color did wonders for her cheeks. "If you'd have your promise back, Mr. Minnett . . ."

"I'm no believer in luck, Anne. But I must have a crew."

"Perhaps in Exeter . . .?"

"Exeter. That'll be another two days." He frowned at her. "You've crewed Harry."

"On occasions; when we was courting." Her head came up, the color deepening. "You wish me to go with you, sir?"

"Do *you* believe in luck?"

"Oh, aye. But I'll not believe the *Rose* is other than good fortune. But . . . I've never crossed the Channel."

"I'll do the navigating—and the helming—if you can take a turn on a sheet."

"I can do that, sir. But what would people say?"

"Has what they've said done you any good, this summer?"

She swallowed, and licked her lips, and looked around the room, almost as if seeing it for the first time. "And after?" She might have been asking the question of herself.

"You'll be my crew, after," he said. "*Golden Rose* will be your home."

Suddenly she smiled, and with the widening of the generous mouth all the care, the misery, the hunger and the despair which had shrouded her seemed to disappear.

"Aye," she said. "She'll make a good home."

Three

Anne found Nick one of Harry's fishing smocks, and a thick cloak; both hung a little short, but at least his stomach and chest were well protected. The alternative was to ride over to Windshot Castle, the Minnett summer home, where he'd be sure to find a change of clothing, but that was ten miles away and he was determined to catch the evening tide. She also found woollen caps for both of them; at any time of the year the Channel could be cold at midnight. But Nick refused the loan of Harry's razor; ideas and possibilities were already drifting around his mind, and there would be time enough to shave in St. Suliac, if all should be well.

Anne herself pulled on thick woollen stockings beneath her gown, and tied up her hair in a bandanna. Gone was her earlier uncertainty, and it occurred to Nick that since Harry's death she had only been waiting for something to do with her life. Now she smiled, and broke into a snatch of song as she worked with him on the windlass to send the mainsail soaring aloft.

No doubt she loved *Golden Rose* as much as he. The ship was in much better shape than he had dared hope; there was in fact nothing that a coat of paint would not set right, saving perhaps a scoop of grease for the pulleys. Time for that when they got back.

Fortune seemed intent on favoring the start of their expedition. The wind was in the west, and no more than moderate; it was sufficient to drive the ketch at a steady eight knots, and as his course was just east of south they would be on a reach the whole way. He set their biggest foresail, main and mizzen, and within half an hour of leaving harbor *Golden Rose* was almost sailing herself, curtseying over the waves, shrugging aside the lonely whitecaps which occasionally surged at her.

By then it was dark, but already with the promise of a moon streaming across the water. And by then, too, Anne had served him cheese and bread and a mug of hot rum, which somehow tasted far better than anything Tom Price had ever produced. "I doubt not that I am half man," she said, facing the wind and taking long breaths. "I had forgot the pleasure of being at sea."

"Aye," he agreed. "I'd rather stand here than anywhere in the world, especially when it is so pleasant. A little different . . ." he bit off the sentence.

Her head did not turn. "To last time, Mr. Minnett?"

"I was thinking of the weather."

"You'll be wanting a spell?"

"Not yet. You turn in, Anne. Relieve me at midnight."

She nodded, and went below. The companion door slammed, and he was alone in the darkness, save for the glow of the lantern.

So then, he could think again, after two days—as for two days he had not dared think. Undoubtedly he had run away, from a situation which had been too sudden to be faced on a liquor-enlarged head. Try as he might he could remember nothing of his night with Caroline. Night? It could scarcely have been more than an hour; yet he was entirely at her mercy.

Unless, perhaps, he were to return with the Benoîts, and already betrothed to Aurora. He smiled at the wind. There was the answer. Could he carry them off, bring Aurora back to England, marry her on the spot, and leave Caroline where she belonged?

What a confusing world it was, to be sure. And now he had compounded the confusion by purchasing himself a boat for an exorbitant sum. But of all the events which had crowded in upon this year, he was only sure of that single one as being right.

Anne looked up at him from the hatch, gathering her

thick auburn hair once again beneath her bandanna. "Midnight, Mr. Minnett. I have a drink for you." She handed it up, and he sipped, felt the liquor tracing its way down his throat.

"On the larboard bow you will see a glow, from time to time. That is the light tower on the Casquets Reef. We leave Alderney and the Race, and the rest of the islands, wide on the larboard beam."

She nodded, closed her hands on the spokes, leaned forward to check the compass course.

"You'll call me, should anything disturb you."

"I will, Mr. Minnett."

He went down the ladder, pulled the hatch shut, stood for a moment in the swaying cabin, sipping his drink. Then he spread his chart, laid off his estimated run from Lyme, and checked it against the bearing he had taken of the Casquets Light to determine his position. It was important to work the tides in the Gulf of St. Malo. But he knew, as Harry Yealm had told him often, that the tides were constant, and related unchangingly to the hour of high water at St. Malo itself; he also knew, as once again Harry Yealm had drummed into him on endless occasions, that high water at St. Malo was a mere half hour before high water at Lyme, and as he had made a note of that, his calculations were simple enough.

He kicked off his shoes; how ridiculous to be at sea in dancing pumps. He pulled off his outer clothing, and hesitated. Both bunks were made up, and the starboard one was still warm. He had the strangest temptation to get in there, snuggle down beneath that blanket which only a few minutes ago had been against her body. He realized that he was as anxious to draw strength from her as she from him.

He used the larboard bunk, pulling the covers to his neck and immediately falling asleep. There was no more soothing motion than that of a ship in a slight sea. The creaking of the timbers, the thrumming of the rigging, the gentle swish of the water past the hull, all combined to remove the last worry from his mind, leaving him utterly content. He was awake again, it seemed but a second later, with the sound of the hatch slamming back.

"Mr. Minnett," Anne Yealm called. "Mr. Minnett."

He knew at once that the wind had dropped. He threw back the blanket, reached for his clothes, and discovered that he could see, beyond the reach of the lantern. But it was an uncertain light, and the clinging dampness which settled on his face and hands warned him what to expect before he gained the deck.

Golden Rose drifted along before a faint breeze, in the middle of an empty world. A gray mist had descended on the ocean, and visibility came to an abrupt halt at the bowsprit.

"Dropped without warning," Anne said.

He joined her at the helm, checked his watch. It was past five in the morning. "The breeze was steady up to then?"

"Oh, aye. We were bounding along."

He returned to the cabin, laid off the fresh position. If indeed they had maintained eight knots since yesterday afternoon, then they were southwest of Guernsey, and the tide would now be starting to set them toward the French coast.

He went on deck, took the wheel. "You'd best have a nap."

She hugged herself, and clapped her hands. "Harry always said fog was worse than wind in these waters."

"Because of the tides. But I think I know where we are. Anyway, we've a couple of hours before we're in any shoals."

"I'll make some breakfast," she decided, and shook her head when he would have spoken. "I'd not sleep now, Mr. Minnett."

He clung to the helm, peered into the mist, and listened for the slightest sound which might denote surf. But in fact the sea was so gentle it could well be breaking on rocks fifty yards away, and yet make no noise. Anne joined him, and they ate; then she took herself forward, to sit astride the bowsprit, her skirt drawn up to her knees, watching and listening.

One hour passed, and then two. Now the mist had turned yellow, to indicate that the sun was up there somewhere, and the morning had even warmed, slightly. But still he could see less than a hundred yards. And by now surely he was immediately north of the passage to St. Malo. If he had made all his calculations accurately—he had a sudden fear of a mistake—the Minquiers Reef, a vicious accumulation of rocks and tide-rips south of Jersey, should by now have been ten miles and more astern. But to be ten miles off course, either behind where he estimated or farther to the east, was simple enough in the mist.

"Rocks," Anne shouted, scrambling to her feet. She pointed to the right, and Nick hastily put the helm to larboard, turning the ship's head away from the danger. He peered into the mist as he did so, hoping to recognize something, but saw nothing more than a flurry of white surrounding the jagged black heads.

"We'll have the main down," he decided, and lashed the wheel. The girl came aft, and between them they lowered the big mainsail, reducing the ship's speed by more than half.

"Where are we?" she asked.

Nick hesitated, and then squared his shoulders. The essence of good navigation, Harry had always said, was a proper confidence combined with a proper caution, combined with a proper care in making, and checking, one's calculations. He called it the rule of the three Cs.

"Off the head of the passage," he said. "But 'tis the marks we want. Or failing that, the Isle Cezembre."

She went forward again. Now they had taken way off the ship they could hear the rumble of the waves on the rocks, away to starboard, and every few minutes they could see the surf. But the tide was nearly slack by now, Nick calculated.

"There," Anne called.

Nick strained his eyes, and saw the island, suddenly

high and topped with green. "Cezembre. Will you harden
those sheets?"

"Aye aye," she said, and came aft.

Nick altered course, to leave the island well to larboard. Moments later the Jardin appeared, and then mark
after mark. Now the mist became an aid, as it left them
all but invisible from the shore. "We've the last hour of
tide," he said. "We'll make St. Suliac easily enough."

She stood beside him. "You're to be congratulated,
Mr. Minnett. Harry himself could have done no better."

He looked down at her, and she turned her face up to
smile. With her hair confined her face was exposed, and
once again he thought of chiseled marble, save for the
colour in her cheeks. He put his arm round her shoulders,
squeezed her against him, and kissed her on the forehead.

"Harry himself would not have been a better crew.
Now we'd best get down that mizzen."

"You'll stay with the ship," Nick said. The shore was just
visible from the anchorage, and seemed quiet enough.
"We've no way of estimating our reception."

"And you?"

He climbed into the dinghy. "I'm a simple seaman,
wouldn't you say? And they've no official quarrel with
England, so far as I know."

"Take care, Mr. Minnett," she said, and he gave her a
reassuring wink. But already she was becoming vague
in the mist, as the ship itself took on a ghostly outline. He
wondered what she would do, were something to happen
to him; she was really being very bold in undertaking this
journey at all. Or was she merely desperate?

In any event, the best chance of avoiding anything
happening to him would be to concentrate on the task in
hand. He brought the dinghy into the side of the dock,
looked up at familiar features. "Good day, monsieur." He
tethered the painter, allowing sufficient scope for the range
of the tide, and climbed ashore. "Monsieur Condorcet in
town?"

"Citizen Condorcet is with the Assembly, in Paris." The

man's face did not relax, and he had always given a cheerful enough greeting in the past. Yet the village had not changed; there were few people about, but in the middle of an October afternoon he had not expected many.

"And Madame Condorcet?"

"She is here." The fisherman turned away, and said, apparently to the river, "Take care, monsieur." His voice was quiet.

"Now you have restored my faith in human nature," Nick said, in English, and also to himself. He walked up the street, smiled at the girl in the butcher's shop, and she hastily averted her gaze.

"You there," called a voice.

Nick turned, faced the soldier. Presumably a garde français, he decided, for although the fellow wore both a moustache and a blue uniform jacket over dirty white pantaloons, and carried a musket, with a bayonet hanging at his thigh, his appearance was decidedly unmilitary. "Yes, monsieur."

"You are from the ship?"

"Yes. I am a friend of Monsieur Condorcet."

The man inspected him. "The *Golden Rose*," he said, slowly. "You are also a friend of Monsieur de Benoît."

At least the fellow was using the present tense. "They have bought our fish at the château."

"Ha ha," shouted the soldier in sudden good humor. "Ha ha ha ha. And they will do so again, at the château. I will tell them." He slapped Nick on the shoulder and walked on.

"Deuced odd," Nick decided, in English. But now he was at Condorcet's door; there was smoke escaping from the chimney. A moment later there were those eyes, bewilderment slowly changing to pleasure.

"Monsieur Minnett." The expression in the eyes changed again, to alarm, as she looked past him. "What brings you here?"

"The wind and the tide, Seraphine. May I not come in?"

She dried her hands on her apron. "You are most welcome." She stood aside, and he brushed her arm as he passed. "Most welcome," she said again, and closed the door.

But he was not here to flirt with Louis' wife. "Are you alone?"

"Oh yes, monsieur," she said. "Come into the kitchen. You'll take a glass of cider?" He watched her stoop, and pour.

"If you'll join me."

Her head half turned, and she smiled. "It will be my pleasure. And you are on the *Golden Rose?* How splendid. But you will have heard . . ."

He sat at the table. "That is why I am here."

"Ah." She placed the two mugs in front of him, then sat opposite, her face ridiculously solemn. "I do not know what has happened to France, Monsieur Minnett."

"Call me Nick," he said. "But you know what has happened to Louis?"

"Ah bah, Louis." She shrugged. "He is an important man, they say. Paris is his home now. Seraphine must exist on what he sends. When he sends it. When it reaches me. If it reaches me."

"And what of St. Suliac?"

"Ah, Monsieur Nick." She leaned forward, and licked her lips. "The military have taken over the château."

"My God. And the Count?"

"Monsieur de Benoît is imprisoned there. There is talk of a conspiracy."

"Against him?"

"By him, monsieur. Which is far more serious. Etienne is also in prison, but in Paris. I do not know the details."

"And Mademoiselle de Benoît?"

Seraphine gazed at him, and her tongue slowly came out and circled her lips. "Mademoiselle de Benoît is very beautiful. Do you not think so?"

"I think all women are beautiful, but in different ways. I have known her a long time. I merely wish to be sure she is well. And safe."

Again Seraphine shrugged, and drank, noisily. "She is at Versailles with the Queen."

"There's a relief. Then we must think of the Count, and Etienne. Where is Etienne imprisoned?"

"I do not know, monsieur."

"But the Count is in the château. Is he in any danger?"

Seraphine finished her cider. "You will eat with me, monsieur? It is so very lonely, living here, with naught but the chickens to feed, and Papa so very busy. I have a rabbit."

It smelt delicious. And he could not afford to offend her. "It would be a pleasure, Seraphine. You were going to tell me of the Count."

She got up, stirred the pot, fetched two china plates. "Everyone is in danger, in France, today, Monsieur Nick. Aristocrats more than others. Even English aristocrats."

"I'll be gone on tonight's tide. But I will take the Count with me."

Seraphine carefully ladled rabbit stew on to each plate, then sat opposite him again. "There is wine."

He sensed, rather than reasoned, that their relationship was slowly changing. But he got up, secured the bottle of vin ordinaire and two goblets, and poured. When he handed her the glass, her fingers touched his for a moment, and she smiled at him.

"It is impossible to fetch the Count from the château, Nick. There is a garrison of soldiers. At least a dozen."

"Yet it is possible. If you will help me, Seraphine."

"I, monsieur? My husband is a member of the Assembly. He has played his part in voting the aristocrats out of privilege."

"Does he know what has happened here?"

She shrugged, picked a chunk of meat out of the plate between thumb and forefinger, and slowly chewed it. "I have not told him."

"Well, I have no doubt at all that he would be appalled. He and Pierre de Benoît have always been friends. Perhaps he would be unable to do anything officially. But I have an idea, and if you will help me, then neither you nor he will be involved, except innocently. The blame will be mine."

She swallowed, and took another piece of meat; gravy gathered on her chin. "You will be killed."

"I don't think so."

"You wish to get me into trouble, monsieur." Her tongue came out, seeking the gravy, perhaps, reaching wide. She had a large mouth. A generous mouth? She sighed inflating the front of her gown. "And I have troubles enough, living here all alone, my bed cold and empty, my larder seldom adequate . . ."

Her gaze held him, and her mouth was still wide. "You are a mercenary young woman," he said. "I have a couple of English guineas in my pocket."

"I do not want money, Nick." She got up and came round the table, sat on it, next to him, one leg swinging beneath the thin skirt. "You are asking me to risk my life; certainly my freedom. And I have not lived at all, as yet. I am but seventeen years old, and Louis, oh, all is ambition there. On our wedding night he spoke of nothing but his ambition."

He could not look away. The skirt was pulled tight, and he could trace the line of her thigh up to her hip. And above was a smiling face and laughing eyes, conspiratorial certainly, but with a complete absence of the underlying viciousness which had characterized Caroline Moncey. Yet Caroline, and woman in general, lurking in his mind, filled his belly. He had lain beside her, had been held in her arms, and whatever her faults she was a magnificent woman.

But here was Louis' wife. "And did his ambition not include you?"

She shook her head, slowly. "He did no more than whet my own, Nick."

She leaned forward, again slowly. Louis' wife. But Pierre de Benoît's savior. There could be no one else. Having come here, and revealed his purpose, he was at her mercy.

As if that truly mattered, at this moment.

She was surprisingly plump; when she lay on his chest she made him gasp, just as when she breathed herself her belly flooded his, and her breasts seemed to swell. She was as full of energy in bed as in her daily life; she squirmed, and moved constantly, guiding his hands not with her own but by subtly changing her position. She breathed rabbit stew and wine on him and he tasted it in her mouth. Her black hair tickled, and smelt vaguely of wood smoke. To lie beside her after Caroline was to leave a paved sidewalk and cross a muddy street.

But the mud laughed, when it was not smiling, and sought only pleasure. Not counting the whores he had paid for their favors, she was the first woman he had known in full possession of his faculties. He seemed to explode, as he cupped breast and squeezed buttock, stroked the soft legs, ran his fingers into the brittle hair. And even an explosion was scarce sufficient. It was dusk before he sat up and reached for his clothes and his watch.

"We cannot go yet." She lay on her back, face reddened with his kisses, body red and white splotches where his fingers had marked. "We need a full tide, and that will not be until ten."

When he had explained his plan she had pretended no knowledge of the sea. But it was not the expedition he had in mind. Anne would be terrified, supposing him a prisoner. As if he was not a prisoner. And how could he face Anne, so quiet and prim, at this moment? And now he was spent, true understanding of what he had done took possession of him.

"You will leave me too exhausted to accomplish anything," he grumbled.

"And can you be sure that it is not my objective, sweetheart?" She sat up, her arms round his waist, and her teeth scoured his shoulder. "Oh, Nick, Nick. From the moment I first saw you, I knew we must come to this. You and me, Nick."

He turned, and found himself lying on her belly once again, while her mouth puckered. "You had best start on the letter. You are sure you can imitate Louis' writing?"

"Well enough for that Sergeant Popel." The eager body ceased moving. "You are cold."

"I am thinking of what we must do."

She smiled, and the smile rippled into a laugh. "Then do what we would rather do. Now, Nick. Now."

He had not known it could be possible, to want so much and so often; his visits to the London whore houses had always left him sated before his money had earned its worth, eager only to escape, to wallow in self hatred. Perhaps because they never laughed.

His mouth was open, and biting on the pillow. And her hands played lightly on his back. And it was now as black as pitch. "Now you will help me," he whispered. As if he cared, now.

"To take the old man away?" She sighed. Perhaps another manoeuvre, as he felt himself being sucked into her body as she expanded her lungs. "If I must. But would you not rather spend the night here?"

"You must," he said, and pushed downward with his hands to raise his body. "Is there a candle?"

Tinder scraped and a moment later the candle glowed. She had raised herself on her elbow, a superb sliver of white in the prevailing dark. "Will you visit me again, Nick?"

He hesitated. "Louis is my friend."

"Would you cuckold an enemy? That were dangerous." She lay back to laugh.

He found the washbasin, and a moment later was dressed. "Will you not come? It is past eight."

"I have just remembered. We cannot break the curfew."

"If that is all we are taken for, we have no problems. Get dressed, Seraphine."

She pouted, and then laughed again, and rolled off the bed. Nick went downstairs, discovered his hands were trembling, and poured himself a glass of cider. Because of what he had done? Or because of what he was about to do? Both were outside his experience. To take a girl, the wife of a friend, to bed, deliberately, was criminal and only to be justified by necessity, as she would have it so.

To realize that he had enjoyed these past hours more than any in his life before but compounded the crime.

And now, to challenge an entire state. Smuggling had never been more than an adventure; he had been too conscious of his own security, because of his name. And after Harry's death, why, he had determined there would be no more senseless risks of that nature. Yet had he set off across the Channel with only delight in his heart at the prospect of once again being at sea, of once again challenging authority. And now he was realizing that there was no apprehension in his mind at this moment; only a swelling anticipation of the next few hours.

"Here is the letter." She wore a cloak over her gown.

He peered at the still drying ink; he had never seen Louis' handwriting. But it was her neck as well. "Then we are ready."

"Not quite." She sat down, facing him. "I doubt my ability to sustain the part you have given me. I wish to come with you."

"To England? What would you do there?"

Her mouth widened as she smiled. "Why, I will be your mistress, Nick. You will buy me a big house, and give me an allowance, and visit me, and we will lie together in bed, and remember tonight, and make love. Does that not sound attractive?"

He gazed at her; there was no humor in her voice. And she had timed her move very well, for a woman who did not understand the sea; his plan was only practical if they were at the château as the tide turned, which left them less than an hour. There could be no argument.

But then, he reflected, having risked so much, and already acted so ruthlessly, why should he argue now?

"If you wish it, Seraphine." He raised his glass. "I drink to your future."

"I will have some too." She drained his glass. "I am terrified. Would you believe that, monsieur?"

"No. Will you not bring some clothes?"

"Those rags? Bah. You will buy me better. Oh, Nick, let's make haste. I am desperate to be away."

"Yet we will be careful. Douse those candles."

She obeyed, and he cautiously opened the door. The moon was already up, but to some extent restricted by the houses, causing patches of brilliance to alternate with impenetrable shadows. And the cobbled street appeared to be deserted.

"What of weapons?" she whispered.

"Eh?"

"Oh la, la," she said, and gave a stifled shriek of laughter. "You would challenge an army, with your bare hands?"

"I was considering surprise, and speed, rather than assault. I have no desire to kill anyone."

"But you may be sure that they have every desire to kill you. Or will have, when they find out what you are about." She reached behind the door, and handed him a blunderbuss. "Louis says I must keep it there, to repel unwelcome strangers. And you may be sure it is loaded, and the flint is new. Now let us make haste."

Suddenly she seemed to have assumed command of the whole operation. But she knew her country, and presumably her countrymen, much better than he. He waited while she closed and locked the door, then followed her down the moonlit street.

The dinghy waited where he had left it; the tide, having fallen, was now nearly full again. *Golden Rose* remained at anchor, and he could see the glimmer of her lantern. He had been away very nearly twelve hours.

"This is what we must use?" Seraphine demanded, standing on the steps with her skirt pulled up to her knees. "My God. Is it safe?"

"Of course it is safe," Nick assured her.

"But the river runs so very fast." She peered at the water. "Suppose I fall in?"

"You will very likely drown." Nick himself got in, sat on the thwart, the gun beside him. He released the painter and held the boat against the dock. "Now, step into the middle, aft there, and sit down."

She took a long breath, and jumped in. The dinghy rocked dangerously. Nick released the dock and the tide swept them out into the stream. He unshipped the oars and pulled for the ship.

"Mr. Minnett? Is that you? Oh, thank God. I have been so afraid." Anne was on deck holding on to the shrouds.

"I am sorry, Anne. It was necessary to recruit some help. Will you assist her on board?"

"But that is a woman," Seraphine said, in French.

"My crew."

"Your . . . my God. I am betrayed."

"Don't be absurd. She is my crew. Nothing more. She is the widow of Harry Yealm. We are friends."

"Friends," Seraphine said in disgust. "A man and a woman are never friends, monsieur. They can only be lovers or enemies."

"Who is that with you, Mr. Minnett?" Anne asked, in English. "She does gabble."

"A French lady who is going to assist us," Nick said.

"What are you saying?" Seraphine demanded.

"That you will pass up that cannon." He changed to English. "Take this gun, Anne. But be careful. It is charged."

Anne leaned over the side, carefully took the blunderbuss from Seraphine and laid it on the deck.

"Now give madame your hand." He spoke French again. "She will help you up, Seraphine."

Seraphine tossed her head, grasped the shrouds, and clambered on board. She attempted to stare at Anne, but only came up to the English girl's shoulder. "Is there no cabin?" she asked.

"Down that ladder." Nick gained the deck, the painter in his hand. "You'll assist me, Anne."

They connected the falls, winched the dinghy from the water and on to the deck. "That woman," Anne whispered. "She is a friend?"

"She is the wife of a very old friend," Nick explained. "He is not here at present, but he is an important man."

"And she will help us?"

"I think so. I'm sorry I left you alone so long; she took a deal of persuading."

Anne Yealm looked aft, to where Seraphine had come back on deck, and was seated on the hatch cover, arms folded across her breast. "I am sure you know best what you do, Mr. Minnett," she said. "I was but afraid for you."

She turned away, and he snatched the tail of her bandanna, jerking it from her hair, bringing her to a stop, and ran his fingers into the thick auburn hair as it came free. "And I am grateful for your fear, Anne."

He released her, and she faced him for a moment, slowly reaching up to restore the kerchief. It was too dark properly to see her face. "I will prepare the capstan," she said, and went forward.

"Ha," Seraphine remarked.

"I had no idea taking two women to sea could be so difficult," Nick said.

"I have a mind to abandon the whole project here and now. It was a senseless scheme in any event, which can only get us killed. And for what? To rescue an old man who serves no useful purpose whatsoever."

"He is your seigneur."

"Bah. There are no such creatures, nowadays."

He took her hand. "Yet will you help me, Seraphine. Or I will never speak to you again."

"Ha." She tossed her head. "And that should concern me, monsieur? As if, with your bed so adequately warmed, you will speak to me in any event."

"I may well use my hand instead of my voice, if you do not stop sulking," he warned. "Now come. The tide is nearly full. We'll set the foresail only, Anne. But once we come alongside, release the main and make ready for sea. We shall doubtless leave in haste." He joined her to heave on the capstan and bring up the anchor. "And you will command the blunderbuss."

"I have never fired such a weapon, Mr. Minnett." She panted as she strained on the bars.

"It does not require aiming. And with fortune, you will not even have to point it. Haste now."

He hurried aft to gain the helm, while Anne pulled on the halliard and the jib ran up the stay. *Golden Rose* slipped gently up the river.

"Oh, la, la," Seraphine cried. "Such activity. And how does it heave so."

"We are in a river, sweetheart," Nick reminded her. "There is really no movement at all. You'd do better to rehearse what you have to say."

"Ha," she said again. But she stood up, and looked forward as the river made a bend and they saw lights. "Oh Nick," she muttered, "I am a fool. I should be home in bed. With you."

He squeezed her hand, squinted into the gloom to make sure of the landing stage. "Drop your foresail."

Anne released the halliard and the sail clouded on to the deck. She let it lie and stood ready with a warp. Nick put down the helm and the *Golden Rose* came round to breast the current as she lost way, exactly alongside the dock. Anne stepped ashore and made the warp fast, came aft for the stern line.

"What is that?" came a shout from above them. "Who is there? Stand, or I fire."

"Come on, come on," Nick muttered, giving Seraphine's hand a last squeeze before releasing it and handing Anne the second warp; then he took one of the heavy wooden belaying pins from the rack at the foot of the mast, thrust it into his belt.

"It is Seraphine Condorcet," Seraphine called, only the slightest tremor in her voice.

"Eh? Madame Condorcet, sergeant," the sentry said.

"Seraphine?" Now the two men emerged from the shadows, where stone steps led from the stage to the gate in the wall. "You should be in bed, girl. What will Monsieur Condorcet say? And on a ship? What means this?"

"Bah," Seraphine said. "I am but obeying my husband, Sergeant Popel, when I could be at home doing much better things. I have a letter."

The sergeant stood on the stage, peered at the ketch. "This is the *Golden Rose*. From England."

"That is right, sergeant," Nick said. "She is my boat. Harry Yealm, at your service."

"Bring the lantern, monsieur," Popel said. Nick held it above him while he unfolded the paper and read, brows dragged together. "Monsieur Yealm," he muttered. "I know this name. You are a friend of the Count's."

"On the contrary, sergeant," Nick protested. "I am a creditor. As is explained."

The sergeant resumed reading, and then grinned. "You hope to obtain money from that old ratbag? Why, he has none."

"Then I shall possess his goods."

"Goods? They have all been confiscated. You waste your time here, monsieur. Take Seraphine back to the village, and she will cook you a good dinner."

"I assure you, sergeant," Nick protested. "I have not come all this way to return empty-handed. This Count you think is destitute. Why, we know he has funds on deposit in Madrid. I will obtain his signature . . ."

"Funds on deposit, you say?" The sergeant pulled at his chin. "He has admitted nothing of this."

"Why should he?" Nick asked. "But as I already know of them, he will scarce deny it to me."

"That is true, monsieur. And it is Monsieur Condorcet's wish . . . I will keep this paper, eh?"

Nick shrugged.

"And you may see the old man. Oh, yes. I will listen to what he has to say."

"I will come too," Seraphine decided. "I would like to watch him squirm."

"You'll stand by, Anne," Nick said in English. "Keep that gun ready, but out of sight. And prepare to cut the warps."

"Take care, sir."

"What do you say to her?" demanded the sergeant, as Nick stepped ashore.

"I told her I will not be long." He climbed the steps,

Seraphine at his side. Her hand brushed his, and he gave her fingers a quick squeeze.

"Women sailors," grumbled Popel behind them. "You'll stay here," he told his sentry, "but leave the child alone. Understand me?"

The sentry winked, and pulled his moustache.

The gate stood open, and they were on the lawn. Before them the château was in darkness, save for a light in the kitchens. "A strange hour to come visiting," the sergeant remarked.

"Tides, monsieur. Tides and winds. They rule our destiny at sea."

"I know nothing of the sea." The sergeant, opened the side door for them, and they entered the kitchens, a vast, nearly empty area with a stone floor and a low ceiling, where the ranges waited silently. Here there were two men, seated at the table, drinking wine and playing cards. They did not trouble to get up, but they raised their heads.

"What is all this noise, sergeant?"

"Visitors for the prisoner Benoît," the sergeant said, with some importance. "Lazy scum. It is up here."

He climbed the staircase leading into the main hall of the house.

"This is your entire garrison?" Seraphine asked.

"I have more," the sergeant said. "Some sleep, some are on leave. This is but a headquarters." He held his candle high, climbed another flight of stairs.

"And what of the servants?" Nick asked.

"Servants? Why, they are all gone. And were happy to leave. He begged but one to stay, his valet. The fellow laughed."

Now they were on the first floor, moving through the darkness, and the silence, for there was not a sound to be heard above the creaking of the floor. The sergeant chuckled. "The old fool will be in bed. We will have him up. Linen nightshirts. What vanity."

He fumbled in the keys at his belt as they stopped before the main bedroom door, turned the lock. "Hey,

Benoît. Benoît, wake up," he bawled. "Be sure your sins have found you out."

"Amen," Nick said; he pushed the sergeant's hat forward over his face, and struck him on the back of the head with the belaying pin.

The sergeant fell without a sound, and hit the floor before Nick could catch him; fortunately the château was a solid old building and the thud was dull.

"My God," Seraphine gasped, staring at the unconscious man. Before she could say anything else, Nick's left hand closed on her throat and his right arm went round her waist, sweeping her from the floor. She shrilled, as he carried her into the room.

"What? What?" called Pierre de Benoît from the bed. "Fire."

For the candle continued to burn, on the floor.

"Ssssh, Uncle Pierre, I beg of you." Nick kicked the door shut behind him.

"Who's that?" The old man could just be seen, sitting up in bed, peering into the darkness. "Who's that? Nick Minnett? It cannot be."

"It is, Uncle Pierre." Nick reached the bed, Seraphine squirming in his arms, her knees kicking into his thighs. "Will you fetch that candle."

"Bless my soul," said the Count, but he got out of bed, and Nick sat down, throwing Seraphine beside him. A moment later the candle was held high, to illuminate the scene. "Bless my soul. Is that not Seraphine Condorcet?"

"It is. And she will scream the place down if we do not make haste." He looked around the room, found nothing in the gloom. "Your nightcap, Uncle Pierre. Please."

Benoît hesitated, then took off his nightcap.

"I will force her mouth open and you will stuff it in," Nick said, and released Seraphine's throat.

"You . . ." she shouted, but his fingers closed on the base of her jaw, holding her mouth wide, and Pierre de Benoît pushed the cap in.

"Hold her there," Nick said, and tore the sheet into strips. Seraphine struck at the old man, but Nick caught her arms, rolled her on to her stomach, and tied her wrists together. "Now her ankles," he gasped. She kicked at his face, but he brought her feet together, pushed her skirts up to her knees.

"Bless my soul," said Pierre de Benoît. "Bless my soul. I wish I could understand what is happening."

"You are leaving St. Suliac," Nick said. "That is what is happening."

"But how? Am I being released?" The Count scratched his head, bald without its wig. "No, that cannot be."

"Get dressed, Uncle Pierre, I beg of you," Nick said. He placed Seraphine on her side, where he calculated she would be most comfortable. It was difficult to see her clearly in the dim light, but her eyes glowed at him like black coals. "It is for your own good," he said. "What, would you be nothing more than a kept woman in England? This way you can pretend to have been hoodwinked by a wicked Englishman, and your reputation will be untarnished." He bent low over her. "And believe me, Seraphine, I am grateful. Not merely for your assistance in this matter." He kissed her on the forehead, and her body heaved once more.

The Count was dressed, the sergeant was showing signs of regaining consciousness. Nick hastily tore some more of the sheet into strips, and bound and gagged him in turn, removing his sword as he did so. "There are two men downstairs," he whispered, "and one on the wall. The rest are sleeping. If we leave by the front entrance can we gain the dock?"

"We can follow the house round," the Count said. "But I cannot permit you to take this risk, Nick. If we are caught they will surely execute you."

"They will surely execute me now in any event, Uncle Pierre," Nick pointed out. "Quiet now."

He tiptoed across the gallery and on to the main staircase, the sword in his right hand. The Count held the candle above them. The château itself was in silence; even the whisper of the wind and river was muted. Only the occasional shaft of moonlight, drifting through the high windows to scatter across the floor, broke the darkness.

"To the left," Benoît whispered as they reached the foot of the stairs.

Nick reached the door, found it bolted. Carefully he drew the steel rod, touched the second, and heard a sound behind them.

"Sergeant," said one of the men from the kitchen. "Sergeant? Is that you?"

Nick drew the other bolt hard, threw the door open.

"The guard," shouted the man behind them. "Awake the guard."

Nick seized Pierre de Benoît by the shoulder, thrust him out, flattened himself against the wall as the man ran forward, presenting his musket. There was a flash and an explosion and a rush of black powder, and the sinister twanging of the ball ricocheting off the walls, clanging against one of the suits of armor. And the fellow was still coming. Nick stepped away from the door, swung the sword left to right, struck the musket from the soldier's hands. Then he was away, once again seizing Pierre de Benoît by the arm and urging him across the garden. At least Anne would have heard the shot and know they were on their way.

But now lights were flaring all over the château, and men were calling. And now too the sentry was running up the steps, pushing the gate to the dock wide and presenting his musket. "Halt there," he bawled. "Halt, or I shoot."

There was a tremendous rumble from immediately behind him, and he gave a shriek and threw up his arms.

"Nick?" Anne gasped. "Mr. Minnett, sir? Are you all right?"

"But who is that?" Pierre de Benoît panted.

"A girl with a blunderbuss," Nick told him, and then they reached her. The force of the explosion had knocked her over, and she was still on the ground. "I am all right, Anne," Nick shouted, kneeling beside her. "What of you?"

"No more than a bruise." She grasped his arm, pulled herself up and he gave her a squeeze.

"Good girl. Let's be out of here."

They ran down the steps and on to the dock, where *Golden Rose* nodded to her mooring. Nick helped Pierre de Benoît over the gunwale, noted that the tide had just turned. "Cast off," he shouted.

Men appeared at the garden wall, lining up as if about to fight a battle, muskets presented. A ripple of flame spread along the wall, and the night came boomingly to life. Something struck the deck with a crack, but the range was too far for accuracy. Nick thrust Pierre de Benoît down the hatch, and saw the dock drifting away as Anne released the mooring warp and the now falling tide took the ship downstream.

He ran forward, and together they heaved on the foresail. "What of the woman?" she gasped, her hair flying in the breeze; she had lost her bandanna.

"I thought it best to leave her behind."

More shots rang out behind them, but these were totally wild; more disturbing was the thunder of hooves. A horseman would probably make St. Malo before they could gain the open sea.

"Now the main," he said. "We shall need all sail."

"But the woman?"

"She will be all right," he promised. "Safer there than here. They know nothing of her part in this." He wondered if Seraphine would have been similarly concerned.

They set the main, and then the mizzen. By now it was necessary for him to take the helm and peer into the darkness, picking out the landmarks, keeping in the center of the stream to gain the best advantage of the current and yet having to be as alert as ever in his life at each bend; for the *Rose* to go aground at this moment, and on an ebbing tide, would mean disaster for them all.

The shouts and the shots faded behind them, and they slipped through a silent darkness. Anne joined him in the stern. "That man," she said. "Do you think he is dead, Mr. Minnett?"

"I doubt that. Perhaps he will sleep on his face for a month or two."

"I did not know what to do," she said. "I heard the shots, and I saw him run up the steps, and then I heard him challenge . . . I did not know what to do, Mr. Minnett."

"I'd say you saved my life. Be sure of that."

"I have never fired a gun before," she said. "I have never even attempted to harm anyone before."

But now she has, and because of me, Nick thought. Just as Seraphine has played at once the whore and the traitor, because of me. Or was it because of the revolution which was taking place in France? What an incredible thought, that people's entire lives, entire characters, could be changed because of some academic argument as to who should govern a country, and how.

Lights. The time for philosophy was past. And not merely lights. The tocsin sounded, and there was the roll of a drum. And there were cannon on the ramparts of the city.

"Will we get through, Mr. Minnett?" Anne asked. Her voice was calm.

"If it can be done," he said. If only the moon would set. But now they were away from the last of the trees and into the broad open flow of the estuary; open for visibility, there was the trouble, but not necessarily for navigation. The river mouth was so littered with rocks it was necessary to stick to a narrow passage, a passage which would be better known to the Malouines than to himself.

Even as the thought crossed his mind there was a roar and a flash of light, and a ball plunged into the sea, perhaps half a mile in front of them; but exactly in the center of the channel. It was March all over again. Would he be as fortunate this time?

"You'd best get below," he said.

"And what will I do there, Mr. Minnett? Those are heavy balls. Should they strike us we will sink."

"Aye," he agreed. "Then stand by your sheets."

Because why should he wait on fortune? He had just been supposing himself unlucky because of the moonlight; but surely there was no such thing as an event so unlucky that it could not be turned to some benefit. His brain drifted back to an occasion, two years ago, when he had entered this river on a beautiful summer's afternoon, and Harry had pointed to a cut, bearing away east from the main channel, which could be used for cheating the tide, in the right conditions. Half tide up, and good visibility, and a steady breeze. Well, it was getting on for half tide *down*, now, and there was the risk; if he touched he'd be done. On the other hand, the wind was steady and fair, and the moonlight was providing visibility a shade too good in most other respects.

Nick peered ahead. Now there were three cannon at work, booming and flashing to his right, dropping their balls with a flurry of foam into the main channel, covering every inch of it. The *Rose* would never get through there, but the gunners were not bothering to close any other stretch of water. They felt sure of their prey, unless the mad Englishman should choose to turn back and surrender.

"Slack away on your larboard sheets," he said. "Only a little."

Anne glanced at him, and then up at the pennant which flew from the masthead to give the helmsman the direction of the apparent wind. "You'll not surrender?"

"Not unless I have to. Bring her round."

She released the sheets, and the helm came up. *Golden Rose* turned out of the channel, while Nick strained his eyes for the marks Harry had shown him. The cannon continued to boom for a few minutes longer, but now the shot was passing directly over the ketch before plummeting into the sea; the passage Nick was taking was much closer inshore than the main channel, and he could see the people on the city walls, while some enterprising soldiers even tried musketry. But the range was too great for small arms, and there was no time for the cannon to be depressed. The main danger lay in the tide and the rocks, now showing above the surface on either side as the ketch, leaning over on a broad reach, gathered speed and fairly boiled along.

Anne grasped the shrouds beside him, and stared at the city. "God above, Mr. Minnett," she shouted. "Suppose we touch?"

"Then we surrender," he said. "Supposing we survive."

But ahead was the open sea, and the city, and the noise, were dropping astern.

"We'll bring her back now," Nick decided. "Harden in those sheets."

Pierre de Benoît's head emerged from the cabin. "I had supposed myself a dead man."

Anne winched the sheet hard, and then sat beside Nick on the deck. "Not with Mr. Minnett in command, sir. He has a way with the *Rose*."

"I was well taught," Nick said.

Anne glanced at him, and her shoulders seemed to droop. "Aye," she said. "You were well taught, Mr. Minnett. I'd best prepare some food." She went down the hatch.

Four

"My God, Priscilla, but my head remains in a whirl." Pierre de Benoît still wore borrowed clothes, and huddled close to the fire. He sipped the mulled wine, sighed, and shook his head, gazed around the soft carpeted luxury of the Minnett's winter parlor as if unable to believe he was there, and cast suspicious glances at the two pale-blue-clad footmen who stood one on either side of the door, as if wondering when they would seize arms and imprison their employers.

"Terrible," Priscilla Minnett agreed. She sat opposite her friend, and refilled his glass herself. She was very obviously mother to both Lucy and Nick; they had inherited her good looks. Hardly a wrinkle creased her cheeks, and her neck was nearly as smooth as when she had accompanied Percy Minnett down the aisle, twenty-five years earlier.

"I must confess I am confused myself," Percy Minnett remarked, and also sought refuge in a cup of hot wine. "You did all this, Nick?"

"You said I should go to sea for a few days, instead of back to Oxford, Father," Nick said.

"My word," Percy Minnett said. "My word. Why, so I did." He peered at his son, for Nick had not bothered to seek a change of clothing before placing Pierre de Benoît on a coach for the safety of London; Percy Minnett had never seen him bearded and dressed as a seaman before. "And we thought you were but taking refuge from . . . but no matter. What have you done with the *Rose?*"

"She is safe in Lyme, Father, with Anne Yealm on board. But it is of . . ."

"There will be a scandal, of course," Priscilla Minnett remarked. "Could you have found no one else?"

"A scandal?" Lucy went into a peal of laughter. "Another one, you mean."

"Oh, come now," Percy Minnett said. "How can you suppose that anyone would link Nick's name with a peasant girl. Why, this house is full of serving girls."

"We do not take them away on small boats," Priscilla Minnett said, primly.

"She is a good girl," Pierre de Benoît said thoughtfully, starting on his third mug of wine. "My God, that this floor would stop heaving. My mind is in a tizzy."

"So you said," Percy Minnett agreed. "Now what you want, old friend, is to come upstairs to bed. You are safe here, you may be sure of that. And there are matters Nick and I must discuss. Urgent matters, to be sure."

"Urgent matters?" Nick shouted. "Christ give me patience. I am sorry, Father. And I do not mean to offend, Mother, but can there be any matter more urgent than Etienne and Aurora? I but wished to bring Uncle Pierre safe to London, and to obtain an order for a thousand pound . . ."

"A thousand pound?" demanded Percy Minnett.

"The cost of *Golden Rose*. I purchased her from Anne Yealm."

"A thousand pound? For a ketch?"

"She is worth every penny, Father. She has proved that, on this last trip. And Anne is in need of the funds."

"My word," Percy Minnett remarked.

"A common fisherman's wife," said Priscilla Minnett.

"You are becoming quite a rake," Lucy said.

Nick stared at them in anger.

"Anyway, I do not understand you," Percy Minnett said. "You wish to be away to sea again, in this overgrown rowing boat? What of Oxford?"

"Oxford can surely wait, Father. Do you not understand?

I learned in St. Suliac that Etienne is under criminal arrest in Paris."

"Etienne? Arrested as a criminal? I do not believe it. Pierre, what nonsense is this son of mine talking?"

Pierre de Benoît finished his fourth cup of hot wine and seemed to feel better. "It is true enough, Percy. Etienne had some quarrel with one of these upstart representatives, and the fellow drew—on Etienne, would you believe it. Why, it was over in seconds."

"Etienne killed him?" Priscilla was aghast.

"Not to my knowledge. But no doubt the rascal will find it painful to cough, for a season."

"And for defending himself the lad was arrested?" inquired Percy Minnett.

"You do not understand affairs in France as they are today, Percy. Why, the word continually goes up that the Court is protected by hired bravoes. Etienne has been charged with attempted murder, at the least, and with conspiracy to overthrow the Assembly. This is their favorite attack on us, that we would resort to force to have done with them, if we dared."

"And would you not?" Percy Minnett demanded.

Pierre de Benoît sighed, and shrugged. "If the King would give us a lead, perhaps. I do not know."

"But why were you arrested, Uncle Pierre?" Lucy asked.

"I am the father of an accused conspirator. They need no more."

"My word," Percy Minnett said.

"Thus you see the reason for haste, Father," Nick said.

Percy Minnett scratched his head, sending his wig askew as he did so, but ignoring his wife's frown. "I cannot see what you hope to do, Nick. Oh, you performed marvels, bringing Pierre here in safety. I congratulate you. I've almost a mind to forgive your other sins. But truly, there was a place which you knew well, and where you were well known, and the garrison was at once small and asleep. But Paris? You have been there but once. And a Parisian prison?—even supposing you knew which one."

"There is talk of La Force," Pierre de Benoît said.

"La Force? Christ in Heaven. The Bastille was not less formidable."

"But I have a plan," Nick said.

"A plan? Why, you are becoming a perfect conspirator."

"A plan, which will work, supposing I act quickly enough. Should I reach Paris before word of what happened in St. Suliac gets there, and approach Louis Condorcet, I am sure he will help."

"Condorcet help Etienne?" Pierre de Benoît shook his head, slowly. "That fellow has become the most republican of them all, if rumor can be believed."

"Rumor," Nick said. "In any event, he will help me. I am sure. I simply mean to purchase Etienne's freedom. If you will give me carte blanche, Father, and with Louis' support, it should not be so very difficult. From what I hear, money is shorter in Paris than anywhere else in the whole world, at this moment."

He wondered what they would say were they to discover that the true reason for haste was to obtain Louis' help before his friend discovered how he had been cuckolded, and his name forged, or that his real purpose in visiting Paris was to bring back Aurora, even if he were to fail in purchasing Etienne's release.

"I really do not know what to say," Percy Minnett said. "Pierre, can you find any faith in this scheme?"

"I cannot argue, for or against, Percy," the Frenchman said. "It is Nick's life, and I owe him mine already. It is also your money we discuss; I have none. On the other hand, it is also the life of my son. The decision must be yours."

"And what of the other matter?" demanded Priscilla Minnett. "All London is by the ears, with Nick galloping off into the sunset, and poor Caroline Moncey left deserted in a country tavern . . ."

"Oh really, Mama, if you'll believe that you'll believe anything. Ask Lucy. She's the true conspirator in the family."

"Me?" Lucy shouted. "Why, I know nothing at all of

the matter. There was a party and cards and ale, and heaven knows what else after."

"Why, you . . ." Nick choked back the words. "For God's sake, Mama, I will deal with this matter the moment I return. You have my word. But can Caroline Moncey's quite unreal plight really be set against Etienne's life? What the devil do you want?"

For Henry the butler stood in the doorway, a silver tray in his hand.

"A caller, Mr. Minnett."

"A caller?" Percy Minnett cried. "I am not to be disturbed today. I had supposed I had made that clear."

"This gentleman will not be turned away, sir. It seems he has discovered that Mr. Nicholas is back in town."

"What? What? Not turned away. Why, the impudent rascal." Percy Minnett strode across the room. "Give me that card. Why, I'll pin back the puppy's ears, by heaven. I'll . . ." He picked up the card, gazed at it, and all the color left his face.

"Percy?" Priscilla Minnett was also on her feet. "What on earth is the matter? Whoever can it be?"

Lucy was at her father's shoulder. Now she took the card from his momentarily paralyzed fingers. "Lord George Moncey." She gave a shriek of laughter. "George Moncey. Now let us see which matter is the more grave, darling Nicky."

Nick found himself on his feet, his heart pounding while a curiously empty feeling spread across his stomach. His life had hitherto been devoid of violence, or even enmity. His own personality, his father's position, had combined to keep him clear of arguments concerning politics or honor which might conceivably have gone as far as a settlement. He knew himself to be an excellent pistol shot, as indeed he had practiced often enough with Louis Condorcet in the woods above St. Suliac, but he had never considered firing at another human being . . . Why, indeed, did his mind immediately jump to the conclusion that such an outcome was inevitable?

"My word," Percy Minnett was saying. "How one's chickens do come home to roost. I suppose we had best see the fellow."

"Indeed you will see me, Mr. Minnett," declared George Moncey, having followed the butler into the antechamber, "or I will have your son's ears. Mistress Minnett; Lucy; I apologize for this intrusion. You understand the necessity."

Like his sister, Lord George Moncey was tall and powerfully built, with fair hair and unusually pale skin; his features were handsome, spoiled only by the smallness of his eyes. He wore a dark green tail coat over matching waistcoat and breeches, and leather boots, carried a fringed bicorne under his left arm, and tapped the floor with his sword cane.

"My word," Percy Minnett said again.

"You are welcome of course, Lord Moncey," Priscilla Minnett said. "And equally we had intended to invite you here to discuss the situation. We but wished to wait until Nicholas returned, in order better to understand what happened."

"Indeed, madam?" Moncey took his position in the center of the floor, gave Pierre de Benoît no more than a glance, and resumed staring at Nick. "And why did he run off in the first place, may I ask, and dressed in that ridiculous garb? And wearing a beard, by God."

"My son had urgent business," Percy Minnett explained.

"Indeed, sir? Can there be business more urgent, or at least more honorable, than a lady's reputation?"

"Why, sir . . ." Percy Minnett began, but Nick was suddenly aware of being angry. Of feeling, indeed, a spasm of the same anger which had overtaken him at the inn.

"If you do not mind, Father," he said. "As this is a matter between Moncey and myself, I will do the explaining."

"My word," said Percy Minnett.

"Well, sir, well? Not that I shall believe a word of it."

"You need not try," Nick said, feeling his heart renew its

pounding; he was as much in control of his destiny at this moment as if he were astride a runaway horse and charging a precipice. "Because where I went, and why, is none of your business."

"What? What?"

"As for your sister, I was the victim of a practical joke—as Lucy will no doubt confirm."

"Why, I . . ." Lucy bit her lip, and flushed very red. "There had been a deal of wine."

"Gad, sir," Moncey shouted. "Gad. You deny you took my sister to bed."

"Lord Moncey, please," Priscilla Minnett protested. "There is no need for vulgarity."

"Vulgarity, madam? 'Tis the absolute truth. And I perceive I am entirely surrounded by vulgarity, here in this room. Touch mud, by God, and be sure some of it finds its way beneath your fingernails."

"My word." Percy Minnett also flushed. "My word."

"You'll apologize for that remark," Nick shouted.

"Apologize? I? Gad, sir, I'd not permit my sister to marry into such a scurvy lot if she went down on her knees. I but propose to take you outside and remove the skin from your arse, sir, and then have done with it."

Priscilla Minnett gave a faint shriek; Lucy threw her arm around her mother's shoulder. Percy Minnett stared at the intruder in horror.

Nick exploded with the fury which had been bubbling in him for the past week. "You'll apologize, sir, here and now. Knees, sir? Why, use your own." He reached for Moncey's collar and shoulders, exerted all his strength, forcing downward. Taken by surprise, Moncey's knees buckled and he all but fell, seizing the back of a chair to sustain himself.

"Nick," Percy Minnett shouted.

"Gad, sir," Moncey bawled, half turning to butt his head into Nick's stomach. Nick fell over on to a chair himself, and Moncey regained his feet, bringing up his stick as he did so. "I'll have at you now, sir."

"Henry," Lucy cried, deserting her mother to run for

the door, where the footmen remained immobile. "You two. Call your people. And quickly."

Moncey's cane came crashing through the air, but Nick rolled aside and it did no more than thump the cushions. Then Nick was up, his hands bunched, and as his assailant turned, he hurled his right fist at the pale face, landing on the cheekbone, sending him tumbling over again, bringing a splash of sudden color to the cream.

"Nick," Priscilla Minnett screamed.

"Nick," Percy Minnett protested. "You cannot strike a man so."

Henry the butler, having arrived in the doorway to join his two companions, watched the scene in amazement.

Nick panted, and Moncey slowly climbed to his feet. Now the red of the bruise was spreading right across his face, and his nostrils were dilating as indeed Caroline's had done when she had been angry.

"Gad, sir," he said in a low voice. "I *will* have your ears. And now." The cane sheath was thrown to one side, and the thin steel blade glinted in the firelight.

"Aaagh," screamed Priscilla Minnett.

"Henry," Percy Minnett snapped. "Fetch a pistol. Quickly, man. The fellow is demented."

Henry hesitated, and then turned and ran for the gun room.

"Now, then," Moncey said, advancing slowly, the blade flickering in front of him. "Strike your betters, would you, you little rat? Gad, sir, I will carve you like a steak."

Nick took a step backward, licked his lips. He had the greatest temptation to charge forward, seize the blade, and wrench it from the man's hand. But that was wishful thinking. In his present mood Moncey would run him through. But then, he reflected, as he gazed at the flickering steel point coming ever closer, does he not mean to run me through in any event?

"Nick." Pierre de Benoît had got up, and freed one of the decorative swords from its hook where it hung beside the fireplace. Now he lobbed it through the air, haft first. Nick sprang to one side as Moncey lunged, dropped to his hands and knees, closed his fingers on the hilt.

"Ha ha," Moncey cried. "Face me, would you? Come on then, come on. It will be more sport."

"Gentlemen, I beg of you," Percy Minnett shouted. "This will end in a hanging."

"Oh, my God," Priscilla Minnett said. "Oh, my God. Lucy, my salts. Quickly, girl."

But Lucy had backed against the wall, was watching the antagonists with a mixture of horror and delight. Nick was again on his feet. For a moment the two men faced each other, motionless except for the slowly moving points, then Moncey, left arm high in the air, gave another shout and moved forward, with quite unexpected speed, the blade contemptuously knocking Nick's to one side, disappearing from view with the rapidity of its motions, passing through Nick's fishing smock and whipping aside again to tear the cloth.

"Ha ha," he shouted, stepping back.

"Mr. Minnett. Mr. Minnett, sir." Henry had arrived in the doorway with a pistol case.

"Now for the other side," Moncey said, apparently to himself. "A little closer to the flesh this time, I think."

Clearly he was a superb swordsman. Whereas, Nick reflected, he had never used such a weapon in his life. But indeed he had. Only three days ago, in St. Suliac, when he had beaten down a thrusting musket with the ferocity of his charge.

"What?" Moncey demanded, moving forward again. "Paralyzed, are you? Now, where is the sport in that?"

Nick took a long breath, and swung his sword, leaping to one side as he did so. The blades clashed, and Moncey turned after him, only vaguely surprised. Priscilla Minnett gave another scream as her son nearly fell over her legs. But Nick was moving to his left to give himself more space, and then hurling himself forward once more, sword arm swinging to and fro with all the speed and energy he could muster. Again the blades clashed and Moncey's expression of surprise became mingled with dismay. He brought his sword up again, attempted to thrust, and had the weapon once more slashed to one side. But this time Nick was close, and his own blade, continuing its flailing movement, bit deep into Moncey's shoulder.

Nick dropped his arm, and stood and panted. Moncey's sword struck the floor with a rattle, and his left hand swung round to grip the wound, where the blood came seeping through the severed jacket. His right arm hung straight, the fingers stiff.

"Oh, my God," he muttered. "Oh, my God."

Nick dropped his own weapon. "Henry," he shouted. "Fetch a surgeon. Lucy. Bandages. Something. Anything."

"Oh, my God," Moncey said again, and slowly sat, while the blood flowed down his arm and dripped to the floor.

Pierre de Benoît stood above him. "It is all but severed," he said. "My God, what a blow."

Priscilla Minnett gave a moan, and fainted. All color had left Moncey's cheeks, and he fell against the back of the chair. But Lucy had lifted her skirt to tear strips from her petticoat, and was now kneeling at his side, while Nick bound the wound as he had seen Dr. Planchet doing to Harry Yealm.

"Oh, my God," Moncey said again.

"My word." Percy Minnett had joined the group around the wounded man. "We must have him to bed. Lucy, see to your mother. Fetch Mistress Ogilvie. What a day! There will be a to-do about this. Oh, there will be a to-do. He called us scum. He called us dirt. Is that what they really think of us, Nick?"

Nick tied the knot. He looked down at the blood on his hands. "Aye," he said. "He called us dirt. A man who would brawl in front of ladies, and in our own drawing room. But you would take his side, Father?"

"My word," Percy Minnett protested. "That is not what I meant at all. Oh, dear me, no. We are in the wrong, Nick, there can be no doubt about that."

"I am in the wrong? For defending myself against a madman?"

"Oh, my, God," Moncey whispered, his head resting. "Oh, my God."

"He is lucky to be alive," Pierre de Benoît remarked. "And it is more than he deserves."

"Of course you had to defend yourself," Percy Minnett said. "It is the cause of the matter. Practical joke or no, it is being said you are no gentleman, Nick. And what will they say now?"

Nick looked at his father for some seconds. Then he sighed. "Aye, what will they say now, Father. Well, then, you had best write to the Earl of Seend and ask for his daughter's hand, on my behalf."

"Nick," Lucy screamed. "Oh, Nick, it will be splendid."

"Nick?" Priscilla Minnett sat up. "Oh, Nick, that were a proud thing."

"That it is," Percy Minnett said. "That is a noble gesture. After . . ." he looked down on George Moncey. "After this."

Nick looked at Pierre de Benoît, and the Count returned his gaze, for a moment. Then he too sighed. "I can see no alternative, Nick. Not now."

"Oh, my God," George Moncey moaned, and fainted.

"A thousand pound." Anne Yealm spread the parchment on the kitchen table, slowly, peered at the words. "I have never seen so much money, written down."

"You had best take it along to a notary, for safe keeping," Nick suggested. "If you know of an honest man."

"But you are in haste to be away, Mr. Minnett. It can remain here until we return." She raised her head, pulled a strand of hair from her face. "Or would you rather tear it up, sir?"

"Eh? What a ridiculous idea." He looked around the kitchen, as spotless as ever, and today with a fire roaring in the grate. As Anne herself had blossomed over this past week. He stood there watching her. Perhaps even more than *Golden Rose*, she represented freedom; but now freedom would be short lived. "We have in any event to wait for the tide," he said.

Anne folded the paper again, tucked it into her bodice. "You are uncommonly serious today, sir. Or do you fear for your friend?"

"Eh? Oh, I fear for Etienne, all right. I believe he is in some danger. But serious . . . why, I suppose I am. My life has taken a sudden turn. I am to marry."

"Sir?" Her head jerked, and then she looked down again. "May I congratulate you?"

"Oh, you may. Or commiserate with me. It is an arranged business. And I have been forced to abandon Oxford into the bargain . . . Well, there is no loss. I'd rather be at sea in the *Rose*, and with you, Anne, than poring over a book. But this marriage business . . . I'm not sure I truly understand that it is happening. And I have crippled a man—my future brother-in-law, to be sure. God, what a confusing world!"

Anne Yealm gazed at him. "A duel, sir?"

"Good lord, no. A brawl. But I did not come down here to burden you with my problems. We have two hours before she floats. Here is five guineas for food, and I really would have you place that paper in security. I am for Tom Price again."

Anne stood up. "But you understand, sir, that for me to accept this money, now, would be a false pretense. You are no longer sure you will have any use for the ship."

"I will always have use for the *Rose*, Anne. I'll hear no more about it. Where will I find Tom Price?"

"On the quay, most like, sir. But why should you want him? Am I not coming?"

"If you will, Anne. But we must change our plans. I do not think we would be very welcome in St. Malo, or indeed anywhere in Brittany right now. On the other hand, it was but a local fracas, and the news will doubtless travel slowly. We are for Havre; from there I can take a stage for Paris. But I'll be gone some time, and I cannot leave you alone on board in a place like Havre."

She picked up her pelisse. "I am sure I would manage, sir."

He crossed the room, took the coat from her hands,

held it for her. Her glance was pure amazement; but the surprise was mingled with delight. "You are still my crew, Anne. Now and always. If you would have it so."

"I would ask for nothing more, Mr. Minnett."

His hands rested on her shoulders, for a moment. He wondered what she really thought of it all, what she really thought of her position. What welcome had she received in the village on her return? He had not waited around to discover, had hired Lyme's only coach and team and whipped Uncle Pierre off to the safety of London the moment they had landed. Anne had been left, to look her own people in the eye, if she could, after having spent several days at sea with a man. And not merely a man. A gentleman, with all the evil connotations that would have for the Lyme fisherfolk.

This was but another aspect of the absurdity of life. Anne regarded him as a creature apart, because he was a gentleman. The Monceys regarded him as beneath them because he wore no coat of arms. And what of the situation now? He had not seen Caroline, but the marriage was decided. Honor was everything.

Then what of Anne's honor? Would any single living soul believe they did not share the same bunk, at sea. Yet the idea had truly not crossed his mind before this minute. She was Harry's widow; it would be like committing incest.

And yet, the thought had crossed his mind, now.

She turned, frowing at him. "Mr. Minnett?"

"As I said, Anne. I am totally confused at this moment. I must find Tom Price."

"And will he sail with us, sir?"

"This time, I have no doubt. I have been, and returned. He'll know I can do so again."

A state of total confusion. For how much more confusing could life be than that he should be sitting in a coach riding across rural France in the middle of the night on his way to visit one of his oldest friends who was now become, entirely without being aware of it, an enemy, and with whose wife, but ten days ago, he had shared the most memorable four hours of his life.

But was not Seraphine herself about the principal reason for his uncertainty? The whole thing had been totally unexpected, and, now he reflected upon it, totally magnificent. Seraphine Condorcet, an utterly lascivious bundle of sexual pleasure. Did Louis know that? And what now? He had left her tied to a bed in the Château Benoît. There could be no questioning her hatred of him. Then what of *his* feelings? There was the true problem. He was going to marry a woman he positively disliked, and indeed even feared a little. He was on his way to rescue a woman with whom he had imagined himself in love, down to very recently, and with whom, he did not doubt for a moment, he could again fall in love, on the slightest pretext. He had crossed the Channel, and left in Havre, a woman for whom he possessed total respect, and indeed a total affection, but who had suddenly, and again quite without knowing, become a woman rather than a friend. And whenever he thought of women, his mind must inevitably dream back to the utter heaven of those four hours in Seraphine's bed.

The carriage was rumbling to a stop, as the fields had at last disappeared and the walls of the city were before them. Dawn was breaking. It was time to come to his senses, to concentrate on the job in hand. It occurred to him that he was in many ways two distinct people; on the one hand a rather shy, confused young man, on the other a cold-blooded agent provocateur who would use his best friend to further his aims. Another cause for confusion? Which was the real Nick Minnett?

And what of the man who had destroyed George Moncey? Whose reputation was at this moment once again going the rounds of London gossip. How many challenges would be waiting for him when he returned? And what would he do then?

Supposing he returned. Because surely here was the greatest confusion of all, that he should once again be challenging a State, and this time at its very heart.

"Passports. Passports."

The soldiers on the gate wore ill-fitting uniforms and had not shaved in days. There was nothing exceptional in their demanding his passport, nor those of the other traveler from the coast; they had been ordered to produce the document several times during the night. But in Havre, and perhaps even in Rouen, there had been a certain humor, a French bonhomie. Here on the outskirts of Paris there was no smiling, no suggestion of a welcome.

And now the sergeant was peering from his passport to his face. "Nicholas Minnett. That is not an English name."

"Yet is that an English passport, monsieur," Nick pointed out.

"Citizen," bawled the sergeant. "Citizen. What is your purpose in Paris, Citizen Minnett?"

"Business, citizen. Business. I am a banker."

"Banker. Bah. Credentials? You have credentials?"

Nick sighed, and opened his satchel. "Which I doubt you can read, citizen. I have here letters, to Monsieur Necker."

"We have had no breakfast," complained the driver, as scruffy as the soldiers.

"Ah bah, get on with you. Monsieur Necker."

The door slammed shut. "I really wonder why I travel," complained the man opposite, a journeyman tailor, carrying a huge carpetbag filled with samples. "These people have lost all civility. All civilization, to be sure." He peered at Nick from behind horn rimmed spectacles. It had been dark when they had boarded the coach, and Nick had resisted all attempts to engage him in conversation. "A banker, you say. Minnett. By heaven, sir, I am proud to make an acquaintance of that illustrious family. Gorman is my name, sir. George Gorman."

"My pleasure, Mr. Gorman. Nicholas Minnett."

"Indeed, sir. Indeed. And you are in Paris . . . You'll not deal with these . . . these . . ."

"You should choose your words with care, Mr. Gorman," Nick said. "These citizens, to be sure. We may not approve of what they are doing, but they are none the less customers of the House of Minnett, some of them. And more of them would be."

"No doubt you are right, sir. No doubt. But it grieves me that an English gentleman should be forced to bend his knee, even mentally, to such a pack of uncouth rascals."

The coach ground to a halt, the hatch was raised. "No farther, citizens," growled the driver.

The door was opened by a soldier, and it was necessary once again to go through the business of producing passports and documents to prove identity and a reason for being in Paris. But was this really Paris? Nick gazed at the pile of rubble, for the coach had stopped in the Place de la Bastille, and realized that the once mighty fortress prison had been dismantled, literally stone by stone. Then he looked at the rubbish which littered the street, and at the people themselves, for a crowd had gathered to oversee the arrival, men and women, and children, ragged and unkempt of person, many armed, all shouting and talking with an arrogance he had not observed on his previous visit. There were a large number of uniformed officials, but no coaches, apart from the mail stage, and no person who could remotely be described as either a gentleman or a lady, while everywhere the red caps of the sans culottes bobbed and waved.

And his own clothes, for he was dressed today as representative of the House of Minnett rather than a seaman, attracted stares and caustic comment, while the bolder spirits clustered round to finger the heavy material of his dark green garrick overcoat, point an accusing finger at his white buckskin breeches, kick mud at his black Hessian boots and jeer at the gold tassels with which they were decorated, while one bold spirit attempted to pull the silken cord which decorated the brim of his grey felt hat.

"Begone with you," he shouted in French as good as theirs, and they retreated. "Give me back my papers, sir," he snapped at the guard. "A man is scarce safe in your streets, it seems. I seek the lodging of Monsieur Condorcet. Quickly, now."

"Eh? Eh? Condorcet, you say?" The soldier looked him

up and down. "Citizen Condorcet, of the National Assembly?"

"And who else, do you imagine?"

"Why, he lives in the Madeleine."

"I thank you. Pass me down that valise, fellow. And will I be safe?"

The soldier grinned at him. "Safe, citizen? Why, we shall see to that. You shall have an escort. You, citizen."

The soldier saluted, and shouldered his musket.

"You will be safe with him, citizen . . ." he peered at the passport for the last time. "Citizen Minnett."

"I trust so, or Citizen Condorcet will hear of it, you may be sure." Nick straightened his hat, followed the soldier, who was already marching down the street, accompanied by several little boys. Several more surrounded Nick, and he lengthened his stride to catch up with his escort.

"I observe Paris has changed, citizen."

"For the better, citizen. For the better. And it will change more. You mark my words. It will change more."

The Seine and its islands disappeared behind them, and with it all the beauty which remained to this stricken place, Nick thought. The streets were immediately narrow and dark, and the garbage, and the stench, increased with every footstep. It occurred to Nick that whatever shape the eventual government of France assumed, its first task would be to make the people once again proud of themselves and their surroundings.

But the soldier was stopping before a somewhat taller house than the rest, although presenting a similarly dilapidated appearance, with windows so grimy it was impossible to see inside, and an overhanging gable so lacking in paint and in general suggesting such decrepitude that it seemed ready to tumble into the street. The front door, surprisingly, was not locked, or perhaps that was not so surprising after all, for there appeared to be no one living on the ground floor, and the furniture was falling to pieces; the rabble of small boys immediately commenced making free with it in some wild chase.

The soldier was mounting the stairs. "Belonged to an émigré," he snorted. "They would run off and find friends in Austria, by Christ. They threaten to chastise us, by Christ, should we so much as threaten the Capet. We shall settle with them, citizen. Oh, we shall settle with them."

"I'm sure you shall," Nick agreed. Or they will settle with you, he thought. And wondered what it must be like to have to leave one's own country, one's own city, one's own house, to the mercies of a mob.

The sentry stopped on the first floor landing, and banged on the door with his musket. "Open up," he bawled. "Open up."

"Is that how you summon a member of the Assembly?" Nick asked in wonderment.

"Ah bah, Citizen Condorcet is only a man, like the rest of us. We are all men in Paris, now, citizen. All men, in France. There is no more rank. You'd do well to remember that. Besides, Citizen Condorcet will have left already. But no doubt the citizeness will see to your requirements until he returns."

"Citizeness?" Nick asked in horror, as the door opened, and he found himself looking at Seraphine.

Five

Seraphine Condorcet stared at Nick for a moment, and then started to slam the door. But the soldier's foot was in the way.

"Citizeness?" he asked in bewilderment. "This is an English milord, with business for Citizen Condorcet. He has papers, and everything. Show them, citizen. Show them."

Nick raised his hat. "Citizeness Condorcet and I are acquainted, citizen."

The soldier grinned, and winked. "Ay, ay," he said. "Well, then, citizeness, will you not let your friend enter? Show her the papers, citizen. She is no doubt afraid of assassination. Everyone in Paris, nowadays, with a husband in authority, is afraid of assassination. Even amongst friends."

"I am perfectly unarmed, citizeness," Nick lied. "And I do have letters for Louis. Why, this fellow brought me here . . ."

Seraphine at last seemed to have her breathing under control. "Louis is at the Assembly," she gasped. "The Assembly sits at the bishop's palace. It is too far. Come in, citizen, come in." She reached out and seized Nick's arm, dragging him through the door. "My thanks, citizen," she told the soldier. "My thanks." The door shut, and she leaned against it, still panting. She wore as usual an utterly simple gown, today in pale green, and wooden sabots on her feet; her hair was loose and there were pink spots in her cheeks. And also, apparently, in her mind. "Can you give me a single reason why I should not scratch your eyes out?" she demanded.

"I'd be unable to see," he said, and looked around him at what had clearly been the upstair withdrawing room, a few months ago. The embroidered drapes had been largely destroyed; only their memory hung in rags from the pelmets. The carpets had been scuffed out of recognition. The upholstered rosewood furniture remained, scratched and with its pink satin covers sadly faded and stained. But there was a roaring fire in the grate. And, as in the house at St. Suliac, a delicious smell drifted in from the back.

"Ha," she said, and left the door to stoke the fire. "You come here, dressed like a fine gentleman . . ." she cast him a surreptitious glance. "Are you really a milord, Nick? I never truly believed Louis when he told me that."

"A very tired and hungry milord." Nick sat down, crossed his knees. Crisis number one had been successfully negotiated, although there were certainly many to come, and where Seraphine was concerned it was impossible to tell when. But she was here. They had proved a successful pair in St. Suliac, even if it had been largely unplanned on her part. This time he was slowly realizing that her presence altered the entire situation. Louis' help remained no more than an idea. Seraphine was here, and the same deception he had used so successfully in St. Suliac could be repeated, with fortune and a few adjustments. "You'll explain *your* presence?"

"Should a wife not be at the side of her husband?" She poked the grate, obtained a shower of sparks and a spurt of flame, and stood up, dusting her hands. "Hungry, you say. There is little to be had in Paris. Not like St. Suliac. No rabbits."

"Then why did you leave? And so precipitately. You were there but ten days ago."

"Ha," she said, clasping her hands in front of her stomach and commencing to stare at him. "There was a great to-do, as you may imagine. Poor Sergeant Popel had a lump the size of his head on his head, poor Private Daniel had a back full of buckshot . . . that whore of yours, I suppose."

"She saved my life." He was not prepared to argue about Anne's status at this moment.

"And poor Citizeness Condorcet had at the very least been criminally assaulted," she concluded.

"By whom?"

"Ah well, there is the point. The man called himself Harry Yealm. But Harry Yealm is dead. So he was an imposter. A bearded fellow, dressed in rough clothes, and a seaman, clearly, that is the best that could be said." She burst into a peal of laughter. "Oh, Nick, you should have seen them putting their heads together, and wondering what was to be done. And deciding that their representative should be informed, and quickly, and who better than by his wife, poor helpless thing." The laughter disappeared as quickly as it had arrived. "You were to take me with *you*, swine. I owe you nothing. I would be doing no more than my duty were I to hand you over to the military. I have a list of charges sufficient to fill a book."

"Except that, having gone along with the general mystery of who or what I was, you can hardly decide that I am your friend and lover, ten days later."

"Ha."

"Although you will have no problem at all if you do not at least give me something to eat and drink, as I am about to die of both hunger and thirst."

"There may be a scrap." She clumped into the kitchen, and he followed, leaned in the doorway to watch her at work. Once again, the mark of Seraphine was clearly in evidence. In contrast to the rest of the house, to the rest of the city, here was all cleanliness and heat and mouth-watering odors. And this had obviously not even been a kitchen, but a pantry, down to the flight of the family. Now a range had been installed, and linked to the fireplace, and there was a pot simmering, and a loaf of bread, all gnarled and fresh. "There is some cheese," she said. "And a bottle of wine."

"That will do admirably." He sat at the table, and wondered if all the world, saving the favored few, lived on

bread and cheese and wine, or beer if it was in England.
"What does Louis think of everything?"

"Ha." She placed the bottle and the cheese in front of
him, watched him eat. "He is furious, as you may suppose.
He is out for the blood of this blackguard. When he has
the time."

"And was he pleased to see you?"

"Of course. I think he was beginning to miss me. Not
that he has much time for me either, even when he is in
the house. It is all business, all politics, all shouting and
brandishing of arms." She sat on the table beside him, as
she had done in St. Suliac.

"And will he be pleased to see me?"

"Of course, Nick. He often speaks of you. But, having
gone to the Assembly, he cannot possibly return before
this afternoon. And even if he did, as you say, you have
ridden all night, and are exhausted. As the wife of your
friend, I insist that you retire. We have but the one bedchamber, the one bed. It is yours for the day."

"And you?"

"Oh, Nick." She seized his head, hugged it against the
bodice of her dress. He could hear and feel her heart
pounding as he swallowed his cheese. "Why were you
such a wretch? Why did you leave me behind?"

"Because of my love for you, Seraphine." By heaven,
what a scoundrel you are become Nick Minnett, he
thought.

She released him. "It is love, to leave behind the object
of your affection?"

"I had supposed us certain to be killed, as we passed St.
Malo." Which at least was less of a lie.

"Ha. And now? Now you are here on great business, as
Nicholas Minnett. You will have no time for poor Seraphine. Except for today. Today, Nick. All today." Once
again his head was sucked into the enormous softness of
her chest. "If you will but finish eating."

He reflected that if it was what she wanted, then perhaps he owed it to her. As if he did not wish it himself?
Whatever his dreams, however confused his desires, how-

ever uncertain he was as to his exact wishes, she remained
the girl he had shared those four hours with, the girl his
memory seeped back to in the small hours of the morning, the girl whose body, and whose desire, was the main-
spring for every thought he enjoyed about any other
woman. She remained, too, the one woman whom he not
only wanted but whom he could take without conscience
and without regret; having done so once, where was the
crime in repeating the offense? Especially as he was in
Paris to compound an even greater felony.

And this time, he realized with a growing delight, he
could watch, and absorb, and remember the more clearly.
Last time was confused in his mind, a compound of haste
and desire and fear and apprehension and uncertainty.
This time he could lean in the doorway and watch her
release the ties for her gown, and then lift it slowly over
her head, for she could no more undress without playing
the coquette than she could permit an untidy kitchen.

The gown settled on the floor, and she wore only a shift
beneath, clinging in folds at breast and groin. But before
she would continue, she must undress him first, with the
care of a valet, pausing to kiss where she chose and hug
when she chose, not passionately, as yet, but with deliberate enjoyment, knowing that all the while passion was
building in both of their minds, both of their bodies,
gurgling with pleasure when he could not keep still but
must slide his fingers over her back, under her armpits
and round the soft folds of her belly before rising to cup
her breasts, to feel the already hard nipples become rigid,
to know that moment of quite overwhelming pleasure
which can only come when two people are about to enjoy
each other with equal passion.

He snatched away her shift, swept her from the floor,
one arm under her knees and the other under her shoulders, carried her to the bed, while she kicked her legs,
amazingly slender when contrasted with the wealth above,
and laughed, silently, but with a widespread mouth, and
seized his shoulder to raise herself up and nibble at his ear.

He threw her on the bed, and she bounced, and lay

back, sighing, and spread arms and legs wide, and rolled her tongue around her mouth, waiting for him, and receiving him with enormous gasps of the most utter pleasure, rocking her body, and then arching her belly with a tremendous groan, her strength at that moment able even to raise him from the mattress.

But he was also spent, and rolled away to lie on his back in turn, if only for a few seconds, for then she was once again above him, leaning on her elbow, gathering her hair to trickle it across his face, mouth huge as she smiled. "Take me with you, Nick," she whispered. "This time. Take me with you. When I saw you this morning, in all those fine clothes, oh my God how wonderful you looked. You looked like a god, Nick. In Paris all is squalor, nowadays. They seek to make all men equal. Equality is always at the lowest level. There is no elegance, no style in Paris any more, Nick. To be unkempt, to be filthy, is to be a patriot. Nick, I will cook for you and sew for you and work for you. I only ask my keep, and a share in your bed. No more than that, Nick."

She licked his chin, his mouth, his nose, his eyes. And I had been waiting to time my gambit, he reflected. And would she not be a dream to have, always there, always willing, always waiting—a French whore, for Nicholas Minnett? As if he did not have problems enough. As if he had not come to Paris for a purpose. As if, having embarked upon a criminal career, he had room for the slightest hint of gallantry.

"This time, my darling," he whispered. "This time. But first I must complete my business. And you will help me."

"Me?" she asked, from his neck where she was busy sucking and kissing. "I know nothing of money and banking."

"Nor should you. I am not truly here for money and banking. I am here for Etienne de Benoît."

* * *

She stared at him. Then she rolled away from him in a flurry of arms and legs. "Wretch," she shouted. "Beast. Horror."

He reached for her arm, and missed, fell on his face. "If you'd let me explain."

"Explain," she bawled, and seized the china ewer. "Explain?" she shrieked, and hurled it.

Nick rolled to one side, and the heavy missile struck the wall behind the bed, and immediately above him. It was full of water, which cascaded on to him, and the bed, and the sheets, while Seraphine's anger dissolved into a shriek, this time of laughter.

Nick sat up, scooped water from his face, pushed back his hair. "Now you have ruined your bed."

"No doubt it will dry. But I have not yet ruined you. I propose to do that now." She ran for the kitchen.

He got up, had reached the door when she returned, brandishing a carving knife. "I'll have them off," she panted. "Oh, I will. You'll not betray any other poor girl."

She thrust at him, and he hastily jumped back, still unsure whether or not she was serious. But certainly she was at this moment highly dangerous.

"Seraphine," he begged. "Come and sit down and talk about it."

"Talk? Ha." She made another sweep with the knife, this time back-handed, taking him by surprise and almost completing her objective. There was no question of argument until she was disarmed. The force of her swing carried her round, facing him for the moment but still spinning. He slapped her smartly on the back of the neck and she made a strangled noise and fell to her hands and knees. Instantly he was astride her, seizing her right hand as it left the floor and twisting it backward.

"Aaagh," she screamed, and dropped the knife.

"I would make a little less noise, or you will have the guard up here again, and what will you say then?" He reached past her, seized the knife, and released her.

"Wretch," she said, and sat down to cry.

Nick placed the knife on the mantelpiece, and got dressed, watching her the while. Her shoulders heaved, but as her black hair was clouding past her face it was difficult to tell if she was genuinely upset.

He tied his cravat, put on his coat, and felt more in command of the situation. "You knew it was my intention to get all the Benoît family safely out of France."

She sobbed, noisily.

"And Etienne is probably in the greatest danger of all."

Seraphine crawled across the floor, and blew her nose on the sodden sheet, noisily.

"And this time," he said, "if you will help me, I *will* take you away." And hated himself.

Her head jerked, and she dragged hair from her face. "Where? How will you get back to England? There are no ships."

"The *Golden Rose* is in Havre, waiting for me. We but need a couple . . . I beg your pardon, I should have said three, fast horses."

"Is that red-headed whore still on board?"

"Mistress Yealm is on board, yes. With another man. She is used to the ship."

"Ha." Seraphine climbed to her feet, picked up her shift. "You expect me to believe you? You, of all people? You are the greatest liar I have ever encountered. Anyway, horses? What nonsense. You have first to find your Etienne, and even that will be difficult. You think Paris is a sleepy little village like St. Suliac? They will have you soon enough. Do you know what the mob does to those they do not like, here in Paris? They parade them through the streets, while they are insulted by the women, and then they hang them from a lamp-post. That is what will happen to you, my friend. And good riddance."

"And what will happen to you, sweet Seraphine, supposing I cry your name all the way to execution?"

She held her gown above her head, and for a moment disappeared from sight. "They told me you were a gentleman." Her voice issued from the material.

"It is all a matter of relativity. There are those in

England, and no doubt here in France, who consider me a common clerk, however much they enjoy the use of my money. Anyway, there is no room for honor in a business like this. Etienne is my oldest remaining friend. I have heard he is imprisoned in La Force."

She settled her gown. "I have no idea." Her head turned. "Oooh, la la." She seized Nick by the shoulder and pushed him into the withdrawing room, closing the bedroom door behind her. He concluded that she must have ears like a cat, because he had heard nothing. But a moment later the door opened, and there was Louis Condorcet.

"Nick," the lawyer shouted. "Nick Minnett. A soldier told me you had come to Paris, and were searching for me. Nick, how splendid to see you. Let me look at you."

He seized his friend by the shoulders, holding him at arm's length. And I must also look at you, Nick thought; if I dare. In fact, Condorcet had changed but little since their last meeting, at Easter. He wore the same black suit, looking somewhat shiny now, and his cravat was perhaps not quite as white as it had been in St. Suliac, while he had abandoned a wig altogether in favor of a flat black hat. But although his smile was as warm as ever, it did not match the almost fanatical glow in his eyes.

"It is good to be here, I'll tell you that," Nick said.

"And on business, eh? Banking matters? Ah, it is good to see the House of Minnett taking an interest in our affairs. Money, there is the curse of the world; but what can we do without it? At the end of the day it is you fellows who command us all."

"Have you nothing to say to me?" Seraphine inquired.

"You? By heaven, I wonder I do not take my stick to you." Instead he threw it, and his hat, into a corner, hurled himself into a chair with an almost equal velocity. "You have heard about her adventures down in St. Suliac?"

"Rumors," Nick confessed. "Seraphine would not speak of it."

"I can well believe that." Condorcet sat up again, hands

waving. "It was the *Rose*, you know; and a fellow masquerading as poor old Harry. By Christ, when I discover who . . . but there was a woman on board. With auburn hair, as I am told. What color was Anne Yealm's hair, Nick?"

"Why . . . I suppose you would describe it as bright yellow," Nick said, and listened to Seraphine apparently swallowing her tongue, as noisily as she did most other things with her mouth.

"Ha," Condorcet said. "We will get to the bottom of it. They snatched old Benoît, you know. Assaulted French soldiers, hoodwinked this silly girl I have married, stole my gun, forged my name . . . By Christ, the list is too long to recount—every one a hanging matter."

"I knew the Sieur de Benoît was in England . . ."

"Sieur? Sieur? There is no more Sieur de Benoît, Nick. Be careful, I beg of you, or not even I will be able to protect you from the mob. The man is a conspirator against the will of France."

"Well, then, Conspirator Benoît. I found it quite impossible to believe he was imprisoned, and in his own château. I could not see how you could permit that, Louis. Did he not help you set up in practice?"

"Ah bah," Condorcet said. "That was charity. You cannot mix charity and politics." He lowered his voice. "Mind you, I understand gratitude, Nick. I am glad the old fool made his escape, because the way things are shaping, life for such as he, and him in particular, may not be very good these coming months. But that is a private opinion, expressed to you alone. Are we being offered nothing to drink?" he shouted at his wife.

She raised her eyebrows at Nick, and went into the kitchen.

"I had heard rumors, of course," Nick said. "Of Etienne being in some trouble . . ."

"Etienne, bah. I repeat, I am happy, in my heart, that old Pierre made his escape. Etienne? Why, he is one of the Court bravoes. Oh, they are out to destroy us, Nick. What, would you believe it? A handful of swordsmen, dagger men, if you like, setting themselves out to destroy a nation?"

"Etienne? I cannot believe . . ."

Condorcet was on his feet again. "From the very beginning, they sought to limit us, to make us smaller than we are, to establish their superiority. You have heard?"

"Well, I . . ."

Condorcet seized the bottle Seraphine brought in, filled their goblets. "It began the very first day. Shall I tell you?"

"You have never told *me*," Seraphine complained, "and you know how interested I am."

"Well then, sit there, and listen. Oh, take a glass for yourself. There we were all assembled in Paris, the people who would remake France, Nick, the noblesse, the clergy, and us, the representatives of the people. We were to parade in procession, led by the Royal Family, to receive our blessing. And how they sported their satins and their jewels, and their swords, to be sure."

"You saw the Queen?" Seraphine asked. "I have never seen the Queen."

"She has more sense than to parade herself now," Condorcet said. "Oh, we have cut her down to size. But then, ah, she thought herself something."

"And is she as beautiful as they say?" Nick asked. Clearly there was going to be no interrupting this flow.

"Oh, she is not beautiful. She has a kind of aura; that is it. A presence, perhaps; these things are not real. But oh, how they strutted. There was but one man amongst them with the wit to understand their days were numbered. Orléans. There is a man of vision. As they marched, he kept dropping back to be closer to us, to let us see where his sympathies lay, although his place was next to the King himself. And then, when we would hold our first meeting, do you know, Nick, they had had our benches constructed lower than their own? What folly. What imbecility."

"And yet you triumphed?" Nick asked.

"Ah, bah. Those were not men. Only privilege. They even sought to exclude us from the hall, soon enough."

"Ah, I have heard of that," Nick said. "But you adjourned to a tennis court, and held your meeting there."

"And proved our strength." Condorcet drank, deeply. "Then they would seek to outmaneuver us with the vote, considering that all voting should be done by orders, so that their two groups would always have the word against our one. We refused of course, demanded voting by heads, for we outnumber them at that alone. Oh, they would wriggle and fight, they would claim their sceances royale and their beds of justice, but we would have none of them. So do you know what happened next, my friend? A resort to arms."

"Here, in Paris?"

"Where else? There was de Bouillé on one side, and de Broglie on the other, some twenty-five thousand regulars in each army, converging on Paris. And here there were the Germans and the Swiss. How those noblesse laughed, supposing us about to be crushed like a walnut. They knew not their people, Nick. Those soldiers, apart from the Germans, of course, they were Frenchmen, and not about to fire on their own countrymen. And we in Paris, why, we were Frenchmen too. We seized arms. We took the power into our own hands, for are we not the power?"

"And you stormed the Bastille," Nick said. "Were you there, Louis?"

"Everyone who would call himself French was there. Storm? Ah bah, there was a lot of noise. But there were scarce a hundred men in the entire garrison, including Delaunay."

"In England it was represented as a great battle."

"They called for help," Condorcet said contemptuously, "and none was forthcoming. So they surrendered."

"And yet you killed them?"

"Oh well, they were symbols, don't you see? Symbols of our triumph, of the rule of the people. Oh, it made the noblesse sit up and think, that. Half of them fled the country, the other half fell to conspiring. Not many of them have been as open about it as Etienne de Benoît, to be sure."

"And for showing open hostility he has been imprisoned?"

"Imprisoned? Why, he is not imprisoned, as such; he is merely awaiting execution."

"What did you say? Execution? But why?"

"He drew his sword and ran through a friend of one of our members. Cut him down, he did. He is really nothing better than a bravo, you know. But that is murder, no less. We will not stand for it. No, no. He will be hanged. I promise you that."

"My God," Nick cried, "but he is your friend."

"Was my friend, Nick. I have just explained that." Condorcet poured some more wine. "Now, what are your plans for your stay? You spoke of letters."

"To Monsieur Necker. I beg your pardon, I meant Citizen Necker. But Louis, if you will forgive me, surely something can be done about Etienne?"

"Something?"

"Well, I have been authorized by my father to offer whatever might be considered an appropriate sum for his release."

"Appropriate sum?" Condorcet's voice rose an octave. "Money for a murderer? Were you not my friend, Nick, I should be angry. Really I would. I beg of you, do not mention the matter again."

"Well then, may I at least ask when he is to be executed?"

"Why, the day after tomorrow, I think."

"Then I should like to visit him. I have been told he is in La Force."

"Visit Benoît? He is not in La Force. He is in the Conciergerie. You would find it far from edifying, I do assure you."

"Yet I cannot visit Paris, immediately before the poor chap's life is removed, and not pay him a visit. Surely you understand that, Louis. He is still *my* friend."

"Ah, well, I suppose . . . you English have no notion of

how one should feel about political matters. I will write out a pass for you to be admitted. Tomorrow afternoon."

"I will forever be in your debt, my dear fellow."

Condorcet was frowning into his wine. "But it would not be well for you to visit him on your own. No, no. The guards might be objectionable; he is not much loved. Nor would it be very sound politics for me to go. People might begin to say that I still have some feeling for the wretched Benoîts. No, no, I have it." He slapped his leg. "Seraphine shall accompany you."

"Me?" Seraphine shouted from the kitchen.

"Capital," Nick cried. "I was about to suggest that very thing."

"No one can possibly suppose she cares anything for a bravo like Etienne de Benoît, and she is known to be my wife. Do you know, it was for that very purpose the scoundrel in St. Suliac, the false Harry Yealm, kidnapped her? Oh, when I catch up with him—because I will, you know, Nick—I will fill every inch of his body full of lead." He seized his wife round the thighs as she came into the room. "You will enjoy yourself, my sweet, parading the streets of Paris with so fine a gentleman as Nick. You will wear your good gown."

Seraphine stared across her husband's head at Nick. "But I do not want to go to prison."

"Only as a visitor, silly girl." Another squeeze. "Now, is luncheon ready?"

"I shall take good care of her, I promise you," Nick said. "But while you are in a signing mood, there is just one thing, old friend. The guard at the gate this morning seized my passport."

Condorcet frowned at him. "Seized your passport? Why, that is not correct."

"I'm sure it isn't. I protested, but the fellow was downright rude. I suppose it was the fact of my being English."

"Now there is a deuced nuisance," Condorcet said. "I will make inquiries. There will be trouble for you?"

"Not in getting back to England—not even in getting

on board the Calais packet—but in leaving this confounded city, so closely do you have it guarded."

"Ah well, you see, this caution is caused by the activities of these very bravoes you seek to admit as friends. We must keep some sort of a check on their movements."

"Of course I understand that, dear friend," Nick said. "And I am not criticizing your rules. I but seek to return to England the day after tomorrow, when my business is complete."

"So soon?"

"Well, really, I could stay longer, but I am afraid I have no desire to be in Paris when Etienne is executed."

"Ah, but while you *are* here, Nick, you will stay with us."

"There is only one bed," Seraphine said from the kitchen doorway, her voice a low rumble of distant thunder.

"We shall make up a bed, out here," Condorcet said. "You have no objection, Nick? There is so much I wish to tell you, so much I wish to show you, so much that you can perhaps have your English politicians understand about our plans, our hopes, our fears."

"It will be my great pleasure, Louis. Unless it really will upset Seraphine."

"Seraphine? Bah. She is just afraid she will have to do a little work around the house for a change. Now, this afternoon . . ."

"I'd be very obliged if you'd write me out permission to leave the city, when I choose," Nick said. "Forgive me, dear friend, but I do tend to worry about detail. It is my banking upbringing."

"Oh, very well. Immediately after we eat." He got up, held Nick's arm, escorted him toward the kitchen. "Now, this afternoon . . ."

"I also have a letter for the Court," Nick said. "I am told it now resides at the Tuileries."

"That is so. We brought them here ourselves, but a month ago. We, I mean the women. When there was no food, and another spate of rumor, they marched out to Versailles themselves, seized the royal party, and delivered them to us here in Paris. Oh, we are a united nation, Nick."

"I have no doubt about it." Nick found himself seated on Seraphine's left. Her cheeks were pink as she served chicken stew. "Then I will not have far to go."

"But the Court . . . Why?"

"I can see I am going to offend you again, Louis. But is not Aurora de Benoît still in attendance on the Queen?"

"Mademoiselle Benoît is living with the Capet family, if that is what you mean," Condorcet said, severely. "And have you still hopes there?"

Nick could feel Seraphine seething beside him; probably jealousy was the only emotion which would make her betray him. "Alas, no," he said. "My heart is elsewhere engaged. But I have promised my mother, and my sister Lucy, who are close friends of Mademoiselle Benoît's, that I would visit her and be sure she is well. You'd not have me break my word?"

"Of course not." Condorcet chewed, thoughtfully. "And it may turn out well. You may hear things, as an Englishman, which are kept a close secret from us, the people. For it is all conspiracy, Nick. All conspiracy. So keep your ears open."

"Oh, I shall," Nick promised. "I shall have a great deal to tell you, tonight."

He allowed his knee to drift to his right, and it brushed Seraphine's. She was holding a chicken bone in both hands, and frowning as she chewed. Now her eyes came up, although her head did not move. And still she frowned.

Nick walked, by way of the Rue St. Honoré. On his last visit to Paris, with Father in the summer of eighty-seven, he had been fascinated, by the very name of the place, to be sure, by the variety of the entertainments, the history behind the buildings, the elegance of the people. On that visit he had not looked twice at any of the ragged shadows, male or female, which had lurked down alleyways and hastily removed themselves from the way of the

noblesse. Now they swarmed everywhere. Each street corner was an impromptu gathering, every other alley a
parade. These people were officially starving; nor, looking
at them, could he suppose the official estimates to be very
far wrong. Their clothes were even more ragged than he
remembered. The odors arising from the gutters and sewers
were even more repelling. The houses past which he
walked were all in a totally dilapidated condition, where
their windows even still contained glass and there was no
damage to the doors, and most had clearly been abandoned by their owners and were now the residences of
squatters intent upon reducing their erstwhile elegance to
a constant level of filth. It was a sobering thought to
suppose London in such a condition, the Tower leveled to
the ground, St. James's Palace patroled by militiamen, the
Mall a throng of beggars.

And yet these people *lived*. There was the biggest difference between Paris now and Paris two years ago. Then
he had reflected on the omnipotence of a few, the inert-
ness of the mass. Now the few had fled or been assimi-
lated, and the mass had come to life. And about the life,
however terrible its threat, however ghastly some of its
deeds, there was a fascinating excitement, a feeling that
he was privileged to be present at the very first rumble of
a volcanic explosion, which might carry this nation, and
perhaps the world, anywhere, with no suggestion that the
point of arrival might be more acceptable than the point
of departure, but with a guarantee that the journey, however long it might take, would be the most exciting, the
most dramatic, the most profound, ever commenced by
man.

And life in Paris was sufficiently exciting at a much
lower level, as well. His expensive cloak no less than his
satin coat and his pique waistcoat attracted continual attention, and there were hands grabbing at the material as
there were voices ever catcalling at his splendor. He wondered if an announcement that he was English would en-
rage or encourage the mob. Instead he kept a fixed smile

on his face, bowed and nodded to everyone he considered likely to return the courtesy, and kept on his way.

The gates to the Tuileries gardens were open, although guarded by soldiers. But Condorcet's letter soon had him admitted, and he was walking up the famous paths, between the famous topiary work; at least, he reflected, the royal gardeners still seemed to be employed.

But the Tuileries had also apparently become a place of promenade for the Parisians. The door to the Louvre was shut, and guarded, and here again he had to produce his letter, to be admitted into a small antechamber, clean and with a polished floor, and inspected by a majordomo, who wore a silk coat and a powdered wig. The tawdriness of Paris disappeared, and he was once again within the elegant embrace of the greatest of Royal Courts.

"Her Majesty's ladies do not receive," the majordomo said. "You have a title, monsieur?"

"I am an Englishman," Nick pointed out. "And I am sure Mademoiselle de Benoît would wish to see you. You may tell her that I have a message from her father."

The majordomo bowed, and left, carefully closing the door behind him. Half an hour passed, most of which Nick spent at the single barred window, wondering if he had unwittingly entered some kind of prison. He watched the constant parade outside, and endeavored not to think about tomorrow, about whether or not he would be successful or was actually living his last day on earth, and about what Louis Condorcet would say of him when his true role was discovered. Thoughts like those could only lead to disaster.

"Ahem," said the majordomo. "If you will accompany me, monsieur."

They walked, along marble-floored corridors, and up a broad flight of stairs. Here the guards were Swiss, in red jackets and wearing tall bearskins, suitably disciplined and impassive, the strongest possible contrast to the unkempt gardes français outside. They passed antechambers filled with elegantly dressed men and women, talking and whispering, waiting for audiences, some of whom came to the doors to gaze at the intruder; they would certainly be able to identify him as an Englishman, from his clothes.

Then another door closed behind him, and he found himself in a withdrawing room, small and delightfully furnished, the chairs upholstered in white and gold, the ornaments, and the clock on the mantelpiece also in gold, the mirrors gilt-framed. The air smelt of scent, and there was no sound. He found it incredible that this oasis of calm magnificence should exist in the very heart of the volcano; he wondered if the people within were truly aware of the tumult without.

The door was opening again. Aurora wore a white satin gown, trimmed with gold thread, and her hair was lost beneath a powdered wig which added two feet to her height. Her shoulders were bare and her décolletage extreme; an enormous pearl hung from a gold chain between her breasts, her earrings were also pearl, and there were rubies glinting in the wig. In the middle of the afternoon she was dressed as if for a ball. And her mouth was smiling, although not even the thick powder could hide the dark shadows beneath her eyes. "Nicholas Minnett." She extended her hand. "How splendid to see you."

He kissed her glove, straightened, still holding her hand. "Mademoiselle. Again I must ask, may I call you Aurora?"

"And again I will say, it is my name." She sat on the settee, motioned him beside her. "Will you take tea?"

"I . . . if you intend to."

"I think so." She rang the little golden bell on the table. "And what brings you to Paris?"

"Ah . . . business. My father's business."

She nodded. "Of course. There is never sufficient money in the world." Her tongue escaped her mouth for just an instant, and then disappeared again. "There was talk of a message . . ." She swallowed the words as the door opened to admit a footman. "There will be tea," she said. "For two."

The footman nodded, and retired. Aurora seemed to notice for the first time that Nick was still holding her hand, and withdrew it.

"From your father," Nick said. "He is safe in England, as you perhaps know."

"I had heard. I am so very grateful. There is talk that it was the *Golden Rose,* but I do not know whether I should believe that."

"It was the *Golden Rose,*" Nick said.

"You know the people? Oh Nick, if you could convey to them my gratitude . . ."

How much did he adore this woman, he thought. What nonsense she made of Seraphine Condorcet, who was all he could aspire to, and what a tragedy she made of Caroline Moncey, who was his undoubtedly deserved fate. But to obtain a smile from Aurora de Benoît he would throw all gallantry to the winds. And all discretion too.

"I commanded her," he said. "She is mine now."

"You?" Her mouth made an O.

"But clearly it is a matter of confidence."

"Oh, yes." She seized his hands. "You, Nick? Then am I your absolute slave, now and always. But command me, I beg of you."

He squeezed her fingers. "Then forget those words. They bring me nothing but pain. And reassure me as to your own safety."

She continued to gaze at him, and then slowly released his hands. A faint frown gathered between her eyes, and he wondered why, having cast all other honor on the altar of expedience, he had not indeed taken advantage of what must have been a genuine offer.

"I am well," she said. "As you see me."

"Which is why I ask."

She looked away, waited as the footman placed the tray beside her, poured the tea herself. "What do you see, dear Nick?"

"I would say, fear and fatigue."

"You are very direct. But then, you were always so. Fear and fatigue. How observant you are. How long have you been in Paris?"

"I arrived but this morning. But I have seen, and heard, enough."

"Have you heard how we were brought here, but a week ago? How our very bedchambers at Versailles were invaded by a horde of harpies? How they decapitated a life guard in front of us, and then had his hair dressed by a barber and paraded him, and another, before us, all the way to Paris?"

"Not that," Nick admitted. "It must have been horrible."

"Horrible," she said. "If I do not sleep, it is not only because of fear of the future; it is the nightmare of the past." Once again she seized his hands. "Have you heard of Etienne?"

He stared into her eyes; a feeling came over him that all might not after all be lost. And yet he had consented to the drawing up of contracts with Caroline—

"I said, I was in Paris on business."

Her frown deepened. "My God," she whispered. "My God. Nick . . ." Her grip tightened. "Oh, Nick. Can you? Dare you?"

"I mean to try."

"But . . . you could be killed."

"I could be killed riding my horse down an English lane, were the animal to rear without warning."

Her tongue came out again, slowly circled her lips, disappeared. "Oh, Nick, but how . . . No, I will not ask. Indeed, I dare not. Nick . . ." she got up. "You must meet Her Majesty."

He rose with her. "I came here to see you."

"You must, Nick. If I am afraid, and exhausted, how much more do you think she is? Please, Nick. You will bring a ray of sunshine, a glimmer of hope, into her life."

"But will she be discreet?"

Aurora's face froze, for just a moment. "We are discussing the Queen of France, monsieur." Then it softened again. "Please, Nick." She hurried for the inner door, opened it, and dropped into a deep curtsy.

He stood beside her. So close, all this time? So close? But he was following her example, and bowing.

"Aurora?" asked the soft voice. "Child? What is the meaning of this? Have you taken leave of your senses?"

"Your pardon, ma'am," Aurora said. "This gentleman is from England. His name is Nicholas Minnett."

"Indeed? Oh rise, Mr. Minnett. I have heard of you. I gather what feeble finances our state can still command arise at least partly from your father's generosity."

Nick slowly straightened, and for the first time looked at indeed a somewhat more splendid edition of Aurora herself, the powdered wig, the mass of jewels, the dangling earrings, the exposed throat, and here indeed was her true beauty, the magnificent whiteness of her long neck, almost like that of a swan. And yet, these physical attributes were all irrelevant, when he met her eyes, and was impaled upon an unimaginable mixture of arrogance and utter charm, which swept over him and reduced him to nothing in the same instant. They suggested that were she minded, she could raise him to a height he did not know existed. This was *l'autrichienne*, the once gay young woman who had shocked even the Court of Louis XV with her frivolity, who had had to wait seven years for her marriage to be consummated, if rumor could be believed, and who had no doubt consoled herself with remembering that one day she would be the most powerful woman in Western Europe. And who now must see that power collapsing about her.

"My . . . my father can scarce have been generous enough, ma'am."

The corners of her mouth twitched, as if she would have smiled. "My surroundings are presently limited, Mr. Minnett; but I am sure my poverty is temporary. I would have you meet my friend, Marie Thérèse de Bourbon, the Princess de Lamballe."

Nick hastily bowed again. The Princess de Lamballe was certainly older than the Queen, and perhaps old enough to be Aurora's mother; not even the powder could hide the faint lines which raced away from her eyes and were beginning to crease the splendor of her neck. Yet not even the lines could for a second diminish the beauty of her face. She was the most magnificent woman he had ever seen. He had supposed that Anne Yealm's face might have been carved from marble by a master sculptor; but here was a bone structure which had been etched by an artist, slowly and laboriously, intent upon creating a vision which could not possibly be forgotten.

And he was meeting her with the better part of her life already gone into history. He bowed again. "Your Grace."

"My pleasure, Mr. Minnett." Her voice was quiet.

"And you are Aurora's lover, Mr. Minnett?" Now the Queen did smile, at their joint flush.

"Mr. Minnett is a childhood friend, ma'am," Aurora protested. "I but wished him to meet you, because . . . You will remember the escape of my father, ma'am?"

"Fortunate man," said the Queen, and sighed. "We had sought to do no less, Mr. Minnett, but alas, argument and delay cost us the opportunity, and so you find us here."

"My father did not manage his escape by himself, ma'am," Aurora said. "It was through the agency of Nicholas here."

For the first time a suggestion of real interest appeared in Marie Antoinette's eyes, and she almost frowned as she gazed at Nick. "Is this true?"

"It is a matter of great confidence, ma'am."

"And it shall be treated with confidence, sir. And now ʋu are in Paris, and visiting Aurora . . ." She smiled. "You play a dangerous game, Mr. Minnett. What, cannot ʋu sit down in London and enjoy your wealth?"

"Wealth, and leisure, Your Majesty, are surely given us to be put to some use."

"Indeed." She extended her hand for him to kiss. "Your visit has been a tonic, Mr. Minnett. Should we, as I trust, surmount our present difficulties, and restore our people to a proper awareness of their duty, then it shall be our pleasure to receive you again, and on a more suitable occasion. Should we, by any mischance, fail to achieve that objective, then we may wish to see you even sooner. Take good care of your young man, Aurora."

Aurora was already backing toward the door, carrying

Nick with her. He had time only to give a hasty bow to the Princess before he was returned to the antechamber, and the door was closed.

"She likes you." Aurora gave his arm a squeeze. "Oh, Nick, the Queen likes you. And admires you. With such support there is no limit to the heights you may scale."

No limit, he thought, and remembered the hungry mobs outside, the contempt with which Louis Condorcet had spoken of her. "I am flattered."

"And now you must leave, before I ask too many questions." Still she held his arm. "And before we are interrupted. Her Majesty waits in that chamber with a purpose."

"And suppose I say I have not come for Etienne alone?"

She frowned at him. "It is not possible."

"I believe it is. It is certainly what your father wishes."

"It is not possible, Nick. My duty is here, with Her Majesty. Please do not tempt me again. But Nick . . . Oh, Nick, God go with you, and protect you, and all your attempts. And bring you back again, soon."

He looked down into those wide eyes, those parted lips he so wanted to kiss.

"Aurora." He bit his lip. "I must tell you something. It is that I am to be . . ."

The door burst inward, and Aurora stepped away with an exclamation of alarm. And with reason, he decided. The man who had entered, and who now closed the door behind him, was quite the most repulsive specimen of humanity he had ever seen. Well dressed, certainly, but there was a button missing from his vest. Wearing a wig, to be sure, but a dirty one. Even these suggestions of a preoccupied personality paled before the enormity of the face, huge and round and jowled, dominated by a beak of a nose and bulldog lips, rendered even more hideous by the blue veins which spread a purple glow across the pallor of his complexion.

"Well?" he demanded. "Well? What means this? You, sir . . ." he pointed at Nick, "are a spy?"

The accuracy of the statement left Nick speechless, and his paralysis increased as he observed the monster put his arm around Aurora's waist and squeeze her against him, his fingers reaching so far as to drum lightly on her breast, while far from struggling to free herself she merely gave a little squeak of discomfort.

"Well?" the man said again. "Introduce me."

"Mr. Nicholas Minnett," Aurora gasped. "Honoré Riquetti, Count Mirabeau."

Nick, at last regaining his senses and about to intervene, found himself again struck dumb.

Mirabeau released Aurora, and frowned. "Minnett? Minnett? Not of the House of Minnett?"

"Percy Minnett is my father," Nick said. "But you, sir . . ."

"Ah, yes indeed," Mirabeau said. "Me, sir. My presence offends you. As it would offend half of Paris, to know I entered here clandestinely, to take tea with the Capet, and talk, of things. You have seen too much, Mr. Minnett; I should run you through here and now." And indeed he was wearing a sword, Nick observed. Then the horrific features broke up into a smile. "But you are an Englishman, and a Minnett, and you have yourself just left Her Majesty, I perceive. Should you know how to be discreet, as a banker ought, then are you forgiven."

"I would prefer my own presence to remain a private matter, Count," Nick said.

"Aha." Mirabeau nodded, and extended his right hand. His grip was powerful, but brief. "Nicholas Minnett. I count today a fortunate one. You will stay in Paris?"

"I leave tomorrow, sir."

"Ah." Mirabeau glanced from Nick to Aurora, and then back again. "But we will meet again. I make that resolution, and I am a man of my word. Adieu." He opened the inner door without knocking, closed it behind him.

Nick scratched his head. "I am totally confused."

Aurora was straightening her gown. "You would be more so, should you be so mistaken as to lend him money.

He is perennially bankrupt. Not that he allows it to interfere with his pleasures."

"But . . . the way he fondled you? The way he entered the royal apartments?"

She shrugged. "As to the one, he cannot keep his hands off any living creature of the female sex, to my knowledge. 'Tis said he has even attempted to embrace the Queen. As to the other, there is much intrigue in Paris nowadays, as you no doubt have observed."

"You trust him? The Queen trusts him?"

Aurora was opening the outer door to peep through and make sure the corridor was empty. Now she closed it again; but her earlier intimacy had gone. "He negotiates, Nick. For power, should he restore it to us, for money no matter what happens. While he negotiates, he is entirely trustworthy. Should the negotiations fail, then perhaps we are lost in any event. But I would not burden you with our fears; you have enough on your mind." She took his hands. "I say again, God be your shield, tonight and tomorrow, dear Nick. Now you must go."

He hesitated, leaned forward and brushed her lips with his own, and stepped through the doorway.

"Charm?" Louis Condorcet was contemptuous. "But of course she has charm; it was taught her as a child. It is her profession, as banking is yours or the law is mine. It cannot alter the fact that beneath it she is a cold and heartless tyrant, intent only upon enjoying her life, caring nothing about the conditions of her people."

Not for the first time Nick had the feeling that Louis was either rehearsing a speech, or remembering one.

"No doubt you are right," he agreed. Today was not the occasion for arguing with anyone. "I know little of these matters."

Louis adjusted his hat. "We shall bring her down," he promised, "and that great oaf of a husband of hers; and all who support them, however much it may grieve us to take such a step. But the country, the nation, must come before all. I will say goodbye for now, Nick. You will see me at supper. Be sure Seraphine takes good care of you. Perhaps, after your visit to Benoît, you will come along to the hall, and hear our debates. You would find them interesting."

"Perhaps I shall," Nick said, and watched the door of the apartment close.

"Ha," Seraphine said, from the kitchen. She had just returned from her morning's shopping, and still wore her pelisse and hood. "I am amazed that you can sit there, and share his food and wine, and lie to him in that fashion."

"So am I," Nick agreed. "But then, you are also amazing, are you not, Seraphine? Did you get the horses?"

"Ha," she said. "I am not yet sure that I will be amazing. I have not made up my mind."

"But you got the horses?"

"Ha."

"Seraphine . . ."

"Oh, I got them. They are stabled around the corner, with a tavernkeeper I know. But there were questions, and they cost every sou of the money you gave me."

"Do questions concern you? You will not be here to answer them." Truly, he was becoming the most accomplished liar in the world.

She pouted, and lowered her head to kiss him. "That thought is all that sustains me. Nick, can we not forget this madness? What is one noblesse more or less? If you were to stay here, with me, this afternoon, I should make you forget all about Etienne de Benoît."

"I'm sure you would," Nick agreed. "But I would remember tomorrow, and then I would hate you. Now, what of the carriage?"

"Oh, you wretched man." She flounced away. "It is ordered for two of the clock. Again there were questions, and expenses . . ."

"Which were again not a problem for the wife of Louis Condorcet, especially with gold coin jingling in her pockets. It is all but two now. We'll go downstairs and wait for it."

"Ha," she said, but she went to the door. Nick swung

his own cloak round his shoulders, felt the weight of the
primed pistol in the pocket, felt his blood tingle as sweat
stood out on his shoulders. This was indeed twice as dangerous as anything he had risked in the sleepy security of
St. Suliac. But he still felt a sense of mission, of uplift, of
exhilaration, from yesterday's meeting with the Queen
and the Princess and, above all, with Aurora. She had let
him kiss her on the mouth. For how long had he dreamed
of doing that? And should he succeed in rescuing Etienne,
why, all things might be possible, married or no.

The streets were less busy, in the early afternoon. And
now too the clouds dropped lower and it began to drizzle.
Once again he was being fortunate. No doubt, when his
luck broke, it would leave him destitute; but for the moment he could only take advantage of it.

"Come on, come on, citizen," growled the driver, "it is
getting wet."

"But you will wait for us at the prison," Nick insisted.

"For another gold coin, citizen. I have my health to
think about."

"It shall be yours," Nick said, and sat beside Seraphine,
who was staring out of the grimy window.

"This rain," she whispered. "Will it not make our escape
more difficult?"

"On the contrary, sweetheart, by keeping people off the
streets it will make our escape easier."

"I still do not see how it is to be managed," she said.
"This is not the Château Benoît. There is no ship waiting,
and it is broad daylight. It is an utter impossibility. We
will all be killed. I know we will all be killed."

"No one is going to be killed, Seraphine, if you just
keep your wits; and your nerve." In fact her nervousness
was beginning to communicate itself to him. He put his
hand into the pocket of his coat, where the heavy pistol
gave him some comfort.

They crossed the bridge to the Isle de la Cité; they
were now beneath the very towers of Notre Dame, and at
the forbidding gates of the Conciergerie. "Well?" de-

manded a bearded soldier. "What business have you here?"

"We are to see a prisoner," Seraphine said. "Citizen Benoît."

"Benoît? He is to hang."

"Tomorrow. So we would see him today," Seraphine explained. "This gentleman is an Englishman, Nicholas Minnett. He is a banker, and this Benoît owes him a considerable amount. Citizen Minnett wishes to obtain Citizen Benoît's signature on a deed."

"Transfers. Deeds. Bah." The guard peered at Nick through the window. "Noblesse stuff. I'd have none of it. We *shall* have none of it, I promise you."

"I have an order here, signed by my husband, Citizen Condorcet," Seraphine said.

"Condorcet? Let me see it." The guard studied the paper.

"It will not be improved by getting wet," Seraphine said severely. If she was really afraid, she was not revealing it.

"Ah, bah." The guard handed back the paper, banged on the door. "Two citizens to see the prisoner Benoît."

A postern gate was opened, and a ragged, unkempt fellow who jangled an enormous bunch of keys, looked out. "He is to hang."

Nick assisted Seraphine to the cobbles. "Tomorrow, friend. Tomorrow. You'll wait, coachman." He handed over another coin.

"For an hour. No longer."

"An hour?" The jailer cackled. "I'll allow you fifteen minutes, citizen. This way."

Nick followed Seraphine through the little door, found himself in the courtyard of the prison, had his nostrils assailed by an entirely new and offensive accumulation of odors. Even Seraphine seemed affected, and held a kerchief to her nose. The yard was presently empty, containing merely scattered straw and piled filth, but there were barred windows in several directions, and faces peered at them; some, true criminals these, booing and catcalling at the sight of a woman, others, no doubt imprisoned for their politics, staring gloomily at this brief glimpse of the outside world.

"Citizen Benoît," grumbled the jailer, mounting three steps to unlock a door set in the wall, and carefully locking it again behind them. "A strange one that. We shall see. We shall see."

"See what?" Nick asked. They walked along a narrow, straw-strewn corridor, and the stenches, of human excreta, human sweat, human fear, seemed to swirl about them. Seraphine continued to hold her nose. It occurred to Nick that he really was the most fortunate man in all the world.

"How he shall behave on the gallows, eh? That we shall see." The jailer laughed again, led them up another flight of stairs, and halted. "A cell to himself, mark you. There is luxury. But then, he has money. Had money, I should say. It is all gone now." The key scraped in the lock. "Well, Citizen, I have a surprise for you, eh?"

The door opened inward. Etienne was on his feet, back to the single window, which in his case was set in the outer wall, enabling him to look down at the Seine and the left bank beyond. "Nick? Madame Condorcet? My God."

"Etienne, dear friend." Nick seized his hands, discovered to his relief that he was not chained. But certainly he looked the prisoner, with a several-weeks-old growth of black beard, and his clothes torn and reeking.

"Make haste," said the jailer. "Make haste. I have not got all day. There are duties."

"Then attend to them," Nick suggested. "And return for us in a few minutes."

"What, leave two noblesse alone? I shall stay. So make haste."

"Indeed we shall," Nick said, drew the pistol from his pocket, and as the jailer's mouth opened in alarm, struck him on the head. The man buckled, and Nick caught him just before he hit the floor.

"My God," Etienne said.

"You are becoming quite an expert," Seraphine remarked.

"But what will you do now?" Etienne asked.

"Make haste, as the man suggested." Nick knelt beside the jailer, stuffed his cap into his mouth, tore his shirt into strips to bind his arms and legs, placed him in a corner. Seraphine checked the corridor.

"It is empty," she said. "But will the guard on the gate not stop us? Or do you mean to challenge the whole of Paris?"

"Not if I can help it," Nick said, and seized her by the throat. "Help me, Etienne. Quickly. Use your clothes."

Seraphine gave a strangled gasp, and kicked him on the ankle as she punched him in the stomach. Finding her fists lost in the folds of his cloak, she struck at his face, but by now Etienne had woken up and was grasping her arms from behind.

"Gag her," Nick said. "But nothing else. And do not tear her clothes, I beg of you."

Etienne stuffed his own kerchief into her mouth, secured it with a strip of the jailer's shirt. He was awake again by now, blinking at once with pain and bewilderment, staring at the people stamping above him as Nick and Etienne wrestled with Seraphine, swinging her round and round as they took off her cloak, and then holding her down on the cot for Nick to unfasten her gown. She tossed and heaved, kicked and attempted to scratch, and soon enough the material ripped, but at last he had it off, leaving her in her shift.

"Now," he panted. "Bind her up, and then put these on. You are a trifle too tall, but that cannot be helped."

Etienne tied Seraphine's ankles together, Nick tied her wrists. Then he knelt beside her. "As you say, sweetheart, I am becoming an expert at betraying friends. You shall not see me again, I promise; and you may claim to be an entirely innocent victim of my deceit. I give you my apologies, and my heartfelt thanks. And I can only apologize to Louis, as well. Tell him I am but doing my duty as I see it, as he surely will always do his."

Her eyes glowed at him. Should I ever see her again, he thought, then certainly she will slip a knife between my ribs. But there was no more time for looking over his shoulder. Etienne was wearing the gown and pelisse, with the hood pulled over his head. "But my beard," he said. "It will not work, Nick."

"It will work," Nick said, and handed him Seraphine's kerchief. "This place offends your nostrils. It did so coming in, there is no reason why it should not coming out. Now remember, take your time." He paused in the doorway. Seraphine and the jailer stared at him. So, what have you done, Nicholas Minnett, he wondered. Of all the women in the world, this girl alone has given you her heart and her body. And now she must hate you, and hate you, and hate you. "I grieve for us," he said, and closed the door.

Six

Lord George Moncey raised his glass, in his left hand; his right hung useless at his side. And for all the smile on his lips his eyes stared gloomily at the long tables, glittering with silver on the white cloths, and with all the jewelry in London on this famous occasion. "Your Royal Highnesses," he shouted, to make himself heard above the hubbub of conversation which had constantly interrupted his speech. "Your Graces, ladies, and gentlemen, I give you the bride and groom."

The assembly rose. "The bride and groom."

Caroline squeezed Nick's hand. His glance took in the length of the huge table, to which had been joined several others to make an inverted U, at Prince George and the Duke of York, at William Pitt and Charles Fox, at Edmund Burke, seated as far from his erstwhile friend as he could manage, at Lord Howe and General Dalrymple, closer at hand, at the Earl and Countess of Seend, at Mama and Father, at Lucy, her bridesmaid's costume the most daring present. And at last at his wife as the toast was drunk.

Caroline wore white satin, and had thrown back her veil. Colour was supplied by the glow in her cheeks, the brilliance of her hair. Whatever the guests, whatever her own parents or her brother, whatever her parents-in-law, indeed, whatever her husband thought of this occasion, she at the least seemed totally happy. Now she leaned forward to kiss him on the nose, and the guests gave a roar of approbation.

But now at last was an end to it. They had eaten, and

toasted, and drunk, and laughed, and cheered, since twelve of the clock, and it was past three. The bells still caroled merrily through Westminster, the servants still bustled with their laden trays, inside the wide open windows the curtains still fluttered in the summer breeze. There had been no greater social occasion in London this year. Lucy had risen, and was bending over Caroline, whispering, and she was in turn rising, and the guests were again standing with her, as she smiled at them all before being hustled away to change her gown.

"Well." George Moncey had acted the best man, but this was the first occasion since the rehearsal that he had actually addressed Nick. " 'Tis done then."

"Many thanks, George." Nick extended his left arm. "I will hope that we shall be friends, as we are now brothers."

Moncey stared at him for some seconds. "No doubt," he said. "No doubt." He turned his back.

"Nick . . ." The Prince of Wales threw his arm around his shoulder. "I saw you carry her off last October, by God, and all but chased behind you. I had no knowledge it was true love. True love, eh, what?"

"Do they not make a splendid pair?" Fox added his pounding to Nick's back. "We must have you in the House, Nick."

"I doubt he can spare the time," Pitt remarked. "Where would we borrow?"

"I would hear more of that remarkable escapade last October," said the Duke of York. "Come on, monsieur, encourage him. Or tell us yourself."

"Why, your Grace, it all happened so quickly, my head is still in a total whirl," Etienne confessed. "We just walked out."

"With you mincing like any madame, eh, monsieur?" shouted the Prince of Wales. "I like that, sir. I like that."

"And holding the kerchief to my nose to hide my beard," Etienne said.

"Leaving the wench in her extremities," Fox said. "Now, sir, there was no way to treat a young lady."

"Ah bah, Charley," Pitt said. "You are too sympathetic toward those wretches. Why, I'll wager you'd have rather seen Benoît hanged."

"Why, if it comes to that . . ."

"No politics, gentlemen," said the Duke of York. "This is a wedding, not a debate. And then you made your departure by the gate, without a problem?"

"We had two passports; mine and one signed by Citizen Condorcet," Nick explained.

"Now there is a gentleman you'll never want to meet in a dark alley," Fox agreed.

"Or in a crowded ballroom, I'll wager," shouted the Prince.

"And then," said the Duke of York, "it was spurs to your horses and a gallop to Havre. What romance. Why, they will be writing novels about you, Nick."

"Mind you, your Grace, it was a near run thing," Etienne said. "We could feel them breathing down our necks the whole way. And indeed, there was a clamor on the dock before we were clear of the harbor."

"It puzzles me, Nick," remarked Lord Howe, "why you did not take your ketch up to Rouen. You know those waters?"

"Not the Seine, to say truth," Nick said. "But I had a better reason, my Lord. The tides were springing. I doubted we should get out."

"The *mascaret?*"

"You should have seen it, my Lord," Etienne cried. "We rode by the river as we made our way, and it was bubbling and foaming. Why, we saw a good-sized vessel ripped from its mooring and dashed to pieces on the shore, all in a matter of seconds."

"It really was quite the most frightening thing," Nick confessed. "Had the *Rose* been in Rouen, she would have been there yet, and forever."

"Aye," the admiral agreed, "it was good sense, good sense, Nick. I wish we had more seamen with your experience in the Navy, indeed I do."

"Still, it is a remarkable tale, sir," Prince George declared. "A remarkable tale. Were there more men of your caliber in France, Nick, and you, Monsieur de Benoît, things would not have come to this pretty pass. Have you heard, sirs? The King has accepted the constitution. Gad, sir, it makes your blood boil."

"On the contrary, your Grace," Fox objected, "why should he not accept a constitution? Your father governs under a constitution."

"By heaven, sir, so he does. And where does that get the country?"

"You had best ask your minister about that," Fox said. "But I will declare to the world, sir, that all that has happened in France must be for the best."

"My dear Charles," Pitt remarked, "you have already declared your sentiment to the world, and on several occasions. But I had supposed we had decided there would be no politics today, especially in front of Monsieur de Benoît. Is not your sister still in Paris, monsieur?"

"Indeed, Mr. Pitt. But she remains with the Queen, and is safe enough. Indeed, now that His Majesty has accepted the constitution, why, I see an end to the present mayhem. France may never be the same again, but surely at least a return to orderly government is now possible."

"And I will say amen to that," Pitt said.

"Nick," whispered Percy Minnett. "Can you spare a moment?"

"You'll excuse me, gentlemen." Nick followed his father from the dining room into an antechamber, where a man waited, dressed in black, and looking highly nervous. "What is the trouble?"

"This fellow," Percy Minnett said.

"An account, Mr. Minnett. I was told to present it as soon as possible after the wedding."

"And so you chose to interrupt the reception?" Nick demanded. "My God, sir, I've a mind to have you thrown out."

"It is of some matter, sir," the man said sulkily. "I'll take it to court, indeed I will. There is still prison for debtors."

"What? What?" Nick snatched the parchment. "Nine hundred and seventeen pounds. Good God. For . . ." He flipped the page, glanced at the close set writing. "Clothes for Mistress Minnett. Shoes for Mistress Minnett. Fans for Mistress Minnett. Jewelry for Mistress Minnett. You've presented this to the Earl?"

"Oh no, sir. Mistress Minnett instructed me to present it to you, sir, as I said, as soon as I chose after she was wed."

"My word," Percy Minnett said. "My word."

Nick gazed at his father. "We had best furnish a note. I am sorry, Father. Truly I am. It seems we may have taken on more than we knew."

"Aye," Percy Minnett said. "I suspected this would be the size of it, from the beginning. I will see to the note." He cocked his head at the burst of cheering from the reception room. "You had best join your bride."

"Oh," Caroline Minnett said in disappointment as she stared out of the window of the coach at the signpost, "this is the west road. Nicky, you are just not romantic; I thought we'd spend our first night at that inn—and make it really our second night."

"We are expected in Somerset tomorrow," he pointed out. "And anyway, I have no great desire to return to that place."

She turned her head to smile at him. "Nicky, you are not going to bear a grudge, I trust."

"I hope not. Are you happy?"

She put her hands on his cheeks to kiss him on the mouth. "Ecstatic. I hardly know whether I am floating or flying. I had never realized how magnificent it is to be a wife. All those people, all those men . . . all those women. Do you know, but six months gone they scarce took my height? But now I am Mistress Minnett. Now they must pay me a proper respect, or you will not lend them any money. Now . . ."

"I should point out that our loaning policy is not governed by personal feelings, at any time," Nick said.

"Oh, you wretched man. What can be a better guide to trustworthiness than personal feelings? I can see I shall have to improve your system."

"I'm sorry, Carrie. Minnett ladies have never, and shall never, interfere in the business of the House."

"Oh . . ." she pouted. "At least I can make sure you only meet the right people. Oh, I have had such a splendid time, this past month, making up lists for our parties. We shall commence with a grand ball, when we return from honeymooning. Then we shall have a ball to celebrate autumn, and another to celebrate your birthday in December, and then of course one for Christmas . . ."

"These things all cost a deal of money. And time."

"But Nicky, darling . . ." she squeezed his arm. "You have the money and I have the time. Although I suppose" —she put her head on one side to look at him—"I really have the money now, as well."

"Believe me, I know there is the reason for everything that has happened," he remarked.

"Nicky. And me a bride of scarce three hours. Why, as I told you when last we shared a coach, dearest one, money means absolutely nothing to me at all, providing I never go short of it. And now that is an impossibility, why, you shall find me the happiest, the most contented, the most willing, of wives. And my motives were of the purest. I saw you, young, handsome, talented, high-spirited, wasting away, chasing behind feckless French aristocrats, who are now paupers into the bargain where they even possess their lives . . ."

"I have no idea what you are talking about."

"Oh Nicky, a man really should not lie to his wife, at least until they have been married a few years. Do you not know that Lucy has told me all about your infatuation for that Benoît girl? Do you not know that all London is well aware there is the sole reason for your foolish adventuring into France, risking your life, if you please, to save a man from a fate he no doubt richly deserved."

"Etienne is my oldest and dearest friend, after Aurora. I'll thank you to remember that, Caroline."

There was sufficient anger in his voice to make her eyes watchful, just for a moment. Then her ready smile returned. "It is no matter, dearest one, as you succeeded. As you always succeed in your endeavors, do you not? Have we arrived?"

London was more than an hour behind them, and the coach was drawing up in the yard of an inn set in the most delightful country surroundings, with a green sloping down to the village pond, scattered with ducks, with the July evening still possessing an hour of daylight, with a distant bell tolling, with the air still and quiet save for the crack of a cricket bat, as the villagers practiced their sport beyond the pond.

"Here for the night," Nick said. "My favorite village." He helped her down while the groom held the door.

"My God," she said, "how absolutely boring. Couldn't we have stopped in a town, where there might be a gaming house?"

Nick sighed. "We are supposed to be honeymooning, sweet. Good evening to you, Mr. Landon."

"Mr. Minnett. What an honor, sir, and a pleasure. And this is Mistress Minnett? Oh welcome, madam. Welcome." The innkeeper seized Caroline's hand to kiss it, and she hastily pulled it away again.

"You'll be inviting us to table next," she declared.

"I would hope you shall take a cup of wine with my wife and myself, Mistress Minnett."

"I am retiring," Caroline said. "I have just been reminded that I am honeymooning. There is champagne in that hamper, and some sweetmeats. I suppose you can supply us with something to eat?"

"Oh, indeed, Mistress Minnett. There is veal and ham pie, and . . ."

"Veal and ham pie," she said. "My God. At least add a few tarts." She swept up the stairs, while Stevens, her maid, who had traveled on the back of the coach with Nick's man, Eric, hastily ran behind her.

"I did not offend your good lady, Mr. Minnett?" The landlord was anxious.

"No doubt you did," Nick said wearily; "it is by no means difficult, it seems. I will be pleased to accept a cup of wine with Mistress Landon."

Landon scurried in front of him, scattering other customers and his own barmaids, reaching for the door which led into the parlor beyond the taproom. "Mr. Minnett is here."

Mistress Landon was short and stout. She wore a white cap and perspired. "Mr. Minnett, sir. It is too long, sir, too long. And for one night? Why, could you find a better place to honeymoon?"

"Probably not, Jeanette," Nick agreed. "But we are bound for Windshot."

"And Mistress Minnett . . ." Jeanette peered past him. "She is well?"

"But tired." Nick raised his cup. "Many thanks for your welcome."

"Begging your pardon, Mr. Minnett, sir," said the valet. "But Mistress Minnett wishes to know if you are joining her or not."

"I am coming now, Eric." Nick placed the cup on the table. "Again, my thanks, Jeanette. Harry. We shall no doubt see you tomorrow."

He went up the stairs, and Eric held the bedroom door for him. The hamper had been opened, and the champagne and sweetmeats set out. Caroline had changed into a negligée, but her mood did not seem to have improved. "Really, Nicky," she complained, gesturing at the bed, the drapes, the candles which had just been lit. "This place is perfectly squalid."

"That will be all, Eric. Stevens. Good night to you." Nick waited until the door was closed, then turned the key and sat down. "I think we should attempt to understand each other, sweet."

"Do we not? Oh, please pour some of the champagne. I am quite parched."

He obeyed. "These people are my friends. I have been stopping at this inn for years, on my way down to Lyme."

"Oh really, Nicky. An innkeeper and his wife?"

"You will no doubt find that, according to your point of view, I have even less acceptable friends."

"Oh, indeed." She helped herself to some pie. "I have heard all about your escapades. They are the gossip of London. What is the wench's name? Anne something or other, with whom you float about the English Channel? Is this what you are trying to tell me?"

"Sometimes you are positively repulsive, Carrie. Anne Yealm crews my ship, and is my friend, to be sure. Nothing more than that. She is as much a lady as you are."

"*Well*," Carrie said, with some emphasis. "No doubt it pleases you to insult your wife."

"Believe me, I am endeavoring not to; but this is what I would speak about. This marriage was entirely your decision. When last we shared a bedroom together, I suggested that we did not love each other, and you remarked that for two people to marry because of love would be the height of absurdity. Correct me if I am wrong. So, I think I am right in supposing you have married me for security, for want of a better word. I have married you because you were in a position to make society demand it of my honor. But now we are married, we may as well accept the fact. Do not expect me to alter my way of life, to give over my friends, to suit you. Have your balls if you must. No doubt I shall play the host to the best of my ability. But by heaven, if I am to play the husband, provide you with everything you have ever desired, then you will also play the wife, and fit your life to mine."

Her eyes were wide, and rigid with anger, for just a few seconds. Then she smiled, with her mouth. "You may believe me, dearest one, I desire only to play the wife to you. And should you have finished your meal, why, sir, that bed over there should allow me to prove myself."

"My God, what a gloomy pile." Caroline Minnett gazed up at the towers of Windshot, holding her hat on to her head. "What on earth possessed your father to purchase such a monstrosity?"

"He wanted somewhere to escape the burden of being

banker to the nation," Nick said. He supposed she was right, although he had never thought of it before. The castle was several hundred years old, and Percy Minnett had only ever troubled to maintain the central keep; thus the curtain walls were beginning to crumble where they were not bound in grass and moss, and at dusk the whole area wore an aspect of the most solemn gloom, while with a sea breeze finding its way across the moor it could be unpleasantly chilly, even in July.

"And do you also use it, dearest one?" she inquired. "For pleasant visits with admiring ladies?"

He glanced at her. He had already formed a resolution that his best course lay in never losing his temper with her, so that in due time she would lose the pleasure of baiting him. "As a matter of fact, I have not entered this gate for two years; but I have ever had it in mind for a honeymoon. Shall we go up?"

For the huge oaken doors at the top of the broad stairs were open, and the candles guttered in the wind, while the yard boys were already unloading the coach.

"You shall carry me up, dearest one," Caroline decided, "as it is your house." She smiled at him, and kissed him on the chin. "Or should I now describe it as ours?"

He shrugged, and swept her from the ground. He was realizing that in many ways he hated this woman, where he had supposed himself entirely indifferent to her. But hate could not thrive on indifference. Last night he had been sober, and even perhaps inclined to rejection. And he had found it impossible. So then, he wanted her, because of her physical magnificence, her physical ability at the art of love, and he hated her, because of the cold-blooded way in which she had set out to entrap him, and even more, no doubt, because of the total success with which she had been rewarded.

And out of that hate, and that desire, would no doubt come at least one child. The Minnett heir. There was a remarkable thought.

The servants clapped, and Morley the butler hastened forward to take Caroline's hands as Nick set her down.

"Welcome, Mistress Minnett. Welcome to Windshot. This is the greatest day in any of our lives."

She freed herself. "And the coldest in mine, I do assure you. Is there no heat?"

"Not with the door open, certainly," Nick agreed. "Morley, it is good to see you again. Maureen, you are looking splendid. And the children?"

Mistress Morley curtsied. "Well and growing, Mr. Nicholas. Madam."

Caroline did not spare her a glance. "I trust there is a fire in my bedchamber," she said. "Will you show me the way, woman?"

Maureen Morley hesitated, then lifted a candle above her head. "Of course, madam." Their heels clicked on the parquet flooring as they went towards the spiral staircase which ran round the walls of this central tower.

"You'll take a glass of hot wine, sir?" Morley asked.

"Aye. We're for rain, I have no doubt," Nick said, and followed the butler into the pantry, where the footmen and the chambermaids lined up to stare at him and bow.

"New people, sir, new people," Morley said. " 'Tis hard to keep them here; not everyone likes the loneliness." He raised his cup. "Your very good health, Mr. Nicholas; and that of your lovely lady."

"Aye." Nick drank. "She is somewhat tired, this evening, Morley. We have been on the road for two days."

"Of course, Mr. Nicholas. Of course. You are going to be very happy, sir. I can see . . ." He broke off to gaze at his wife as she came in.

"Mis . . . Mistress Minnett awaits you, Mr. Nicholas," Maureen Morley said, her voice hardly more than a whisper.

Nick frowned at her, at the tears in her eyes, gripped her shoulders and released her again as she winced. "Maureen? What in the name of God has happened?"

She took a slow breath. "Happened, sir? Why, sir, nothing has happened. I would say Mistress Minnett is tired, and anxious to get to bed."

Stevens stood behind her in the gloom of the corridor. "The mistress calls for you, sir."

"What happened, Stevens? By heaven, I'll not leave this room until I know." He held Maureen's shoulders again, and again she winced. "She struck you?"

The housekeeper licked her lips. "The mistress is tired, Mr. Nicholas. And perhaps things were not quite to her liking. And . . ."

"She struck you?" Nick said again. "With her hand? No, no, she could scarce have so hurt you."

"She used her cane, Mr. Minnett, sir," Stevens said. "Six blows."

"Six blows of a cane?" Nick repeated, feeling the entire keep appear to rock beneath his feet. "By Christ."

" 'Tis no more than exhaustion, sir," Maureen Morley insisted. "By tomorrow . . ."

"Six strokes of a cane, by Christ." Nick thrust Stevens out of the way and ran along the hall, thence up the stairs. He could not remember ever having been so angry in his life. He could not, indeed, ever remember having been angry before in his life, if this was anger. He threw the bedchamber door wide, stood in the entrance, eyes for a moment dazzled by the roaring fire, the glowing candles which framed the bed.

Caroline sat up, wearing her white lace nightgown, her golden hair loose and shrouding her head and shoulders. "Dearest one," she said. "Must you always pause to drink with the servants, when you could be drinking with me?"

Nick closed the door behind him. "What happened here?"

Caroline frowned at him, apparently in bewilderment. "Happened? Why, nothing, so far as I know. I cannot pretend this is my ideal of a sleeping chamber; heaven knows how we shall fare when that fire dies. But by then, no doubt, we shall be capable of warming each other. And at least I am in bed. I know, dearest one, you may feed me."

The food waited on the table.

"Feed you?" he demanded. "Feed *you?* You struck Mistress Morley."

Caroline's bewilderment appeared to grow. "Mistress . . . oh, you mean the housekeeper. I believe I did. Servants grow lazy, and indeed insolent, when they are left to themselves for long periods. They begin to suppose themselves the equals of their employers."

"You . . ." Still he endeavored to control his temper. "What was the cause?"

"Why, as I recall, I considered the sheets to be damp. And that woman—what did you say her name was?—said, Oh no, madam, you must be mistaken; they are perhaps a trifle cold. What insolence, to question her mistress."

"And so you struck her with your cane? Maureen Morley? Six times? Maureen Morley? My God, she held me in her arms as a babe."

"Then it is time she was made to realize that you are no longer a babe, Nicky. I do believe I am going to have to take you in hand, and make a man of you."

"You . . . you . . ." It came over him that *he* was about to strike *her*. With a tremendous effort he threw her arm away from him, so violently that she rolled right across the bed. Then he turned and strode from the room, banging the door behind him.

* * *

He realized that out of three nights he had so far spent with Caroline, or intended to spend with her, he had fled on two. But what to do now? To return would be total surrender. Supposing he wanted to. But even to remain in the castle was distasteful to him at this moment.

He went down the stairs, discovered Morley, anxiously hovering. "Mr. Nicholas? Can I fetch you something?"

"Aye," Nick said. "You can saddle me a horse, Morley. I need some fresh air."

"Yes, sir." Morley hesitated. " 'Tis starting to rain, sir. And the wind is up."

"Saddle the horse," Nick said, and put on his cloak. Suddenly he knew where he should go. Lyme Regis was only ten miles away, and he had not visited the *Rose* all summer. Preparations for the wedding, combined with the increasing responsibility Father was giving him in the bank, now that he had definitely put the completion of his university career behind him, had kept him in London throughout the fine weather, and, he was realizing, had slowly built up a mass of apprehensions and desires within himself, an overtiredness and an irritability which had always been in the past dissipated by a brief voyage on board the *Rose*. It should have been done sooner. Certainly he should have gone to sea for a week before his wedding, to place himself in a properly contented mood.

Remarkably, it was Caroline's own reference to Anne Yealm which had put the ship back in his mind.

The horse stood at the foot of the steps, Morley holding the bridle. And it was indeed raining, quite hard. "Shall I come with you, sir?"

"You go to bed, Morley."

"Yes, sir." Still the butler held the bridle. "And when Mistress Minnett asks after you?"

"Tell her I have gone into Lyme to look to my ship. I shall no doubt be back by morning." He kicked the horse, and cantered out of the yard. Beyond the windbreak of the castle the breeze whipped at his face, and the rain, driven by the gusts, seemed heavier. But it was splendid to be out in the open, galloping into the night, with *Golden Rose* at the end of it. And Anne Yealm? Just to see her face, to know the presence of her strength, would be to restore his confidence in himself.

But it was the fresh air and the rain and the wind which was really doing him good. He wondered if Louis Condorcet had not spoken the truth, back in St. Suliac how many ages ago, when he had suggested that his true future lay in the Navy, rather than in sitting behind a big desk and deciding which of his friends and acquaintances were good financial risks.

Louis Condorcet. He had heard nothing of Louis, or Seraphine, for nine months; but things in France seemed to have settled down, for the moment at any rate. As Charles Fox had truly said—was it only yesterday?—now that Louis Capet had accepted the Constitution, and would rule as an Englishman might, there could be no more cause for strife, and France would resume its elegant, ambitious, quarrelsome journey through history. Why, soon enough he might be able to return, to see his friends.

As if he had any friends, in Paris, now.

It was one in the morning when he walked his horse down the deserted, wet cobbles of Lyme's street, and on to the dock. The tide was low, and *Golden Rose* sat up on her legs on the sand. Nick guided his horse down one of the sloping ramps used by the fishermen to careen their boats, and across the beach to his ship, pausing there, with the wind now gusting to a gale and the rain drops slashing at his back and shoulders, to admire the lines of this magnificent vessel, the way in which her brightwork was polished, her sails neatly furled, her hatch covers in place, her warps coiled in a perfect cheese. Anne's work. It was her only work now, and he paid her a pound a week for her trouble. The best crew a man could ever want. The best friend a man could ever want.

And tonight he needed a friend. He urged his horse back up the ramp, and to the gate of the little cottage, dismounted. Did he ever think of her as a woman? How could he do otherwise? Anne Yealm had none of the elegance of Aurora de Benoît, the arrogant femininity of Caroline, the utter beauty of Marie Thérèse de Lamballe, the pure sexual energy of Seraphine, but she provided a serene strength which was almost motherlike in its protective umbrella. To think of Anne as other than Anne would be sacrilege. Thus had Caroline committed sacrilege, last night.

He banged on the door, and it opened in seconds.

"Mr. Minnett? My God, you must be soaked. Come in sir. Come in."

She held the candle high above her head, and he stepped inside. A blanket was shrouded around the shoulders of her white cotton nightdress, and she appeared as no more than a tall shadow with red gold hair. Her face was only just losing its sleep flush, and she smelt of clean sheets.

He closed the door. "I am sorry to wake you up."

She placed the candle in a holder, lit another. "I was awake, sir. I lie awake, and listen to the wind, and the rain, and wonder what it must be like to be at sea, on such a night."

"And also, perhaps, if you will ever be at sea again?"

She poked the fire, stooping her back to him. And what a contrast, this living room, now, to when he had first come here after Harry's death. The comfortable furniture was restored, and with it the enormous pleasantry of the room.

"I know you are a busy man, sir. And now you are wed?" Her head half turned.

"Yesterday morning." He took off his coat and hat. "I mean, the day before yesterday."

"Then may I congratulate you, sir." She took his wet things, arranged them on the horse in front of the flames. "But . . ." The blanket had slipped from her shoulders, and she let it lie on the floor.

"I should be honeymooning? Indeed, I am honeymooning, Anne. I but felt the need of some fresh air."

Her gaze shrouded him for a moment. "I'd best get you something warm to drink, sir," she decided.

And certainly he was very tired. He sat down in the chair by the fire, watched the flames dancing up and down, smelt the damp rising from his boots, enjoyed the warmth spreading through his body. Perhaps he dozed. When he awoke she was standing beside him, a steaming cup in her hand. "Coffee," she said, "laced with rum; as in the ship."

"The ship." He drank, and left his hand against hers. "We must to sea again, Anne. We have lain idle too long. You must be entirely bored."

She remained standing, beside the chair. "I have enough to do, sir. If you stay until daylight you may inspect the *Rose,* and tell me where I have done wrong."

"I have already inspected the *Rose,*" he told her, "and

am entirely pleased. But a ship should be sailed, not admired from the beach. Perhaps, when I have sorted out this marriage of mine, I will be able to spare the time . . . It would be nice just to cruise . . ." He yawned.

"Would you use the bed, sir?" she asked.

His eyes opened again.

"I can make up a pallet here by the fire for myself," she smiled.

He shook his head. "You use your own bed, Anne. And lock your door."

"Sir?"

"Perchance, on a belly full of hot rum, I may dream. I will stay here. Now . . ." He paused at the rumble of wheels, the thud of hooves, on the road outside. The almost immediate and most peremptory rat-a-tat on the door.

"A busy night," Anne remarked, and crossed the room.

Nick sat up, knowing who it was before the door was opened, unable to summon the will from his half asleep mind to call her back.

The door swung on its hinges; a blast of cold air and slanting rain accompanied Caroline Minnett into the room. "Madam?" Anne shut the door.

"Caroline stared at her. "My God. The fisherwoman."

Nick was on his feet. "What do you want?"

"Want?" Caroline turned away from Anne, looked round the room. "What should a bride want, on the second night of her marriage, but her husband's arms?"

"Then go home and wait for them. I shall be back in the morning. We shall both be in a better temper by then."

"Indeed?" Caroline carried a riding crop, and slashed her own boots with it. No doubt she had intended more, but had decided against it in view of Nick's presence. "I doubt you will be able to manage me, when you have wearied of these filthy surroundings."

"Madam, you nauseate me," Nick said. "Get out."

"Oh, I shall, sir. I was warned about your tastes. Touch mud, they said, and you will be sure to be defiled. I'll not

encumber your bed again, sir, you may be certain of that."
She turned back to the door.

"Madam, I am sure Mr. Minnett can explain," Anne
said. "I am but the crew of his ship."

"You are a common whore," Caroline told her. "Had I
not had a tiring day I would take the skin from your back.
Get away from me, wretch. The smell of fish afflicts me."
She pulled the door open, and stepped into the rain.

Anne looked at Nick. "She is very angry. And very beautiful."

"No doubt." He got up. "I had best follow her and see
what can be done." Then he slapped himself on the back
of the head. "No, by heaven, I'll be damned if I will. Let
her think what she wishes. I'll sleep right here, Anne. Do
you get to bed. By tomorrow, as I say, she'll have
survived her temper."

"But, Mr. Minnett, sir . . ."

"Bed," he said firmly. "And lock the door, Anne. Now
more than ever."

"So there it is," Nick said. "I returned to Windshot the
next morning, as I had said I would, and she was gone.
Without leaving an address. I could do nothing better than
come here."

He sat before his father's desk in the Threadneedle
Street office, and drummed his fingers a little nervously on
the arm of his chair.

"A pity," Percy Minnett said. "A pity." He looked tired,
and his face was an unhealthy color. No doubt he was
too fond of his port, but there was more certain ill health
in his system than indulgence.

"You'd not have had me ride behind her in the rain like
a whipped dog?"

"Pride," Percy Minnett said. "Pride. I doubt it goes well
with a marriage." He raised his hand. "I do not condemn.
I well know that you were coerced into this business, and
by me as much as anyone. Well then, what do we now?"

Nick surveyed the parchment which lay on the desk in
front of him. "An establishment of her own," he said.

"That is already rented. The Godolphin House in the Mall. The bill for next year's rent, and for a complete redecoration and refurnishing has already arrived." Percy Minnett sighed. "You'll observe she wishes no divorce, and she has pointed out, or her advocate has pointed out, that you have no grounds for divorcing her."

"Well then, pay her damned rent and her damned bills," Nick said. "No doubt it had to come to this, before very long. At least there are no children to become involved."

"And you?"

"I have managed quite well without a wife down to last week, Father."

Percy Minnett left his desk to stand at the window and look down at the street. "The cost will be enormous. I do not grudge you, or her, that. No doubt there were faults on both sides. And a Minnett wife, even one so rapidly estranged from her husband, must never want. But the scandal of it. Have you seen your mother?"

"I called at the house, and was told Mama had retired, and would see no one."

"She'll not see you, and there is a certainty. Do you know what they are saying?"

"I neither know or care. I know which side carries the blame."

"You say she struck Maureen Morley. She has not related that. She says you left her bed to seek another's, on your second night. And no one is even prepared to leave it at that. They say that you are incapable."

"Oh, do they?" Nick said. "Well, then, at least that must make nonsense of the original scandal, that I raped the bitch."

Percy Minnett turned. "I cannot for the life of me see the slightest aspect of amusement in this dreadful business."

"Oh, believe me, Father, I am not amused. I am still devilish angry, if the truth were known. And the way she bandies Anne's name . . ."

Percy Minnett frowned at him. "You care more for the reputation of a . . . a . . ."

"A friend, I am sure you intend to say, Father."

"Oh, heavens above. I do not know what to make of you Nick. You have a streak of waywardness . . . Well, what is it, man?"

John Turnbull, chief clerk to the House of Minnett, hovered in the doorway. "Mr. Addington, Mr. Minnett. With another gentleman. He says his business is most urgent."

"Addington? I suppose I had best see him. Nick, we'll continue our discussion later. In the meantime, you had best return home and endeavor to make friends with your mother."

Nick nodded, and stood up. He turned for the door, bowed to the Secretary of State. "Mr. Addington."

"You're not leaving, Nick?" Addington was a short, sallow man with somewhat indeterminate features. "But 'tis you we wish to see."

"Me?" Nick looked at his father.

"Oh, you as well, Percy." Addington took his companion by the arm. "Allow me to present Monsieur Joachim Castets."

The Frenchman smiled; he was scarcely taller than the MP, but wore a black beard and moustache, which gave his brown cheeks an almost gasconade appearance. "You should call me citizen, Mr. Addington."

"But . . ." Nick was astounded. "We have met. Not a year ago. At an inn on the Dover Road. Only then you lacked a beard."

Castets bowed. "Indeed we have met, Mr. Minnett. I might even hazard that it was the information I gave you that day started your career of fame."

Addington smiled. "You'll stay, Nick."

"And you'll sit down, I hope, gentlemen," Percy Minnett said. "You too, Nick. No doubt you'll explain what this is about, Henry."

"A most confidential matter," Addington said. "But one which carried the blessing of Billy and the entire Cabinet providing that it never becomes known."

"Indeed?" Percy Minnett placed his fingertips together

and regarded the Frenchman with a stare which no one who knew him only socially could possibly suppose he possessed. "As you would scarce have come to see me, gentlemen, did it not concern finance, perhaps I should make it clear at the outset that affairs in France at this moment do not inspire confidence. I have no faith in the future value of assignats."

Castets glanced at Addington.

"If you will be patient, Percy, and make your decision after you have heard what Monsieur Castets has to say?"

"Well, sir, speak up."

Castets cleared his throat. "You are au fait with recent events in Paris no doubt, Mr. Minnett?"

"I am, sir."

"We had supposed, with the King accepting a constitution, that the worst of the crisis might be past," Nick ventured.

"Ah, sir, but what a constitution. He retains but the vestiges of executive authority, and in fact, Mr. Minnett, as he remains virtually a prisoner in Paris, he retains no authority at all. Nor is this the worst. No doubt the majority of the members of the Assembly are honest fellows, who desire only to see an improved, a stronger, a greater France. But there is a lunatic fringe, built around the club of the Jacobins . . ."

Percy Minnett frowned. "Club of the Jacobins? A religious order?"

"By no means, sir. They merely hold their meetings in a convent abandoned by such people. This club had its origins in the Breton representatives, led by one Condorcet . . ." he paused, to glance at Nick.

"Louis Condorcet. He is an old friend. Or perhaps I should say was."

"Indeed, sir, was would be more appropriate. He has sworn the most dire vengeance against you, sir, since you used his signature, and his wife, to facilitate the escape of Etienne de Benoît from the Conciergerie. But that is by the by. He is, to be sure, one of the most rabid, but he has surrounded himself with a crew as dangerous as himself—Marat, a journalist fellow; Desmoulins—oh, they are creatures of the gutter, who openly call for the destruction of the King and indeed all forms of nobility or even talent, and demand the rule of that very gutter from whence they arose."

"My word," Percy Minnett remarked. "And these are all Breton deputies, you say? I had supposed Brittany one of the most peaceful of the provinces."

"You would no doubt find it changed, Mr. Minnett," Castets said. "But these men are not all from Brittany, of course. The club's doors are wide open for anyone with a pronounced revolutionary bent. Red is their color, sir. The color of blood."

"And these men, it appears, are exercising all their wits, and all their undoubted influence with the Paris mob, to dispossess the monarchy," Addington said, "with perhaps worse in mind."

"But surely," Nick argued, "Lafayette can control the Paris mobs."

"He has not done so very successfully so far," Addington commented. "Not a day passes but we hear of some poor fellow dragged off to the lanterns and hanged amidst scenes of indescribable humiliation."

"Lafayette thinks only of Lafayette," Castets growled. "He seeks to ride the tide of popular opinion, as a man might cling to the back of a runaway horse."

"Well then, sir, surely the army . . ."

"The disaffection has alas reached even the army, Mr. Minnett. Oh, there are loyal troops to be found, but these are mostly guarding the frontiers. To march but a battalion nearer the capital raises the mob. I tell you, sir, the King, and the Queen, and their gentlemen and ladies"—he gave Nick another glance—"are in daily danger, and daily grow more bereft of the prospects of survival."

"They must be got away," Addington said. "At least out of Paris."

"Indeed, sir, you are right," Castets said. "But now we

come to the truly secret part of this affair, gentlemen. The Royal Family has a friend."

"Mirabeau," Nick said.

Castets frowned. "How knew you that, sir?"

"That is *my* secret, sir."

"Ah. Yet is it true, and no longer sufficient of a secret. Honoré Mirabeau is my friend, more he is my employer. I honor his action. Whereas others take exception to the rumor that the Court is paying his debts, and that he is considering accepting office."

"And is he?" Percy Minnett demanded.

"No doubt he is, Mr. Minnett. And why not? He is the one man who can perhaps save France from the abyss. But to do that he must also save the Royal Family."

"Count Mirabeau supposes, with reason," Addington said, "that were their Royal Highnesses removed from Paris, say to Nancy or some such place, where they would be under the protection of the frontier army, and a general such as the Marquis de Bouillé, they could then deal with the Assembly, and the Paris mob, on more equal terms. Certainly without the daily risk of being murdered."

"An entirely sound concept," Percy Minnett agreed. "I am surprised it has not been done before."

"Ah, sir, it is not easy," Castets said. "The Royal Family, the Tuileries, Count Mirabeau himself, are constantly under surveillance by spies of all parties. The situation is tested, every so often. A lady is sent to visit relatives, perhaps, outside the city. And with every horse that is harnessed there is an outcry, and guards appear to ask questions, and deputations from the Assembly are close behind. Oh no, sir, when it is decided to take the step, it will have to be a decisive and possibly dangerous maneuver."

"Believe me, monsieur, I can understand that," Percy Minnett agreed. "What I do not understand is how or why it should concern the House of Minnett."

"Ah," Castets said, and gave Addington a somewhat nervous glance. "Well, gentlemen, as I have endeavored to make clear, should this maneuver fail, there will be no alternatives for the Royal Family. They will have to flee the country. Now there are, of course, several alternative routes which are being considered, but one of these must obviously be by sea."

"The Navy?" Percy Minnett looked at Addington, who cleared his throat.

"Ahem. I am afraid that this is not possible, Percy. Oh, you may believe that His Majesty's Government has every sympathy with King Louis and his family, but the fact remains that England is at peace with France, and must, if it is at all possible, remain so. The world just cannot afford another war within seven years of the last one. Even more important, this country cannot afford another war while we are still recovering from the last. No, no, England can in no way be involved in French internal affairs."

"My word," Percy Minnett said. "My word." At last he looked at Nick.

Now it was Castets' turn to clear his throat. "It seems that not only is Paris gossip filled with the remarkable achievements of Monsieur Nicholas Minnett in removing Etienne de Benoît from the Conciergerie, in broad daylight, and his father from St. Suliac, but Her Majesty herself met the young man, and has confidence in him, and even more to the point, Count Mirabeau has also met Mr. Minnett, and now he wishes to do so again. To discuss possibilities and eventualities."

"My word," Percy Minnett said. "I have never heard anything so preposterous in my life. You have just stated that all Paris, all France, knows how Etienne de Benoît got away. You have just said that Louis Condorcet has sworn to have my son's blood. And now you wish him to return, openly? Does this sense of madness affect everyone in France, monsieur?"

"Undoubtedly such a course would be suicide for any ordinary person, Mr. Minnett," Castets said soothingly. "But Monsieur Minnett is not an ordinary person, now is he? He is heir to the House of Minnett. And there is one great passport to safety in this imperfect world, sir. Money. As you should know better than anyone, France is bankrupt. Pouf, you will say: France has been bankrupt for a hundred years. Well, sir, she is a little more bankrupt now than before. Necker has fled. Well, he always dreamed of more than he could accomplish. But yet the Paris mob starves. The Assembly, even the Jacobins, are well aware that there is a force which could, and will, sweep them all away if the simple problem of providing at least one meal a day per head is not solved. The man who can solve that problem, sir, will have France in the palm of his hand."

"I have already said, monsieur, that there is no good argument for me to advance money to the present French government." Percy Minnett's voice was cold.

"And I agree with you, sir. But it could do you no harm to listen to their proposals. It could do your accredited representative no harm to listen. And such a representative, sir, on such a mission, would be protected by every man in France. Whatever his antecedents; whoever his personal enemies."

"A clever scheme," Addington said, "and committing no one. Billy and I will have precise instructions for you, Nick, should you accept the task."

Percy Minnett looked at his son. "You would return, to Paris, knowing the hate you inspire there?"

But Nick's heart was already singing at the thought of seeing Aurora again. And this time, perhaps, of being able to assist her as he had assisted her brother and father. Why, as his own marriage was in any event in total ruins, and her life was similarly in a state of catastrophe . . . "Indeed, Father, I think Monsieur Castets' arguments are entirely convincing."

"And when Louis Condorcet slaps your face?"

"I doubt he will risk that, sir," Castets protested.

"And in any event, I have but to decline. As representative of the House of Minnett my time and my honor are not my own."

"And suppose he stoops even lower than that, in his hatred?"

"Well, then, Father, I must be sure my back is always guarded." Nick seized Castets' hands. "Tell your Count that I will be with him as soon as it can be arranged."

Seven

"Passports. Passports." The year might never have passed. It might almost have been the same soldier. "Minnett? Minnett? You are French."

"I am English, monsieur, as my passport indicates."

"Monsieur? Monsieur? Citizen, Englishman. Citizen. Step down, citizen. Step down. I am to search the baggage."

So then, a year *had* passed, and France had descended a little further into hell. Nick stepped down, together with the three men who had accompanied him in the coach from Calais, watched their boxes being distributed over the cobbles, and investigated by grubby hands, while Eric anxiously hovered.

It was just dawn, and cold for August. There were few people about at this hour, although around them could be heard the sounds of awakening Paris, the stealthy rustle of a great city preparing for another day of turmoil and anxiety, the faint whiff of baking French bread, hanging on the still air, combating even the odors of the gutters and the sewers.

"And that satchel," said the sergeant.

Nick shook his head. "These are private papers, citizen."

"Private papers? How can an Englishman have private papers in Paris? I have the power of arrest, citizen. How would you like to spend the night in the Conciergerie, eh? Those who enter the Conciergerie do not come out again, except to be hanged."

"I have heard of the Conciergerie," Nick said. "I also have letters here for the Count de Lafayette, I beg your pardon, for Citizen General Lafayette. No doubt his powers are even greater than yours?"

The sergeant glared at him, and was interrupted by a bystander, who had arrived on foot, but well enough dressed. "Citizen Minnett? The coach must be early. I am Jacques L'Onglon, at your service."

"Nicholas Minnett, Citizen L'Onglon, and extraordinarily glad to see you."

"You know this fellow?" the sergeant inquired.

L'Onglon nodded. "He is an English banker, here to talk with the government. You'll come along with me, Mr. Minnett. Is that your man?"

Nick nodded. "You'll bring the bags, Eric."

"Man? Servant?" bawled the sergeant. "There are no servants in Paris, citizen. Make him carry his own bags."

Eric gave the sergeant an apologetic smile, and hurried behind Nick and L'Onglon.

"We have arranged lodgings for you with Citizeness Aumone," L'Onglon explained. "It would be best for you to deal exclusively with my principals, you see." He scratched his nose. "Your name is well known in Paris, and in certain quarters well hated."

"Indeed, citizen?" Nick had already decided that his best course lay in diplomatic nonchalance.

"Indeed, citizen. It would be well for you to remember that. The government has guaranteed your safety, of course, but in return it must ask for a pledge of correct conduct."

"Which of course I offer," Nick said.

"Thank you, citizen. Then all should be well. This is the place."

Madame Aumone turned out to be a large woman, heavy rather than fat, who folded her arms and regarded Nick and Eric as if they were peculiarly noxious beetles. However, the rooms were comfortable enough, and inevitably there was bread and cheese and wine for breakfast. L'Onglon sat with them while they ate, and while Nick washed and shaved following the meal; Nick wondered if he was going to be overlooked every moment he was in

Paris; he was distressed to discover that there were two pallet beds made up in his sitting room. Clearly any secret meeting with Mirabeau was going to be difficult. Immediately after breakfast the secretary had him walking toward the Tuileries once again. "Citizen Roland, and Citizen General Dumouriez are waiting to see you, Mr. Minnett."

"Ah," Nick said. "It will be my great pleasure to meet them. Then there is Count Mirabeau . . ."

"Count Mirabeau?" L'Onglon demanded. "You mean Citizen Riquetti."

"Of course, citizen. Of course. But his is a name we hear much of in England."

"No doubt," L'Onglon said disapprovingly.

"Is he not a member·of the government?"

"He would *be* the government, Mr. Minnett; but he is not concerned with financial matters, saving his own. We will enter here."

A guard opened a postern gate for them, and they ascended a flight of narrow stairs which eventually debouched into a wide hall. They were in the Louvre. Nick wondered what it must be like for someone like L'Onglon, clearly a simple clerk in his heritage and upbringing, to be walking these marble floors about the nation's business. Undoubtedly it was a heady brew the French commons were presently imbibing.

Another guard stood before huge polished doors, but at a nod from L'Onglon he threw them open. "Citizen L'Onglon, and Mr. Minnett, from London," L'Onglon said. "Citizen General Lafayette."

"My pleasure." Nick shook hands. The general was considerably younger than he had expected, with glowing eyes and a splendidly contemptuous tilt to his head, and yet with a curiously indecisive cast of features. He wore a white uniform, but with the tricolor, the blue and red of Paris combined with the white of the Bourbons, as a cockade in his belt.

"Citizen General Dumouriez."

Now here, Nick decided, was the true professional soldier; but then no doubt Dumouriez had obtained his rank as a consequence of the revolution, whereas Lafayette still held his despite it. He possessed a lean, thoughtful face, with brooding eyes which entirely lacked arrogance, and yet looked at Nick, as they seemed to look at everything, with an air of meticulous inspection, as he might be reconnoitering a battlefield.

"Citizen Roland."

A great hearty fellow, tall and broad and red faced, with a booming voice and a happy smile. "Mr. Minnett. An honor for France. Today, gentlemen, today, Mr. Minnett, I feel we are at last accomplishing our purpose. Now I would have you meet the true spirit of the revolution. Mr. Minnett, my wife, Manon."

It occurred to Nick that of all the women he had met over the previous year, here was perhaps the most remarkable; yet she was far from being the most beautiful. Indeed, she could not truly be described as beautiful at all, in a classical sense. About average height, she was attractively plump; he estimated that she was in her middle thirties. And she was plainly dressed in a red gown. Her face matched her body, smoothly rounded, with a big nose and fleshy lips. Her black hair was loose. But her brown eyes glowed with a tremendous quality of fervor, and seemed to light up her entire face, giving her appearance at once an intelligence and an intensity he had never known before. She was a woman one would wish to please and please, and please, whether by deed or word, because to please her at all would be a tremendous achievement.

Her hand was soft, her grip firm. "Mr. Minnett. At last I meet the man who set Paris by the ears."

He bowed to kiss her knuckles. "I am sure you flatter me, madame."

"Citizeness, please, Mr. Minnett. And I do not flatter you. Indeed, as a good patriot, I have every reason to hate you, although not so much as Citizen Condorcet perhaps. But I understand you are here today in a different role. Gentlemen?"

"I shall take my leave," Lafayette decided. "Money matters bore me, and depress me. Mr. Minnett, Citizen L'Onglon is my secretary, and will see to your requirements, and your safety. No doubt you will dine with me in due course."

"It will be my pleasure," Nick said.

"Now come and sit down," Roland said, offering the chair on his right as he himself sat at the head of the long table, Dumouriez on his left. Madame Roland sat at the far end, where paper and pens had been placed for her. L'Onglon discreetly took a seat at the side of the room. "We must be brief, and frank," Roland said, "as indeed I would have it no other way. You are familiar with the current situation in France, Mr. Minnett?"

"As familiar as an Englishman may be, citizen. I understand that you now govern France under a constitution, by which the King expresses his executive authority through appointed ministers, much as we do in England."

"General Dumouriez and I do not yet control the affairs of France, but it is anticipated that we shortly shall do so, once the constitution is ratified by the Assembly; we of the Gironde will certainly possess a majority in any new House."

Nick nodded. In view of his true mission, it made very little odds whether he spoke with government or opposition.

"Unfortunately, France is not England," Dumouriez remarked.

"Even more to the point, Frenchmen are not Englishmen," Roland added. "We have our political parties, of course, Mr. Minnett as do you. Even in England, I understand, interparty feeling runs high. Yet Whig and Tory are equally agreed on the efficacy of your constitution, on their loyalty to the Crown. Here we pursue a more dangerous game. We call ourselves Girondists, because most of our support comes from the area around Bordeaux. We flatter ourselves that we are moderate, that we have discovered the best solution for France in its present situation, and that given time, and some fortune, we may en-able the people to understand that as well. The Jacobins and the Cordeliers hold very different points of view. They encourage a gutter press, written and inspired by men like Marat and Desmoulins, who openly call for the end to the monarchy and, by implication, an end to us."

"And the word end, as used by Citizen Marat, admits of only one interpretation," Dumouriez said.

From the corner of his eye Nick watched Madame Roland, writing industriously.

"Which is all merely a preamble," Roland continued. "In the hopes that you will be able to understand that while we may sit here in comfort and discuss certain possibilities, it is really a matter of life and death for us all."

"We need money, Mr. Minnett," Dumouriez said. "God knows we need it for every possible purpose, but we need it in the first place to buy food."

"It is I suppose an inevitable concomitant of revolution," Roland said. "Oh, the concept is tremendous. We shall overturn the landlords, and make a paradise of equality. But without a landlord, why should people sow? And unless they sow, how can they reap?"

"And those who are prepared to work still refuse to sow because they say the government is merely going to take all their produce in taxes," Dumouriez said. "But what can we do? We must tax."

"It had been supposed that once the tax-free privilege of the nobility was removed, your troubles would be over," Nick suggested.

"Oh indeed, supposing the noblesse continued to support their vast estates, and pay taxes on their enormous incomes. But the swine have all fled the country, and their estates are merely decaying rubble. You find that amusing, Mr. Minnett?"

"No, citizen; but I suspect it is inevitable." He consulted his notes. "The borrowing record of recent French governments is very bad, as no doubt you know. We have had Turgot borrowing to pay the debts of the war, and Necker borrowing to pay the debts of Turgot, and Calonne borrowing to pay the debts of Necker, and Brienne borrowing to pay the debts of Calonne, and then Necker again resting his entire reputation on convincing the nobles that they must submit to taxation to pay the debts of Brienne . . . My father fails to see where the security can be obtained for financing on the scale you seek in the present climate."

"We have of course obtained possession of a vast amount of property, Mr. Minnett," Roland said. "Perhaps to an Englishman this may smack of a criminal business, however, it is there, and . . ."

"And was used to secure the assignat issue," Nick said. "My information is that the value even of assignats has dropped tenfold."

"More than that, as we are being blunt," Dumouriez said.

"Because they were overissued, Mr. Minnett," Roland insisted. "Now, sir, we are prepared to embark upon a plan of tremendous economy, of paring every last expenditure to the bone. We are prepared, sir, to offer all the security in property that can possibly be asked . . ." He gazed at Nick's face. "But this will not be enough."

Nick felt a good deal of sympathy for their arguments, and also found himself believing in both their patriotism and their honesty. But his feelings did not enter the matter at all. He was here merely as an agent, and not even a financial agent; the pretense of money had got him safely into Paris, it could now be dropped—as Billy Pitt had shown him how.

He sighed. "As you know, gentlemen, I am here not merely as representative of the House of Minnett, but on behalf of Mr. Pitt as well. The sums you seek can scarce be guaranteed by any private establishment, even one such as my father's. You are seeking nothing less than the support of the English treasury. And sirs, however much you may repudiate the policies of the Bourbons over the past two hundred years, there yet remains the fact that you hope to be the ministers of a government which has proved Great Britain's most inexorable enemy throughout that period. We live, gentlemen, by trade. That wealth which is your envy, and which you now seek to your aid, is earned by the endeavors of our citizens in our colonies, by the courage and endeavor of our seamen who bring it safe to London and Bristol. To borrow of that wealth, you will have to offer security in kind."

Dumouriez was aghast. "Our colonies?"

"You can have no fear for them, general, if you do not doubt your ability to repay the loan."

"By Christ," Roland said. "You have come here merely to refuse us, sir."

"I have come here to listen to your proposal, gentlemen, and to clarify the situation," Nick insisted, and hated himself, as he did increasingly when required to lie. "We do not seek to humble France. On the contrary, in England there is a large body of opinion which sees in this revolution of yours all that is bright for the future of civilized man. But yet is every living man haunted, and supported, or weighted down, by his past. What will we see, should France be restored to greatness by our money? A French navy once again battering at our West Indian colonies? A French army once again designing on the Netherlands?"

"What will you see, Mr. Minnett, should the present government be unable to withstand the demagoguery of the Jacobins?" Manon Roland spoke quietly, but her words seemed to fill the room. "Then you may well see an explosion which will alter the course of history. And not merely French history, sir. France is today a volcano, restrained from erupting only by relieving fissures through which the angry energy can escape, a little at a time. Refuse to open those fissures wider, Mr. Minnett, and I wager you will hear the rumble in London itself."

Nick gazed at her. He had never had business dealings with a woman before. "You may believe that I will report the situation to London, madame."

She smiled. "Citizeness. You must try to remember, Mr. Minnett. And how long will it take you to do that, do you think? We are not talking of years, now. Even months may be too long."

"We had supposed you came empowered to make a decision here and now," Dumouriez said.

"Indeed, you had supposed correctly," Nick said. "And my decision has been given. If I now seek to temporize, it is because I do understand the seriousness of the situation, as expressed by Madame Roland. I beg your pardon, madame; Citizeness Roland. Yet am I, as are you, tied by the requirements of my government. I can only endeavor to have them think again."

"Well, sir," Roland began, and checked at a sudden uproar from outside. "What the devil is that?"

L'Onglon was on his feet, and moving toward the door, which was now thrown in with tremendous violence before he could reach it. "Where is he?" shouted Louis Condorcet. "Where is the blackguard? He shall not escape me this time."

"Quickly, monsieur." In her agitation, Manon Roland forgot her own strictures. She ran around the table, seized Nick's arm as he rose to face the door, whence both Roland and Dumouriez had hastened, and pushed him toward a smaller door at the back of the room. A moment later they were through, the door was slammed behind him, and she was hustling him down a narrow corridor, still holding his arm, her hair fluttering, exuding a most delightful natural scent.

"Should I not have faced him?" Nick asked. "He has every right to bear a grudge."

"Oh indeed he does," she agreed. "And what would you have done? Accepted a challenge?"

"I am not afraid to meet him, citizeness," Nick protested. "I am at least as accurate a shot."

"No doubt. And believe me, Mr. Minnett, no one questions your courage. That has been amply displayed by your presence in Paris at all." She stopped, to catch her breath, and to open another door, which led into a small antechamber with a single chair, and indeed a single window, looking out at the river. "But either way would be an absolute disaster, would it not? What, a member of the Assembly kill Mr. Nicholas Minnett, a representative of His Majesty's Government? Or equally, what, a representative of His Majesty's Government kill Citizen Condorcet, a founder member of the Jacobin Club? Believe me, sir, the Paris mob needs too little to be stirred to violence as it is."

"You make no moral judgements."

She glanced at him, stood by the window. "France is undergoing a profound moral change, Mr. Minnett. So, as a Frenchwoman, I had best reserve judgement until I see where we eventually arrive, however much, as a spouse, I may abhor you."

He frowned at her. She spoke quietly, but her words had an edge. "I do not understand."

Again the quick glance, and now there was color in her cheeks, and she had stopped panting. "Do you know that Seraphine Condorcet confessed all, and especially her liaison with you?"

"But . . ." he bit his lip. "I left her bound and gagged."

"So there was no need. But she, being a true woman, Mr. Minnett, discovered her anger submerged in misery, at being left at all, after your promise, and when reproached by her husband with carelessness, blurted her true feelings. It caused quite a scandal, even in Paris, especially when it was considered that this was the second occasion you had made use of her in such a fashion. You cannot blame Condorcet for hating you more than any man on earth."

"Nor do I," Nick said. "And Seraphine?"

"Ah, Seraphine. I cannot tell you of her. I know she was divorced. Then she wisely chose to disappear from public view, and public recrimination. I imagine she has returned to her home. Where was it?"

"St. Suliac."

"I do not know Brittany very well."

"So I am regarded as a total scoundrel," he said.

At last she turned, and crossed the room, and sat in the one chair. "By many."

"By you, Citizeness Roland?"

She hesitated, and then shook her head. "No, Mr. Minnett. You are not a scoundrel. That were too simple, and you are not a simple man. You are, in fact, a highly dangerous man, although perhaps you do not yet realize it. From what little I have been able to gather of your accomplishments, from what little I have seen of you today, I would estimate that you possess that rare gift, the ability to submerge every personal consideration to the business you undertake. We are beginning to see such men emerging in France today. Sometimes I wish my husband were one of them. And then, at other times, I am grateful that he is not. A man such as you, Mr. Minnett, will accomplish great things, in the eyes of the world, should he survive the undoubted numbers who will wish to kill him; he will also cause much hardship and misery, by the very determination with which he pursues his course. Oh, he will regret this, Mr. Minnett, but that will not alter his course one iota."

He tried boldness. "I could almost say you sound as if you admire me, Citizeness."

"If I wish such a quality in my husband, from time to time, do I not wish it in myself, all the time?" Her gaze shrouded him. "I admire you, Mr. Minnett. I envy England the possession of you. In retrospect, I envy Seraphine Condorcet her hours with you. But I would not undertake even a minute such as she knew. It is not sufficient for my lover to have a handsome face, a virile body, a passionate nature. My lover must also love me with all of his mind, at least while sharing my embrace."

Was she baiting him? He seized her hand. "And if I told you that I did indeed love Seraphine, with every aspect of my being, while we were together? That I hated what I must do, with every aspect of my being?"

Now her smile was real, and sad. "Yet you did it, Mr. Minnett, with courage and determination and flawless panache." She rose, but did not withdraw her hand. "You have never loved anyone, Mr. Minnett, physically or mentally, with all of your being. And to show that I do not judge you harshly, I will add that you do not even love

yourself with that abandon, or surely you would not risk
yourself in so profligate a fashion. But I pray, Mr. Minnett, that you do learn to love; or all your fame will
amount to very little, at the end."

Her hand was gone, and she was moving to the door.
"Don't follow me, Mr. Minnett. I will make sure that Condorcet has been removed, and then I will send one of my
servants for you. He will see you safe back to your lodging." She paused, her hand on the door. "I am sure we
shall meet again, Mr. Minnett, and I look forward to that
occasion. For the moment, I beg of you, do what you can,
for France."

"No," he wanted to shout. It is but another deception.
There will be no money. There was never to be any
money. It was all nothing more than a conspiracy to bring
me safe to Paris.

But he said nothing, and the door was closed, and he
was alone, with his heart pounding and his brain tumbling, unable to deny the truth of much of what she had
said, or indeed, all of it, searching for the excuses which
he knew were there, the trick played upon him by Caroline, the death of Harry, his rejection by Aurora, and
knowing that still every word she had said had been true,
and that these were but excuses, and then starting, violently, as the door again opened, and staring in amazement
at Joachim Castets.

The little man smiled at him. "Do not look so surprised,
Mr. Minnett. Nothing in France today is quite what it
seems."

"But . . ."

"I am the Count's servant, yes. I am also a faithful servant of the Girondins, or so it is believed. Now come, I
am to escort you home, and once there, you will remain
concealed all afternoon, eh?" He laid his finger on his nose.

Nick decided to wait and see what was going to happen. He followed Castets into the corridor, and then
through another paneling door and down a succession of
staircases, sometimes obviously close to the mainstream of

life in the palace, at other times moving through a silently empty world. At last Castets opened an outer door which led on to the bank of the river itself. Here there waited a rowing boat with two oarsmen, into which Castets and Nick got, to sit in the stern as their crew breasted the current, heading upstream for the jutting bow of the Isle de la Cité. Nick gazed at the towers of the Conciergerie, almost lost against the greater towers of the cathedral in the background, and felt a chill, although it was by now past noon and the day was quite hot.

"Here," Castets said, and the boat pulled into a flight of steps tucked in the shadow of a high building. Castets handed over a bag of coin. "Our thanks, citizens."

The men nodded, but did not answer. Nick jumped ashore, and followed Castets on to the street, busy enough now. But today the crowds seemed less concerned with their new found freedom than determined to enjoy themselves; even his English clothes and tall hat caused little interest beyond the odd coarse comment. Within seconds they were delving down a series of noisome alleyways before emerging at the back of what was obviously a house of considerable size. The door was bolted, but Castets knocked thrice and it was opened to allow them inside before being bolted again.

"There," said the agent, taking out a kerchief to wipe his forehead. "We have disappeared from the face of Paris."

"The Count is upstairs, Monsieur Castets," said the woman who had let them in, and who, Nick now discovered as his eyes became accustomed to the sudden gloom after the glare of the street, was young and handsome.

"This way," Castets said, and led the way along the corridor until it entered the main hall, and thence up the grand staircase. Clearly the house had once been the Paris hotel of some noblesse, and was now entirely occupied by Mirabeau. Then why, Nick wondered, did he not suppose it was the Paris hotel of the Riquetti family? Because there was an air of encampment, of nouveaux riches about the place; expensive drapes hung above dirty floors and over even dirtier windows; the entire house smelt of garlic and baking bread, and was filled with young women, who peeped out at him, and giggled when he would return their gaze.

"The Count is easily bored," Castets observed, and threw open double doors at the top of the stairs to give admittance to a large and comfortably furnished withdrawing room, but one which was as untidy and dirty as the rest of the house, with several spaniels scattered around the floor, now leaping up at the intruders, and dominated, as might be expected, by the reclining figure of the Count himself, sprawled on a chaise longue, barelegged while a young girl manicured his toes, and with another girl serving him wine.

But was this really the Count? Nick frowned at him. The features were the same, repulsively ugly and compellingly strong; but the color had gone, and the purple veins looked ghastly against the pallor of his skin, while his eyes were heavy, and seemed to require a great effort to turn toward his guest. Even more disturbing was the slowness of his movements, the uncertainty of his grip.

But the voice had not changed. "Nicholas Minnett," he rumbled. "This is a good day, sir. A good day. Off with you, Mimi. Take your sister. Tell Charlotte we shall eat now. In here." He smiled at Nick. "I find sitting at table uncomfortable. Ah, it seems my sins are finding me out. Sit down, Mr. Minnett. Sit down. Joachim, some wine for my guest. And for yourself, you rogue. You have completed your business?"

Nick sat down. "I have completed my subterfuge, if that is what you mean."

"Bah." Mirabeau drank, deeply and loudly. "You would lend money to those fools? It would be giving it to the scoundrels of the gutter. You think it will buy food? It will not even buy their lives."

"I must confess I am . . ." Nick checked, as Mirabeau's finger brushed his lips, and now three young women brought in small tables, one to be placed in front of the men, while others followed with dishes of pâté and toasted bread, boiled chicken legs and stalks of celery, and a liberal number of wine bottles to replace those being exhausted.

"Do you approve of my household?" Mirabeau shouted, and gave a bellow of laughter. "So I enjoy the flesh, Mr. Minnett. Do we not all enjoy the flesh? Or would we not, had we the means? I enjoyed the flesh even while I lacked the means, Mr. Minnett. Oh, times were hard. There were letters du cachet out for me, time and again. I am intimately acquainted with the interior of Vincennes Prison, I do assure you. But now, now they are happy to settle my debts for me, because I am valuable to them. And once they would not allow me within their gates. Times change, Mr. Minnett. Times change."

The girls departed, and Castets got up and closed the doors. Mirabeau was already chewing a drumstick, while the dogs waited expectantly. "You were about to say you are confused, Mr. Minnett. But it really is very simple. We are in the midst of a revolution. Revolutions, if allowed to pursue an uninterrupted career, are like uninterrupted rivers; flowing fast and violent, as they do, they gradually eat away all the top soil, all the trees and the grass and the beauty in life, and carve their way down to bedrock, hard and grim and ugly, where do they not eventually reduce all to mud. But dam a river, and why, you might arrive at a pleasant and placid and beautiful lake, filled with power, to be sure, but yet quiescent and controlled, from which perhaps one might permit a tumbling millstream to furnish whatever energy you require."

"And are not the Rolands and their friends endeavoring to build such a dam?" Nick asked.

"They are endeavoring to do nothing, Mr. Minnett, save stay afloat on the front of the flood. They presume that if they can do that long enough, the river will lose its impetuous energy. And they would be right, *could* they stay there long enough. But that is impossible, Mr. Minnett. This river is too great for half measures. Already it is tumbling down to a muddy bottom, where all is churned, where nothing can be controlled. The Assembly passes laws and decrees, the mob ignores them. The judiciary sets a prisoner free, the mob seizes him and hangs him as he leaves the court. To control such a force, a man must have more ability than Roland de la Platière."

"And Madame?"

"Ah. You are smitten. And why not? Manon is an unusual woman. And yet, Mr. Minnett, as she is a woman, she is of no account in this situation. Which is probably as well for the rest of us."

"But you assume *you* can control this flood of which you speak."

"I can do so, Mr. Minnett. Nobody else, that is certain. And even I must play a strange, a dishonest game. I am a Jacobin. I attend their club, I make inflammatory speeches, I stand for the people. I even rub shoulders with your enemy, Condorcet. They suspect I am in the pay of the Court, but they cannot prove it, and even if they could, they would not dare. I have the mob. And the man who possesses that force can dominate the world."

"Why do you not?"

Mirabeau finished his chicken, and drank. "Mobs are fickle things, Mr. Minnett. No, no. The revolution has accomplished enough. We have overturned the noblesse. I hate them. They were parasites who battened upon the blood of France—my own family not excepted. But now they are gone. Now the King is constrained to rule as a monarch, and not a god. Yet must he rule, because if he does not, then it will be somebody far more sinister. We are working toward this end. It will take time, it will take patience. There is always the possibility of some impetuous spirit, some gutter journalist, driving things to extremity. This is why you are here."

He paused, to stare at Nick from beneath those overhanging brows.

"I understand that," Nick said. "Tell me what you plan."

"I hope, rather than plan, Mr. Minnett. Yet must I also plan. And my plans must even confuse me, lest my enemies discover them. You have a boat, called the *Golden Rose*. Did I request it of you, could you find her in some French port? You know Brittany, I understand."

"And Brittany knows me, alas."

"St. Malo and the Rance. There are other rivers, other ports, no farther from Paris."

Nick thought. "Yes. There is the Trieur River, which is desolate enough toward its mouth. There is a village, Lézardrieux, where the *Rose* could enter and lie."

Mirabeau snapped his fingers. "The map, Castets. Show me, Mr. Minnett."

The map was unrolled on the floor, and Nick placed his finger on the little port.

"Aha," Mirabeau said. "Yes. That is good. Now, Mr. Minnett, when I send, you will come? Immediately? This could be the life of a king and queen, and a certain young woman, we are discussing."

"I will come," Nick said. "Providing I can be sure the message comes from you."

"Aha," Mirabeau said again. "I have thought of that. Joachim."

Castets went to a rolltop desk in the corner, opened it, and took out a small jewelbox. This he placed on the table in front of his master.

"Your ship is known to only a few people, Mr. Minnett," Mirabeau said. "Certainly to only a few people in a position to give you this."

He lifted the lid of the box; sitting on a blue velvet pad was a gleaming golden rose, flower petals and stem all made from the precious metal, the whole perhaps the size of a man's thumb.

"But that is absolutely exquisite," Nick said. "May I touch it?"

"Take it out. Examine it very closely. It is a process known as filigree, in which threads of gold are worked together. It is very costly, and very rare. You will not see its like again."

"And you will send me this?"

Mirabeau took back the ornament, and replaced it in

the box, which he closed and handed to Castets. "When
next you see that rose, Mr. Minnett, I shall expect your
ship to be in Lézardrieux twenty-four hours later."

Nick shook his head. "That is not possible, Count Mirabeau. It is two days from London to Lyme, and at least
one across the Channel. You must give four days' notice."

Mirabeau stared at him for some seconds. "Very well,"
he said at last. "You will have four days. But on the
fourth day after receiving this rose, Mr. Minnett, your ship
must be in Lézardrieux."

"You may count on it," Nick said.

"Winter or summer, snow or sun, gale or calm?"

"Only total calm need concern us, Count, and that is
rare enough for any length of time in these latitudes. You
may count on it."

Once again the long stare. Then Mirabeau nodded.
"Yes," he said. "I believe I can count on it. Then have
we completed our business, and the sooner you are away
from Paris the better. But before you go, there is someone
would have a word with you. Knowing that you would
be here, she persuaded me to arrange this meeting, against
my better judgement, to be sure. Joachim."

"If you will come with me, sir," Castets said.

Nick got up, held out his hand. "Until we meet again,
Count Mirabeau."

Mirabeau squeezed his fingers, but with a strange lack
of strength. "Why, Mr. Minnett, I doubt that we shall
meet again. But I will pursue my course with the more confidence, knowing that I have in you a trustworthy friend.
Now I must rest. I attend the Assembly this evening."

Nick nodded, and followed Castets through the door,
his heart beating with a pleasant anticipation. They went
along the hall outside, and the servant opened another pair
of doors. "Mr. Nicholas Minnett, Citizeness Benoît."

Had he ever doubted that it would be she? But then, his
mind was still obsessed by the fact that he was to be
responsible for the safety of the French Royal Family,
should events make that necessary and, more recently, by

Manon Roland's strictures on his character. Had Aurora perhaps seen that streak of hardness long ago, and had decided against ever considering him as a husband?

The doors closed softly behind him, and only then did she move. Her hair rested on her shoulders, and her yellow gown was simple, lacking pannier or bustle, clinging to hip and breast and shoulder. She wore no jewelry. On a sudden she was once again the girl with whom he had fallen in love.

"Nick," she said, and came forward, her hands outstretched. He took them and kissed them. "Your courage astounds me," she said. "Do you not know that half of Paris, headed by Louis Condorcet, is seeking your head?"

He smiled at her. "I also know that the other half, instructed by the government itself, is determined to preserve my head. The two seem to be balancing each other rather well."

"You can joke?" She drew him back to the settee, made him sit beside her.

"I can also weep. I can also be confused. You here?"

"Riquetti is our agent. I speak of the Court. We see him daily."

"Ah. And even you are drawn into the web of intrigue."

"Even I, you mean, am engaged in a fight for survival."

He frowned. This was not the graciously arrogant woman of the Tuileries last October. This was even less the contemptuously arrogant woman of the Château Benoît, two years ago. But now he was realizing that this also was *not* the unaffectedly friendly playmate of his childhood. Here was a breathless, somewhat nervous coquette.

"And now you are to be a part of that fight, Nick," she said. "Oh, I am so happy. And on a sudden, so courageous, where before I knew only fear."

"Did you ever doubt I would be here when you needed me, Aurora?" He kissed her hands again, and checked himself. Perhaps she had not heard. All things were possible, and certainly in Paris. "You know I am married?"

"Oh yes, Nick. And estranged, on your honeymoon. She must be a total ogre. My heart bleeds for you."

Could this possibly be Aurora? He would have released her, but her fingers gripped his tightly.

"Yet am I still wed. I have no legal cause to complain of her."

"Then forget her." Suddenly she did release him, and rose, walking impatiently about the room, picking up ornaments and fingering them, replacing them on the tables. "Although I wish . . . But no matter."

"Yet say it," he said. "Please."

"That you were free? To sweep me from my feet, and into your bed." She returned to stand by the couch. He was shrouded in her perfume. "I do not deserve so much, having refused you with all the carelessness of youth. I know better now. But believe me, I am only being selfish."

No, he decided, this was not Aurora de Benoît. But it was an entirely entrancing creature; this was a coquette with the charm to make Seraphine Condorcet no more than a serving girl.

"To me, you are being utterly magnificent," he said. And wondered if he meant it. They were the words he had always hoped to use of Aurora, and so he was using them now. And yet he did not know if he meant them. He could not forget Manon Roland's lecture. "Do you have news of your father and Etienne?" he asked. "They are both well, and attended my wedding."

"Papa," she said. "Etienne." She sat down again, beside him, still holding his hands. "There are living monuments to how much I owe you. No, I have little news of them, Nick. I only know that, as they are in England, they are free of France, and therefore happy. But they cannot help me. Only you can do that."

"As I shall. As I have sworn to do so, the moment I am needed."

"Needed?" she cried. "Can you ever be needed, more than now?"

"But Mirabeau has explained . . ."

"'Riquetti considers only Her Majesty and the King, which is his duty. I am but a lady-in-waiting. My peril at this moment is greater than anyone's."

Nick frowned. "Because of Etienne's escape?"

She gazed at him, seeming to be summoning all the intensity of her personality. "In a sense. You know that the Jacobin monster, Louis Condorcet, has divorced his wife. Indeed, it is because of you, a liaison she confessed."

He felt his cheeks burning. "I know not what to say."

"About her? Why, what should you say? Why do you have to be ashamed? She was a common slut. Should you ever have required the use of her body, then it was her duty to yield it to you."

Nick scratched his head. "A point of view, certainly."

"But having divorced her, Nick, Condorcet must think of another wife. You remember our conversation in St. Suliac? My God, it seems as if then we were on another planet."

"Condorcet?" Nick was aghast. "But he is a lawyer, and you . . ."

"I am noblesse? Does that matter in France, today? Am I not reduced to plain Citizeness Benoît, as Marie Antoinette is herself reduced to plain Citizeness Capet."

"And he has always loved you," Nick said thoughtfully. "I suppose . . ."

"Love?" she cried, and was away again, bouncing to her feet and parading the room. "Oh really, Nick, what can such a creature know of love? Lust, certainly. He seeks the use of my body as you sought his wife. But there will be no tenderness in his embrace. He seeks only to leave the marks of his fingers where I must always suffer shame."

Nick scratched his head again. He could not really believe that a girl like Aurora de Benoît was using such words, expressing such thoughts. He would not even have believed it possible for her to think of them, in her most private moments.

"But of course that is only the half of it," she continued. "The Jacobins' whole scheme is to bring ourselves down to their level; they know there is no prospect of raising themselves to ours. And thus am I become a symbol. A Jacobin marrying a queen's lady? There would be a triumph. He says our bridal carriage would be drawn through the streets of Paris by every sans culotte alive."

"He has spoken to you, then?"

"They make themselves as free with the palace as they would like to be free with our persons."

"And what was your reply?"

"That I must have the consent of my father. This he refused to accept, as Papa is an émigré and without any rights in France. Then at least, I begged, let me inform him of the matter. And to this he consented. And who knows, the mails travel slowly, when they travel at all, in these days."

"Then you must come with me, tomorrow," Nick said.

"I cannot. My duty lies with the Queen."

"But . . ."

She threw herself at his feet, knelt, held his hands tight, resting her heaving bodice against his thigh. "Women have duties as well as men, Nick. I would not attempt, I would not dare attempt, to sway you from yours. And so long as Her Majesty is in Paris, and in danger, I must remain at her side. Yet I am optimistic that she will remain here only a short while longer, as Riquetti will have told you. And when she leaves, then, Nick, will I be free to leave too. And then, Nick, we may have need of you in great haste, great urgency, great danger."

"And I have sworn to come, Aurora. But had I not, then I do so now, again and again."

"Oh, Nick. Oh dearest, dearest Nick."

Her mouth was close, her lips parted. Once before she had held herself thus, for a moment, and he had acted. He could still remember the taste of her lips, the swiftly withdrawn touch of her tongue. He lowered his head to kiss her, and this time the tongue remained. And more than that. He found his fingers on her shoulders, and they were slipping from his embrace as she raised herself from the floor to join him on the couch. His hands touched her thighs, about which he had only daringly and on occasion allowed himself to dream, and he discovered to his amazement that he could trace the contours of the flesh; she wore nothing more than a shift beneath her gown.

Here, in the house of the greatest rake in Paris? But before his brain could register he discovered her own hands busy with his breeches, and his face was shrouded at once in her hair and her mouth. Coherent thought was impossible in the seething presence of such a lifelong dream. She was everything he had ever hoped for in a woman. The voluptuous arrogance of Caroline, the bubbling sexuality of Seraphine, both seemed to come together in a combination of desire and knowledge and anxiety, and eventually, satisfaction, as she gave a great sigh, and lay on her back, her head drooping over the edge of the couch, her golden hair trailing on the floor, her mouth wide and her tongue swollen.

"My God," she whispered. "My God, Nick. You and I, Nick. You and I. When the time comes, let it be you and I."

He knelt above her, only now able to look down at the swell of her breasts, strangely small, and with even more strangely flattened nipples; but then, her desire was no doubt spent. And at the flutter of her rib cage, which seemed barely covered with skin tight drawn. At the high mountain ridge of her pelvic girdle, within which the skin once again seemed scarcely supported by flesh beneath a pale white desert only thinly protected by scrub. And then at surprisingly well fleshed thighs and hips and legs. Which were, he supposed, being able to think at last, her most lovely features, but doomed to lie hidden forever beneath her gown, available only to her husband and her lover.

Her lover. He still could not believe it had happened, or indeed that it could ever happen, when he thought of all his other memories of this coolly confident girl he had known for so long. And yet she lay, and waited for him to mount another assault, moving her tongue now, round and round her equally swollen lips, staring at him the while. And certainly he wanted to. He would stay here, in her arms, forever had he the chance.

Here? Suddenly he was alert, and heard a sound. The slightest creak, which might only have been his imagination. But he had spent too many hours at sea, his mind attuned to the smallest alteration in wind or sea.

"Nick," she whispered. "Nick."

He left the couch, tiptoed across the room, ignoring his nakedness, threw the hall door wide. Castets stopped his flight, and turned.

"By God, sir," Nick said. "Do you answer for yourself, or your master?"

"I . . . I . . ." Castets looked to his left.

"He answers for me, sir," Mirabeau said. He now came around the corner of the wall.

"And is this your idea of sport?" Nick demanded. "Should I call you out, sir, would you consider that sport too?"

"No doubt you are an expert, sir," Mirabeau said. "I shelter beneath my immunity as a minister, your immunity as my guest. And as for sport, sir, have you not had yours? Why, sir, there is the best sport in the world."

"By God, sir," Nick shouted. "Immunity or no . . ."

"Nick." Aurora was on her knees on the couch. "Please, Nick, can we not just enjoy our time together?"

He stared, from her to the Count to Castets. And he had once supposed himself angry with Caroline. "I have been tricked and betrayed, by those anxious to get their hands on my money," he said, speaking more quietly. "This is the first occasion anyone has found it necessary to trick me to obtain possession of my honor. I had supposed that was available to all who deserved its benefit, without recourse to stratagems."

He reentered the room and began to dress.

"Oh come, sir," Mirabeau said from the doorway. "Did you not trick and betray Seraphine Condorcet, for your own ends?"

"I did," Nick admitted, "and have regretted it ever since. More so than ever now." He glanced at Aurora, still kneeling, still naked, Aurora de Benoît, naked in the presence of Honoré Riquetti. Now his very last doubt, his very last hope, had disappeared.

"And your promise of succor?" Mirabeau demanded.

"I do not break my oath, Citizen Riquetti." Nick bowed to the couch. "Citizeness, your servant. You have been too good to me. But I shall repay your charity, by my own." He crammed his hat on his head and left the room.

Eight

The curtains were drawn, the bedchamber was dark; even the occasional rumble of a passing carriage on the Lane was muted in the hushed interior.

Nick stood by the door. He hated the smell of medicine, the stertorous breathing from the bed. He hated the knowledge that he was in the presence of death, slow and malignant. But hate was a part of his nature. He hated himself, for what he was, for what he had been, for what he would undoubtedly become. Father's illness was merely another symptom.

And yet, what a futile business hating was. This should have been proved even to his satisfaction, only a month ago. Mirabeau was dead. All the signs of collapsing health Nick had noticed last August had been too accurate. And with that awful, dominant figure had gone the last hope of the French Royal Family. Certainly now he would not see Aurora again.

Supposing he wanted to. But, oh yes, he wanted to. Supposing he could be sure whether it had been the man he had hated for seducing the girl, or the girl for being seduced. Supposing he could be sure it was possible for Nick Minnett to hate Aurora de Benoît.

Dr. Crosby straightened, sighed, turned away from the bed. He nodded to the waiting manservant, and the door was opened. The doctor took Nick's arm, and escorted him outside. "No change. But then, no change for the worse either, so far as I can see, Nick. Which must be a hopeful sign."

"Yet he will not recover."

"Ah well, if you mean fully . . . He will never sit behind his desk again, Nick. That must be your responsibility now."

"It has been my responsibility for the past six months, Alan." But there was no necessity to hate Alan Crosby; the good man had delivered him into the world—supposing that was an achievement to be proud of. Nick shook his hand. "You'll call tomorrow?"

"Indeed I shall. And meanwhile, rest . . ." The doctor sighed. "Rest. There must be the answer."

"You'll show the doctor out, Eric," Nick said, and took himself along the upstairs gallery to his mother's boudoir, gave a brief rap on the door, and entered. Both Priscilla and Lucy Minnett were at their needlework; both looked up as he entered. "Father is doing very well, Alan says," he announced.

Priscilla Minnett's eyes were red, but more from lack of sleep than weeping. She was not a woman who wept. "Now we may have the truth, if you please, Nick."

Nick sat down, allowed his legs to flop. He was tired. He was tired all the time nowadays. And his head was heavy with the port he had drunk last night at Dundas's table. "There is the truth, Mother. He is holding his own, which is as much as can be expected."

"I shall sit with him for a while." Priscilla Minnett stood up, and hesitated, then held out a letter. "Will you read it?"

"It is not addressed to me, I am sure."

"She doubts that would be worth her while."

"And she was always accurate in her conclusions."

His mother stood above the chair. "Nick, the whole business was unfortunate; but surely there were faults on both sides. And if Caroline genuinely seeks a reconciliation . . ."

"Genuinely? Oh come, Mother, do. She merely wishes to be sure I continue to pay her bills."

"Well, there are some accounts attached, to be sure, but . . ." Priscilla Minnett bit her lip. "This is not a matter I would normally discuss, Nick, but it should not escape your attention that you are the last male Minnett, and with your father grievously ill . . ."

"I should make sure there is someone to carry on the business? Believe me, Mother, I am sure Carrie would find that as distasteful as would I." He got up, kissed her on the cheek. "I must get down to the office."

"Nicky." Lucy put down her sewing and jumped to her feet, accompanied him into the corridor, fingers tight on his arm. "Will Papa recover, Nicky?"

He shook his head.

"Then . . . Nicky, what are we to do about Paul?"

He glanced at her. Eric hovered at the end of the corridor with his cloak and hat and stick, but the valet was still out of earshot. "I understand that Father was not in favor."

Lucy pouted. "Oh . . . it's just that Paul has had some bad luck at the tables recently. But he is so sweet, and he comes of a very old family. The de Lanceys fought with the Conqueror."

"And have been interbreeding with other members of that decrepit army ever since."

"Oh really there is no need to be vulgar."

"In any event, he cannot possibly support you," Nick said.

"Ah, but that is because Papa would not make him a reasonable advance. Now Nicky, now that you are in charge of the business . . ."

"I do not propose to make him any advance at all."

"Nicky."

"Don't suppose I dislike the fellow; he is no worse than all the rest. But he has long since exhausted his credit, and I'd not put you in the same position as regards him that I am regarding Carrie. Now I really must get down to the City."

"Oh you . . . You are a beast," she shouted behind him. "You have no feelings. You don't have blood in your veins at all, Nick Minnett, but ink. Carrie was right when she said you are nothing but a clerk, you . . ."

Her voice disappeared behind him as he went down

the stairs, and sought the fresh air of the courtyard, where his horse waited. The afternoon ride to the House was the best part of the day. He was out in the open, he could feel the sun on his cheeks, and he was by himself, in the midst of crowds, to be sure, but yet not required to do more than raise his hat or nod to any acquaintance, male or female. Christ, to be able to turn his horse's head to the west, and just ride, and ride, and ride, until he came to Lyme, and thence put to sea . . . But he had not seen *Golden Rose* this year, and it was again May. Anne wrote to him every month, reporting on the weather and the work she had done on board. He treasured the letters, because they transported him out of the business and social world in which he now existed, and because he could imagine her, sitting at her table, slowly and carefully forming each word; she was still only in the process of teaching herself to write a fair hand.

But Anne was a woman, and the sex was not for him. In a flush of excitement he had opened a Pandora's box filled with the creatures, and discovered that they were only adorable at a distance. Carrie, out for money. Seraphine, out for sex, and cruelly mistreated for her pains. Lucy, out for marriage to some rascal. And Aurora, out to do the bidding of her mistress and her lover. Was there a woman in the world who was not merely out for herself? And thus Anne, for all her pretense of simplicity, undoubtedly had something in view.

Besides, he was too busy. He threw the reins to the ostler, and the doors of the bank were opened wide by the waiting majordomo. He strode through the public hall, and the clerks and tellers bowed. He climbed the broad marble stairs, and the office boys lined up to salute. His secretary opened the double doors of his office, also carefully bowing, one hand under the tail of his coat, and then hurried forward to hold his chair, while Turnbull stood to one side, a baize-covered folder under his arm.

"Good afternoon, Mr. Nicholas. And how is Mr. Minnett today?"

"Unchanged." The folder was in front of him, and he

opened the cover. "He will never walk again, Turnbull. His right side is quite gone. Indeed, he will never sit again. I am afraid you now have me permanently. What of that matter I charged you with?"

"Well, sir, so far as I can ascertain, there is no one by that name living in St. Suliac. There was a Dr. Planchet, but he has moved on."

"Damnation."

"Oh, we shall find the young lady, sir, given time. My agents have put it about that there is a legacy . . . It is really a great deal of money, you know, Mr. Nicholas. Perhaps too great."

"You may regard it as a debt. What's this?" He frowned at the first piece of parchment.

"Lord Rathbone's account, Mr. Nicholas." Turnbull cleared his throat, a trifle nervously. He still felt uncertain with this young man. Percy Minnett had been a shrewd banker, who had disguised his acute business sense beneath a charmingly absentminded demeanor. His son did not trouble to disguise his feelings at any time.

"Up for renewal of credit," Nick demanded, "for the fifth time this year, and still rising?"

"It is secured, Mr. Nicholas."

"Just." Nick flicked the papers pinned to the account. "Stock in Ratsey's? I have heard they are in difficulties."

"Well, sir, they were heavily invested in France, you see, and . . ."

"And they are our competitors. You'll tell Lord Rathbone we require settlement, and this week, or we'll utilize this issue."

"Sir?" Turnbull was aghast. "Foreclose on the Rathbones?"

"Are they so different to anyone else?"

"Why, sir . . ." Turnbull bit his lip. "Mr. Minnett gave me to understand he would carry his Lordship for some time."

"He has done so, for some time. And as I have just made clear, Turnbull, you are now struggling beneath my weight, not that of my father."

"Yes, sir." Turnbull mopped his neck with a kerchief, and tried a new approach. "Yet will we be wasting our time, Mr. Nicholas. As you have just pointed out, Ratsey's stock is at present in decline. Should we place that amount on the market it will be further depressed, and we will not even realize the amount of the Rathbone loan."

"Quite," Nick agreed. "I have no intention of placing any Ratsey stock on the market, Turnbull. But as I have just reminded you, they are our competitors, and this is a large slice of their issue. You'll make me a list of any other of our debtors who are covered by Ratsey stock. I'd like it on my desk tomorrow."

"But Mr. Nicholas . . ." Turnbull again took refuge in his kerchief. "Is that ethical?"

"It is most certainly legal, Turnbull. As for ethics, when I understand what is morally right in this world, and what is not, be sure I'll let you know." He folded the Rathbone papers on his right, frowned at the next set. "Benoît?"

"They must live, Mr. Nicholas. And our credit is all they have."

Nick turned the page, ran his finger down the escalating balances. "What does he use money for? Burning?"

"It is a remarkable expenditure, sir," Turnbull agreed. "No doubt the young man gambles."

Nick tapped his chin. He had seen neither Pierre nor Etienne since his return from Paris last summer. Nor had he wished to. "You'll write to the Sieur de Benoît, John," he said to his secretary. "Request him to call upon me here, as soon as is convenient."

"Yes, sir, Mr. Nicholas. But Mr. Nicholas . . ." Turnbull twisted his kerchief in his hands; it was sopping wet. "The Benoîts, why . . ."

"They are our oldest friends," Nick said, "and so I am not refusing an extension. But I must discover where it will end, Turnbull. Is there anything else?"

"No, sir." Turnbull took a long breath. "I am told the Sieur de Benoît is scarce in better health than Mr. Minnett, Mr. Nicholas; and Mr. Etienne is naturally distracted about his sister, and as you say, sir, he is your oldest friend . . ."

Nick closed the folder and stood up. "I have no friends, Turnbull. Not as head of the House of Minnett. And indeed, none as Nicholas Minnett. You'd best remember that." He snapped his fingers and the secretary hurried forward with his hat and stick. "I am to Brooks's for cards."

Nick turned over his hole card, placed the knave beside the seven and the three. "I pay twenty-one, gentlemen."

"Ah bah," George Moncey threw his four cards on to the pile in the middle. He still used only his left hand, carried his right tucked into his coat. And he still looked at his brother-in-law with eyes of hatred. Yet play he must. And lose he must, when Nick Minnett dealt.

"You have the luck of the devil," Dundas said, also adding his cards to the pile.

" 'Tis not luck." George Grenville considered his for some seconds longer; he held two kings. "He gambles high, that is all. Would I be right in supposing, Nick, that your last card was that three?"

"You would," Nick said.

"Dealing, you took three to seventeen. There is the maneuver of a madman," Moncey protested.

"Or someone who cares not whether he wins or loses," Dundas said. "Nick is in that happy position."

"Which but means, as I am trying to establish," Grenville insisted, "that unless he is very *un*lucky, he will beat us poor impoverished devils far more often that we will beat him."

Nick had accumulated the cards, placed them on the bottom of the pack. "Now you are finished your dissection of my character, gentlemen, shall we have another hand?"

"Not I," Grenville said. "Since I have started playing with you, I have had to set myself a limit, and will lose no more than a hundred a night. Dundas?"

"Too dear for me," the First Lord agreed. "You have had your pleasure, Nick."

Nick glanced at his brother-in-law, but Moncey merely got up and walked away from the table.

"He is devilish rude," Dundas murmured, "and likes you not at all, Nick."

"Aye," Grenville agreed. "Neither do his cronies. I wonder they have found no excuse to call you out, Nick."

"They'll not risk that," Dundas said. "Not after what happened to Moncey himself, and Nick is well known as a superb shot. They have gained the opinion that he fights in the same spirit as he plays."

"No doubt. But I trust you walk with a servant when you go abroad after dark, Nick." Grenville stood up. "I must be away. Tomorrow?"

"Tomorrow," Nick agreed, and watched his friend walk across the room. "Am I that fruitful a source of gossip, Harry?"

"'Tis nothing to be ashamed of, in your case," Dundas said. "You'll take a glass of port? I see Billy has just come in. Well, sir, how goes it in the Commons?"

Pitt sat down and stretched his legs. The waiter was already waiting with a tray and glasses, and he tossed his off without drawing breath, reached for another. Some color entered the pale cheeks. "Fox and Burke are at it again. They generate so much hatred a man must doubt his senses to remember what bosom friends they were but two years ago. And all I desire is to pass those navy estimates. You had best do your utmost in the Lords, Harry, or we shall be back where we were in the seventies."

"But did you not get the debate started?"

"Oh, indeed. Now it has degenerated into an argument concerning the morals of the late Catherine. Was she ever really mounted by a horse, Nick?"

"I suspect that to be a complete libel. Yet Russia is your design?"

"Oh, indeed," agreed the Prime Minister. "Paul is a madman, and they will covet Constantinople. Besides, who else can I conjure up to build ships against? Prussia still thinks about Frederick, Austria has this trouble in the Netherlands, and France . . . My God, France. Believe me, Nick, obtaining money from the Commons for the good of the country is almost as difficult as obtaining money from you for the good of my own pocket."

"We'll have done with shop," Dundas hastily said. "You'll have a hand?"

"With Nick?" Pitt demanded. "I'll need my head examined for bumps."

"So remarked our earlier company," Nick said, and took a second glass of port.

"After you had fleeced them, no doubt. The fact is, Nick, you play cards with the deadly earnestness of a bravo setting about a duel."

"Grenville's very words," Dundas said. "In reverse."

"And equally true," Pitt said. " 'Tis supposed to be sport, you might like to remember. All life is supposed to contain some sport, yet you have none at all. You will consume yourself with that inner anger, unless you learn to dissipate it in some harmless vice. There cannot be a man in the world who has not discovered a beautiful woman can have hands as dirty as an ugly one."

" 'Tis not hands we discuss," Dundas said, and gave a bellow of laughter.

"By Christ, sir," Nick snapped, starting up.

"Sit down. Sit down," Pitt commanded. "I'll not have my minister filled with lead; at least, not until I have my new navy. He was in any event no more than joking; and I had an ulterior motive in mentioning the lady. Have you any news of Paris?"

"Should I have?"

"From her, no. From her brother, perhaps. You know he raises a private army."

"Etienne? By heaven," Nick said, and slapped the table. "So that . . ."

"Aha. His debt grows, does it? Well, if you would do your government a favor, allow it to do so, Nick."

"The scheme smacks of madness."

"Perhaps. And then, perhaps not. He considers a descent on the coast of Brittany, according to my information. And the news which comes my way from Rennes suggests that the idea may not be as harebrained as you suppose. The Breton deputies may have been the most fiery of any in Paris, but those they left behind are beginning to wonder where are the benefits they were promised two years ago."

"And you'd connive at insurrection?"

"Privately, Nick. Privately. Certain it is that something must be done. Since Mirabeau's death things have gone downhill very rapidly. You heard about the St. Cloud episode?"

Nick shook his head.

"Why, the Royal Family merely sought a holiday, but a few miles from Paris. Lafayette gave his consent, as did Bailly, and off they set. But no sooner did the word reach the faubourgs than all of Paris was hot in pursuit, women to the fore as usual, seized the lot, and marched them back in total humiliation."

"And *was* Louis trying to escape?"

Pitt tapped his nose. "He would certainly wish to do so now."

"Without Mirabeau he has no hope whatsoever," Dundas said.

"Perhaps. There remain the plans that Mirabeau laid."

Nick discovered that Pitt was staring at him. "By Christ," he said, "do you ever cease business, Billy?"

"When I sleep," Pitt said. "Sometimes, at any rate. Will you honor your pledge, Nick?"

Nick gazed at him as if hypnotized, and the Prime Minister put his hand in his pocket and brought out a small jewel box. The lid flipped back to reveal the shimmering gold rose.

"But where is your ship, Mr. Minnett?" Castets peered from the window of the coach. The two men had hardly spoken on the journey from London; the Frenchman had been able to add little to what Pitt had told Nick in any event, and the sight of the man had reawakened all of Nick's resentment against Mirabeau's machinations.

"She rides to her mooring." He pointed. The tide was

half up, and *Golden Rose* had just left the sand. How good she looked. How good Lyme looked, as the berline rumbled down the hillside. What a fool he was to have let business consume so much of his time. Indeed, any man who permitted that, however urgent the necessity, was but wasting his life. Here was a rising tide and a freshening breeze, good visibility and a moderate sea, and a ship.

And friends. The coach tumbled over the cobbled street, and people came out of their shops to wave. " 'Tis Mr. Minnett," they shouted. "Mr. Minnett, come for the *Rose*."

The harbor once again opened in front of them. Castets was still staring. "That, monsieur?" he demanded. "You'd take the King and Queen of France to sea in so frail a bark?"

"She'll go where your three deckers dare not," Nick said, "and ride the Channel as well as they, into the bargain." The coach was slithering to a halt beside the harbor wall, and a few minutes later they were in a dinghy and being rowed out to the ketch; their luggage consisted of no more than a change of clothing.

Tom Price peered at them from the deck. "Mr. Minnett?" He reached down for the painter, and to squeeze Nick's hand. "Well, glory be, sir, we'd not expected you down so early."

"The matter is urgent, Tom. We'll put to sea. Where's Anne?"

"I am here, Mr. Minnett." She knelt on the foredeck, the pumice stone in her hand, and indeed the decks gleamed as if freshly laid.

"She works at this boat like it was her own," Tom Price said. "But then, she'll work the harder for Dick Allardyce."

Anne had risen and come aft; her hair was lost beneath her bandanna and the breeze, and the exertion, had brought flame into her cheeks. Now the glow deepened.

"Eh?" Nick asked. "Oh, Citizen Castets, Tom Price and Anne Yealm, my crew."

"But . . ." Castets took off his bicorne to scratch his head. "An old man and a girl? What farce are we about, Mr. Minnett?"

"We'll talk of that when we are in mid-Channel, monsieur, and you find your bunk. Stand by your capstan, Tom. And what is this talk of Allardyce, Anne?"

"Why, sir, he has asked for my hand."

But why had it not happened sooner? She was a superb woman, and she was not yet twenty. She was born to be wife to a sailor. "Well," he said. "You are to be congratulated. But Dick even more so. And I hear he has his own ship."

"He has, sir," she said. "And will you not miss me?"

Her eyes were very clear as they ranged his face. "I shall indeed," he said. "I have no idea where I shall find another crew. Or at least one at once as pleasant and able."

"You will not find another crew, Mr. Minnett," she said. "I have refused Dick's offer."

"But . . ." Nick glanced to where Tom Price was fitting the bars to the capstan.

"Oh, the folk here suppose I am but playing the woman; yet my decision has been taken."

He frowned at her. "You'd grow old, scrubbing the decks of the *Rose?*"

"If the decks of the *Rose* have need of my stone, sir, then why not?"

For a moment longer they gazed at each other. "You'd best release those sail ties," Nick said.

Castets watched her walk away. "Your mistress?"

"My crew, monsieur. And watch your tongue. I made no promises to you."

The Frenchman shrugged. "My life is forfeit in any event. I but borrow the time to breathe. But if that woman is *not* your mistress, Mr. Minnett, then perhaps you seek to borrow too much time, as you are indeed profligate in the wasting of it." He went below, and a few minutes later *Golden Rose* was at sea, with the chalk hills of Dorset fading into the afternoon behind them, and the open Channel ahead. And then the narrow reaches of the Trieur River, sheltering behind the Roches Douvres reef. Nick wondered he was not excited at the prospect of once again risking his life and his ship, this time in the cause of royalty itself.

And was there not the slightest prickle of anticipation in his blood at the thought of once again seeing Aurora? So she had been mistress to a monster, to be used as and when Mirabeau had seen fit; or perhaps even when he had found it amusing. There could be no telling how many men she had bedded on that couch, at his command, and for his entertainment. And yet the memory of her, kneeling naked on the settee, arms outstretched, remained in the forefront of his mind. Eight months, and it had been replaced by no other, as her arms had been replaced by no others.

Perhaps there was the trouble. Perhaps instead of throwing himself into cold-blooded business and even colder-blooded card-playing, he would have done better to have thrown himself into a long debauch, to have placed her where she properly belonged, as just another woman.

But Mirabeau was dead, and the Royal Family was about to flee France forever. They would be exiles, and to a large extent helpless. In fact, Billy Pitt had more than hinted that they could well become a charge on the House of Minnett, should he be so minded. Aurora would quite literally be cast adrift. There was temptation.

"Midnight, Mr. Minnett." Anne wrapped her cloak tighter around her as she came out of the cabin; the spring breeze became chill once the sun was gone.

"Is all well below?"

"Oh aye, sir. I think the Frenchman sleeps."

"Do you not like our friend?"

"He looks too hard, Mr. Minnett. His eyes are like fingers on my flesh."

"Aye, well, he is French," Nick said. "He is also a spy and a messenger, and lives in constant danger."

She offered no opinion on that, sat on the deck beside him. "Is it true we shall return with the King and Queen of France, Mr. Minnett?"

"And others. We shall have a full ship."

"The King and Queen of France," she repeated, half to herself. "I doubt I shall be able to do a thing."

"I had never supposed you concerned with rank, Anne. I had never supposed you concerned with anything but the business of living."

Her head began to turn, and then straightened again. The breeze had freshened, and wisps of red hair escaped the kerchief. He looked down on her neck, and suddenly remembered Marie Antoinette's, so smooth and slender and white; Anne's was thicker and stronger, but no less compelling. He wanted to touch it. Indeed, he could, no doubt. But what then? With this girl he shared a remarkable rapport. To touch her would be to shatter that relationship. And what would remain? There was a question. He could achieve sheer heaven, here on earth. Perhaps. But perhaps he would turn their relationship into a bitter hell: on the evidence of his own experiences so far, this was much the more likely.

But most likely of all, she would accept whatever he wanted, and perhaps even pretended to be happy. He would never know whether she hated him for taking that advantage, or whether she was merely a bored servant carrying out her duties: that would be the worst of all.

"Not to marry Dick Allardyce would be a grave mistake, Anne," he said. "He is a good man. And he was a good friend to Harry."

"Harry had many good friends, Mr. Minnett," she said. "Dick was not the closest." She smiled. "Besides, it is not suitable. Anne Allardyce? There is not a name I'd contemplate." She got up. "You'd best to your bunk, Mr. Minnett. You'd not be falling asleep, before the Queen."

"You may enter, Mr. Minnett," said the majordomo, and Nick pulled his coat straight and hastily patted his cravat. The huge gilded doors swung inward, and he heard his heels clicking on the polished parquet as he followed the gold and white cloth jacket of the servant. Swiss guards stood to attention on either side of the long corridor, but this apart the palace seemed empty. And yet he was aware of a great stealthy whisper, which seemed to penetrate the very walls.

"Mr. Nicholas Minnett," the majordomo said, bowing over his staff until his wig seemed about to slide over his ears.

Nick also bowed, and straightened. "Your Majesty."

It was almost a question. The man immediately in front of him was indistinguishable from the three who stood on one side, unless he was less distinguished than they. He was fairly tall, and a trifle heavy at both shoulder and belly. He wore an undressing robe and no wig; his pale hair was thinning. His face was quite remarkably reminiscent of a pig's, and was totally lacking in expression, although he smiled pleasantly enough, and his eyes rolled around Nick and past him to the back of the room. "Hum," he said. "Hum. There is much to be done, Mr. Minnett. Much to be done."

"I am ready, Your Majesty."

"No doubt. Castets has been telling me. No doubt. You'll know my brother?"

The Duke of Provence sniffed. He was an altogether larger man than Louis, and had a better mouth and chin and shrewder eyes; but his expression was not so pleasant.

"And Count Ferson," Louis said, waving his hand at the best dressed man in the room, after Nick himself. The Swede wore a sword and high boots, and looked intensely military. He sported a small moustache, and his eyes gleamed.

"We share the same harness, Monsieur Minnett." He turned to the King. "And now, Your Majesty . . ."

"Ah," Louis said. "Now. It is always, now."

"We are two days behind, as it is," the Duke grumbled.

"Time," said the King, sadly. "Always time. But it rests with the ladies. You'll wait, Mr. Minnett." He heaved himself to his feet, and Castets hurried to the back of the room to open the door. The Duke of Provence turned to follow his brother, and then stopped, to glance at Nick.

"Castets says you sail the Channel, in a small boat."

"Not so small, your Grace. It is as safe a ship as there is."

"Hm," said the Duke. "Hm." He followed the King.

"I wish I might understand what is happening," Nick said.

"No more would I," Ferson agreed.

"I was given to understand the family would be awaiting my arrival in Lézardrieux. Instead I found a message requiring me to come to Paris. There was a risk in the beginning; I am not entirely welcome here."

"Who is?" Ferson asked.

"And then I was assured that I was coming merely to escort their Royal Highnesses to the coast. But I see no signs of preparation."

"The coast," Ferson said, thoughtfully. "I am here to see them safe to Bouillé, or Brussels, should they decide."

"Brussels?" Nick demanded. "By sea?"

"Good heavens no. I am to be coachman. Ah, it will be a business."

"But . . ." Nick checked. The doors were open again, and the King was returning, this time accompanied by Marie Antoinette, with whom there were several ladies; Nick recognized the Princess de Lamballe immediately, but none of the others. Aurora was not there.

"This is Mr. Minnett," Louis said.

"We have met." The Queen extended her hand, and Nick kissed it. "He is faithful support, I hope. Did you have great difficulty in reaching us, Mr. Minnett?"

"Monsieur Castets' passports proved sufficient, Your Majesty, but I cannot say for how long they will do so."

Marie Antoinette smiled. "Why, until they are discovered to be forged, sir."

"Your Majesty," Ferson said. "It is eight of the clock, and we had intended our departure some time ago."

"Two days ago," grumbled the Duke.

"All is ready," Ferson said. "I have secured the key . . ." He showed it to her. "The carriages, the soldiers await you on the way . . . but time, Your Majesty. Time is of the essence."

"I must have my dressing-case, Count Ferson. You'd not have me arrive in Brussels destitute?"

"Your Majesty, the wife of the King of France and the sister of the Emperor can never be destitute." This the Princess de Lamballe.

"The new case will be here," the Queen declared. "Campan, Campan, when did you say?"

"It was promised, Your Majesty," said one of the other women. "But truly the Princess is right. It is very dangerous. I am sure there is rumor . . ."

"What nonsense," the Queen said. "It is ordered for my sister; now, can there be anything more simple than that? And she, fortunate creature, resides in Brussels already."

"Brussels," said the King. He had sat down again before the table, and rested his chin on his hand. "I had not considered Brussels. I cannot leave France. There would be madness. Bouillé . . ."

"I am sure we have considered every possibility, sire," said the Queen. "From Brussels we can look to our requirements with confidence. Even Bouillé cannot withhold the mob forever."

"An entire nation," the King said. "If only I knew what to do. If only . . ." He raised his head to look at Nick, as if seeking instruction. "They will cut off my head."

"Sire?"

"They cut off the head of Charles I. Your people did that, Mr. Minnett."

"More than a century ago, sire. Nowadays people are more civilized."

"English people, perhaps, French people . . ." An alarmed expression crossed his face. "The children. Where are the children?"

"They are asleep, Your Majesty," said Madame Campan. "I thought it best, until the hour of departure actually was upon us."

"By God, madame," shouted the Duke in sudden anger, "the hour of departure was upon us forty-eight hours ago. You play fast and loose with all of our lives. Children, Louis? What of my children? What of my wife? We wait here, while you fiddle with your locks, while Marie here waits on a jewel case . . . By heaven, this is not a play. Carry your jewels in your hand, if you must, but let us be gone."

There was a moment of scandalized silence.

"Really, Stanislaus," Louis said at last. "Above all, we must be calm, and logical . . ."

"There is a regiment of horse, Your Majesty, waiting at Varennes," Ferson said. "They have been waiting from dusk. We cannot make that distance before dawn, as things are now proceeding. I beg of you, sire . . ."

"Hum," said the King. "Hum. What to do, eh? What to do? There is the question, eh? What to do?"

Nick withdrew to the back of the circle, found himself next to the Princess. "Your Grace," he whispered. "This is madness."

The Princess sighed. She alone wore no outdoor clothes, and indeed was dressed for the ball. "Indeed, Mr. Minnett," she agreed, also speaking very quietly. "I would rather lose my tongue than speak disrespectfully of His Majesty, but sometimes I pray that he could possess just a shade of the spirit of his ancestors. And Her Majesty, poor soul, is reluctant to impose her own vigorous character upon his decisions. Yet as Count Ferson says, it is become a matter of life and death. Heaven knows, I thought Mirabeau the most vicious of men, but I would give all I possess to have him here for half an hour."

"And do you not mean to accompany their majesties, your Grace?"

She gave a brief shake of the head.

"But . . . to stay here, will that not be very dangerous?"

She smiled. "Even the fanatics in the Assembly Hall will scarce seek to avenge themselves upon a poor widow, Mr. Minnett. Oh, Lafayette will look severe, but I doubt it will amount to more than that. I may even be banished back to my husband's estate, supposing it still exists. I should like that."

"Yet would I be happier with you in my care as well, your Grace, if I do not seem too bold."

She frowned even as her smile widened. "You are far too bold, Mr. Minnett. What, do you not seek Aurora?"

"Not my Aurora, your Grace. Riquetti's."

Marie Thérèse de Bourbon gazed at him for some seconds. Then she nodded. "Yes. Sometimes it is necessary to condone painful events, Mr. Minnett. Aurora served her majesty, as do I, and she was part of the price to be paid."

"And was happy to do so, I'd wager."

"It is perhaps a necessary self-deception, to convince oneself one is happy in whatever one is called upon to do. You do not ask after her?"

"No, your Grace."

"Ah. Nor would it avail. She has not been seen at the palace for several days. But that would not concern you."

"No, your Grace. Had anything happened to Citizeness Benoît, assuredly you would have heard of it. No doubt she seeks a replacement for Count Mirabeau."

"And they say the heart of woman can be hard, when hurt. You are obviously a young man who will take his place in the world, and make his mark, Mr. Minnett. I would ask you only to be sure you do not leave too many bruised minds behind you on your road to glory. But I would also have you begin that road now. Listen."

She half turned her head, and Nick followed her glance, towards the royal party, where idea and counter idea, plan and counter plan, exhortation and protestation, continued to flow around the head of the King.

"Dare I, your Grace?"

"Dare you not, Mr. Minnett, as it was your promise gave them hope in the first place?"

Nick hesitated, then squared his shoulders and crossed the room once again. "Your Majesties," he said. "My Lord Duke. Ladies. Please. I am here in fulfilment of an oath. I would be failing in that oath did I not now implore you all to make haste, and forget this quarreling, and take your places in your carriages."

They gazed at him.

"Should we leave now, Your Majesty," he said, "we can be at Lézardrieux by dusk tomorrow, and long before any force can be sent behind you, you will be at sea, whence no government reigns absolutely. And the day after that, I shall have you safe to England."

"England?" Louis demanded. "What a problem. What a problem, eh? England, you say?"

"Or any other country you may wish, Your Majesty." Nick felt his desperation increasing.

"England," Marie Antoinette declared. "The sea. No, no, that is not for us. We have made up our mind, young man. We shall go with the Count here, and take the road for Belgium."

Nick stared at her in utter horror. "But Your Majesty . . ."

"Now, we shall make haste," the Queen decided. "Campan, you will awake the children . . ."

"Your Majesty," Nick shouted, as she stopped, and turned once again toward him, her brows drawing together in a most imperious frown. "Your Majesty," he repeated in a lower tone. "The road to Brittany, and the *Golden Rose,* was selected by Count Mirabeau himself."

"And is Count Mirabeau my master, Mr. Minnett? Was he, when alive, do you think?"

"No one supposes that, Your Majesty, but I had presumed the plan for your departure had been left to him."

"Indeed, he proposed it." Her tone softened, and she almost smiled. "But he proposed more than one, and I have selected the one I prefer. This is no reflection on you, Mr. Minnett. But it is logical, would you not say, for my husband and I to retire toward a frontier which is ruled by my own brother, and where the main part of our support is gathered, rather than toward a rocky and dangerous shore, swept by gales when it is not obscured by fog. I know Brittany, sir, I do assure you."

"There will be neither gale nor fog, Your Majesty, at

least none *Golden Rose* may not encounter with safety."

"I lack your confidence, sir," she said. "Monsieur Castets has told me that this ship of yours is but a hundred feet in length, and crewed by but an old man and a girl, and quite lacking in armament. Where is the safety in that?" Still she smiled at him, almost with pity. "We seek the Marshal de Bouillé, with all his army, encamped just beyond Nancy . . ."

"Where there was but recently a mutiny," Nick protested, "in which some of Bouillé's own men took part."

"Nonetheless, there is the émigré army . . ."

"There is an émigré army now forming in England, Your Majesty."

"Indeed? But a nameless rabble. All the princes of France await us beyond the Rhine."

"Passports," Nick cried. "How will you pass the frontier?"

"Ah." The King seemed to wake up. "That is all taken care of, my boy. My wife travels as the Baroness de Korff, a German lady of quality, who is going home, accompanied by her two daughters . . ." He gave a little squeak of laughter. "Poor Louis will have to pretend he is a girl, what? And by her valet." He got up, and someone handed him a flat, round hat. And indeed, once he had put it on, Nick realized that he did look no more than a valet. "What? What? It will be sport."

Nick filled his lungs with air in sheer desperation. "There will be no passports needed, Your Majesty, in Brittany. And even the best of forgeries may be detected. I beg of you . . ."

"Now you are causing an unnecessary delay," Marie Antoinette said. "Campan, you will rouse and dress the children. My mind is made up. I will wait no longer for the dressing case. Count Ferson, are you ready?"

"To die, if need be, Your Majesty." The Swede clapped Nick on the shoulder. "The fortune of war, my friend."

Nick watched the royal party hurrying toward the doors to the bedchambers. Hurrying, now, where they had delayed for two days. And hurrying toward the most dangerous of routes, for surely it was the route which everyone would expect them to take. There was not a Frenchman who was not aware of the presence of Bouillé, and scarce a Frenchman who was aware of the presence of *Golden Rose* in Lézardrieux.

He looked toward the Princess de Lamballe, who had remained in the room. "I would seem to have failed."

"I did not expect you to kidnap the King and Queen, Mr. Minnett," she said, with a gentle if somewhat sad smile. "And at the very least you encouraged them to begin their journey, and that was the main object of my exhortation. I must attend Her Majesty." She held out her hand. "God go with you, Mr. Minnett. Should we meet again, I would trust it will be in a France restored to her former sanity, and her former glory."

He seized her hand, held it to his lips. "But you I shall kidnap, your Grace. I have no similar faith in French gallantry, at this moment."

Her smile seemed even more sad as she shook her head. "You attend your duty, Mr. Minnett, and I will attend mine. Be sure that in both those resolves lies at once our safety and our honor. Adieu."

She withdrew her hand, and he watched her walk across the room toward the door. He realized he was once again surrounded.

"Mr. Minnett," said the Duke de Provence. "It was long decided that my family and I should travel by a different route to my brother. Monsieur Castets has persuaded me that it would be best to travel by your boat."

"Monsieur Castets"—Nick glared at the little man—"I should wring your neck. I should have wrung your neck months ago."

"Oh, come now, Mr. Minnett," protested the spy. "What would you have me do? Her Majesty asked about my crossing, and about the size of your ship. I told her. She asked me how many decks, and I said but one. She asked me how many guns and I said none, to my knowledge. She asked me how many crew, and I said an old man and a girl. Now, monsieur, tell me, where did I lie?"

"If ever there was a time for lying . . ."

"Recriminations accomplish nothing, Mr. Minnett," the Duke pointed out. "Unlike the King and Queen, we are ready to leave this instant."

"Aye, well then, let's be about it."

"Then follow me," Castets said.

They numbered eight by the time they reached the side door for which the spy had secured a duplicate key; the Duke and Duchess, two children, two servants, Castets, and Nick himself. And still, incredibly, in view of the delay and argument, there had been no alarm, and the Louvre seemed to be settling into a midnight slumber. This Royal Family, Nick concluded, for all its apparent misfortunes, was more fortunate than it deserved.

Castets had been peering at the street. Now he returned to them. "All is clear," he whispered. "We must proceed on foot, over the bridge, and to a rendezvous on the left bank. There our berline is waiting and we shall be away. Your passports are ready, your Grace?"

"We have them here," the Duke grumbled. "Lead on, man, lead on."

Castets opened the door again, sidled into the night, and Nick held the door for the fugitives to pass out. He came last, closing the door gently behind him, turning the key in the outside of the lock and then placing it in his pocket, and felt his blood, and his muscles, freeze at the sound of hooves and marching feet.

"We are betrayed," whispered the Duchess.

"Take this," Castets pressed a pistol into Nick's hand, as if a single shot would be much use against the guard. He found himself against the wall, still in the comparative shade of the doorway, the Duchess leaning against him, one of her children tight in her arms, and still, remarkably, sleeping. The Duke was immediately in front of him, holding the boy, with Castets before them again, while the maidservant and the valet huddled behind.

Now they could see the approaching body of men, a squad of gardes du corps, accompanied by a group of mounted men.

" 'Tis Lafayette," the Duchess whispered in Nick's ear. "Oh, my God, what brings him here at this hour?"

Whom would be a better question, Nick thought. But he contented himself with squeezing her hand, and praying that neither child would awake.

The party clanked on, the sound of the hooves faded into the night. "Safe," Castets breathed. "My God, your Grace, but I had supposed it all over with us then."

"It may yet be with the Queen," Nick muttered. "Should we not . . ."

"We'll make haste," the Duke decided. "Come, Mr. Minnett, you have taken the burden of my safety on your shoulders. You'll not forget that should, by any unhappy mischance, the King and the Dauphin be taken, then am I King of France."

"Please, Mr. Minnett," begged the Duchess. "I am sure the King's party is as capable of guarding themselves as are we."

Nick sighed, and nodded. "So be it, your Grace. Lead on, Joachim. We'll be in Lézardrieux this time tomorrow."

Nine

Nick walked the weary horse into the yard, threw the reins to the boy. Eric waited for him by the step. "Thank God you are back, Mr. Nicholas. Thank God. We have been so alarmed . . ."

"My father?"

"Is as you left him, sir. No better, but no worse."

"I must go to him. Mother is in?"

"Oh yes, sir." Eric hurried beside his master. "But there is also Mr. Pitt . . ."

"Here? What has happened?"

"Well, sir, as to that . . ."

Nick ran up the stairs, burst into the withdrawing room. "Billy? Mother." He gave his mother a kiss on the forehead, squeezed Lucy's hand; incredibly, his sister appeared to have been weeping. "Some disaster has happened here."

"Not here, Nick," Pitt said. "But to the Royal Family of France. Where have you been this last week?"

"Why, I took my passengers up the coast and landed them at Ostend. That was simple enough; we had a fair wind and did the journey in scarce more than twenty-four hours. But that fair wind was foul for Lyme, and so these last six days we have been beating back down Channel."

"Your passengers, you say?" Pitt demanded.

"The Duke de Provence, his wife, his children, two attendants, and the man Castets. They did not enjoy their day at sea, I will admit, but they are now safe to Brussels."

"Thank God for that at least," said Priscilla Minnett.

"But the King and Queen? Are they not also in Brussels?"

"Why, they were stopped at Varennes, and arrested," Pitt said.

"Like common criminals," said Priscilla Minnett.

"At Varennes?" Nick scratched his head. "But if they reached so far then surely they were safe? There was a regiment of horse, waiting outside Varennes, to escort them to Bouillé."

"There had been a regiment of horse," Pitt corrected. "But the royal coach was several hours late in arriving at the rendezvous, and the troops had been withdrawn. Oh, it seems to have been a mismanaged affair, from start to finish."

"It was that. The Queen refused to trust herself to the *Rose,* and I could not change her mind. But what has happened now?"

"Why, as your mother says, they have been arrested and treated as common criminals."

"They say there is a guard on duty in the Queen's bedchamber," Lucy said. "He is withdrawn only when she must change her linen."

"And the King is similarly constrained, as well as the Prince," said Priscilla Minnett.

"Good God." Nick sat down. "Ferson?"

"Oh, he is safe enough in Belgium," Pitt said. "His responsibility was to deliver the Royal Family to their berline, and this he did."

"The Princess de Lamballe?"

"Has been arrested, as privy to the conspiracy to escape."

"Damnation. I should have taken her by force," Nick muttered.

"And you ask about no one else?" Lucy cried.

"Should I? Oh, very well. What of Aurora de Benoît?"

"Married," Lucy wailed. "Married, to that monster Condorcet. Taken from the side of the Queen and forced to live with that . . . that red-handed revolutionary. And a divorcee, to boot. He has entirely foresworn religion, like all of his kind. But can Aurora ever be more than his mistress, in the eyes of God?"

"Aye, well . . ." Nick wondered how much of that was Condorcet's revenge on him, personally, for Seraphine. "At least she is not in prison, like the rest of them."

"She might as well be," Priscilla Minnett declared. "Indeed, surely prison would have been preferable. Do you know, poor Pierre has suffered a stroke? Just like your father, only worse. They say he will never speak again."

"Aye." Nick sighed. "And I have been gossiping here when I should have visited Father." He stood up.

" 'Tis more than just gossip," Pitt remarked, also standing. " 'Tis what happens now."

Nick frowned at him. "I can understand your personal concern, Billy, but surely what occurs in France is of no matter to us?"

"You think so? What do you *think* will happen now?"

"Why . . . I have no idea. What of the constitution?"

"It exists; they pay lip service to it. Even the King, as I understand the situation, is paid lip service as a king, while the guards remain on his door. Yet the country is rapidly sliding into the grip of extremists. But there is still worse, alas. Leopold will not stand by and see his sister mistreated. There are already threatening noises coming from Vienna."

"War?"

"Which the Condorcets and the Marats and the Desmoulins would no doubt welcome. A revolutionary tide must be directed, constantly, and at far-flung objectives, lest it consume those who would ride it."

"Aye," Nick thought of Madame Roland, composed and apparently self-confident, yet entirely aware of the danger in which she and her husband stood. He wondered what change in her situation the débâcle of the King's flight would mean. And wondered why he cared. "But surely we need take no part in it?"

"In a general European war, which might involve God alone knows what changes in the balance of power? I do not see how we could avoid it. Besides, the nation is working itself up to it. Support for the revolution is fading. You'll have heard about that business in Birmingham?"

"Priestley's house?"

"And others. Burned to the ground, and him lucky to escape with his life, because he would celebrate the anniversary of the fall of the Bastille. There is a kind of madness creeping over all Europe," Pitt said sadly. "I feel it growing every day. War. My God, surely that is not to be my fate. We need peace, Nick. Peace to recover, and peace to build."

"Aye," Nick said again. "I take your point. I must go to Father. You'll excuse me, Mother, Lucy."

"And me. Mrs. Minnett, if you will." Pitt accompanied Nick into the corridor. "I would have a talk."

"About war?"

"About preventing war, if it can be done."

Nick glanced at him. "You will scarce hope to employ me in that role, Billy. I imagine half of France starts rattling its saber at the very mention of my name."

"And I'm all in favor of that, Nick. Supposing it rattles its saber at the other half."

Nick hesitated at the door to his father's room. "You would encourage civil war?"

"If they are fighting each other they can hardly be fighting anyone else. And supposing we look at our own history, while a civil war is actually in progress, the life of the King and Queen may be considered safe; they are far too valuable as hostages and far too dangerous as martyrs."

"But your government cannot officially take this point of view." Nick smiled at his friend. "I have said before, I wonder at times how you sleep at night."

"And I have admitted, badly," Pitt said, "save with the assistance of a few bottles of port. But having been given the task of preserving and if possible increasing England's wealth and fame, why I will carry it out to the best of my ability, you may be sure."

"And I must back Etienne de Benoît's little army, you mean. A very bad investment, Billy."

"You will not lose by it, Nick. You have my word. I cannot ask for funds to equip the émigrés; but I can direct the investment of government funds, and they shall find their way into the House of Minnett, or a subsidiary. I have heard rumors concerning Ratsey."

"Aye," Nick said. "When I can possibly spare the time to concern myself with my own affairs. 'Tis a major matter you now propose, Billy, I am but Father's attorney. I will have to put it to him."

Pitt laughed, and slapped him on the shoulder. "Why do you think I am here, Nick? I have already put the business to Percy."

"And him scarce able to lift his hand?" Nick said. "Oh shame on you."

"His brain is as good as it ever was," Pitt insisted. "He knows that he can no longer bear the entire burden of the House. The decision must be Nick's, he said; he is the head of the House of Minnett, now."

"You are a rascal, Billy," Nick said. "You will need double your usual ration of port this night."

"I am already looking forward to it," Pitt agreed. "Now, shall we go in and acquaint him with your decision?"

Nick reined his horse at the crossroads, inspected the signpost. It was a hot May day, and had rained earlier; his cloak was still damp. The road was inches deep in mud. But it was spring, and he was in Dorset. The trees were green, the fields were green, and with the disappearance of the clouds the sky was an endless blue.

And there was the tang of salt in the air. He was not more than twenty miles from Lyme.

"Is that the road, Mr. Nicholas?" Eric urged his mount forward.

"Aye," Nick touched his horse's flanks with his spurs, and turned down the left-hand lane, mud splashing from his hooves. The road led between high banks, topped with trees, which occasionally deposited a cascade of water on his beaver hat. But a few moments later it debouched into a field, beyond which was a lonely farmhouse. And suddenly there was noise. They heard the sounds of men shouting, accompanied by the rattle of musketry, watched the black powder smoke rising into the gentle breeze.

"A battle," Eric said. "Here?"

" 'Tis but the preparation for a battle," Nick said. "They are doing no more than burn my money."

He walked his horse forward, across the farmyard, and a door opened, to reveal a man in a white uniform and belts, with a white cockade in his black bicorne. He carried a musket with a fixed bayonet. *"Gardez-vous."*

"I would have supposed, as you mean to keep the existence of this little army secret, that you would at least challenge me in English," Nick said. "Where is the general?"

"With the army, monsieur. But you cannot go to him without the password."

"Minnett," Nick said.

"The road to the right, behind the house, monsieur."

"What nonsense," Eric grumbled. "Do they not know the sound of their muskets can be heard beyond that hill?"

Nick did not reply. But the man was entirely right. His stomach seemed to be slowly filling with lead. It was not merely the amount of money which was literally being burned, as he had remarked; it was the complete futility of the idea of a handful of men opposing a nation. And it was not the first time he had felt this way; he had known it only a few days ago, in Paris, as he had watched the Royal Family fluttering like moths, and with the success of moths too.

The road led up, and over the hill. At the top he reined, to look down at the open field. There were, he estimated, perhaps three hundred men down there, marching and wheeling, forming line, the first row kneeling, the second standing, and delivering volleys which immediately had them surrounded in black smoke. They wore white uniforms and black hats, every man with a white cockade tucked into his brim. Their lines were seldom straight, and the volleys were the most ragged he had ever heard, even on volunteer outings. But at least they were well armed, with sword and pistol as well as musket and bayonet; the House of Minnett had seen to that.

The commands were given by three men on horseback, somewhat to the right of the regiment, and at the foot of the hill. They were dressed exactly like their men, except that they carried no muskets.

"Etienne," Nick shouted, and cantered down the hill.

The horsemen turned, and the soldiers turned as well, to stare, and to present their arms. Fortunately, as they had just delivered a volley their pieces were empty, Nick recalled with some relief.

"Nick," Etienne shouted in reply, and took off his hat to wave it. Then recollected himself and turned back to his men. "The regiment will fall out," he bawled.

The men dropped their muskets, threw themselves on the damp ground; hats came off and coats were unbuttoned, and Nick saw to his consternation that flasks were immediately produced and handed round.

"Nick," Etienne shouted again, cantering toward him. "What a pleasant surprise. You'll not have met Philippe de Montmorin."

The second in command was even younger than Etienne; he did not seem much older than Nick himself. And his eyes burned with excitement, perhaps even fanaticism.

"It is an honor, monsieur," he said, "to shake the hand of our benefactor."

He reached across his horse's head, and Nick squeezed the gloved fingers. "My pleasure, monsieur."

"What do you think of them, Nick?" Etienne's eyes were also alight with excitement and anticipation.

"Well," Nick said. "I . . ."

"There is not a man out there who has not got noble blood," Etienne said. "Those are men, Nick. Men. They will show Condorcet and his friends what happens when they tamper with our King and Queen, eh, with my sister, eh?"

"Aye," Nick said.

"You have heard of that, Nick?" Etienne's voice rose an octave. "You have heard of that swine Condorcet? He was once your friend."

"He is probably my greatest enemy now."

"But you doubt we shall succeed?"

"Doubt? Three hundred men?"

"*Men,* Nick. No screaming rabble."

"I have visited Paris, Etienne, several times in the last two years. That rabble will also fight."

"Not like my people, Nick. Fighting, winning, is in our blood. And besides, it is not just a matter of three hundred men. I receive my information as well. My Bretons are tired of this revolution. They have been tired of it for over a year already, but now, now the Assembly takes another step toward its own perdition. You have heard of the priests?"

"That they must now take a civil oath? I have heard that, Etienne."

"And those that have not taken the oath are dismissed their livings. But this is the majority. And what will a good Frenchman do without his priest? Why, I have heard that in Brittany, where a legal service is held, but a score of people attend; the remainder walk ten, fifteen miles to hear a non-juror in an open field. Now they are angry, Nick. They cannot be born, they cannot die, they cannot marry, without their priest, and the government has decreed that they shall have no priests. I will tell you this, Nick. My people lack only a leader, a name they can follow. But there is not a soul in Brittany has not heard of de Benoît. I have but to plant my standard and they will come flocking."

"And Brittany will conquer France?"

"Now you seek to make fun of me, Nick. But I am serious. If it comes to that, why, Brittany has only been a part of France these past three centuries, and then by marriage. We could be independent again. Rennes will be my capital, eh?"

"I was not making fun," Nick said, very quietly. "I had presumed your intention was to rescue the King and Queen, and your sister. You will not do that from Rennes. You may well raise an army, but you will have a French army thrown against you. Would it not be better to coordinate your attempt with the invasion planned by the émigrés from Belgium and the Palatinate? And link that in turn with the invasion planned from Savoy? The Duke of Condé himself is in Nice."

"Ah bah," Etienne shouted. "Condé? This is not his grandfather we speak of, Nick. This one, why, he but concerns himself with who takes precedence at ceremonial occasions. Invasion? Why, do you not suppose I have been in correspondence with them, all this while, begging for concert? But Peter will wait upon Paul, and Paul is quarreling with all. Should we wait for those Court layabouts, the King, God bless him, will have died from old age before a sword is drawn in his defense. But let the army of Etienne de Benoît but land, and unfurl its flag, and recruit, and march on Paris, and they will be stung to action. Do you not see, Nick? We shall spur them on."

Nick frowned. "There is the best argument you have yet put forward. The only argument, in fact."

"But you are still not convinced. Then come and meet my bravoes, Nick. They are but a cadre. Imagine each of my men at the head of ten, a hundred soldiers. Think what great deeds we can accomplish then." He wheeled his horse away, galloped toward his scattered regiment, reined and flung himself from the saddle. Nick followed more slowly, also dismounted.

"Gather round," Etienne shouted.

"Gather round," bawled Philippe de Montmorin, who had joined them.

"I would have you meet our benefactor," Etienne shouted. "This gentleman is Mr. Nicholas Minnett, the banker, whose money pays for your food, your uniforms, your weapons, and your bullets, my friends. Come and shake the hand of the man who will go down in history as the savior of France."

They gave a great shout, and gathered round Nick in such a frenzy he supposed he was in some physical danger. They grasped his hand and pounded his back; an array of names and faces passed before him, in such quantity that he could remember none of them. But every eye contained the same glow of fanatical determination to do or die, and he reminded himself that Etienne was right about at least one thing; where Louis Condorcet and Roland de la Platière had grown up with farm tools in their hands, and rabbits as their principal antagonists, these men had held swords and pistols since they had been old enough to talk, and they had not regarded their weapons as toys, but had indeed exercised themselves in the military art, if only against each other, for almost every day of their lives.

After all, Alexander had conquered the known world, at odds of several thousand to one.

"Well?" Etienne shouted in his ear. "Are they not splendid? Are you not proud to have helped raise such an army?"

But then, was Etienne de Benoît another Alexander?

Nick laughed. "Aye," he shouted. "They are splendid. And as they are partly mine, Etienne, I will keep an even closer eye on the affairs of this army. Providing you will be sensible."

Etienne frowned. "Sensible?"

"I too am in correspondence with the émigrés of Belgium and the Rhine. And with the Austrian Court. They assure me that an invasion will be mounted immediately should their majesties appear in danger, but preferably next spring."

"A year? But Aurora . . ."

"If you would accomplish great things, Etienne, personal feelings must not be allowed. A year will give you time to increase and improve your army." He seized his friend's hand. "But wait a year, and I will march with you. You may leave the accumulation of a fleet to me."

* * *

"A fleet." Anne Yealm clung to the rigging of *Golden Rose* and gazed at the twelve sloops, cutters, ketches which had gathered in Lyme Bay, riding to their anchors. "Why, 'tis a marvelous sight."

"Aye," Nick agreed. "Put one frigate amongst us and we'd hit bottom so fast you'd think we were made of stone."

She glanced at him. "Have you still no faith in this venture, Mr. Minnett?"

Nick sighed, and watched the boats being rowed out from the shore, each one filled with eager young men. It had cost him a year to raise this number of private boats able and willing to cross the Channel; every step had had to be taken in the deepest secrecy. In that time Etienne had trained his little band, and even recruited another score of blades, buoyed up and driven on by the constant rumor of the disintegration of the French state. And in that year Louis XVI and his unhappy family had found themselves ever deeper in the clutches of the Assembly, who were themselves ever deeper in the clutches of men like the gutter journalist Marat, and the fanatical Jacobin Condorcet. Under its own decree, the original Assembly had dissolved itself, and at the same time passed a law making it impossible for any of its members, the group who had drafted the constitution under which France was now officially governed, to belong to the new Assembly, the body which would put that constitution into practice. This was a sufficiently cockeyed way of carrying on government, however noble and even Grecian it might appear on the surface. On the surface, there was the rub. For Marat and Condorcet, and other names which were now beginning to be heard, such as Maximilian Robespierre and George Jacques Danton, both also lawyers, were even more powerful now they were out of the Assembly. They controlled the Paris mob, with their newspapers and with their street corner oratory, and the mob in turn controlled the Assembly.

Or most of it. As they had foreseen, the Girondists had secured a majority in the new House, and the Rolands were probably the most powerful people in France at this moment. And so it was the Rolands or, to be more precise, Madame Roland, whom no one could doubt was the real force behind the government, that he was now going to oppose in arms. And yet, where was the alternative? Manon certainly had no greater love for the King and Queen than anyone else. Were she to be confirmed in her power, then they might find themselves forced to abdicate.

And would that not be the best possible thing? He had himself seen enough of the total lack of energy in Louis XVI to recognize that as a king he must be a disaster, nor could he suppose that the overweight, ill-tempered man he had carried to Ostend would be greatly more successful.

But now at last events were shaping. Their information from Coblenz indicated that the Austrians were ready to move; their army was to be commanded by Europe's foremost soldier, the Duke of Brunswick. So now at last Etienne's diversion had a chance of success.

And Nick Minnett was going to war, if only as an observer. There was a senseless occupation for a banker. But he had an ulterior motive for wishing to return to Brittany; a year's search by every financial agent he could contact in France had failed to discover any trace of Seraphine Condorcet, and of all the people he had used over the past two years, she alone troubled his conscience. Besides, he was but accompanying the fleet to see the expedition away to a sound start. He had promised to be back in London in a week.

"The general approaches," Anne said, having decided that he was not, after all, going to reply.

He raised his head, watched the boat rowing toward *Golden Rose*. Etienne had had a new uniform made for the start of this venture; his white coat shone in the morning sunlight, his breeches gleamed. He wore gold epaulettes, and a sparkling leather baldric to support his sword. His bicorne sported the largest white cockade Nick had ever seen.

"Nick," he shouted as they approached. "To sea. To sea. The time for secrecy is past. You may be sure there are sufficient spies overseeing our loading. We must be in France before they can send word."

"We shall be in France tomorrow morning," Nick said. "Is all prepared, Tom?"

Price scrambled on board behind Etienne and de Montmorin. "Aye aye, Mr. Minnett. There are letters."

"Haste," Etienne shouted, ranging the deck. "Haste."

"We've an hour for the best tide." Nick sat on the hatch cover, opened the satchel, took out the letters, thumbed through them quickly. One from Mother, wishing them godspeed; Father sent his best wishes as well. He was no better. One from Turnbull, with a breakdown of banking affairs over this past month. But there was nothing Turnbull himself could not deal with. One from Billy Pitt, unsigned but nonetheless wishing fortune to the expedition.

And one from Caroline? He frowned, and read more carefully. "How my heart goes out to you," she wrote, "as you undertake this great adventure. Oh, Nick, Nicky, should you not have come to visit your wife before placing your life in danger . . ." and more of the same. Finishing with a postscript, "These small accounts are attached for your generous consideration." He flicked the papers, mentally totting them up. Seven hundred pounds, for jewelry and furs, and entertainments.

"Is all well, Mr. Minnett?" Anne asked.

He shuffled the letters together, restored them to the satchel. "Oh aye, Anne. In this bag is the entire representation of my life. But that life belongs on the beach over there. Once we raise anchor, I am a free man."

"Then let us be off," Etienne cried. "Haste, haste. Fair stands the wind for France."

"Aye, and haste would be sound policy," Nick said, half to himself. "If Carrie herself knows of our venture, then surely there can be no one in all England not in the secret. You'll prepare to raise anchor, Tom Price. Anne, you'll take the boat for the shore."

"Sir?" She frowned at him. "You have not sailed these past two years without me at your side."

"We are going to war," he explained, gently. "War is no place for a woman."

"The war will surely be fought on land, Mr. Minnett," she said. "I shall not leave the ship."

"Should a French man-of-war sight us, Anne, we shall be blown out of the water."

"Did that not apply when last we left Lézardrieux?"

"I suppose it did. But . . ."

"Mr. Minnett," she said, and seized his arm. "If you find freedom on board the *Rose,* what do you suppose of me? I am your woman, sir. 'Tis an accepted fact in Lyme. In all Dorset. When once I said no to Dick Allardyce, there was I finished for the people here. They peer at me from around street corners, and look the other way when I would approach them."

He scratched his head. "They always seem happy enough to have me visit them."

"You are a man, sir, and a gentleman. Your way is not their way, and they can only stop and stare and envy; but I played with them when we were children. Their envy toward me is filled with malice."

"But . . . you know none of that rumor is true."

"I know that, sir; and you know it. But there is no one else can *know* it; certainly no one will believe it. Sir, were they to suppose you had withdrawn your protection from me, they would spit in my face and take the clothes from my back."

"By Christ," he said. "By Christ." And indeed, he had understood that it might come to this, long ago, and then forgotten about it. He was Nick Minnett; he was inviolate. And his life was far too busy for considerations of rumor and counter rumor regarding the daughter of a lighthouse keeper. So, what misery had he inflicted upon her in his endeavors to make himself happy?

Color was flooding her face, almost matching her cheeks to her hair, and her fingers slowly relaxed, dropping her hand from his sleeve. "I was insolent, sir. And stupid. You bear too many burdens to be bothered with mine. I shall go ashore now."

"No," he said. "No. You'll stay afloat, Anne. I promised you the *Rose* would be your home. So it shall. Tom Price," he called. "Stand by to make sail. Anne, there is the signal prepared. Run it up the yardarm and make sure the other captains follow. Etienne, if you'll open that bag over there you'll find a bottle of port. We'll toast our departure. God and the King."

Etienne raised the bottle, drank deeply, and passed it to de Montmorin. "God and the King. And now for St. Malo."

Nick shook his head. "That would be madness. What, attack a walled town, lacking cannon and with but three hundred men?"

"But . . . all my men suppose we make for the Rance."

"Aye. But as all of France no doubt expects our coming, our only secret is that there is a long coastline from Dunkirk to Bordeaux. Once we disappear to sea this night, no one can tell where we shall drop anchor tomorrow. I have had this in mind from the beginning. We are for Lézardrieux."

"They are here." Philippe de Montmorin's horse was a lather of sweat, and the young man himself hardly seemed better off; his hat was askew and his boots and breeches were splattered with mud as he clattered over the cobbled main street of Lézardrieux, reining his horse before the church. Here, where the village cross dominated the square, Etienne had unfurled the white banner blazoned with the fleur de lys, and beside it, the black wheatsheafs on the white ground of Brittany, and the green and gold banner of the House of Benoît. Here there was a table erected on trestles, and here waited Etienne and his officers, and his scribes, ready to enter the names of the recruits on their roll.

Supposing any really were coming. The army had been encamped a week, and so far had mustered twelve recruits, and these had been for the most part dragooned.

Nor was Etienne making himself very popular, Nick reasoned, by quartering his men on the unfortunate inhabitants of this tiny village.

But his friend's enthusiasm had never waned for a moment; he merely blamed Nick for setting them ashore in this desolate spot, even if they had disembarked without the loss of a shot fired. Now he paraded the square, arms waving as usual. "I knew it," he shouted. "I knew. How many, Philippe?"

"Now, that I cannot say." The second in command had been gone four days, riding round the neighboring villages, drumming up support. "But there are many men on the road."

"And horses?" Nick asked.

"Oh aye, monsieur. Horses. We shall mount some light cavalry yet. All we now need are guns."

"There are guns in St. Malo," someone muttered.

"And guns in Rennes, which is not so well defended," Etienne declared. "Did you get to Rennes, Philippe?"

The young man shook his head, and downed a glass of wine. "I was warned against it. 'Tis held in force."

"Ah, but we will soon have the force, eh, Nick?"

"Aye," Nick said. From where he stood he looked down at the river, flowing between the wooded banks and high cliffs, a scene of remarkable beauty dotted with the anchored hulls of his craft. His skippers were anxious to be away. He was anxious to have them away. The appearance of a single man-of-war off Isle Brehat would leave them trapped.

"There," shouted one of the sentries, and ran to the corner. As if he had given a signal, doors and windows opened, men and women and children ran on to the street, staring and chattering while the dogs barked. The inhabitants of Lézardrieux might be hoping to see the backs of this band of itinerant aristocrats, as the supporters of the old order were now being called in France, but they had also managed to get caught up in the excitement of the invasion.

And now, down the street from the highroad which led

over the bridge to Paimpol, there came a body of men. A terribly small body of men, Nick realized with a sinking heart; not more than a hundred, of whom only twenty odd were mounted. And their arms were of the poorest quality, fowling pieces and a few rusty muskets, while only their leaders carried swords. But arms were the least of their problems; he had sufficient stacked down by the water's edge for three times this number.

And at the least they marched with spirit, and waved and shouted at the inhabitants.

"Benoît," shouted their leader, a big fellow with a black beard who rode a white horse and carried a most serviceable-looking sword, although his clothes were threadbare and filthy. "Benoît. Are you there in truth?"

"I am here." Etienne stood in front of his men, hands on hips, and peered at the newcomer. "I know your voice, you villain, but not your face."

The big man dismounted. "Jean-Louis Charette, at your service."

"Jean-Louis? But . . ." Etienne scratched his head. "Nick, let me present the Vicomte . . ."

"Citizen Charette," Charette insisted, and seized Nick's hand. "Citizen Minnett. I have longed to make your acquaintance. There is scarce a conversation in France that does not include your name."

Nick felt his fingers about to crack, and hastily withdrew his hand. "The pleasure is mine, citizen."

"Citizen?" Etienne bellowed. "Citizen? What charade is this, Jean-Louis?"

"Why, none at all. Is that wine?" Charette seized the bottle and drank from the neck. "Pass them back," he shouted. "My men are dry."

Montmorin looked at Etienne, and received a quick nod.

"Charade?" Charette looked around the village. "What a desolate spot."

"We landed unopposed," Nick explained. "We lack cannon."

"Aye." Charette nodded, drank some more wine. "Charade? Why, this is a serious business, Etienne." He lowered his voice. "But we must proceed with caution. These good people wish to throw off the yoke of the Assembly. They are not sure they wish us all restored to our privileges. That can come later, if it must come at all."

"I'll have no part in such subterfuge," Etienne declared. "Why, next you'll be telling me to strike the flag."

"I *am* telling you to do that. The black and white will do us for the present."

"Monsieur, you are a traitorous dog," Etienne shouted.

"Citizen, did I not suppose you are not as stupid as you sound, I would carve your head from your shoulders this very instant," Charette replied.

The two men glared at each other, while the crowd in the square stared at them in turn, aware that there was a dispute between their commanders even if unable to hear what was being said.

Then Charette smiled. "Ask Citizen Minnett. He is a famous sailor, I am told. Does he attempt to sail against a strong tide? Or does he not prefer to take advantage of the current, and let it work for him? The tide here is Brittany. I am a Breton, Etienne, and so are you. I have lived with these people for the past year, ever since I was outlawed. They will follow me and fight for me, and I will follow you and fight for you, so long as you prove to me you know what you are about. Now, you need guns. There are guns in Rennes."

"I have heard there is a regiment of gardes français in Rennes," Montmorin objected.

Charette gave a burst of laughter. "And you will not fight them? But you have come here to fight, citizen, and be sure gardes français are easier to beat then regulars. The advantage is all yours."

Etienne sat at the table, peered at his map. "There are guns in St. Malo. And less soldiers, I have been told."

"And very high walls," Charette pointed out. "Not to mention a frigate anchored off."

"A frigate?" Nick demanded. "I must get my people to sea. They will know we are lying up this creek by now."

"Yet they will not leave St. Malo," Charette pointed out. "Not only will they be unwilling to trust themselves amongst these rocks, but her crew is the best defense the city has. And do not underestimate them."

"Nonetheless," Nick said, "I will send my people to sea."

"The others, Mr. Minnett," Tom Price said. "Anne and I will not desert you on this shore."

"And what help will you be if a frigate comes along?"

"This gentleman has just said that is unlikely, Mr. Minnett, with respect. You tell us where you march, and we'll keep the sea just off the coast, so should you need us you'll know where to be."

"Now, you listen to me, Tom," Nick said.

"The little girl and me talked it over, sir. So long as you are in France, then we're staying too."

Nick glanced at the three Frenchmen in some embarrassment.

"There are pressing matters," Charette said. "We must take a decision."

"And quickly," Montmorin said. "There is scarce sufficient food left in this village for another two days."

"So we march on Rennes," Charette said. "You may reckon on another hundred men joining us before we reach the city. They are enthusiastic enough, but afraid. They have been rioting, from here to La Vendée; the women have hanged more than one priest before his own altar. But openly to take the field, there is another matter. They wish to be sure that we mean business. Let us march with our banner flying and our muskets primed, and they will flock to the color. All we lack is a band."

"A band?" Montmorin cried. " 'Tis a battle we are about, not a parade."

"Not even a battle," Etienne said. "At least until our numbers are grown and we have secured cannon. We take the road for St. Suliac."

Both his lieutenants looked at him in surprise.

"You seek cannon in St. Suliac?" Charette asked.

"I seek the Château Benoît."

"Is that what you came to Brittany for?" the big man shouted. "Merely to repossess your home? By heaven, then I take my men back to our hills this very instant."

"Be quiet," Etienne said, "and listen to me. This is my army, marching under my name. 'Tis my neck they will stretch the longest, should we be defeated. St. Suliac is my domain, or at least that of my father. There I am known and respected and loved. There we will find our best recruits. And there too we are in close proximity to St. Malo. There are cannon in St. Malo, and I have sufficient friends within the walls of the city. We have never had much to do with Rennes, but the name of Benoît is even given to a street inside St. Malo. And there too, messieurs, should we have to fight, I know the country. I know every branch on every tree."

"And you will have to fight, even there," Charette said. "There is a garrison in the village, placed there since Citizen Minnett's raid of two years ago."

"Well, then that is even better," Etienne declared. "We shall fight them, and we shall beat them. Now, there is the way to find recruits. Let us send but a few gardes français running into St. Malo crying *sauve qui peut*, and Brittany is ours. Do you not agree, Philippe?"

Montmorin hesitated, and then nodded. "There is much good sense. A victory, even a small one, will enhance our fame."

"Charette?"

The big man pulled his beard. "It will do for a start."

"Nick?"

Nick looked at their faces, so eager, so confident, and then at the faces of the soldiers and the townspeople, all listening to the argument. Whatever decision they made would be known to every garde commander in the province by dusk. And St. Suliac was at least only two days' march away.

"Aye," he said. " 'Tis best, I imagine."

" 'Tis there they will make a stand. Or should, at the least." Etienne de Benoît reined his horse at the top of the slight rise, looked down the wooded lane at the river, and the bridge; there was no ford nearer the mouth of the Rance, and St. Suliac was but five miles to their left.

Certainly the bridge looked empty enough; it was only just visible through the early morning mist which clouded upward from the water. But then, the entire forty miles they had marched the previous three days had seemed through a deserted country. Within hours of leaving Lézardrieux they had tramped through the port of Paimpol, with flags flying and their single drummer beating the time, and had bivouacked for a midday meal while Etienne and Jean-Louis Charette had harangued the mayor and the townspeople from the steps of the church. They had received four witless youths to their ranks, and they had seized and hanged another witless youth who had fired a blunderbuss at their general. And they had been stared at from behind shuttered windows.

Had Etienne been shaken by the lack of support? If so, he disguised it well. It had been his decision, as the people would not rise in his favor, that they should where possible bypass the villages, so as to conceal their lack of numbers. "Once we have gained a victory," he said, "then they will flock to join us. Then we will be turning men away."

So then, perhaps, the moment was at hand. The émigrés were getting restless with what seemed an endless march. But Nick was more interested in the sea; they had caught but a glimpse of the bay of St. Brieuc yesterday afternoon as they had topped a hill, and he had pulled out of the column to inspect the quiet ocean, and had made out the cluster of sails which was his little fleet, standing close by the shore, using all the local knowledge that Tom Price and Peter Lownd possessed, for should the frigate decide to abandon St. Malo and sail to destroy the aristocrats' lifeline, the yachts' only hope of survival would be amongst the shoals where the warship dare not venture. But not a man had as yet taken his ship home. There was loyalty.

And of the frigate there had been no sign; just as to this

moment there had been no sign of any gardes français, much less any regulars.

Etienne continued to watch the bridge through his tele-scope, while Charette and Montmorin walked their horses impatiently to and fro. "Well?" demanded the big man.

"I see nothing. And yet . . . unless they mean to stand siege in the château, it were surely best to attempt to hold us this side of the river." He chewed his lip.

"Yet must we cross," Montmorin said.

"Supposing they are entrenched on the far side, with a roadway that narrow, twenty men could hold us here all week," Charette objected. "And should they by any chance have a cannon trained on the bridge . . ."

"I am considering that very possibility," Etienne said. "There is a ford, but two miles farther up, where at low water it is possible to cross. What is the state of the tide now, Nick?"

Nick studied the rocks, as he had been taught by Tom Price.

"All but dead low."

"Well then, I shall need the fittest, say fifty of them. Get them out, Philippe."

Charette frowned at him. "You will avoid a battle?"

"I will make sure I win a battle. Do you know the ford?"

Charette shook his head.

"Nick?"

"I have never been farther up than St. Suliac."

"Ah. And Philippe is a stranger to these parts. I will command the encircling movement. Charette, you will command here. You have a watch?"

Charette felt in his fob, brought out a massive gold timepiece.

"Do we agree?" Etienne compared it with his own. "Half past eight. At ten o'clock you will commence the assault. Advance confidently to the bridge, but cautiously as well. When you are fired upon, line the bank and re-turn shot. Lose no lives unnecessarily. We have none to waste. When you hear our muskets, behind the enemy, then rush the bridge."

"And suppose we are not fired upon at all?" Charette grinned.

"Then cross the bridge and wait for us. Believe me, friend, it is better to be too cautious than to be too bold and suffer unnecessary loss. Are they ready, Philippe?"

"Fifty of the youngest and strongest we have, general."

"Good. One hour and a half, Jean-Louis. Nick, you are here as an observer. I'd not have you forget that. One hour and a half, Jean-Louis."

He dismounted, placed himself at the head of his small band, and led them off the road and across the gentle heath to the right of the main body. They watched them go for several minutes, then they disappeared into a copse.

"Perhaps," Charette said, apparently to himself. "Perhaps he has more spirit, and more ability, than I had first supposed. You'll tell the men to fall out for an hour, Citizen Montmorin. And you, Citizen Minnett, had best take the rear."

Nick dismounted and stretched his tired muscles. "I can scarce observe from there, Citizen Charette."

"You have no sword."

"I have two primed pistols." Nick patted his horse's neck. "And another in my pocket. But I promise, I shall take no part in the fighting, unless the situation is desperate."

"Bah." Charette walked back up the ridge, parted the leaves once more, looked down at the bridge. "We waste our time, parading around the countryside. There is no one there."

Nick sat down, and then lay down, his hands behind his head. The sky was blue, and gave every promise of a superb spring morning. The heat was already beginning to disperse the mist, and the grass was drying. It was incredible that in an hour's time men would be shooting at each other, and attempting to kill each other.

Charette stood above him. "You know that should we be defeated, and taken, they will hang us all?"

"I assume that, certainly."

"Nor will it be a dignified death."

Nick smiled. "I doubt that hanging can ever be a dignified death."

"I meant that in civil conflict, everything is so much more terrible than in a proper war. There are women, and boys. There are insults and humiliations." He squatted. "Do you understand these things?"

"I would not have supposed you afraid, citizen."

"They will not take me alive," Charette declared. "So I have no cause to fear that. I but wonder why you, an Englishman, and a millionaire, should choose to crawl around muddy lanes with us, when your best prospect is a rope and a knife in the crotch."

"I grew up here," Nick said, "at least partly. Etienne is more than just a friend. And besides . . ." He pulled his nose. "It is impossible to explain."

"Try."

Nick shrugged his shoulder up and down the damp earth. "Were I not careful, my life would become the safest, the most civilized, the most pampered, in all the world. I am safer than my king, because the mob scarce knows of my existence. I am wealthier than he, certainly. I have but to snap my fingers, to possess."

"I do not think you are trying very hard," Charette said.

"Perhaps you are not trying hard enough to understand, Jean-Louis. I play at cards, and gamble with a recklessness that frightens my friends. But it has no interest for me. I do not even have the political excitements, such as they are, of my friends. Women? Why, they all wish something from me. Mostly money. And to get it, they will give me anything or everything they possess."

"And you grumble?"

"I think to myself, live that life, Nick Minnett, and no other, and find your powers failing, at fifty or sixty, or whenever, and look back and see, what? What moment in time will you pinpoint as having been good to be alive?"

"You will remember today?"

Nick smiled at the bearded face. "Oh yes, my friend. Should I survive, I will remember today."

"Aye. So will I. It is ten o'clock." He turned, to find Montmorin at his shoulder. "There is no call for quiet, as if they are there they will know we are taking this road by now. Form ranks and march down the hill." He mounted, and the men fell in behind him, muskets clattering against sword bayonets, muddy white breeches stamping into even more muddy gaitered boots, against which the homespun browns and blacks of the new recruits stood out in stark contrast. "You'll take the rear, Mr. Minnett."

Nick hesitated, and then nodded, and pulled his horse out of the line. He had not come here to get killed, and he could accomplish little at the head of the column, where a chance ball might put an entire end to the future of the House of Minnett; it was a paralyzing thought that the Monceys might possibly get their fingers into those accounts and those investments.

The men marched by, smiling and waving at him as if on parade. They were confident enough. But then, they had been brought up to believe that each of them was worth a hundred of the peasantry, and even the local recruits, who were themselves peasants, had inhaled some of the arrogance of their companions.

Nick held his horse's bridle, led it to the top of the ridge, looked down through the trees. Charette and Montmorin were first, walking their horses; behind them the other dozen mounted men also proceeded slowly, apparently unsuspecting that there could be any danger. But Charette was at the very front, his black beard replacing his absent cravat to shroud his bullneck. He was the most obvious target, as he was the obvious leader; if he had indeed lived as an outlaw for the past year, any national guardsmen would know his name.

A shot rang out, and then another, but no one fell. "Take cover." Charette was already out of the saddle, running to the left, while Montmorin moved to the right, and the young men behind them were also spreading out, dropping into the shelter of the bushes which fringed the river, and returning musketry. The banks became clouded with black smoke, intermingling with the mist; the noise was tremendous. And yet apparently no one was hurt. And the men guarding the bridge had not fired a cannon, so presumably they did not possess one.

The firing continued for some fifteen minutes, and then died away. The smoke eddied above the river, and the echoes slowly dissipated themselves in the hills. But hardly had they done so when there was a fresh volley, followed by a series of hurrahs, from the far bank. Instantly Charette was on his feet, his sword drawn. "Come on," he bellowed. "Come on. Charge them."

Bayonets were hastily fixed, and the émigré army ran at the bridge. A single shot was sent from the far bank, and that went wild. The men crowded together, and one fellow cried out in pain as he received a bayonet thrust from his neighbor. But by now Charette was across, and bounding into the bushes, Montmorin at his elbow, the rest spreading out as they reached dry land. The trees shook and the bushes rustled; there was the occasional flash of flame and puff of black smoke rising into the sky, mingled with the high pitched cries of the combatants. Then these too faded.

Nick mounted and rode his horse down the road. At the western end of the bridge two men waited with the other horses, and these they now led across. On the far side the grass was trampled, and Nick's mount checked and attempted to rear as it all but trod on the lifeless body of a blue-coated guardsman. Farther on were another two men, lying together, and then a group of wounded, huddled around a tree, clutching bleeding arms and legs and bellies and chests, and guarded by three of the émigrés, still with fixed bayonets.

Beyond the bushes the ground once again opened up into heath, and here the majority of the victorious army were gathered, drinking wine, exchanging experiences. In the distance the fleeing national guardsmen could still be seen, and on the way they had discarded muskets and cartouches, which lay scattered about the road.

Etienne's face was flushed, and he had not sheathed his sword; the blade was discolored with blood. "Did you see them run, Nick? Did you see them run?"

Nick scratched his head. "This was a battle?"

Charette grinned at him. "They are not always so easy. Now we march on St. Malo, eh, general?"

"Now we march on St. Suliac," Etienne said.

"But St. Malo will be in a panic."

"We shall drive them into an even greater panic. Bring those fellows over here."

The wounded guardsmen were prodded to their feet and driven up the road, muttering and moaning, rolling their eyes as they faced the officers.

"Rascals," Etienne shouted, grasping the hilt of his sword in both hands, the point thrust into the earth in front of him. "You are rebels against your king. I should have you hanged."

The men stared at him, and one gave a sudden moan and sank to his knees, then flopped forward on to his face. One of the émigrés knelt beside him. "He is dead."

"There are still three left," Etienne said. "And I am a magnanimous man. Take yourselves off. Tell them what happened here. And tell them too that this is but the advance guard of my army. There are six thousand men on the road from Paimpol, commanded by the Prince of Condé himself. We were but sent ahead to clear the road. Tell them in St. Malo that if they would save their lives, they had best surrender when I approach their walls, for believe me, the Prince of Condé seeks only to avenge the insults offered to his king. Tell them I shall be at the walls of St. Malo this time tomorrow morning, when the gates shall be opened to me. Thus may I intercede with the Prince for all of your lives. Go now, and tell them."

The men rolled their eyes some more, and exchanged glances. "It will be hard, my lord," one said.

"Hard? Hard? To save your life?"

"My lord, you say if we do not surrender we shall all

be hanged. But if we do surrender, then also shall we be hanged."

"The man is out of his mind," Charette growled. "How can you be hanged if we promise you your lives?"

"Because we were but sent to hold the bridge, my lord, depending the arrival of the army."

"Army?" Etienne frowned at the man, then sheathed his sword and seized him by the coat. "Which army? There is no army in Brittany, save mine."

"An army was dispatched from Paris, my lord," the man gasped. "As soon as word was received of your landing. A messenger came to us last night, saying they are at Rennes already, and will be here tomorrow. Three thousand men, my lord. I do not know how they will fare against your six thousand, but they are coming." He rolled his eyes some more. "There will be a great battle."

Nick watched the color slowly draining from Etienne's face. "Three thousand men," whispered the general. "Three thousand men?"

"Ah bah," Charette said. "I do not believe him. And even if he speaks the truth, an army is only as good as its commander, its reputation. We have won here. Those fleeing rascals will have spread the tale of our victory. We shall be famous. Charette, Benoît, Montmorin, let them know who we are. And who shall they oppose to us?"

"Who?" Etienne demanded, shaking the man like a rat. "Who?"

The guardsman licked his lips. "The army is commanded by Citizen General Condorcet, my lord."

Ten

The officers stared at the guardsman for a moment, and then Etienne de Benoît burst into laughter. "Condorcet? A general?"

"Appointed by the Assembly, my lord," the guardsman gasped. "He asked for the command, sir."

"Why?" Charette demanded.

"Because it is well known in Paris, my lord, that this army is commanded by Etienne de Benoît, and financed by the English milord, Nicholas Minnett." His eyes rolled toward the civilian greatcoat and beaver hat worn by Nick.

"And he would be avenged upon us?" Etienne laughed again. "Why, truly is it said that men destroy themselves."

"You know this fellow?" Charette asked.

"A country advocate."

"He will know the country as well as you, Etienne," Montmorin said. "And he has three thousand men."

"And are not each of ours worth ten of his? Besides, I can assure you, Philippe, I am worth more than ten of him as a general. Leave it to me. We shall tomorrow gain a victory which will truly make us famous. But we must prepare. He will be happy to march on St. Suliac, and we will be happy to defend it. He will come by this road, and like us he will expect to find the bridge defended. He knows of the ford as well. Now, we will leave three horsemen here, and three more at the ford; the moment the republicans appear, they will ride for us and inform us of their numbers and their armament."

"But we will not defend the bridge?" Charette asked in bewilderment.

Etienne shook his head. "In the long run that would be futile, and we must bring them to battle while St. Malo is still in a tizzy about the defeat of the gardes français. Else we may well be caught between two fires, should the garrison make a sortie up the river while we are engaged with the republicans. Have no fear. We shall choose our ground well, by St. Suliac. Nick?"

"I am sure you know best what you do, Etienne."

Etienne frowned at him. "You do not agree with me?"

"I think the odds of ten to one are considerable, even supposing we make sure of every possible advantage. On the other hand, should we gain the day, then I agree we will be regarded as invincible. It is a gamble."

"And you are against gambling?"

"I usually gamble where I care not whether I win or lose."

"Ah, but we already have a trick in our favor, would you not agree? Condorcet."

"As to that, he has a powerful reason for hating us both. Hate can give a man a strong impetus toward success."

"It can also blind him to proper measures," Etienne insisted. "No, no, my plan is best. Now for your part in this. I would have you summon your ships up the river, and command them to lie at anchor off St. Suliac, so that we may retreat on them and leave again, should the cause arise."

Nick stared at him, and then Charette. "There is madness."

"Aye," agreed the big man. "No army fights with a will when a retreat has been so openly prepared."

"I was not thinking of the morale of your army," Nick objected. "The only way into the Rance is to pass before St. Malo. That is, to pass under the guns of the frigate."

"She will not follow," Etienne said. "She cannot. There is insufficient water."

"Yet will she make sure my people never leave again, or yours," Nick objected.

Etienne chewed his lip, glanced at Charette.

"The Englishman is right," Charette agreed. "I would have ordered things differently, but as we are here, and as you wish to fight on ground of your own choosing, then let us fight, and win, or die; the only alternative is to re-embark your men now, while there is time." He thrust his beard at his general.

"Philippe?"

"To sneak away now, after having gained a victory, would seem total cowardice to me."

"Hm. And what will you do with your ships, Nick?"

"I am inclined to send them home," Nick said. "They are totally unarmed, and exposed not only to the weather but to the French navy. If Condorcet marches on us with an army, then you may be sure the navy is also interested in us."

"And you will go with them?"

It was Nick's turn to glance at Charette and Montmorin, and then at the émigrés, waiting around them, leaning on their weapons, muttering amongst themselves. Already reaction to their success was setting in; they were wondering how they would fare against an army.

"I will stay," he said. "Until after your battle, at the least. It would do your men no good to see me desert them now."

Etienne clapped him on the shoulder. "I knew you would not fail me. Then we must make haste. You'll ride to your ships, give them your instructions, and return to us at St. Suliac. My headquarters will be the château. Haste now. Philippe, you'll come with me. Charette, to horse."

But Charette waited while the other two hurried away, and then peered at Nick. "You are sure what you do? This Benoît, oh, he has courage, and perhaps even ability; but he is too optimistic. It is not a good characteristic in a general."

"Would you have me abandon you?"

"I have nowhere to go, Mr. Minnett. I succeed here, or I die, or I return to my hills and my forests."

"Then for you it is simple enough. But I have been caught up in this business from the start. I will stay for the finish. And should we be defeated, why, then I look forward to seeing these hills and forests of which you speak."

Once again Charette peered at him, then thrust out his hand, and squeezed Nick's fingers. "I would we had more support of such sober strength. Go, and return."

The tide was only just beginning to rise. Nick tethered his horse to a bush, and walked across a seemingly endless desert of sand, toward the distant ripples which marked the sea. And the twelve little ships, nodding to their anchors, inside the outer fringe of rocks, protected for the moment from any naval assault. But the mist had lifted, and the horizon was empty. It occurred to him that the Malouine authorities were treating this invasion with contempt. As well they might, with three thousand men on the march from Rennes.

And yet, who could tell what might be happening on the far side of France, how many armies might be pouring across the frontier to dissipate the ragged forces of Dumouriez? The man had struck him as talented, more so, indeed, than Lafayette; but neither could compare with Brunswick. Surely.

He watched a boat leave the side of *Golden Rose*, and pull for the shore. They must have been watching through a telescope.

He splashed into the shallows to save the dinghy from grounding, climbed over the stern while Price backed the oars. "How goes it?"

"We are blessed, it seems, Mr. Minnett. Just enough wind to keep us moving when we choose, a mist which clears every morning and gathers again at dusk, and not another ship to be seen. No doubt it was all arranged."

"No doubt," Nick said.

"And you, sir?"

"Oh, we have gained a victory, over a handful of

gardes français. No doubt it will go down in history as a decisive battle, at least if left to us. But the real battle will be fought tomorrow or the next day. At St. Suliac, if Monsieur de Benoît has his way."

"And then, sir?"

"Aye, there is the question." They came under the stern of *Golden Rose,* and Anne waited for them on deck, her hair scattered in the gentle breeze. He had not been to his ship for more than a week, and how good she looked, how safe and secure, how separated from the indecisions and imponderables ashore.

"Mr. Minnett," she said. "Are we to leave now?"

"Would you?"

She hugged herself. "This empty coast terrifies me."

Nick climbed aboard. "Aye well, it is over now. Tom, you'll go round the fleet. Tell the captains I would have them weigh anchor at full tide and stand out to sea."

"To sea, Mr. Minnett?" The boatswain frowned at him.

"There is no more you can do here, Tom. And tomorrow or the day after we fight a decisive battle."

"And suppose you lose, sir?"

" 'Tis no thought to take into battle, Tom. Those men will conquer or they will die. Either way it is no concern of these good fellows. You'll take my orders. I'll have this fleet in mid-Channel by dusk."

Price hesitated, then nodded, and glanced at Anne. "Aye aye, sir." He thrust the oars into the water, slowly pulled away from the side of the ketch.

"No doubt you can find me something to eat," Nick said. "I breakfasted early."

"Oh yes, sir." She went down the companion ladder into the cabin, and he followed her, watched her place the inevitable bread and cheese and a bottle of wine on the cabin table.

"You'll join me."

"I'll take a glass of wine, sir." She sat opposite him. "What will you do with your horse?"

"Why, ride him."

"But . . ." The cup was to her lips; now she put it down. "Are you not coming with us, Mr. Minnett?"

Nick shook his head.

"But, sir, this is no quarrel of yours, any more than it is ours. Fight a battle? Why, sir, there is nonsense for Nicholas Minnett, surely."

He drank wine, and swallowed, watched the color flame into her cheeks.

"I am insolent, as usual. I wonder you do not take a stick to me, sir."

"Aye. Well, I am grateful for your solicitude. But you do not understand. We fought a battle this morning. Oh, it was a skirmish; but we won it. Our people are presently buoyed up with the confidence which comes from a victory. They do not know I am ordering the fleet to sea; they suppose I but visit you to keep you informed of the situation. They expect me to return."

"And if you do not they will lose heart?"

"I believe they may very well. They are desperate men, engaged upon desperate measures. I represent an outside influence, an outside confidence, if you like."

She drank wine, holding the mug in both hands and watching him over the rim. "Do you believe you will win?"

"I do not. But I am not a soldier."

"Then we will stay, sir. The others need know nothing of it. I am sure Tom Price can find his way up the Rance under cover of darkness. And should you need us, why, we shall be there."

Nick pushed his plate aside, leaned forward. "Then I will indeed take a stick to you, Anne. I'll not have it."

"But Mr. Minnett, sir . . ."

"You'll return to England, and in one week's time you'll come back, but to Lézardrieux. Just you and Tom. He knows the river. If we are defeated, I can hide until then. If we are victorious, I will wish to reembark in any event, as the army will then be proceeding upon a campaign and will no doubt need additional supplies of money and arms. One week today, Anne. Keep the Channel if you wish for that time, but keep it outside the reach of

French cruisers, or where you may run for shelter should it become necessary. I'll have no argument on this, and I'll have no disobedience."

She refused to lower her eyes. "And supposing you are killed, sir?"

"If I am not in Lézardrieux this time next week, or if there is no message from me, then I shall be dead. There is an end to the matter."

"An end to the matter?" It was the first time he could ever recall her voice being raised to him.

"Listen to me." He reached across the table, held her hands. "You have naught to be afraid of, Anne. I have made a will, and left it with my chief clerk, Jonathan Turnbull. He is an honest fellow, and will carry out my instructions to the letter. The *Rose* reverts to you, as sole owner, to be done with as you choose. And you will receive a pension of ten pounds a week for the rest of your life, to be paid by the House of Minnett."

She had lowered her head to look at his hands on hers; now her eyes came up again, her brows drawing together, her expression unlike anything he had ever seen before, on any woman.

"It is a fair sum, Anne. Ten pounds will free you from want forever."

Slowly her tongue came out and circled her lips. He felt her fingers twitch as she would have withdrawn them. But he retained his grip.

"What is the matter?"

Once again she licked her lips. But the movement in her fingers ceased.

"Anne?"

"Do you suppose, sir, that I care for money, or even the *Rose,* where your life is concerned?"

It was his turn to look down at the fingers, which had suddenly tightened on his own. What had he thought once? What had he thought a million times? What did they say of her, and her millionaire lover?

He raised his head, to meet her eyes again, saw the expression he could not understand slowly fading to alarm.

Then he raised his hands, carrying hers with them, to kiss her fingers, and inhale the smell of her flesh. Once again they tightened, but this time together with his.

"Everything they say of me is true, Anne," he said. "They say I cannot love, and that is true. They say I cannot feel, and that is true. They say I can only lust, and that is true. Do you remember the night I made you bolt your door?"

"I did not lock it, sir." Her voice was so faint he scarcely heard it.

"Yet must you now, Anne. Withdraw your hands, Anne. Go on deck. I beg you, Anne. For both our sakes."

It was her turn to move. She stared at him, and he felt her fingers once again tightening, and her arms as well. She gently brought his own hands across the table, and kissed his fingers.

Nick stood up, and Anne stood with him. They leaned forward together, and their lips touched. Her eyes remained wide, and the soft caress of her lips sent a long thrill coursing from the nape of his neck all the way down his spine. For how long had his entire system cried out for him to do just this? And very slowly he was realizing that perhaps she had been waiting just as long, for him to do this. Because, amazingly, her lips remained closed, and yet warm and anxious. Only when he licked them did they part, hesitantly, and her own tongue slipped between her teeth, again with reluctant delight, before vanishing again.

And now, too, she was gone entirely. She slipped out of his fingers and moved away, while he gazed after her in consternation. Perhaps after all he had made a dreadful mistake. Perhaps after all he had wrecked their relationship.

She went aft, to the companion ladder, and climbed the steps. He wanted to cry out, to call her back, to apologize, and promise not to touch her, whilst at the same moment he wanted to touch her more than anything else in the world.

She stood there on the third step, from whence she could reach the hatch, and quietly pulled it forward. Then the door was also closed, and the bolt was shot, to plunge the cabin into a heated gloom, to shut out the gentle soughing of the breeze, and leave only the even more gentle flicking of the wavelets against the hull, further to isolate them from the world.

Nick stumbled across the cabin, caught her in his arms as she fell off the steps. For just a moment she was again hesitant, then her mouth was wide. He thought he could stand there forever, feeling her body against his, her breath mingling with his, her wine tinged saliva mingling with his. For the first time in his life, as he held a woman in his arms, he wanted to do no more.

But oh yes, he wanted to do much more. Slowly he backed across the cabin until his knees touched the bunk, and he allowed himself to fall, carrying her with him. She landed on top of him, carefully restraining her weight. He lost sight of her for a moment, beneath a cloud of sweet smelling red hair, then a shake of her head restored his vision. But now he must begin again, for she was waiting, her eyes wide, and solemn.

"You must show me, sir," she whispered. "I know nothing of love."

"But . . ." He did not dare say the name.

"He was a fisherman, sir. I could count the occasions on the fingers of my hand. And perhaps . . ." Her mouth widened into a half smile, for just a second. "I sometimes felt he was afraid of me, being so much the elder."

"You are a woman to fear, Anne."

"Me, sir?" She frowned.

"You are too lovely. God should not have put so much splendor in the keeping of one body, one mind, for surely He must have robbed all the rest."

"Then make me as all the rest, sir," she begged. "You, sir, you."

His hands had done no more than hold her shoulders. It required a conscious act of will to slide then lower, down the rough wool of her gown, into the small of her back, and beyond, to the gentle rise of her buttocks. She wore nothing beneath the wool. Why should she, as she was a simple fisherwoman? And as he closed his hands, her eyes widened, and closed, and opened again, wider than before.

"Then call me Nick," he whispered.

She shook her head; her hair flicked his face.

"I cannot be your master, Anne."

"You are my master, sir. I wish you to be my master. What would you have me do, sir?"

He kissed her again, and listened to the sound of the dinghy. But when he would have sat up, she gently pressed him back.

"What, sir?"

There was a noise on deck, and then silence. A moment later the dinghy pulled away from the side. Tom Price was not a fool.

But Anne's body was gone. She had taken one burden upon herself. She released the tie at her waist, lifted the gown, slowly. He knew she was not a coquette; her hesitation was that of sheer modesty, of a last uncertainty perhaps. And yet, as he had said to Charette only a few hours before, this day he would remember, at the moment of his death.

He knew her ankles and even her calves. He had seen them often enough as she had knelt on the deck with her brush and her pumice stone, as the wind had playfully flicked her hem. He had no knowledge of her thighs, so straight and yet so entrancingly rippled with muscle. Her hips were wide, but only in general keeping with her own powerful body. Her groin was thickly matted and the pale hair, to his amazement, did have a tinge of red to it. Her belly pouted, but again, as with her legs, was hard with muscle, like her arms and shoulders.

For by then he had caught them, as the gown fell to the floor, to bring her close and lose his face in the total glory of her breasts, so large, so firm, so irresistibly nippled; the word contemptuous came into his mind. Aye, she was the woman to be contemptuous of all mankind.

Because she possessed more, by just breathing, than any other human being in the world, than any Minnett, who had ever lived, or who would ever live. And most amazing of all, for all her honest modesty, her honest uncertainty, she *knew* what she possessed.

She allowed him a brief eternity in that soft sweated cavern, and then she hugged him tighter yet. "Now, sir," she muttered. "Now, sir." She was strong enough to move him aside to make room for her own body, to cloud down on top of him, and she was on a sudden passionate enough to remain moving after his own energy was spent, her hair filling his eyes, his ears, his nose, her mouth sucking at the lobe of his ear, her huge breaths inflating all the splendor of her body to raise her from him before even more entrancingly, allowing herself to rejoin him again, shoulder on shoulder, nipple on nipple, belly on belly, thigh on thigh, knee on knee.

"Now," he whispered. "You will call me Nick."

Her head raised, and she stared at him, from a distance of no more than an inch. Her breath rushed into his as she smiled. "No, sir."

"But, dearest girl . . ."

"No, sir," she said. "Now I know you are my master." Her smile faded into a look of anxiety. "May I touch you?"

"I should like you to."

Her hands were soft, and it required no more than a touch. Then he was on top of her, and her nails scraped flesh from his back. And then the cabin was quiet, save for the lapping of the waves. Her passion was as spent as his.

But the tide was rising. He could feel the slight roll of the ship as the shelter the rocks gave from the ocean swell slowly diminished.

"Anne," he said into her ear.

"No, sir," she said. "I would have no future. I would have no past. I would have only the present."

He pushed himself up, looked at her in turn. "We shall have that, I promise."

"Now, sir."

He sighed, and kissed her on the mouth, and sighed again. "When I return."

Her gaze shrouded him; there were strands of auburn hair across her face, quivering as she breathed. He thought here again was a picture he could never forget.

"Lézardrieux," she said. "One week today."

From the top of a rise he looked down on the beach, now fast disappearing, and at the sea, covering more and more of the rocks, and at the little ships, their decks a bustle of activity as they prepared for sea. He could identify no one on board *Golden Rose*. But one would have thick auburn hair, and a quiet, consuming passion which was the most exciting he had ever known. Manon Roland had said, "You have never loved." She had suggested he had not known how to love. He had presumed her right, because she was Manon Roland. Now he *knew* she was right, because now he knew how deep a passion love could demand.

He raised his hat, then turned his horse's head and sent him bounding across the heathland. He could not believe it. He could hardly believe it had happened, he could not believe that it was possible for anyone to be so utterly happy. He found it difficult to believe that it was possible to have shared such a totally undemanding hour. As she had truly said, in her arms there was no past and no future. There was only the present. The present would last forever, and it would begin again in but a week's time.

He was so happy he burst into song, and allowed his imagination full play. But there were so many endless delicious problems to be solved. Should he move her from Lyme, or should he just make sure he visited the village more often? Should he become a father? Oh, indeed, he wanted to become a father, for the first time in his life, supposing Anne could be the mother. And there were no secrets to be imposed, between them or upon them. All the world already took her for his mistress, and accepted the situation. All either of them had to do now was enjoy it.

He had ridden for more than an hour without realizing it, and now he once again bounded over the lip of the heathland, looking down on the valley and the road winding beneath him, and at the cloud of dust which eddied into the afternoon air. Desperately he pulled on his reins, brought the horse to a standstill, stared at the marching men. Endless men, in blue coats and tricolor striped trousers, toiling along the road, their muskets shouldered. In front of them rode a squadron of dragoons, he estimated, for they were uniformed little differently to the infantry, and in front of the dragoons there was a cluster of blue-coated horsemen with epaulettes on their shoulders and swords at their sides, riding beneath a tricolor banner. As they marched, they sang, a tune he had not heard before, but which swelled out of their lungs and cascaded across the afternoon, made even his own blood tingle.

They had not, apparently, seen him; or they did not consider a lone horseman worth worrying about. He remained still for some minutes longer, attempting to estimate their numbers, and deciding that three thousand was a very reasonable conclusion, and then feeling his belly fill with lead as he made out the end of the column, debouching through the valley, and consisting not entirely of supply wagons, as he had at first supposed, but also of four cannon, bouncing along behind their teams of horses. And then of a company of men in white, with bearskin and blue facings, and long black gaiters, and even longer rifled muskets; the gardes were being stiffened with a detachment of fusiliers.

He kicked his own horse, turned for the bridge. He crammed his hat on his head, whipped his mount into a gallop, now several miles ahead of the slow moving army. Sweat stood out on his face and neck and was immediately dried by the wind, and now he calculated again, but more seriously. The republicans would not reach the bridge before dusk, he estimated. There was time. Supposing they possessed the materials.

He clattered through the little copse where the aristo-crats had stopped that very morning, and down the road to the bridge. A man showed himself for just a moment; he wore a white uniform and a white cockade. "Whoa," Nick shouted, bringing his mount once again to a halt. "Whoa."

Three men came out, having recognized him. "What haste, Monsieur Minnett," cried the sergeant. "We have seen nothing."

"Well I have." Nick walked his horse across the bridge, noting with concern how solid was the masonry. "They are perhaps three hours away, foot, and horse and guns. And regulars."

"Guns?" The three men exchanged glances. "Regulars? My God. What must we do?"

"Destroy the bridge," Nick said. "They'll not get cannon across the ford. It will take them until the end of the week to go round by the bridge at Chatelier, and I will wager Louis Condorcet will wish to have us immediately. You stay here. I'll return in an hour."

Once again he put his spurs to his horse and sent it clattering down the road, riding now with the Rance on his left hand, the increasing woods on his right, urging his tiring horse ever faster, until the old stone walls of the Château Benoît loomed in front of him around a bend in the road.

"Halt there," called a sentry on the wall.

Nick merely waved, and rode beneath the archway and into the courtyard, reined in dismay. Three men sat on the step, and smoke rose from the chimneys of the house itself, but these signs, and the presence of the sentry, were all that suggested even a small army was in the neighborhood.

"What cheer, Monsieur Minnett," said one of the men. "You look as if you had seen a ghost."

"Aye," Nick said. "Several thousand ghosts. Where is the general?"

"Here, Nick." Etienne came on to the porch, accom-panied by Montmorin. They had discarded their hats and their swords, and smoked pipes. "And is your fleet now safe?"

"I imagine so." Nick dismounted, drew the back of his sleeve across his forehead.

"You need a glass of wine, dear friend," Etienne said. "And I have just the thing inside. Those scoundrels knew nothing of wine, fortunately; they drank the new bottles, and left my vintages alone. My God, Nick, but I will tell you this; it is good to be home again."

Nick scratched his head, wondered if it was possible that Charette had been right, and Etienne had undertaken this entire expedition merely to regain possession of his family home. "I have seen the republicans."

"Ah," Etienne said. "Jean-Louis will be pleased. He is spoiling for a fight. They are close?"

Nick shook his head. "They will scarce reach the bridge before dusk, so they will hardly be upon us before dawn. But they have cannon."

"The guns from Rennes," Montmorin said.

"Ah," Etienne agreed. "Well, that is reasonable enough."

"Cannon," Nick said again, a feeling of despair filling his entire being. "They will knock this place flat before you even see them."

"The Château Benoît? Oh, no," Etienne said. "The woods will protect us. I have thought of that. The château is merely my headquarters. Jean-Louis is now arranging his people to cover the road."

"If those guns cross the bridge," Nick said, "you will not stop them with woods."

"And how do we stop them crossing the bridge?" Montmorin inquired.

"We blow it up," Nick said.

"Blow up the bridge?" Etienne cried. "That is solid stone."

"A barrel of powder will at least so weaken it they will not risk the cannon on it," Nick argued. "Or better yet, should they attempt to cross, they might end up in the river."

"A barrel of powder," Etienne mused. "Aye, there is a good thought. A barrel of powder."

God give me patience, Nick thought; he is beginning to sound like the king. "Then let us be about it," he shouted. "There is a cart in your stable. Have a horse, two horses, harnessed to it, and load on one of our barrels."

"But they are not here," Montmorin said.

"Eh?"

"I deemed it best to send them down river, with Charette. He is billeting his men in St. Suliac."

"Billeting his men?" Nick cried. "With the republicans but a few hours away? Harness up that cart and send it behind me." He ran down the steps, vaulted into the saddle, whipped his exhausted horse once more on the road, this time along the way he knew so well. The last time he had ridden here Louis Condorcet had been at his side, and he had been filled with satisfaction at having conned *Golden Rose* through a storm, and with the expectation of seeing Aurora de Benoît. What a remarkable three years that had been.

St. Suliac opened before him, and he cantered down the street; people peered at him from behind half-opened shutters, while white-coated infantrymen milled about outside the pension. "Charette," he shouted. "Colonel Charette."

"Mr. Minnett." The big man came out of the inn, hands on hips. "Are they close?"

"Close enough. And with cannon."

"Cannon, by God. We must fight them in the wood."

"Aye. We must also stop the guns coming north of the river. You've a barrel of powder to spare?"

"I stowed them by the landing. But transport?"

"Behind me," Nick said. "Give me a glass of wine, I beg you, Jean-Louis. I am all but exhausted."

"Come inside, man. Come inside." Jean-Louis himself filled their glasses, while the innkeeper's wife and daughter watched them from the back parlor. "These poor people do not know whether to love us or hate us. No doubt it will depend upon the battle."

"And the battle will depend upon those cannon," Nick said, draining his glass. "I have brought the cart."

"And the videttes," Charette bawled, running outside again. "What are you doing here?"

"We are lost," shouted the sergeant. Indeed, he had lost his hat and looked decidedly frightened.

"Eh?" Charette peered up the street. "There is no one behind you. And keep your voice down, man. What has happened?"

"Why, a troop of horse appeared and ran at us," said one of the other men.

"And you did not stop them?" Nick demanded. "Only two horses could pass that bridge abreast."

"Maybe. But there were too many," the sergeant said, speaking in a lower voice now he had his breath back. "We deemed it best to withdraw."

"And what of the bridge?" Charette asked.

"Why, colonel, the republicans have it. They are crossing now."

"It is dawn, Mr. Minnett." Charette shook Nick gently by the shoulder.

He awoke with a start. He had not intended to sleep. But the night had seemed endless, as it had been filled with sound, an immense stealthy rustle, following the brief exchange of shot which had sent the reconnoitering horsemen galloping back along the road whence they had come. Condorcet knew where his enemy was, as no doubt he had presumed they would be. And thus the two armies had lain to their arms, and waited for light.

The slight mist clouded off the river, hanging in ghostly wisps from the eaves, swirling up around the tall chimneys of the Château Benoît, making the trees of the wood imperfect shadows. As yet the sun had not risen, and the light was the colorless uncertainty of a spring dawn.

"Here, drink this." Charette poured wine into a cup, held it out. "Will you eat?"

Nick sipped and shook his head.

"Then to your post. Here is a sword, should the worst

befall us. You will hold the house, should it come to that. These fellows will be your immediate command, but we shall fall back on it should it become necessary."

Nick nodded; even after the wine, his throat was too dry for words. Charette walked to the door, and the forty white-coated émigrés clustered the winter parlor, leaning on their muskets and gazing at the Englishman who had brought them here.

The downstairs windows were already closed and bolted and reinforced with hastily nailed baulks of timber; this had been accomplished last night. "We'll take the upper floor," Nick said. "Two men to a window. We are but spectators, at this stage, my friends."

They smiled at his apparent confidence, and he led them into the hall, waited for their general to descend. Etienne walked slowly, glancing at the portraits of his ancestors as he came. He had slept the night in his own bed, knew that he was this day putting his family home at risk; but he would fight the better for that.

He reached the ground floor, and Nick saluted. "Good luck, Etienne."

"And to us all." Etienne squeezed his hands, gazed at the pale faces around him. "Remember, we fight for our King, our country, our honor, and our lives. That scum out there, however numerous, possess no such impulses. They will test our mettle, to be sure. But let us withstand no more than two assaults, and they will melt away into the pigsties from whence they came. Two assaults, my friends. We shall be exposed to no more. God go with you."

The émigrés came to attention, and he saluted them as he hurried for the door. Then they were climbing the stairs, Nick at their head. He paused at the door to the master bedchamber, at the very spot he had given poor Sergeant Popel a bump on the head. Three years ago, and he was back where he started; only now he was to be on the receiving end. "Two in here," he said. "And so on, along the entire front of the building. You, and you, take the side and rear; they will hardly manage to come at us from there."

He himself climbed the small staircase to the second floor, and the servants' attic. From the big dormer window he looked down on the courtyard, on the stables, where the horses were restlessly stamping, aware that a moment of crisis was approaching, on the walls surrounding the yard and the garden, lined with white-coated musketeers, and even on the road beyond; amongst the trees, as the light grew, he could discern other white coats, the picked marksmen Charette had taken out with him to slow the advance. How few they looked. But they had the advantage of the ground. And perhaps Etienne was right in suggesting they also had the advantage of spirit.

The stealthy whisper was growing, and taking on more positive characteristics; Nick could identify the clatter of horses' hooves, the tramp of marching men, the rumble of wheels. Then the morning was punctuated by a musket shot, and another, and as if this had been a signal to the very heavens, the sun broke through the mist, flickering shafts of light between the trees, picking out the white uniforms hastily retiring.

Nick stared along the road, made out the horsemen, clustered to a halt as they identified the walls of the château. But now the rumble was closer, and the cannon came into view. Closer at hand, he saw Charette, waving his sword, and at the command the long line of white-coated infantrymen, each man secured to that moment behind a tree trunk, rose and presented their muskets.

"Fire." Charette bawled. Black smoke clouded into the mist, for a moment obscured even the shafts of sunlight. But the range had been maximum. One of the dragoons fell, and two of his companions dismounted to assist him to his feet; then the group withdrew up the road, to join the cannon, which were being wheeled into place by the sweating artillerymen. And now, behind them, as the mist continued to lift, Nick could make out the columns of blue-coated infantrymen, leaning on their muskets, smoking, no doubt chattering amongst themselves, ready to deal with this band of outlawed aristocrats.

"Down," Etienne bawled, walking up and down the

wall, Montmorin at his side. "Lie down. I will tell you when to rise."

Nick watched the horsemen by the cannon; at this distance he could not identify Condorcet. He felt like a spectator, as indeed he was, for the moment; but a spectator who was entirely divorced from the reality of what was about to happen. He saw the flashes of red, watched a corner of masonry burst into a cloud of dust, looked back at the black smoke billowing into the trees.

Then the entire morning was obliterated by the rumble of the cannon, the thudding of the balls, the crashing of the garden wall as it was systematically reduced to rubble. Turgot had created an artillery for the use of the Bourbons, and here it was being used against them. And now the shot was taking effect; a steady stream of men were being brought back to the shelter of the house itself, and even they were being chased by the flying iron, as two of the guns were elevated almost to act as mortars, and the shot came plunging over the outer wall and into the courtyard, fortunately doing little damage on the soft earth.

"There is no hope for us," a man muttered at his elbow. "They need not come to close quarters."

"They cannot destroy us down that narrow road," Nick said. "That cannonade is but to encourage them and, they hope, discourage us. There."

An hour had passed, and the morning was suddenly silent. Black smoke continued to rise above the guns, but they were being manhandled aside now, to make room for the assault. The guardsmen marched, six abreast, raising their muskets to salute their general as they passed the mounted officers waiting by the side of the road. They suggested a moving stream of bobbing red pompoms, of glittering steel bayonets. And now their officers placed themselves at their head, walking on either side of the drummer boy who beat the time, and whose sinister music came rumbling through the trees.

Charette rose from his ditch, waved his sword again. His musketeers stood up with him, and delivered a volley.

But the column continued to advance, its officers and drum still to the fore; perhaps half a dozen men had fallen.

"Back," Charette bawled. "Fall back."

The white-coated soldiers retreated through the trees, to halt again before the walls, at Charette's signal; their year of training in Somerset had not been wasted. Now they were joined by their comrades on the wall itself, lining up with presented muskets, Etienne and Montmorin marching to and fro behind them.

"Fire," Etienne bawled.

The garden disappeared for a moment beneath the smoke, the morning rumbled. And the head of the column dissolved before the hail of shot. Both officers fell, and the drum was silent, rolling slowly across the suddenly red-stained earth, to trickle into a ditch. Behind it the blue-coats lay piled, flung about like toys, and behind them the column was halted.

"Load," Etienne was shouting. "Quickly now. They will not stand another volley."

But the column was already withdrawing, summoned by a bugle call, while the officers trotted their horses forward to see what had happened.

"Now the cannonade will be resumed," muttered the man beside Nick.

He did not reply, watched the column leaving the road to rest in the ditches, while another regiment tramped forward to take its place. But this made no sense. Forced to advance down the narrow road, unable to deploy until they were so close they were practically under the muzzles of Charette's musketeers, there was no way Condorcet could mount an assault so long as the defenders had powder, and Nick knew there was enough powder to kill every man in the republican army; he had seen to that. But surely Condorcet was no fool, intent upon merely sacrificing his soldiers and his own reputation.

Etienne looked up at the windows, and waved his hat. "Sport, eh, Nick," he shouted. "Sport."

"Aye," Nick said, half to himself, and frowned at the column. It was not advancing, but was waiting, with fixed bayonets, staring at the dead and dying bluecoats on the road in front of them, at the distant gray walls.

Something struck the wall beside him, a loud slap which sent a flick of dust wisping into the air. He turned, looked into the trees to the right, saw the white coats and the blue facings, the bearskins and the long rifled muskets of the fusiliers. Indeed, Condorcet was no fool. He had taken a leaf from Charette's strategy and sent his small force of regulars through the trees. Now the musketry was general, and Nick watched one of Charette's men throw up his arms and fall back as if kicked in the face; only he no longer possessed a face. And the fusiliers were more accurate and capable of more rapid fire than the aristocrats; their muskets were rifled. Bullets slapped and crackled all over the garden and the front of the house; Nick heard a scream from downstairs, and went bounding down the staircase, to find one of his men doubled up on the floor, blood trailing away from his belly as his legs writhed and saliva seemed to spit from his mouth.

"Keep down," he said. "Keep down. They cannot hit you unless you show yourselves. Corporal, help me with this poor fellow."

But as they attempted to lift him, the spasmodic movements ceased. Nick stared at him in horror. It was the first man he had seen killed outright at close quarters. Suddenly they were no longer toys, and he was no longer an onlooker. And suddenly, too, the battle was closer. He stood up, looked through the window. The fusiliers continued to fire, the musket balls continued to hum into the courtyard and splatter against the walls; in actual fact the defenders were suffering few casualties, but they were only amateur soldiers, and their own ability to return fire was hampered by the constant tendency to duck into shelter. As Louis Condorcet had foreseen. Now the second column of blue-coated infantrymen came on at a run, bayonets glittering. Charette was waving his sword and calling his men to order, withdrawing them through the gate and into the yard, pausing to assist one fellow who collapsed at his feet, then releasing the dying man to hurry through the gate and bang it shut. Etienne screamed his commands, running up and down the wall, summoning his men to their feet. Montmorin was dead; Nick could see his body, draped over the parapet, his sword trailing away from his lifeless fingers.

The aristocrats rose and delivered one volley. Several of the attackers fell, but the impetus of the charge was unbroken, and they had reached the end of the trees; their officers were bawling commands and they were deploying in line, pausing to kneel and themselves deliver a volley, at close range to send the defenders scurrying once again for shelter, before they ran at the rubbled stone which was all that was left of the wall, clambering over the debris, hallooing and shouting. Nick watched Etienne face the onslaught, surrounded now by only a few of his men. The first bayonet thrust was swept to one side, and Etienne thrust in turn, bringing a spurt of blood and a shriek of agony from the guardsman; but while his sword was still embedded in the dying man, another bayonet disappeared up to its hilt in his side. Etienne made no sound. He half turned, releasing his sword, to look down at the fatal steel for a moment, then the blade was withdrawn, taking with it an explosion of blood, and an explosion no doubt of pain as well, for now Etienne screamed, and fell forward. But the scream ceased before he hit the ground, and he disappeared beneath trampling feet as the guardsmen surged forward, while from the side the fusiliers also advanced, fixing their bayonets as they ran.

Nick came to his senses. "Give fire," he bawled, "give fire." But he possessed only forty men. The rest of the army had disappeared. Charette had disappeared. Etienne was dead. Montmorin was dead. He found himself doubting his own senses, as his aristocrats loaded and fired into the now dense mass of bluecoats beneath them. For a moment they were checked, held by the solid mass of the door, but then the weight of their bodies sent the oaken panels crashing in.

"The stairs," Nick shouted. "With me." He ran from

the room, found his men beside him. The hallway was packed, and the first men were clambering upward, firing as they did so. Gigantic bees buzzed to and fro, shattered the paneling, ripped the huge paintings into grotesque grimaces, brought glass clouding down from the shattered chandeliers. The hallway and the gallery became filled with acrid black smoke, which made it impossible to see or to breathe. Nick fired into the sudden darkness, while he coughed and choked, then retreated against the wall to draw his sword, and had it knocked from his hand by a falling body. Desperately he dropped himself, to his knees, scrabbling on the ground for a weapon, and being suddenly alarmed by the mysterious cessation of tumult.

All was shouting and cheering, punctuated with screams. "Take them out," someone was shouting. "Take them out. Hang them. There are trees enough."

Hands seized his shoulders, pulled him to his feet, thrust him forward; he was surrounded by the smell of breath and sweat and excreta, of fear and bloodlust. He gasped for breath, and found himself tumbling down the stairs, reached his knees at the bottom, expecting to feel a bayonet thrust at any moment, wondering if he would indeed feel it or if he would die first, and was again dragged to his feet, to stare through the shattered door at the piled bodies of the aristocrats, white coats sadly mudstained and blood-stained and powder-stained, to listen to their screams as the wounded were dragged by their legs through the rubble toward the trees, where laughing guardsmen were preparing nooses; there were four men already dangling, their faces turning black as they kicked and choked.

"Come on, come on," shouted a voice in his ear, and a boot crashed into his buttocks to send him staggering again, while a wave of laughter swept over him. "To the tree. You'd not keep us waiting."

He staggered into the yard, into the warm morning sunlight, sucked air into his lungs, for the first time realizing that he was indeed about to die, and faced Louis Condorcet, strange in his military uniform, his tricolor sash belting his blue frock coat, his gold-trimmed bicorne sporting a tricolor cockade and a high red pompom. His scabbard was decorated with gold, and there was not a speck of dust on his white breeches. He might just have come off parade.

And he was smiling, as well he might. "No, no," he said to the men surrounding Nick. "You'll not hang this fellow. He is reserved for better things."

Eleven

"*A la lanterne,*" they screamed. "*A la lanterne.*" They crowded the street, leaned out of the upstairs windows to howl obscenities; even the escort of cavalry failed to keep them entirely at bay, as they rushed under the horses' noses or under their tails to push their wine-laden breaths into the cart and spit and jeer.

But by now Nick was almost able to ignore them. There had been too many previous occasions, beginning at Rennes, and repeating themselves with every town and village through which they had passed, when he had supposed himself about to be torn to pieces. No doubt he was still destined to be torn to pieces, but not until he had apparently been paraded through Paris, and perhaps before the Assembly as well.

Besides, his other discomforts had grown so great, a jeering mob was almost a relief. During the week he had lain in his cart, bound hand and foot, his head banging, every muscle in his body aching. His clothes were torn and dirty, and hourly becoming more filthy, his belly rumbled with hunger when it was not rumbling with the sight, and the stench, of Etienne's head slowly putrefying on its lance; it played the part of his banner. He had found it difficult to convince himself that he was not living some terrible nightmare; it was impossible to believe that he had actually held Anne in his arms, that he had once been clean and free from pain, that his belly had been full and he had been happy.

Impossible to believe that she might still be waiting for him in Lézardrieux. But oh God, he prayed that she was not. The thought of Anne undergoing but a fraction of his own humiliation and misery was unbearable. No doubt Charette was the lucky one. He had either fallen in such a way that he had not been found, or he had made his escape. The republicans considered that he had eluded them; this was the one blot on their triumph.

But for the rest, they had enjoyed themselves. They had gained a famous victory. They had dragged wounded aristocrats to the trees around the shattered house and they had slowly, but so slowly, suspended ropes around their necks and dragged them, kicking and squirming, from the ground. They had cut off the heads of the dead, and set them on pikes. And they had taken a selection of the living, and made them trail behind their column, and hanged one at the village cross of every town in Brittany, as a warning.

And Nicholas Minnett, bound like a hog going to the slaughter house, left to wallow in his own filth, fed a crust of bread and a cup of water twice a day, they had preserved for the amusement of their general. He spent at least an hour a day riding his charger beside the cart, smiling down at his victim, taunting him, reminding him of better days, promising him worse to come. As now.

"Awake, Nick," he shouted. " 'Tis Paris, man. Do you not remember Paris? Oh, you have had some good times in Paris, Nick. You'll have better, I do assure you." He waved his hat. "Make way there," he bellowed. "Make way."

"Condorcet," shrieked the mob. "Condorcet. Show us the villain. Show us the spy."

"Aye," Condorcet agreed. "Get him up, there."

Two of the gardes français climbed into the cart beside Nick, pushed his shoulders up, made him sit and stare at the men and women and children, faces crazed with bloodlust and wine and hunger, parading beside him, shouting their imprecations and their threats. They were already well into the city, and beneath the shadows of the houses, and every window was filled with shouting humanity, waving hands and tricolor banners. Slowly

Nick forced his clamped jaws apart. "You'd think I was the whole Austrian army," he said.

One of the gardes winked at him. "Aye, citizen," he whispered. "You'll have to do. These people, they know that when the Austrians come it will be as conquerors, and they will weep, not cheer."

When the Austrians came. Supposing they came. Supposing they came soon enough for Nicholas Minnett.

The procession had reached the bridge, and here it halted, while the shouts gave way to cheers. Nick saw a cavalcade approaching, and wished the earth would open to swallow him up. Roland looked slightly uncomfortable, and as the morning was well advanced, distinctly hot. Manon's face was expressionless, save for a slight indication of contempt—perhaps for the overheated crowd, more certainly, in their eyes at the least, for the prisoner. She reined her horse beside the cart. She wore a huge brimmed summer hat, and her eyes were lost in the shade. "You have done well, Citizen General Condorcet. Well."

"Well?" shouted the man beside her, a young slight fellow with protruding teeth and a mop of fair hair. "Well? He is the new hero of the republic. He has won, where your Lafayette and your Luckner, aye, and your Dumouriez, do no more than tremble at the sound of an Austrian drum."

"Oh indeed, Citizen Desmoulins," Manon agreed. "But then, these poor rogues lacked the services of an Austrian drum, did they not?"

"Nonetheless," said another horseman, close behind Desmoulins, "a victory gained is a victory, and will be so remembered." He reached across his horse's head to take Condorcet's hand. "You will be famous, Citizen Condorcet." Then his head turned, to allow his pale blue eyes to fall on Nick. The eyes suited his face, entirely pale, with a tight shut mouth and flaring nostrils to his small nose. "And no doubt, Citizen Englishman, the manner of your death will also be famous, and a warning. We do not desire death, citizen, of you, or of anyone. We desire peace, and goodwill. But will we return violence tenfold, a hundredfold, a thousandfold. None shall escape our vengeance once they lift a sword against France." His mouth widened into the semblance of a smile. "And now, General Condorcet, we have a special reward for the victor."

The horses parted, to allow another mount through. The rider was short and slight, with yellow hair floating in the breeze; like Manon Roland, she wore a large hat and a silk gown, and she smiled at the mob who cheered her presence.

"Oh, my God," Nick said. "Aurora?"

"Do not make so free with my wife, you hound of hell," Condorcet said. "Citizeness Condorcet."

Aurora reached the cart, and looked down at Nick. For a moment her face was quite expressionless, then she searched her mouth, slowly and deliberately, and spat in his face.

Nick did not even bother to turn his head; a faceful of saliva did not seem especially unpleasant after his recent experiences. Aurora threw back her head and gave a peal of laughter, while Condorcet grinned his pleasure. "There," he said. "Two very old friends reunited. And now, Manon, I think we will ride away from the cart, and leave our Englishman to these good people. Oh, fear not, we may watch from the windows. It should be very amusing."

So soon? Nick gave a start, suddenly realizing how he had not truly supposed this could ever happen. He was Nicholas Minnett. This could not happen, in fact. He found himself staring at Manon Roland, who was returning his gaze, her face expressionless save for her eyes, and that expression he could not interpret.

"Are you mad, Condorcet?" she asked. "There has been no trial."

"Trial? Trial, for a man captured with arms in his hands opposing the forces of the revolution? I would have been within my rights to have hanged him on the spot."

"But you had more sense," Manon pointed out. "And now it would be doubly mad. This man is Nicholas Minnett. He is a personal friend of Pitt, and he is heir to the House of Minnett. He is the most valuable possession we have in France at this moment, perhaps more valuable than the King himself; and you would carelessly remove his life, in the settlement of some private feud?"

"Valuable? Nick Minnett?" Condorcet demanded.

"Maximilian, I appeal to you," Manon said, pink spots appearing in her cheeks.

The pale man pulled his nose. "There is sense in what you say, Manon. Good sense. He must be imprisoned, while we consider what best advantage we can obtain from his capture. Oh, I understand your desire to have done with him, Louis, but we must never allow ourselves to be led into the paths of blood by personal feelings. Only the good of the State can have any effect upon our decisions."

"Bah," Condorcet said. "His life is of no account."

"I would like to see him hang," Aurora said regretfully.

"Citizen Robespierre is right," Manon Roland said. "This man is far too valuable to be wasted. You will relinquish your prisoner to me, Citizen Condorcet."

"To you?" Condorcet shouted.

"No, no," Desmoulins agreed. "If necessary, we shall appeal," and he looked around at the clustered spectators to leave no one in any doubt to whom his appeal would be directed.

"The Englishman will be closely confined," said the pale man, who was, it seemed, the Maximilian Robespierre of whom Nick had heard. "No doubt he will be glad once again to see the inside of the Conciergerie, of which he must have fond memories."

"Aha," Condorcet cried. "Capital. Capital. It is full of his friends. Ah, you will be safe there, Nick, I promise you. See to it. To the Conciergerie."

Nick turned his head to gaze once again at Manon Roland. Her expression remained cool, but he was sure she was trying to reassure him with her eyes. Manon Roland. She had once expressed an interest in him, and seemed to hate herself for it. Far more likely, she was concerned solely with what she claimed, the possession of him. Yet for either purpose, she would do her best for him, as she saw fit.

The cart was rumbling on, and once again he was surrounded by the baying voices, the demoniac faces which stared at him on every side. But they meant nothing to him now. There were too many other things crowding in upon his consciousness. Aurora de Benoît, or should she now be exclusively Aurora Condorcet. Why had she been absent, last year when the royal family had attempted their escape? Before then she had been the most faithful of maids. And they had been betrayed, there could be no question of that. It was possible to suppose that the whole episode had been allowed by the republicans merely to force the King to commit himself beyond recall. In that case, Aurora might be even more guilty than he supposed.

It had been her own brother's head waving above the cart, and she had shown not the slightest interest, save in seeing Nick's head up there beside Etienne's.

The cart was across the bridge to the Isle de la Cité, and he was once again looking up at the gargoyles of Notre Dame, and then the walls of the prison. At least the jailer was different, but also knowledgeable. "Minnett," he croaked. "Ah, but he has been here before. We know of you, citizen." He seized Nick by the shoulders, the guards having released the bonds holding his ankles, and thrust him through the narrow doorway so violently that he stumbled and fell, his hands being still tied behind his back.

"Up," bawled the jailer. "Up." He kicked Nick in the thighs and then in the ribs, and he struggled to his knees. "We'll have no lounging here. Money. You have money? Turn out your pockets."

Nick reached his feet, sucking air into his lungs, gazed at the barred windows, the pale unshaven faces of the men, the equally pale faces of the women, surrounded by coils of greasy, unwashed and undressed hair, and at one in particular, black eyes sparkling as she clung to the bars and pressed her face against them.

"Nick," Seraphine screamed. "Nick. Oh, Nick."

Her face disappeared in the mass straining for the light, but reappeared almost immediately. Seraphine. In prison, certainly, but so was he now. And she was alive, and as exuberant as ever.

An elbow crashed into his ribs. "Money, lout," said the jailer. "Or you starve."

"I have no money," Nick said. "It was taken from me by the gardes."

"And you a famous merchant," the jailer laughed. "Ah, 'tis the common pit for you, my friend. You can starve with the cutthroats and footpads down there."

"A private cell for this one," said the garde officer, who had followed them into the courtyard. "And bread and wine."

"And who is going to pay for that?" demanded the jailer.

"I have here a paper signed by Citizeness Roland," said the officer. "She'll pay the keep, and you'd best see he comes to no harm."

"Citizeness Roland. Ah, bah." But the jailer thrust Nick toward the steps up which he and Seraphine had climbed that fateful day two years ago. He looked over his shoulder at the women's block, found Seraphine's face, and gave her a smile.

"Nick," she shouted again. "Oh, Nick."

The door was opened, and he was thrust in, and thence into a cell, bare of anything save straw, and stinking. The jailer slit the rope holding his wrists, and he could rub his hands together, after a week, and feel the delicious agony of returning circulation. The officer of the guard stood in the doorway, watching him.

"I thank you, friend," Nick said.

"You have nothing to thank me for, Citizen Minnett," the soldier said. "While it pleases Citizeness Roland to keep you alive, I will see to that. When it pleases her to have you hanged, I shall see to that also."

The door slammed shut, the key turned, and Nick was alone in the darkness.

For an hour in every day the prisoners were allowed into the central courtyard, a milling mass of evil smelling misery, to exchange gossip and despair, and sometimes, a mutual pleasure.

"Nick," Seraphine screamed, pushing people aside as she ran toward him. He caught her in his arms, held her close, wondered if he smelt as noisome. "Oh, Nick," she wept. "What are you doing here?"

"I ask myself that, sweetheart. But you?"

She shrugged, on his chest. "I have been here a year."

"A year? My God."

"Well, you see, after that business . . . Oh, Nick, how I should hate you. How I do hate you." She released him to stamp on his toes. "Hate you, hate you, hate you. You are a despicable monster."

"Believe me, sweetheart, I know that."

"But how I have missed you." She clung to him again. "I went back to St. Suliac. Louis showed me the door. Showed me? His words. He beat me until my bottom was raw, and then he kicked me out. I will show you the mark of his boot still. He called me a whore, Nick. Oh, he was cruel."

"Aye. And so you went home. I looked for you there."

"But that was more than a year gone, Nick. Papa was desolate, and he decided we must leave, when I told him what had happened. Ah, he knows human nature better than I. Or did."

"Where is he now?"

"In heaven, Nick. I am sure of that. We were set upon by a band of robbers, and poor dear Papa was killed. They robbed me of everything I possessed, Nick, and turned me loose."

"But you survived."

"I found work. But I could think of nothing better than to return to St. Malo, where I supposed I had friends. Only then I discovered that as I was no longer Citizeness

Condorcet there was a warrant out for my arrest. My God, I thought I would be hanged on the spot. Instead of which, they sent me to Paris, for interrogation."

Nick was aghast. "They put you to the question?"

"Oh, they showed me the screws, but there was no need to use them. I told them everything. I kept them entertained for hours. At the end of it they sent me here; and left me here. I am quite forgotten. I will rot here, Nick." Her mood had changed again. "Oh, how could you leave me behind, twice? I should scratch your eyes out. I should . . ."

"I am sorry, sweetheart, believe me," Nick said. "Listen to me, should I get out of here, and I think I will, I swear to take you with me."

"Ha."

"This is no trick, Seraphine. You have lain heavily on my conscience these last two years. And now I swear, absolutely and irrevocably, when I leave these walls, you leave with me."

"When? Ha. You think you will escape? You need help, Nick. And who is going to help you, eh? Tell me that."

But that would have involved too much of a risk. Instead he gave her a hug and a kiss; as they were being recalled to their cells, he told her to look forward to tomorrow. As did he. Even in this dire extremity, she was a ray of utter life, alternating sunshine and rain, to be sure, but nonetheless pulsing with humanity. This time he would keep his word. She had once said with prophetic insight, "You are asking me to risk my life, certainly my freedom." Yet had she taken that risk, out of animal passion perhaps, but nonetheless gallantly and effectively. She deserved whatever her reward. So he dreamed of Anne, and would dream of Anne for the rest of his life; Seraphine would soon make other friends, develop for herself another life. He would buy her a little cottage, down in Lyme, and settle on her a pension, and enjoy her happiness—provided, of course, he got out of here.

So instead of Anne he found himself dreaming of Manon Roland, of that face and those firm lips and those glowing eyes. He encouraged himself with the memory of her expression when last he had seen her. But as days became weeks, and spring became summer, and the heat increased the stench and the disease and the misery with which he was surrounded, as more and more people, humble or great, were thrust into the already narrow confines of the prison, as the Austrians and Brunswick made threatening noises, but still failed to cross the frontier, and as the republicans became more and more suspicious of all who did not utterly subscribe to their principles, he found himself beginning to despair. His misery was only alleviated by a visit from the Duke of Sutherland, the British ambassador.

"Nicholas Minnett," Leveson-Gower said, hands on hips. "By God, sir, but you are a sorry sight. Not that you deserve anything better. How mad can a man be?"

"News, George, I beg of you," Nick said.

"I wonder you do not suggest a hand of cards." But he came closer, appeared to look out of the barred window. "You pose us a difficult problem, Nick. Billy will have you out, depend upon it. Yet will it take time, and in Paris sometimes twenty-four hours is too long. Offend no one, I beg of you."

"I'll wait," Nick promised. "If you will tell me Father is well."

"As well as may be expected, with his only son in prison."

"Mama? Lucy?"

"Praying for you, I have no doubt."

"The House?"

Leveson-Gower pulled a face. "One could say it is operating normally. I have recently had a letter from Turnbull informing me that I am exceeding my limit, set by you, as I recall."

"Your limit is this moment removed, George. You have my word. Now, I have a charge for you."

"Carrie?"

"I have no doubt Carrie is taking care of Carrie. There is a girl, living in Lyme, called Anne Yealm. She is my

agent there, for the *Golden Rose*. Have Turnbull see to
her every requirement, George. Promise me that."

The Duke removed his hat, and seemed inclined to remove his wig as well. "You sit here, awaiting death, and
you wish me to see to the welfare of some fisherwoman?"

"Or there will be no credit at all. I do promise you
that."

Leveson-Gower sighed. "Locked away in a French prison, and still the most powerful man in Europe. Anne
Yealm. She shall be taken care of." He turned for the
door, paused, and looked over his shoulder. "Give us
time."

Time. Soon he found himself sharing a cell, but his companion in distress was at once old and ill, and did no
more than lie on his straw, feebly trying to cover himself with his cloak, despite the temperature which was
surely hot enough to cook a meal, and shivered. His misfortunes seemed to have affected his mind, and he did not
seem to realize that Nick was there at all.

For this Nick was grateful. As weeks became months,
for the first time in his life he began to feel fear. Not of
death. Sometimes in the small hours of the morning, as he
lay awake and listened to the groans and screams from
all around him, to the dry cough of his cell mate, he would
have welcomed a tramping of feet which would have indicated a march to the gallows. His fear was of being
forgotten, like Seraphine. It had happened in other French
prisons often enough. Men had lain in the Bastille or in
Vincennes until they had forgotten there was an outside
world.

He prayed for another visit from George Leveson-
Gower, but the Duke did not come. He began to imagine
fears. He had no positive information regarding Anne.
Perhaps she had never regained England. Perhaps in
some way the Monceys had managed to interfere with his
provision for her. Perhaps . . . Perhaps . . .

Sometimes he thought he was about to join his companion in madness. On the thought of Seraphine, busily
going about the business of living in this hell, and then the

presence of her, ready to sing because a guard had carelessly left her an extra crust of bread, or ready to commit
murder because some other prisoner had absently stepped
on her toe, gave him hope. He began to realize that perhaps, in her total absorption with the business of living
every second of every day, she had a better understanding
of the meaning of life than anyone else.

But despair was always lurking, and at times became
unbearable. When, on an August morning, the guard
handed him a letter with his morning meal, he was for a
moment too bemused to open it. Then he snatched at the
envelope, gazed at the clear round hand.

> Minnett. Your father is dead. For this you have my
> sincere condolences. Yet is this fortunate for you.
> The revolutionary tribunal was for condemning you
> to death, and indeed this is no more than you richly
> deserve, for taking arms against the republic, which
> contains within it all that is of hope for the future of
> mankind. In the changed circumstances, however, as
> you are now the head of the House of Minnett, I
> have hopes of prevailing upon them to release you.
> Pitt is adding his efforts to mine, and is prepared to
> offer a ransom for your head, providing it remains
> on your neck. So be of cheer. Your crimes are too
> great for me to consider being your friend, but be
> assured that I am sufficiently interested in keeping
> you alive. The last time you were in Paris you chose
> to betray your trust. Can I believe that the next time
> you will come with fair proposals and truth in your
> heart?
>
> But be also on your guard. There is an increasing
> spirit of anger, justified, in the streets of Paris.
> Should Brunswick move against our armies, it may
> be difficult to answer for the lives of any suspected
> person, even Nicholas Minnett.

There was so signature, but he knew it was from
Manon. Suddenly life became a brighter prospect, and the

dangers which lay head, or the moments of despair, became nothing more than problems, and he was used to solving problems.

"How came you by this?" he asked the guard that evening.

"I found it, citizen."

"Well then, could you take an answer, and leave it where you found this?"

"I could not, citizen. There is no answer. Nor would there matter if there was. You will soon be taken from here, and executed."

"Eh? I have not yet been brought to trial," Nick protested, assuming the fellow was amusing himself.

"Trial? Trial? We have no need to try such as you, citizen. You are an enemy of the state, and we have no more room for enemies of the state. The Austrians have crossed the frontier."

The rumor rippled through the courtyard, seemed carried from person to person in a continuous whisper. Seraphine seized Nick's arm, digging her fingers into his flesh. "Have you heard? The Austrians are in France. They will be here tomorrow."

"Perhaps."

"They will kill all republicans." Her forehead puckered as she seemed about to weep. "To spend so long in this place and then be slaughtered by a horde of Austrians . . ."

"They are unlikely to slaughter any inmate of this prison, sweetheart," he promised her.

"You will look after me, Nick. Swear you will protect me."

"I have already done so. I shall not leave this prison without you, Seraphine."

"Oh Nick, you do love me after all." Her arms went round his neck as she hugged him. Moments later they were separated and driven back to their cells. This day for the first time he was happy once again to be confined. There was too much crowding in upon his mind, apart from his duty to Seraphine. Father. He wondered he felt no greater grief. Of course in many ways it was a blessed relief. To be left a cripple, unable to move even an arm, forced to accept the treatment of a babe, while his brain was still as active as ever. There was horror.

Yet had Father's death placed an enormous responsibility upon him, and he was not there to bear it. Indeed, it had no doubt been criminally irresponsible of him to accompany Etienne on that mad, futile expedition. At least he had learned his lesson, should he survive. But then, he would survive. He had Manon's word for that.

It was impossible not to feel exhilarated. The relief was too great. Had he been afraid? He had despaired, from time to time. He could not deny that. The shelter of the Minnett name had seemed too intangible in this living hell.

He sat up. The gigantic whisper of sound, which had filled the courtyard a few hours earlier, had begun again, seeping through the cell blocks themselves. Doors clanged, voices protested, a woman screamed away in the distance, while outside the prison there came a faint roaring, like surf on a beach, dominated by the melancholy clanging of the tocsin.

His cell mate had heard it also, and ceased dragging his fingers through his beard. Now he also sat up, looked at Nick with his usual private, cunning stare, then got up and peered through the barred window which opened on to the corridor.

"The Austrians," Nick said. "Can they be here already?" His heart pounded.

Again the covert stare, this time over his left shoulder. Then the jaws unclamped, slowly. "There is no gunfire."

How remarkable, Nick thought, that a lunatic should be so clear thinking. Yet there was certainly something happening. A royalist coup perhaps. Feet came closer, sabots thudding on the floor of the passageway. Then the door was hurled in, pushing the madman against the wall. Two of their jailers stood there, but they were accompanied by another man, a huge fellow, naked to the waist, and with a red cap on his head. His appearance, with bloodshot eyes and a fringe of scattered beard, was rendered the more alarming because there were damp red splashes on his chest and shoulders which could only be blood. And he carried a blood-stained sword in his right hand.

"Two more," he said. "Bring them down."

One of the gaolers, the man who had brought the letter from Manon pointed. "That is the Englishman, Minnett."

"He is in prison. There is a certainty of guilt," said the big man. "He must answer for it."

"There has been no trial," Nick said, his exhilaration draining away in a sudden sweat of horror.

The big man grinned at him; his teeth were broken and black. "Oh, there will be a trial, citizen. There will be a trial. Outside."

The lunatic had already been thrust into the corridor. Nick stumbled behind him as the jailer seized his arm and pushed him through the doorway. He gazed at the scene in horror. Most of the cell doors were open, and men were being taken out, begging and sobbing, thrust forward by their guards. The noise welled up from below, and there was a sound of chanting, punctuated by a long scream, which ended as if an axe had fallen. My God, he thought; an axe.

"This is a massacre," he said to the gaoler.

"It is them or us, citizen."

"But . . . what of the letter?"

"I warned you it would not save you, citizen. Paris will save itself."

Another push and he was stumbling down the steps, cannoning into other men. The door to the courtyard was closed, and guarded by four gardes français, but outside the baying noise was tremendous; it seemed all of Paris had assembled there. The prisoners were pushed to their left, into a crowded guardroom, where a table had been set up. Behind it sat two men and a woman, each wearing the red cap, none with the slightest expression of pity or even humanity on their faces. And in this room, Nick was horrified to discover, there were also women. He looked around, and saw no Seraphine. Already dead? Oh my God, he thought.

The table was flanked by gardes français, with fixed bayonets. And the ghastly tragedy was proceeding. "Next," shouted the man in the center of the three judges, and a man was dragged before the table, white hair straggling on to the shoulders of his satin coat, now sadly torn and greased, lips trembling as he tried to keep his nerves under control. And will I be any the bolder when it is my turn, Nick wondered?

"Your name."

The old man coughed. "Philippe Augustus de la Court."

"An aristocrat."

"Once, citizen. I have lived in Paris these three years."

"You are accused of plotting against the republic."

"Accused, citizen? I have been accused of nothing."

"You are in this prison, citizen. Is that not accusation enough? Come, confess your crime."

"I have plotted nothing. I swear it. I know nothing of any plots."

"You have frequented the house of Pierre de Benoît in England. Confess it."

"I visited England last year, citizen, surely. Citizen Benoît is an old friend who is also ill. It was my duty."

"To discuss plots. You have confessed to associating with an enemy of the republic. There is proof enough. How say you?" He glanced to his left.

"Guilty," said the man.

"And you, citizeness?"

The woman grinned at the old man. "Guilty."

"Philippe de la Court, guilty," said the president. "Next."

The old man stared at him. "But I have explained," he cried, his voice slowly rising. "I was visiting an old sick friend. We talked of nothing."

"Next," said the president again, and two of the guards seized de la Court by the arms.

"I am innocent," screamed the man. "I have always supported the revolution. I am for the republic. *Vive la république!*"

The door was immediately in front of him, and the soldiers thrust him forward as one of the guards pulled it open. The noise of the baying voices rose and rushed into the room, and the man tried desperately to dig in his heels, to prevent himself from moving. But the soldiers were too strong for him. He was pushed outside, and the baying became a paean of triumph. Philippe de la Court uttered a single high-pitched scream, followed by a wail which slowly died. The door was slammed shut, and the baying became once again part of the afternoon.

"My God," said the man next to Nick. "Oh my God. There is no hope for any of us."

"Do *you* still hope, Monsieur Minnett?" said another voice, almost at Nick's shoulder.

His heart gave a great lurch, and he turned. Marie Thérèse de Bourbon wore a plain blue gown, and this layered in dust and sweat. Her hair was loosed, and there was no jewelry. He had never seen her other than elegant and utterly beautiful. Now she was disheveled, and that magnificent auburn hair was streaked with gray; but she was still utterly beautiful. Auburn hair? He realized it was the first time he had seen her without a wig. "Your Grace." He seized her hands.

She smiled, and shook her head. "I am Citizeness Bourbon, Mr. Minnett, as you would do well to remember."

"But . . . here?"

"Oh, I am become used to the interior of prisons. I was in La Force until yesterday. Then I was transferred to the Conciergerie, although I did not suppose I would reach here alive. Paris has gone mad, it seems."

"But you still hope."

Her fingers tightened on his. "Answer me first."

Gently he brought her forward, until she leaned against him, gazing at him with wide eyes. After months in prison, after the hunger and the filth and the despair of all of that time, this remained the woman he would most admire, throughout his life. And now his face was against her hair. "I hope, Marie. I hope, with reason. And this I swear, that I shall take you with me."

Her head moved, her face turned up, her eyes once again searched his face. "And this time I will come, Mr. Minnett. You may believe I have often wished I had accompanied you last year."

But you will accompany me now, he thought. My God, what am I doing? Am I that susceptible, or do I merely wish to take all the female sex beneath my protection? And this woman was actually old enough to be his mother. Why, she could be Anne Yealm in twenty years' time, in every way. Could any man have ever been so blessed as to know two such women, or perhaps to have known but one such woman, but at two different stages of her life?

Her lips were parted. Gently he lowered his own, and was interrupted by the shout of "next," booming in his ear, at the same moment as fingers dug into his arm.

The princess continued to gaze at him, the dismay and terror in her own face no doubt reflecting the expression in his. Slowly their fingers released each other as he was dragged backward across the room, and turned to face his judges. He discovered that he was trembling. He had never supposed himself afraid of death before, but death had been anticipated from illness, surrounded by his family, at sea, fighting to keep *Golden Rose* afloat, or, more recently, from a sword thrust or a flying bullet. Death at the hands of a baying mob was a wholly different concept.

"Nick," came a scream from the other side of the room. "Oh, Nicky." Seraphine attempted to burst through the cordon of watching soldiers, and was seized and hurled back. Seraphine. How long had she been there? But at least she was there, and still alive. Seraphine. Another woman he had promised to protect.

"Your name," said the judge.

"Nicholas Minnett."

"You are the English agent provocateur."

"I am an English banker."

"Banker, bah. We have no more bankers in France."

"Then perhaps you should discover a few, citizen," Nick retorted, amazed at his own courage. But suddenly he was aware of that rumbling anger which seemed to seize him at moments of peril. By God, he thought; condemn me to death, and I shall at the least throttle you before they drag me out.

The president was staring at him, but the judge on the right had been peering at the list in front of him, and now he was whispering to his superior.

"Aye," said the president. "There are matters for which you must answer, Citizen Minnett. Be sure you shall. But the moment is not yet. Hold him in custody."

A rush of air came up through Nick's lungs and forced itself from his nostrils. He could not really believe that he had been reprieved. Surely this was Manon's doing. She was working for him, and overlooking him, from a distance. His guardian angel. But would she also be a guardian angel to Seraphine Condorcet and the Princess de Lamballe?

"Next," the judge was shouting, and he was thrust back into the ranks of prisoners. He searched their faces, and watched her being taken out. Her cheeks were pale, her mouth tight closed. There might have been a tear in her eye, but she tossed her head to dispel it, and then saw him looking for her and gave a quick smile. He turned, was sucked back into the people around him, and looked past their heads as she was placed before the table, a small, slight, utterly splendid figure between the two guards.

"Your name?"

"Marie Thérèse de Bourbon."

"Ah," said the president. "You are the Queen's creature."

The princess gazed straight into his face. "I have the privilege to be the Queen's friend, citizen."

"Which is the same thing. There are many crimes attributed to you, citizeness. You are accused of having had a share in the plot to secrete the King and Queen and take them from France, in the spring of last year."

The princess tossed her head again. "And thus I remained in the Tuileries after they had gone, citizen?"

The president met her gaze for a moment, and then lowered his own, to the paper. "You are accused of having secretly corresponded with the enemies of the republic, of being a sympathizer with the Austrians."

"I am a Frenchwoman, sir," the princess said. "I was born a Frenchwoman, and I shall die a Frenchwoman. I have no love for the Austrians. I have taken part in no plots. I have but done my duty, which is to serve my mistress the Queen. I have ever supposed that, in so doing, I have also been serving France. Should it be decided that my duty lies elsewhere, then show me that direction and be sure that I shall follow it with equal devotion. But do not accuse me of plots against my country."

The room had fallen silent at the quiet voice speaking so clearly and with such deliberate self-confidence. The judges stared at their would-be victim, and then at each other, and then at their lists. Finally they looked at each other again. "I find the accused acquitted," said the president.

"Acquitted," said the man on his left.

"Acquitted," said the woman on his right.

"Marie Thérèse de Bourbon gazed at them for a moment in disbelief.

"Be off with you, citizeness," said the president. "Next."

The guards held her arms and moved her aside, marched her to the door. She turned her head and gazed into the crowd, perhaps seeking him, Nick thought. But she was free, and saved. She no longer needed his assistance; indeed, it might yet be he who needed her.

The door was opened, and the baying reached a new crescendo at the sight of the slight female figure.

"She is acquitted," shouted the soldier holding her arm.

The noise grew to a screech, as of all the devils in hell.

"Acquitted," the soldier shouted again. "You are to let her pass."

He stepped aside, and the princess was alone in the doorway. She stared outside, and then half turned her head, as if she would seek some support from inside the prison.

"You must go," said the soldier.

The princess hesitated, for a last moment, then she tucked her fingers into her skirt slightly to raise it from the ground, lifted her chin in that so memorable gesture of defiance, and stepped outside, beside the garde français who stood there.

"Acquitted," the man bawled. "Acquitted, by God." He swung his sword, and struck her on the nape of her neck.

Twelve

Nick never knew whether or not the Princess died instantly. He could only watch in horror, as did everyone else in the room. Marie Thérèse de Bourbon's knees gave way as if she were a puppet, and her master had released the strings; she collapsed in a heap on the step, while blood flowed from her neck and soaked her gown. Even the baying of the crowd outside was muted, for a moment, while inside the room it was possible to hear the sound of breathing.

The murderer was also silent, for a moment. Then he raised his head, and inflated his chest, almost like a gorilla. "The Queen's spy," he shouted. "There she lies, the Queen's spy."

The president of the court was on his feet. "I had pronounced her free," he shouted. "We had all pronounced her free."

"Bah," yelled the assassin in reply. "You are a stupid old man, afraid of a woman, afraid of a name. She was the Queen's intimate. She confessed to that, before you. And we all know the Queen is an Austrian bitch, intent upon bringing us to the gallows. Do you deny that, old man?"

"I had set her free," muttered the president. He sat down again. "You have committed murder."

"I have executed a spy," the big man insisted, and turned again to the mob outside. "Is she not a spy?"

"A spy," they roared. "A spy. You have executed a spy. Raise her up. Raise her up, Santerre. Let us look at her."

"Look at her," Santerre bellowed. "Aye, you shall look

at her. You. And you. Strip the carcass. You. And you. Bring water. They called her the most beautiful bitch in the empire. Bring water, and we shall wash her clean, and strip her naked, and you may judge for yourselves."

"Aye," they screamed, men and women and children. "Bring water, and strip her, that we may look at the spy."

"My God," Nick shouted, trying to force his way forward. "Will you permit such a . . . such an obscenity? The woman is dead. Is that not crime enough?"

A hand seized his arm, jerked him to one side, even as the man Santerre once again peered into the room, seeking the cause of the outburst.

"Would you lie beside her?" demanded the guard who had acted as Manon Roland's messenger.

"I would rather that than watch her body defiled."

"Then would you be a fool. As you have just said, the woman is dead. No matter what they do to her, it is nothing, compared with that fact."

Nick frowned at the man; his vision seemed to be obscured with a red mist. Yet he recognized that this was hardly the surly brute who had helped to march him down from his cell. Had he been acting then, or now?

The jailer winked. "They are distracted. You are to come with me. Quickly now. There may be no second chance."

They had retreated against the wall. Around them, prisoners, jailers, soldiers, were all watching the exposure of the Princess de Lamballe's body, while beyond the doorway the crowd bayed their delight.

"Out there?"

The jailer shook his head. "Another way. A secret way."

And what could he do, but die beside her? Manon was giving him the chance to live, and perhaps avenge. And Seraphine had taught him how to live, from moment to moment, day to day, to draw breath every morning and say, "At least I am alive."

"There is someone I will bring with me."

"I was paid for you, Englishman. There can be no one else."

"Then you will be paid for no one at all, my friend, for I shall stay."

The man chewed his lip with indecision.

"A moment," Nick said, and once again slipped into the crowd. People gazed at him, curiously, but he could not compare with the ghastly attraction being presented in the doorway as the dead body of the most beautiful woman in France was seized by the hair and dragged half to its feet to face the crowd.

"Water," Santerre shouted. "Bring more water. She is still bleeding."

Nick reached into the throng, seized Seraphine by the shoulder. She gave a little shriek, turned her head, saw him, and fell silent. He dragged her to the back.

"Oh, my God," she said. "Nick. Do you see what they are doing? Do you hear them, Nick? They say they will cut out her heart and present it to the Queen."

The jailer scratched his head, removing the red cap to do so. "A woman? Englishman, you are mad."

"She comes, or I stay," Nick said.

The jailer shrugged, and turned away. A door at the rear of the room stood open, and they followed him down a corridor.

"Nick?" Seraphine whispered. "What is happening to us, Nick?"

"Someone is keeping her word to me, and I am keeping my word to you, for a change. Now be quiet."

He held her hand, and they hurried through a maze of passageways, past empty cells, the doors of which swung open. The howling, baying noise behind them receded, slowly, and they went down a flight of stone steps, oozing damp. The jailer opened a postern gate, and they stood on the banks of the Seine; the water rushed by only a few inches from their toes. Nick was amazed to discover it was still afternoon, although dark with clouds and chill with a gusty wind which created wavelets even in the river.

"Oh dear," Seraphine said, "another river? I do not like rivers."

"They have a way of taking one to freedom," Nick promised her. The jailer was searching amongst the piles to the left, and now pulled on a painter, to bring a dinghy down to the landing stage. He stepped in, fumbled under the seat, and passed up two red woollen caps. "Put these on."

"And they will suffice?"

The jailer grinned. "Monsieur has not looked in a mirror recently. You resemble the most bloodthirsty of all sans culottes, my friend. Now get in."

Nick handed Seraphine down; she collapsed into the bilges, and he sat above her. The jailer unshipped the oars, released the painter, and the current swept the boat into the stream. Moments later they were free of the island, and the shadow of the prison; Nick had to blink his eyes as they watered in the sudden glare of the September afternoon. It was six months since he had seen more than a glimpse of the sun.

"Free," Seraphine whispered, and raised her head, able at last even to look at the water without shuddering. "Free," she shouted. "Will this boat take us to the sea?"

"I doubt that, sweetheart," Nick said. "I doubt that."

The jailer was already pulling for the bank, not fighting the current but merely guiding his small craft to the right, until it slipped into another dock. "Quickly now."

He tethered the painter, and the three of them scrambled ashore. Then he was off again, leading them through the maze of alleyways which clustered the waterfront, while around them Paris seethed, and people shouted or screamed, and muskets were fired, and the tocsin clanged in a steady, mournful dirge. Every so often they encountered bands of marauding sans culottes, but as the jailer had promised, they were greeted with cheers, slapped on the back, given half empty bottles of vin rouge to drink, and invited to join the festivities. Once they had to halt on a street corner, and chant and cheer with the mob as some unhappy man, stripped to his shirt, was slowly hoisted, kicking and gasping, to the top of a lantern post, and left there to dangle to his death. But at last they gained an empty street and a side door, and a knock from the jailer gained them admittance into a darkened hall.

"Two gifts, from the Conciergerie," said the jailer.

A candle was thrust into their faces. "Two?" asked Joachim Castets.

"By heaven," Nick said. "I should have known you would be involved. Shall I throttle you now, or wait a more appropriate time?"

"You would do well to thank me, Mr. Minnett. But we contracted for no doxy."

Seraphine once again seized Nick's hand.

"Yet does she accompany me, or I will return to the street."

Castets hesitated, while the jailer stamped his sabot. "I have not been paid the balance."

"You will be paid," Castets promised. "Sit down, sir, in that kitchen. You will find a bottle, and I am sure you are famished after your journey. Mr. Minnett, you had best come with me."

"And I, citizen?" Seraphine demanded.

Once again Castets hesitated, peering at her and then at Nick from beneath the flickering light of the candle. "Aye," he said at last. "You too, citizeness."

He led them up a flight of stairs, and they escaped the gloom of the boards which had covered the downstairs window. Castets doused his candle, and rapped on a door. It was opened by a somewhat severe-looking woman, dressed entirely in black.

"Take this young woman," Castets said.

"No," Seraphine shouted. "I'll not leave you, Nick."

Castets sighed. "And have her bathed, and dressed in something decent. One hour, citizeness."

"No," Seraphine muttered.

"It would be best, sweetheart," Nick said. "I think they mean us well. And you will remember, Monsieur Castets, that I go nowhere without her."

"I will remember."

"Come in, child. Come in," said the woman in black.

"Food," Seraphine said, releasing Nick. "Is that chicken stew I smell? Oh, citizeness, I am so hungry."

The door closed, and Castets was hurrying Nick to another one. Here he found himself in one of those shabbily splendid withdrawing rooms he had come to expect in Paris of the revolution; this one was dominated by an enormous hip bath in the very center of a once priceless carpet.

"You will undress, Mr. Minnett," Castets said. "Those rags are scarce fit for burning."

The door closed, and Nick discovered that he was alone. For the first time in two months. Alone, and not immediately in danger of his life. He crossed the room, stared at himself in the mirror. His beard was black and straggled. His hair was lank, and hung on his shoulders, like a disordered wig. His once fine clothes were threadbare, and stiff with dirt. He found it incredible that the Princess de Lamballe should have been able to recognize him.

The Princess de Lamballe. He wondered he felt no extreme revulsion. Strangely, all he felt at the moment was guilt. And this surely was unjustified. For a few seconds he had supposed her the fortunate one.

He took off his coat, threw it on the floor, joined it with the rest of his clothes. He watched the door open, in the mirror, and saw two men bringing in steaming pitchers of water, which they emptied into the bath. They returned once again, and then he was ready. They did not even look at him, and he decided it was best to wait, to see what next Castets had in store for him. Castets. Probably the guiltiest man in France, looked at from the point of view of any single party. And yet a friend in need.

Nick sank into the tub, almost screamed with the delight of feeling the hot water seeping over his system, already beginning to melt away the accumulated grease and dirt of a six months' imprisonment. He raised his head as the door once again opened, watched Manon Roland enter the room.

* * *

She carried a soap filled bowl, a brush, and a razor, smiled at his obvious embarrassment. "Oh come now, Mr. Minnett. I am a wife of more than twenty years. And you are also married, I believe. Although your wife would scarcely recognize you now."

But she, at least, was instantly recognizable. She had changed not at all since their first meeting. All the tension and all the disappointments she must have suffered in the past two years had marked her face not at all, and her eyes were as clear as ever. Now she knelt beside him, scooping up her pale blue gown to make room for her knees.

"I hardly know what to say," he said, "except to thank you."

"And even that should keep." She wet her brush, leaned forward to lather his chin. "Before I pick up my razor, you had best explain this creature you seem to have accumulated."

"Creature? She is Seraphine Condorcet."

Manon rocked back on her heels to frown at him. "I hope you would not lie to me, Mr. Minnett. At least on a personal matter."

"Perhaps you should ask her."

"Seraphine Condorcet," she said, and began lathering again. "I am glad, Mr. Minnett. Perhaps there is hope for you yet."

"I have searched for her, these two years," Nick said.

"And found her by chance. And will take her to freedom." She smiled. "I was prepared to be strict; but I imagine I can discover another passport." She stropped the blade. "Almost I am proud of you, Mr. Minnett."

"If you were not before, Manon, why did you go to this trouble, and this risk, to pull me from that mob?"

She placed her hand on his chest, gently pushed him back into the warm embrace of the water. Then she began to stroke the razor down his chin, holding his face steady with the thumb and forefinger of her left hand. She concentrated, and her face became set, and tense, and absorbing in its character. "Because you are valuable, Nick. But there is a difference between value and admiration. Now they are come together."

"Yet did I betray you once."

Still the razor stroked, slowly up and down; now her tongue emerged from between her teeth, caught by her lips. "You were obeying the orders of your master. This I have discovered. I correspond with your Mr. Pitt, Nick. Oh, clandestinely, to be sure. I do all manner of remarkable and occasionally objectionable tasks, for the good of France"—once again she leaned away from him, to admire her work—"even down to shaving escaped convicts who are enemies of my country, at least on the surface."

Nick stroked the suddenly clean flesh. "And you do so, admirably."

"Oh indeed. I would also cut your throat, admirably, did I suppose my country would benefit from it. But Mr. Pitt will discuss nothing, save you are safely back behind your desk in Threadneedle Street. So be it."

"And what would *you* discuss?"

She commenced work on his other cheek, leaning across the tub to do so. Her left arm brushed his face, and he inhaled the scent of her flesh. "Ah well, there is a problem. As Mr. Pitt and I would discuss different things, Nick, I have some hope that you will at least show as much gratitude to me as you have to Seraphine Condorcet." She cleaned her razor, stroked again. "The monarchy is finished. The Prussian invasion has finally decided that; this is what I have always foreseen, have always anticipated. Do you know, Nick, once, when I was but a girl, and long before I met Roland, I visited Paris, and was taken to Versailles. I suppose I was eighteen; I cannot remember. There, for the first time, I was made to feel like dirt. I speak four languages, Nick. I am an expert in history, and in foreign affairs, and I write a fair hand. I am content with a needle, happy in my kitchen. I lack only experience of motherhood, and for that I am not alone responsible. I am told I am not without charm and not without beauty. Surely I am the equal of any woman in the empire, any woman in the world."

"You are superior to most."

She smiled; she remained enough of a woman to appreciate flattery.

"Yet was I made, on that occasion, to feel like horse dung, because I had no patent of nobility. That is not the way we were meant to live, Nick. In the beginning, we elevated certain distinguished men, and a few distinguished women, to lead us into battle, to promulgate just laws for all. Somewhere in history that admirable concept became debased and corrupted. You have, I believe, spoken with both of the Capets. Have they, has anyone, the right to treat me like dirt?"

"No."

"Then, you see, you are a republican like myself. Take away the magic of kingship, and what have you?"

"We took it away a hundred years ago, Manon, and have been the happier for it, I agree."

"We delayed, and are the more miserable for it. Hark."

She had finished, and now rested the blade on the carpet. And as he listened, he heard the waves of sound coming toward them.

"They are approaching," she said. "They have accomplished some great deed. But you do not have to be afraid. They still love the Rolands." She stood up, handed him a towel, then went to the window.

"But there is your fallacy," Nick said, as he stood up in turn and dried himself. "They must be ruled."

"As people, not cattle. They . . ." her voice died, as she stared through the window, and the noise of the shouting seemed to shroud the entire house.

"What is the matter?" Nick hurried to her side, felt the blood drain from his own face. The mob swayed, linking arms and chanting, while their leaders stood in front, pikes held high, thrusting them up at the windows. Nick gazed at the features of the princess, uncannily calm even in death, shrouded in tangled auburn hair which seemed to mingle with the blood which still dripped from her neck.

But the head was not alone. Pikes on either side flourished her breasts, others brandished even more intimate portions of her body. "Oh Christ," Nick muttered, and it was a prayer for vengeance. He realized that she must quite literally have been torn apart.

Manon Roland drew the curtains with a tremendous gesture, and remained staring at the velvet cloth, hands still twined in the material.

"That," Nick said, and he did not recognize his own voice, "is not dirt?"

"They have been wronged," Manon said. "Cruelly wronged. For too long."

"By the princess? There was no sweeter human being alive."

Manon's shoulders trembled, and tears rushed down her cheeks. "So the innocent suffer. Who can say who the next will be? The princess was a friend of Marie Antoinette's. She was happy to be that, for too long. There is her crime. Now you must leave, and quickly."

"And suppose I would rather stay here, and die, taking as many of that scum with me as I could?"

"You are a sensible man, Nick. Surely. Where would be the value in that? You would not command a line in history. Whereas, were you to live and take your part, you will command chapters. There is much to happen, during your lifetime and mine, Nick. We stand on the threshold of the greatest events in all history, and we are in the center of them."

"Then tell me what you foresee? The King and Queen?"

She hesitated. "They cannot survive, Nick, as King and Queen. Yet will we try to arrange their survival, as human beings."

"It will mean war, between England and France."

"Perhaps. But more as a gesture, perhaps, than out of conviction. It will be up to people like us to see that it is as short and bloodless as possible." She seized his arm, looked into his face. "Work for Pitt; there is your duty. But work also for me, Nick, because there is your destiny."

"And when Brunswick takes Paris? Then you will know

what it is like to be at the mercy of a mob, and these will be Prussian hussars, not French sans culottes."

"Brunswick will never take Paris, Nick. Those people out there may be capable of acts of bestiality, but they are also capable of heroism. They have only just discovered that they are alive, so in their exuberance they destroy beauty; they will surely die before they will consent once again to enslavement. A nation, Nick, given that determination, cannot be defeated."

There could be no argument with such conviction.

"And will I ever see you again, Manon?"

"Yes, Nick. Yes. When I have tamed that mob, then will you be more than welcome in Paris."

He gazed at the parted lips, the burning eyes, and remembered that both Marie Antoinette and Marie Thérèse de Bourbon had used almost identical words.

Manon saw the disbelief in his eyes. "But you will have to help me accomplish that, Nick. Promise me."

He sighed, and nodded.

"Then listen. I must leave you now. I have stayed too long as it is. Over there you will find clothes. Your own clothes, Nick, delivered by a special messenger. Outside you will find Castets, and your Citizeness Condorcet, and passports for the pair of you. Now listen. I arranged it with Pitt. You will ride for Rouen. Remember, Nick, Rouen. Not Le Havre."

"And will I find a ship in Rouen?"

She smiled. "Your own *Golden Rose*. I told you, I arranged it with Pitt. Almost certainly you will be pursued, at some stage, and it would be too dangerous to send you on a French ship, or even the Channel packet, supposing you could make Havre without being overtaken. Rouen is nearer, and you will know how to con your own vessel. It has called in the way of trade, and but waits for a cargo before departure. It has been cleared by the authorities, who know nothing of its part in Brittany. Once on board her, I trust you will be safe; the lower stretches of the Seine are too wide to worry about cannon. Now go, and reach England safely, that you may visit Paris again, safely." Her fingers ate into his flesh, and she reached up, kissed him briefly on the cheek, and then was gone.

For some seconds Nick remained staring at the door. Too much had happened in the past twenty-four hours, too quickly. He would have savored his meeting with the princess for days; but that was overladen by the horror and the unexpectedness of her death. He would have remained in a state of angry shock for days, but that had been overladen by the suddenness of his removal from prison, the delight of once again meeting the incomparable Manon. He would have remained in a state of pleasant relaxation for days, had it not been for the ghastly sight at the window, the dismemberment and mutilation of so lovely and so splendid a woman. But now again his horror and his anger were caught up in the excitement of knowing that the *Golden Rose* was here, in France, only a few miles away, indeed, and waiting for him.

And with the *Golden Rose,* Anne? After all these months, all these misfortunes, all these horrors, Anne was there, waiting in Rouen? In Rouen? Now the horror returned. Anne, seized as a spy? Anne, confined in the hideous recesses of the Conciergerie? Anne, delivered to a mob and torn apart?

He panted, and rushed at his clothes, dragged them on, and burst outside on to the gallery, to find Castets and Seraphine waiting for him. Seraphine had been given new clothes to wear, although they were several sizes too large. She had also eaten, apparently; there was gravy on her chin. And she was once again happy.

"Nick," she screamed, and threw herself into his arms. "I am to be your wife. Is that not splendid?"

Nick grasped her wrists to disengage himself and frowned at Castets. "What farce is this?"

"It is on the passport, Mr. Minnett," the little man explained. "Citizeness Roland decided it would be least likely to arouse suspicion if you traveled as man and wife. See, it is written here, Citizen Manet and Citizeness Manet,

traveling to Rouen on official business. Here is a brief-
case with a government stamp, and everything."

Nick took the documents, scrutinized them. They meant
his life. And Seraphine's. And perhaps Anne's and Manon's, as well.

"Just for a night, Nicky," Seraphine said, squeezing his
arm. "Just for a night. It will be all I ask."

"When can we leave?"

"Whenever you are ready, Mr. Minnett," Castets assured him, and looked into the room he had just left. "But
you have not eaten."

"Eaten?" Nick demanded. "Were you not at the window just now? Did you not see?"

"Ah," the spy said, "the Princess. It is sad. Such a
pretty woman. But the dead must bury the dead in these
times, Mr. Minnett. The living have enough to do merely to
keep themselves in that state."

"And she was an aristocrat," Seraphine pointed out.
"Here, I will carry the food." She ran inside, seized the
bottle and the bread. "You will soon become hungry. I
will be a good wife, Nick, you may rely on that."

"Aye," Nick said. "Well, let us begone."

"There are horses outside," Castets said. "Yours has
two pistols, and so has the lady's."

"Pistols?"

The little man laid his finger on his nose. "This time,
Mr. Minnett, it would be unwise for you to be taken alive.
I do not think even Madame Roland could save you then."

"And you are not coming with us?"

"My business is here." Castets was already leading them
down a flight of stairs and toward the door to the courtyard. Nick wondered what game he was playing now,
sure he was that they would not escape.

Seraphine at least had no doubts. She squeezed his
arm. "At last, Nicky. At last, I am actually going with
you. Oh Nick, I am so happy."

They stepped into the yard, where the drizzle had become steady, and was now being pushed along by a breeze

from the east. It would no doubt be a throughly unpleasant night.

They mounted, and Nick checked the primings on the
pistols. These at the least were genuine.

"I will wish you God speed," Castets said. "Even if
that is an outmoded expression in France today. Perhaps
we shall meet again, Mr. Minnett."

"I have no doubt at all that we shall, Monsieur
Castets." He raised his head to gaze at the windows to
the house, but saw nothing in the rapidly gathering darkness.

"I will open the gates," Castets said. "Now remember,
sir, give no impression of haste. Walk your horses until
you are clear of the barriers, and then give all the spur
you may. And avoid crowds. They will hardly suspect
you, but they may well force you to some act of horror."

Nick nodded, and walked his horse forward, Seraphine
at his side. The gates swung open, and they emerged on
to the street, empty now, as the dusk and the rain had
driven most of the mob indoors. Although he could still
hear chanting in a distant part of the city, where, no
doubt, the tragic princess's remains were still being displayed in triumph.

"Oh Nick," Seraphine muttered, her mood changing with
its invariable rapidity, "I am so afraid."

"Then conceal it. Ride straight, and with confidence."

He set what example he could, guiding them down a
succession of side streets. As Castets had said, it was a
task he had performed before, with Etienne disguised as
this very woman at his back. But then, perhaps, he had
not quite understood the possibilities were he taken.

They waited in an archway, praying that their horses
would make no sound, while a band of roisterers approached and passed them, singing the *Marseillaise*, the
tune he had first heard rising from Condorcet's army as it
had marched to victory; they were brandishing weapons,
dragging some screaming victim in the direction of the
river. Nick could almost hear Seraphine shudder, but the
people were too drunk at once with liquor and with lust

and with power, to notice them, and only a few moments later they were at the barrier, where half a dozen gardes français lounged in the doorway to a pension.

"Halt there," shouted the sergeant.

"Keep your courage, sweetheart," Nick muttered. "It will be but a few moments more." He reined his horse. "Good night to you, sergeant."

The sergeant pulled his bicorne lower over his eyes as he came into the rain, still carrying his glass of wine. "No one may leave the city this night, citizen. Surely you have heard the proclamation?"

Nick sighed, loudly. "Oh aye, citizen; I have heard the proclamation. But apparently it does not apply to servants of the Rolands. Do you not suppose I would rather be home in bed, with my pretty wife, than riding through the rain?"

"Girondins?" The sergeant peered at Seraphine, who allowed him a brief glimpse of her face before drawing her pelisse closer about her. "You have papers?"

"Of course I have papers." Nick pulled out the wallet. "Jean Manet at your service. And Citizeness Manet. I should be obliged if you'd not get them wet."

Two of the guard had followed their commander into the street. "Read those," the sergeant said to one of them, "in the light."

The man nodded, and took the wallet into the house.

"He was a lawyer," the sergeant said, and grinned. "It is good, to have a lawyer, in one's command. How is the city, citizen?"

Nick had been looking beyond the barrier, at the empty cobbled street which led between the houses. Out there was surely safety, as everyone who would destroy the aristocracy would be inside this night. "Oh gay, sergeant. Gay."

"Aye," the sergeant said, with satisfaction. "We have dealt with the traitors tonight. Ah, my friend, it should have happened too long ago. They say we have done for ten thousand."

"That could well be so, sergeant."

"Aye. Then we shall not have them at our backs when the Prussians come, eh? And then we shall kill another ten thousand. Did you see the princess?" He gave a roar of laughter. "A man was by just now who says they are going to shoot her legs from a cannon. There is sport, eh?"

"Great sport, sergeant," Nick said. "Saw her? Why, I was there when she was struck down."

"You were there, citizen. Then let me shake your hand." The sergeant reached up to squeeze Nick's fingers, and winked. "I am envious. Was she as pretty as they claim?"

"Oh pretty, citizen. Pretty. A devil disguised as an angel. Ah, it was a sight I shall always remember."

"Sergeant." The lawyer returned from the house, waving the wallet. "The papers are in order, sergeant. But the name is not on the list."

"Well then," Nick said, "you will see that I am not a dangerous fellow, sergeant. May we pass? This rain gets no drier."

The sergeant pulled his nose. "You do not understand, citizen. That list is of citizens who *may* pass."

"Eh? What nonsense are you speaking?" Nick cried, feeling his stomach begin to fill with lead. "My papers are in order."

"Oh indeed, citizen," the sergeant agreed, "and no one may pass in any event, without the necessary papers. But as an additional safeguard, Citizen General Condorcet has issued all the barriers with a list, of everyone who will be needed to leave the city this night, and your name is not on it."

"Citizen General Condorcet?" Nick demanded.

"Oh, my God," Seraphine muttered.

"But how could the Citizen General foresee who would have to leave, and who would not?" Nick inquired, keeping his voice calm with an effort. "This is official business I travel on. In the rain, sergeant. In the rain."

"It is hard, citizen. This I know." His face brightened. "But not so hard. The Citizen General is but a mile from here. He gave me an address to which I could refer in case of doubt. So, Citizen, if you and the lady will come inside and have a glass of wine with me, I shall send one of my men, and I swear that within an hour the Citizen General will be here personally to sign your passports. Oh, he is a beaver for work, that Condorcet. Citizeness, may I assist you down?"

"Ride," Nick shouted, and snatched the pistols from his holsters. His first shot brought down the sergeant, his second went scattering into the totally surprised soldiers. Seraphine was already urging her mount forward, for once wasting no time in argument or recrimination, and now she leapt the barrier with all the practiced skill of the country girl. Nick was immediately behind her, digging his spurs into the horse's flank to make the animal respond.

"Shoot them down," screamed the sergeant from the ground, where he had fallen. "Shoot them down."

The gardes lined up along the barrier, and musket fire rippled into the air.

"But that corner," Nick shouted. "But that corner, and we are safe."

"Oh, God," Seraphine screamed, as her horse cascaded over the wet cobbles. "Oh, God. Oh . . ." She released the reins and tumbled over her horse's neck.

Nick reined in with all the force he could manage, leapt from the saddle, knelt beside her. She lay on her face, gasping for breath. And behind him, feet ran on the cobbles.

He stood up, snatched the two pistols from Seraphine's horse, which had fortunately stopped beside its rider. As the first of the gardes came round the bend, he fired, and the man hastily retreated, returning shot, but without taking aim. It had indeed been the merest mischance that Seraphine had been hit.

"Oh God," she moaned, trying to get to her knees, and falling again. "Oh God. I am bleeding, Nick. Leave me here. They can only return me to prison. Leave me here, Nick."

"Not this time, sweetheart." He seized her round the waist, remounted, setting her on the saddle in front of him. Another bullet came perilously close to his head, and he discovered that he had lost his hat; the rain was pounding on his hair. "Come on," he bawled at the free horse, and kicked his own once more into action. Sparks struck from the cobbles as the iron shoes scattered across the surface, and then he was round another bend, and the houses were beginning to thin. "We're through," he said. "Now for Rouen."

"Rouen," she whispered, and put both arms round his body. He released the rein for a moment to give her a squeeze, and discovered his fingers to be sticky.

"Are you in pain?" he shouted into her ear.

"Just a little," she said. "It is nothing. Nothing. Oh Nicky, you could have left me. You should have left me; but you didn't. You must love me, Nicky. After all, you must love me, just a little."

He looked down at her face, turned up to him, suddenly chalky white even in the darkness. "Aye," he said. "I love you, sweetheart. More than a little." He pulled rein.

"Why are we stopping?" She attempted to sit straight, and sighed, then fell back into his arms.

"Because you are losing too much blood." He dismounted, carrying her with him. How heavy she was. Or perhaps he was more weary than he had supposed.

The second horse came up to them, and paused beside its companion. Nick laid Seraphine on the side of the road, attempted to unfasten her gown, encountered ribbons and bows and all manner of ties.

"You will have to help me, sweetheart," he said. "We have not that much time."

She made no reply, and he frowned into her face, then lowered his head still further, to touch the wet cheeks with his own. It was September, and the rain was not cold, but her cheek was like ice.

He knelt, by her side, his head bowed, the rain drumming on his face and neck and shoulders, while the horses waited patiently. He supposed he wept. It was difficult to decide, with the water in any event pouring down his cheeks. And no doubt, he thought, with that part of his brain which always remained disengaged from any emotion, any participation in what was happening about him, he was overstrained by the utterly horrifying events of this day. But now for the second time in twenty-four hours he had watched a friend die.

The earth shook to the sound of hooves. For some moments the sound of them scarce penetrated his consciousness. Here was more than a friend. Here was a companion in the art of subterfuge which he had perfected, a companion in bed for some of the tumultuously happy moments of his life. Here was a woman he had twice betrayed. In fact, her life was his charge, and as with so many other lives, he had forfeited it at the end.

The noise came closer, and he raised his head. He retained a single unfired pistol. He could settle one of them, at the least. Perhaps Condorcet would be at their head.

But what then? *Golden Rose* waited for him in Rouen, with Anne and Tom Price on board. They would wait, and wait, and wait, those two, until he came, or until they were arrested.

He stood for a moment longer, looking down at the still body of the dead woman, then he leapt into the saddle and kicked the horse once more. Behind him there came a shout, and on the still rising wind he heard the sound of a shot. But the range was far too great, and now he was away again, galloping down the road, looking to his left at the gently flowing river, the ultimate highway which would carry him to safety. He looked over his shoulder at the cluster of horsemen, only occasionally visible as they topped a rise, coming, always coming. But not gaining.

He rode. And rode and rode and rode. It is some sixty miles from Paris to Rouen, and he could not remember how long it took him. His horse began to wheeze and stumble. He dismounted, and changed to the faithful companion who had accompanied them all the way. But still the pursuers clung to his heels. He clattered across bridges and through towns and villages. People opened their windows to stare at him, and then hastily closed them again. Tonight was no time to be abroad. The tocsin had no doubt sounded throughout France.

And then, the city. The wind was now whistling, and the branches of the trees were waving like signalers. But the rain had stopped, and the sky was beginning to clear. It would be a brief storm. He did not care about the weather. Tomorrow he would be in mid-Channel, at the helm of the *Rose,* and the horror that was France would be forgotten.

Supposing he gained the ship. "Halt," shouted the guard on the barrier, and the horse instinctively checked.

"Ride," Nick bellowed, kicking the exhausted animal once again in the ribs, and at the same time drawing his pistol and firing. The garde gave a strangled exclamation of pure surprise and fell over backward, and Nick was through the barriers and once again striking sparks from the cobbles as he galloped for the docks. Behind him there came a rising hullaballoo, as the sleepy guard was awakened in time to encounter his pursuers. But now he was back within sight of the river, slowing his mount to a grateful walk as he studied the craft alongside. And indeed the harbor was crowded with craft, all securely moored; the tide was low, and he looked at nothing but mastheads, clustered together beneath the level of the dock. Most were empty, but several retained their pennants, floating in the wind; and there, even in the semi-darkness of the night, was the golden rose on its blue background.

He flung himself from the saddle as his horse gladly came to a halt, gave the animal a last pat on its neck, and scrambled down the ladder. "Ahoy," he shouted. "Ahoy, Tom Price. Anne. Are you there?"

But even as he climbed his heart was sinking. The ketch was made fast to the dock wall, with springers and breast ropes out in every direction; but on her outside there was another boat, also securely made fast. And he could hear once again the thunder of hooves on the cobbles.

He reached the deck of the boat at the foot of the ladder, scrambled across, and almost fell over the gunwale on to his own ship. A tousled head appeared from the hatchway. "Mr. Minnett? Oh, thank the Lord for that."

Tom was pushed out of the way by Anne, still wearing her nightgown. "Mr. Minnett? Oh, God, we thank Thee. Mr. Minnett, are you all right?"

Nick regained his breath. "Aye. For the moment. But only the moment. How did you let this fellow outside of us, Tom?"

"Why, he seeks shelter, Mr. Minnett. They all do. And we cannot leave until dawn, in any event."

"Dawn?" Nick shouted. The clock on the church had shown but half past two as he had galloped by.

"The *mascaret*, Mr. Minnett," Anne explained. "The tides are springing, as you see, and tonight is the fastest, in fact."

"You should have seen it, at three o'clock this afternoon, sir," Price said. "It came bubbling up there, why, most of these vessels were already alongside and yet one was ripped from her mooring. You'll see her wreckage on the far bank come daylight."

"Three yesterday afternoon," Nick muttered. "Then it is on its way now."

"Oh aye, sir," Anne said, and seized his arm. "But there is naught to fear. We bob a little, and grind against our fellows, but we are well secured here. And once it is gone, why, the river settles down rapidly enough. But Mr. Minnett, sir, to have you back, safe and sound . . ."

He looked down into that face of which he had dreamed so often and for so long. It had not changed; it was all the woman he had ever wanted, all the woman he would ever want. Now he must take it to its doom, as he had taken so many other faces to their doom.

"Safe and sound," he said. "Fit only for the gallows, Anne. We must put to sea. Tom, cut the rope holding that fellow. Anne, bend on the foresails. We'll need them both. I'll see to our lines."

Her fingers relaxed as she stared at him. "To sea? Now? But that is suicide."

"Less so than to remain here."

As if to punctuate his words, there came a cry from above them. "There," shouted a voice he recognized too well. "There is the ship. I'd know her anywhere."

" 'Tis blowing half a gale," Price said. "That sea will be twice the size of yesterday. And in the dark . . ."

"Cut those warps," Nick shouted. "Anne, get that sail up. What, would you rather hang?"

"Stop there," Condorcet shouted. "You cannot escape me now, Minnett. Stop there and surrender, or you will all be killed."

Nick ripped the axe from its bracket, ran forward, cut the first of the lines with a single sweep. On the starboard side Price had woken up to the greater danger, and was slashing the fisherman's lines with his knife. A man appeared on deck.

"What?" he shouted. "What, monsieur, are you mad? You are casting me adrift."

For the river had already seized the ship to pull it away from the dock.

"So make fast farther down," Nick shouted, and cut the last of his own ropes. As he did so, Anne sent the first of the foresails up the forestay, and the wind plucked the *Rose* by the bow to pull her round, while the force of the current took her away from the dock and downstream, broadside on.

Nick ran aft for the tiller, and was struck by a flying figure. And then another and another, hitting the gunwale and sending him tumbling over.

Condorcet was first on his feet, pistol presented. "Put back," he bawled. "Put back, or I shoot."

Nick crawled for the tiller, brought it up into his belly, and *Golden Rose* turned as the jib filled. "Set the other one," he bawled. "Tom Price, get the mainsail up. We need all the speed we have."

"Mad," Price groaned. "Mad. We are dead men." But he strained on the halliard.

"Mad," Condorcet shouted. "I will shoot you, Nick. Do not suppose I shall not."

"Then you'd best shoot yourself as well," Nick told him. "There is no one else can con this ship through the *mascaret.*"

"The *mascaret?*" Condorcet looked forward, where the second foresail was just breaking out and instantly filling, to send the ketch racing through the water. "The *mascaret?*"

"Aye," Nick said. "Perhaps you'd like to listen."

Seeping up the river, against the wind, there came a roar, a sound which made all the chorus of the Paris mobs no more than a murmur, a sound to send his stomach tumbling and his brain reeling, but to send his blood tingling through his veins as well.

"My God," Condorcet said, and the arm holding the pistol dropped to his side. "You mean to kill us all."

"I mean to save us all," Nick said, "if it can be done. Put away that pistol and tell your men to do likewise, and then get to shelter. The cabin were best. Tom Price, set this mizzen."

"Too much canvas, Mr. Minnett," Price grumbled. "Too much canvas for this wind."

"We'll not do it at under ten knots, Tom. Remember? Harry's words. Now get that sail up." And what had he replied? "There'd be something, to take the *Rose* through the Seine bore." Something indeed. If it could be done.

Even up the river, the wind was gusting gale force, and as he attempted to keep *Golden Rose* in the center of the stream it meant a steady wrestle with the wheel, judging his distance from the banks, thankful now for the brilliant moonlight which had replaced the clouds, and for the suddenly clear early morning air. Rouen had already vanished astern around a bend, and he could feel the ship gathering speed all the time.

Anne was at his side. He had not noticed her coming aft, so hard had he been concentrating. Now he felt another hand on the helm, and her shoulder touched his.

"I hardly know whether I am dreaming or not," she cried into the wind. "To have you here, Mr. Minnett, again . . . I had given you up for lost."

"But my people have cared for you?"

Her head turned up, the wind swept her hair from her face. "They have cared for me, Mr. Minnett. If you suppose that was all I sought."

"Anne." He released the helm long enough to squeeze her waist. "If I have survived, it is because there is a dream of you, always in my mind. Should fortune give me but one hour more . . ."

"Fortune will give you that, Mr. Minnett," she said. "Do you know who came to see me, while I waited, day after day, in Lyme? It was Mr. Pitt himself. I was so afraid I could hardly speak. He brought me my instructions for this voyage. He said, bring him back, Anne Yealm. He said, we need him, the nation, his family, his bank, and most of all, I need him. There is much to be done."

Nick laughed at the wind. Much to be done. Supposing it were possible. Then his laughter died. *Golden Rose* swept round a bend, and entered a long flow of straight river; the wind was now immediately astern, and the ketch raced along, canvas tight, rigging whining, in this uncannily calm water making her best speed. But the calmness was ending, and within sight. The noise was now all but deafening, and not a quarter of a mile away he looked at what might have been wind driven surf on a reef, only the reef was moving, coming toward him as fast as *Golden Rose* was driving at it.

"Get below," he shouted. "You'd not swim in it, anyway."

Price scrambled into the shelter of the cabin hatchway, where the Frenchmen were huddled, their faces ashen even in the darkness.

"Go on," Nick shouted at Anne.

She shook her head. "You'll need another hand. I would watch it."

And indeed they both stared forward, although Nick
gave a hasty glance aloft to make sure every sail was full.
It would be necessary to take the bore head on. He
looked past the bowsprit. The advancing wave was perhaps eight feet high, he calculated. It rose dark from the
level of the river itself, although most of the noise seemed
to come from down there; on the top it curled forward,
and broke, and this foaming crest was perhaps three feet
more. And as he stared, he realized with a surge of real
horror that it was not just crest; the sea was bringing
with it all the flotsam it had accumulated on its long
journey up the river, including masts and spars and timbers from at least one ship.

"Aieeeeee," Anne screamed, whether in fear or exulta-
tion he did not know. The *mascaret* was upon them, a
solid wall of water stretching right across the river,
towering above the bowsprit. Nick tensed every muscle,
stamped his feet on the deck, clung to the helm, throwing his right arm round Anne's waist to bring her between him and the wheel. If they went, then they would
go together.

Golden Rose drove straight into the center of the wave.
Her bowspirit vanished in foam, and then her bows attempted to lift, but already the massive tons of water
and wood were crashing on to her decks. The ketch
seemed to come to a complete halt at the first impact;
it could only have been for a second but it was the
longest moment of Nick's life. The entire night seemed to
stop with them. As if in a dream he saw six feet of water
obliterating the decks and moving aft, absorbing hatches
and masts and shrouds. As if in a dream he discovered
himself actually beneath the surface, gasping for breath,
inhaling salt water and choking. As if in a dream he felt
Anne's body floating up his chest, and released the helm
to grasp her and pull her back.

And then his dream ended, in the tremendous booming crack from above him. Instinctively he wrapped both
arms around the helm, crushing the girl, discovering that
he could see again, that the ship had plunged through

the maelstrom and now rolled in a tremendous chop, swung broadside on by the force of the wave which had whipped the helm from Nick's hand. And the dream was back as, looking up, he saw the mainmast, slowly folding into two. It had broken at the spreaders, perhaps fifteen feet above the deck, and hung there, for a moment, while the sail ballooned, then there was another tremendous crack, and it plunged for the deck.

Nick released the helm again, held Anne's shoulders and forced her down. The entire ship seemed to jump out of the water and settle again, and the roll threw him away from the girl and against the bulwark. But by now his brain was functioning again. The river was settling back into its normal flow, and the bank was coming too close. He ran forward, threw the chocks for the anchor aside, listened to the roar as the chain hurtled through the hawsepipe and the bower plunged into the mud. *Golden Rose* came gently to a rest, still bobbing as the wind whipped up the tide, but in no more than a gentle sea. And the roaring *mascaret* was already gone, around the next bend and pursuing its way up the river.

He looked aft. The mainmast still formed its angle, slowly drooping further toward the deck and the river; the sail clouded amidships. But there was no other damage; the break had occurred above the gooseneck fitting for the forestays, and the jibs still set. And now people were coming out of the cabin, staring around them as if seeing the river and the sky and the ship for the first time.

He sighed. Now, too, enmity would resume—and he was unarmed.

Louis Condorcet picked his way through the rubble. "Your ship is wrecked, Nick."

"I can sail her, with mizzen and foresail."

"Ah, then had you not best do so?"

Nick frowned at him.

"That was Seraphine, on the road," Condorcet said. "Do you know why I hated you most, Nick? Because I thought you did no more than use her."

"I did no more than use her," Nick said. "On two occasions."

"But at the last you risked your life to save hers, and that is something to be proud of. And then, to challenge the *mascaret*. You are become a legend, Nick. Your ship is become a legend." He smiled, with all the charm Nick remembered from their youth. "To take you back would be to risk giving the mob an Englishman as a hero. If you will permit my companions and I to take your dinghy, we will go ashore."

"And then? I have heard the Prussians will be in Montmartre in a week."

Condorcet shrugged. "Then perhaps I shall be a fugitive. But we will fight them, Nick. We will fight all who oppose our revolution, you included. Remember that, should our paths cross again. For the time . . ." He held out his hand. "Here is to the memory of our boyhood."

Nick squeezed the fingers, remained standing by the anchor capstan as three Frenchmen launched the dinghy and pulled for the shore.

"What now, Mr. Minnett?" Price asked.

"Fetch me the axe," Nick said. "We'll cut away that topmast, set a jury staysail, and then it's home, for Lyme."

It took them but half an hour, and *Golden Rose* slipped down the river, under foresail, trysail and mizzen, still making a steady six knots. It would be a long haul back to Lyme, but with the wind in the east it would be a simple and pleasant crossing. Nick looked over his shoulder, watched the sun slowly climbing into the sky above France. Oh, indeed, there was much to be done. Much to be done in his own life: he could only shudder at the list of accounts Caroline would have for him by now, at the list of borrowers, good, and bad, that Turnbull would have accumulated, at the investments which would require adjusting and calculating; at the latest suitor Lucy would have discovered. He also anticipated his mother's continuing disapproval of his escapades. And much to do, for Billy Pitt and his dreams of an England bestriding the world? That would have to be considered.

And what of France? Much to do there as well, perhaps. An understanding of his own attitude first. A decision between his instincts, which told him that everything Manon Roland had said was true, and his birth and background and upbringing which whispered to him to abhor all revolution, all change, all disturbance in the established order of things. But of one thing he was sure; he would help Manon to create her new state, no matter what.

And much to do, now and tomorrow, and the next day, with *Golden Rose*. And her crew. He watched the companion hatch slide back, and Anne Yealm came on deck. She had tied on a bandanna over her hair, and her face was exposed and lovely, as he liked it best. And she carried a steaming mug of coffee braced with rum, and a hunk of bread and cheese. "Breakfast, Mr. Minnett."

He released the helm, and she grasped the spokes, checked her course with the compass, and then raised her head to look at the sea and adjust her movements to the heave of the deck. Nick sat on the hatch-cover, and watched her, while he sipped his drink and felt the hot liquid spreading through his body. Oh aye, there was much to do.

About the Author

After living in Guyana and Nassau the Bahamas, and visiting nearly every continent, Mark Logan has settled down with his family in Guernsey, one of the Channel Islands. Mr. Logan is the author of more than 25 books published under several pseudonyms. *The Captain's Woman* is the first book in a series to be published by The New American Library, Inc.

More Big Bestsellers from SIGNET

☐ **LOVER: CONFESSIONS OF A ONE NIGHT STAND** by Lawrence Edwards. (#J7392—$1.95)

☐ **THE SURVIVOR** by James Herbert. (#E7393—$1.75)

☐ **THE KILLING GIFT** by Bari Wood. (#J7350—$1.95)

☐ **WHITE FIRES BURNING** by Catherine Dillon. (#E7351—$1.75)

☐ **CONSTANTINE CAY** by Catherine Dillon. (#W6892—$1.50)

☐ **FOREVER AMBER** by Kathleen Winsor. (#J7360—$1.95)

☐ **SMOULDERING FIRES** by Anya Seton. (#J7276—$1.95)

☐ **HARVEST OF DESIRE** by Rochelle Larkin. (#J7277—$1.95)

☐ **SAVAGE EDEN** by Constance Gluyas. (#J7171—$1.95)

☐ **THE GREEK TREASURE** by Irving Stone. (#E7211—$2.25)

☐ **THE KITCHEN SINK PAPERS** by Mike McGrady. (#J7212—$1.95)

☐ **THE GATES OF HELL** by Harrison Salisbury. (#E7213—$2.25)

☐ **TERMS OF ENDEARMENT** by Larry McMurtry. (#J7173—$1.95)

☐ **THE FINAL FIRE** by Dennis Smith. (#J7141—$1.95)

Other SIGNET Bestsellers You'll Enjoy Reading